Inferno City

Faith Webb

Published by Faith Webb, 2024.

This is a work of fiction. Similarities to real people, places, or events are entirely coincidental.

INFERNO CITY

First edition. November 12, 2024.

Copyright © 2024 Faith Webb.

ISBN: 979-8230567394

Written by Faith Webb.

Chapter 1: Into the Flames

I was never one to shy away from danger. My father always told me it ran in our blood—this unshakable compulsion to throw ourselves headfirst into the unknown, whether it was a burning building or a turbulent storm. Growing up in the shadows of his fire-fighting legacy, I learned early on that there were only two options when the flames rose: charge in or get out of the way. So, when the alarm blared through the station, my heart didn't race with panic. It raced with anticipation.

Oldtown had always been a city of contradictions. A place where cobblestone streets wound between towering buildings, their facades as old as the city itself, yet somehow always fighting off decay with fresh coats of paint and a fresh generation's optimism. It was an odd kind of beauty, like a piece of antique furniture with a stubborn streak of wear that added character. The district had lived through centuries of history, from the clamor of revolution to the quiet dignity of families weaving their legacies. But right now, the very heart of it was a roaring inferno, hungry and unrelenting.

The fire had started in the warehouse district, but it had spread faster than we could've imagined. The gusts of wind had turned the flame from an inconvenient brushfire into a full-scale monster. The air was thick with smoke, and the sky above was a smear of red and orange, as though the heavens themselves had caught fire. My lungs burned with every breath I took, but I didn't let it slow me down. I had a job to do. We all did.

I could feel the heat before I even stepped into the blaze. The temperature was suffocating, pressing against my skin like a hundred heavy blankets, threatening to drag me down. But the gear we wore was good—better than good, actually. Still, it wasn't the suit that kept my legs steady as I sprinted toward the burning building. It was the knowledge that I was not alone.

At the edge of the crowd, I noticed him—the man who would come to haunt my thoughts for weeks to come. Tall, broad-shouldered, his back straight like a soldier's even in the chaos of it all. His movements were precise, deliberate. His eyes, dark and sharp as a hawk's, skimmed over everything, taking in the scene like a chessboard. He wasn't here to help; he was here to control, to command. And it was impossible not to notice how he moved among the team—his presence drawing attention like a magnet. People obeyed him without a second thought, a word, or even a glance.

But it wasn't just his commanding presence that caught my eye. It was the coldness with which he watched the fire, the way his jaw clenched as if he were seeing something I couldn't. Something deeper. Maybe it was the smoldering heat, but for a second, I thought I saw something else in his gaze—a crack in the armor. It disappeared as quickly as it had appeared, but it was enough to make me wonder.

I don't like people who hide things, especially not in a field where we all have to trust each other with our lives. But trust isn't given freely, and neither is it earned in a single moment. So, as I passed by him to grab a hose and start soaking the nearest wall, I didn't let myself think about it. It wasn't the time for questions, and it certainly wasn't the time for distractions.

Except, for some reason, that man, with his sharp eyes and brooding air, stayed with me.

The day wore on, the fire taking its sweet time to yield, and I was pushed to the limits of exhaustion. My muscles burned, my lungs screamed for air that was a little less thick with smoke, and my hands, blistered beneath the gloves, ached with the weight of the hose. But even as I stumbled from one task to another, there was no escaping him. Every time I looked up, I saw him. Just a flash—a dark figure moving through the smoke, his silhouette cutting through the haze like something unreal, something out of place.

At one point, I found myself standing in front of a building that had started to collapse, the flames licking at the edges, licking at the foundation. A teammate had gone down to check the lower levels, but the heat was so intense it was hard to see if he was okay. I was trying to make my way over to him when I heard it. A voice, deep and unwavering, coming from behind me.

"Get out of there."

I didn't need to turn around to know who it was. The authority in his voice could've stopped a freight train.

"Not yet," I said, my voice barely audible over the roar of the fire. "Someone's in there. I'm not leaving until I know he's safe."

"Then you'll be joining him," came the flat reply. "And if you think I'm letting you put yourself at risk, you're mistaken."

His words had the edge of an order, but there was something else there, too. A flicker of something I couldn't place. Maybe it was concern—though I'd never admit that to anyone—but I wasn't about to let him control me, not like that. Not here. Not now.

"I'm not asking for permission," I shot back, turning just enough to meet his gaze. My chest was tight, and I could see the tension in his face, the way his eyes seemed to study me, assessing my every move. It was like he was looking for cracks in my resolve.

"You don't have to ask. But if you're going in there, you'll do it with a plan. Not like this." His voice dropped low, the edge sharper than before. "You're not invincible, you know."

He didn't wait for me to answer. Instead, he turned away, his long legs eating up the distance between us in seconds, his movements all fluid precision. I watched him go, the hairs on the back of my neck prickling, as if the air had shifted in the space between us.

But as much as I hated to admit it, I knew he was right. He didn't need to say anything else. The tension between us was palpable, and as I looked back to the building, I understood: This fire was about to show me more than I'd bargained for.

The fire had become an animal, an insatiable beast gnawing at everything in its path. We'd managed to contain parts of it, but there was no denying the beast was strong, and its hunger, relentless. With each passing minute, I felt like I was trapped in some bizarre game, one where the rules kept changing, and the stakes were the lives of people I'd never met. My focus should have been entirely on that, but every few seconds my gaze would flick over to him—this enigmatic stranger whose very presence seemed to spark something inside me, something that made it harder to breathe as the smoke thickened and the flames surged higher.

He wasn't the sort to make small talk. No, he was all business, moving with sharp precision, his orders coming out in clipped sentences that left no room for argument. Yet somehow, I couldn't stop wondering about him. The man had the kind of stillness about him that made you question what was going on behind those unreadable eyes. What was it about him that seemed to demand your attention, even in the midst of all this chaos? Was it the authority he carried, or was it the way he looked like he didn't quite belong here, in the middle of this world I had devoted myself to?

When I finally caught sight of him again, it was from the corner of my eye. He was standing near the edge of the crowd, his back straight, his eyes scanning the surroundings as if he were cataloging every detail in his mind. A small group of volunteers had gathered near the building I was working on, trying to put out smaller flames that had begun licking their way up the side. As they worked, I moved towards the front of the building, ducking beneath a section of burning timber. The heat was unbearable, but I kept going, focused on the task at hand. I knew better than to let distractions cloud my judgment.

But there he was again, right in my path.

"Watch your step," he said, his voice cutting through the noise like a blade.

I didn't need to look up to know who it was. That deep, authoritative tone had an unmistakable pull, like gravity itself. "I'm fine," I muttered, pushing past him without breaking my stride.

He didn't follow, but I could feel his eyes on me, the weight of them pressing against my back. There was something about it—the way he watched without speaking—that sent an unexpected tremor through me. He was like a force of nature, something that couldn't be ignored. The question was: why did he seem to think that I, of all people, needed his watchful eye?

I didn't like being treated like I was in over my head. I wasn't, but for some reason, he thought I was. He was determined to make me aware of my limitations, to remind me that the fire didn't care who I was, or how much training I had. It would swallow me just as easily as it had swallowed entire buildings, families, and businesses.

My mouth was dry, but the heat in my chest was even worse. Something about his aloofness made me want to do the exact opposite of whatever he expected.

As the hours passed, I kept my distance, pretending that my thoughts weren't constantly looping back to him. In truth, I couldn't tell if I was more frustrated with his constant presence or the fact that I couldn't shake the feeling that he had more to say than he let on. His behavior was colder than the icy winds that sliced through Oldtown's streets on a typical winter day. Yet I found myself increasingly drawn to him, trying to decode the mystery beneath that icy exterior.

It wasn't until we were forced to retreat, the fire's rage too much for any of us to control, that things shifted. The wind had turned, pushing the fire back onto itself in a dangerous spiral. We were being called back. A decision had been made by higher-ups—one I hated, but one I understood.

I was taking cover behind a building, eyes squinting against the smoke, when I heard his voice again. This time, it wasn't cold, or commanding. It was laced with something else—something I wasn't sure I wanted to acknowledge.

"Are you listening to me?" His voice was quieter now, but still firm. "We need to get out of here. Now."

I turned to find him standing much closer than I had expected, his eyes locked onto mine. The air between us had thickened, the tension palpable.

"I'm fine," I shot back, unwilling to let him see how shaken I was by the prospect of retreating.

He didn't respond at first, just stared at me, his expression unreadable. There was something about the way his jaw tightened that made my heart race. He was angry—or at least, he was frustrated. But with me? Or with the situation?

"I don't think you are," he said finally, his voice low. "But that's not my decision to make."

For the first time, his cool demeanor cracked just enough for me to see the fire beneath. There was something raw in his tone, something urgent. Something desperate.

But before I could speak, the ground rumbled beneath us, and a shower of debris fell from the building we had been fighting to save. It was a reminder, I suppose, that we were still in the middle of something far more dangerous than either of us wanted to admit.

For a second, I wondered if he would grab me and pull me to safety. But he didn't. He just stood there, watching me as though measuring my next move. Something in his gaze shifted, and for once, I realized that maybe he was seeing me for who I was—not just the rookie on his team, but someone capable of handling herself in the chaos.

I could feel it now, the pull between us—this strange understanding that neither of us had asked for. And as the fire raged behind him, I couldn't help but wonder if, when the smoke cleared, there would be anything left to salvage between us. Or if we would both be consumed in the aftermath of a battle neither of us were prepared to fight.

The next few days blurred together in a haze of smoke, exhaustion, and adrenaline. Despite our efforts, the fire had left its mark on Oldtown. I couldn't escape it, couldn't stop thinking about how much had been lost in that one night. Buildings, homes, memories—all gone in the blink of an eye. But as I trudged through the aftermath, the weight of it settling heavy on my shoulders, my mind kept returning to him. The man who had stood at the edge of the chaos, eyes locked on mine, as if he had seen right through me. I wasn't sure what unsettled me more: the way he had made me feel like I was an inexperienced rookie or the fact that, for all his cold precision, there had been a flicker of something else—something almost human.

I hadn't expected to see him again so soon. In fact, I was halfway through my third cup of coffee in the break room when he walked in. No fanfare, no introduction—just the same imposing figure, with that intense gaze that always made me feel like I was under some kind of silent scrutiny.

"Mind if I sit?" His voice was rougher than I remembered, like gravel sliding against metal. I barely spared him a glance, still trying to nurse the caffeine that had yet to put a dent in my exhaustion.

"Do you mind if I say no?" I replied, not bothering to hide the sarcasm.

A corner of his mouth lifted, just slightly, and that alone was enough to make me feel like I'd made a mistake. He pulled out the chair opposite me and sat down, the wood creaking under his weight as if it too felt the weight of his presence.

"You're a hard one to get a read on," he observed, his gaze never leaving me.

"Maybe I just prefer not to give you the satisfaction of a reaction," I shot back, wondering where this conversation was going, but already regretting the direction it was taking. The last thing I needed was to get caught up in some strange power struggle with a man who had no problem pushing my buttons.

"Uh-huh," he hummed, leaning back in his chair, a barely perceptible sigh escaping his lips. "You've got that whole 'I'm an island' thing going on, don't you?"

I didn't respond right away. His words hung in the air, and I realized he was right. I'd built my life around the idea of being self-sufficient, never needing anyone to step in and fix things for me. Maybe it was stubbornness, or maybe it was fear. The idea of letting someone in, even for a second, was like handing them a piece of your soul and waiting for them to either break it or walk away.

He studied me like a puzzle he was determined to solve, and for a brief moment, I wished I could slip under the table and escape into the crowd. But instead, I did what I always did—I forced a smile that didn't reach my eyes.

"You've got me all figured out, huh?" I said, my voice laced with a challenge.

He didn't flinch. "Not yet. But I will."

There was something unnerving about how confident he sounded. I had no idea who he was, why he was here, or what made him think he could walk in and read me like a book, but I wasn't going to give him the satisfaction of seeing how rattled I was.

"You're lucky I'm not a betting woman," I quipped, swirling my coffee cup absently. "Because I'd bet money you're not nearly as good at this as you think you are."

He leaned forward, narrowing his eyes, but this time, there was no trace of amusement in his gaze. It was all business. "You're wrong about me," he said, his voice low and controlled. "But you'll figure that out soon enough."

I didn't respond. For the first time in our conversation, I didn't have a snarky comeback, didn't have a sharp word to cut through the tension. Instead, I just stared at him, feeling the pull of something I couldn't quite place.

There was a part of me that wanted to believe him, wanted to trust that he had the answers to questions I hadn't even asked myself yet. But there was another part—more guarded, more wary—that knew better. I wasn't about to let some stranger waltz in and start peeling back the layers of my life. Not when I wasn't ready for it.

"I'll see you around," I said abruptly, standing up and grabbing my jacket from the back of my chair.

He didn't try to stop me. He just nodded, as if he had already anticipated my exit.

That night, sleep came fitfully, a series of fragmented images and restless turns. My dreams were a twisted version of reality, where the fire came back in waves, burning hotter and faster each time, and he was always there, standing just out of reach, watching me struggle to keep my footing. But this time, it wasn't just the fire that was closing in. It was something else, something much closer, something that I couldn't shake.

I woke up with the sense that something was about to change—something that would pull me deeper into his orbit. I wasn't sure if that was a warning or an invitation, but either way, I couldn't deny it. I was in too deep. And there was no way out.

When I arrived at the station the next morning, I could feel the shift in the air. The usual hum of activity felt different, almost charged. It was as if everyone was waiting for something to happen. And when I walked through the door, there he was again, standing near the briefing board, his gaze already tracking me.

"I think we're about to have a problem," he said, his voice flat, but there was an underlying tension in it, something I couldn't ignore.

Before I could respond, the doors slammed open, and the fire chief stormed in, his face tight with fury.

"We've got a situation."

Chapter 2: The Fire Investigator

The station hums with the low buzz of ringing phones, muted conversations, and the occasional sharp cough that echoes through the walls. It's an unremarkable soundscape, one I know by heart. But today, as I step across the threshold of the fire department, it feels different. Almost like stepping into a room full of glass walls, where every move is scrutinized. Everyone's eyes are on me, even if they aren't. And if I'm being honest, that alone is enough to make my skin crawl.

Callum is already there, standing near the evidence board like a statue chiseled from stone. His broad shoulders seem to eat up the space around him, and for a second, I wonder if the air is thinner because of him, or if it's just me. He doesn't look up when I enter, doesn't acknowledge my presence, and I almost respect that about him. Almost. I've worked with a lot of people who think their greeting is a form of currency. Callum doesn't seem to care about any of that.

I sit down at my desk and keep my eyes glued to the pile of paperwork in front of me. It's not that I'm avoiding him—okay, maybe a little—but I need to focus. There's too much work to be done, and I refuse to be distracted by his presence. Still, I can feel the weight of his gaze from across the room, like a storm cloud slowly rolling in. And when he finally speaks, it's like the crack of thunder.

"Sergeant Hughes," Callum says, his voice deep and precise, the kind of voice that demands attention. "We've had a string of fires. You've been keeping up with the investigations?"

The question is straightforward enough, but the way he says it—like he's inspecting me from top to bottom—makes me bristle. My hands tighten around the pen I'm holding, and I try to ignore the sensation of my pulse picking up.

"Of course," I answer, doing my best to sound as confident as possible. "I've been tracking the patterns. Each one seems to follow a similar set of conditions. No accelerants, but the burn behaviors suggest something more than just a random cause." I pause, hoping the words come out as sharp as I mean them to. "I've identified a few key elements, and I'm compiling the evidence now."

There's a brief silence, too long for my comfort. I glance up to find him staring at me, not with the interest of a colleague but with the calculation of someone who's just sized you up and found you wanting. His lips curl just slightly, like he's about to say something, but then he stops himself.

"I see," he says, as if he's evaluating my every word. "And have you considered the possibility that the fires might be... accidental?"

Accidental.

The word hangs in the air between us, insidious and irritating. It's a theory that I've already dismissed a dozen times, but hearing it from him—this man who has been doing this for years, who's seen more flames than I can count—irks me in a way I can't quite explain. It's not that he's wrong. It's just that I don't have the time for doubt. I'm close. And I won't let him or anyone else make me second guess that.

"It's not accidental," I reply, the words coming out sharper than I intend. "The burns are too precise, too deliberate. This isn't just some careless mistake. There's a method here." I try to calm myself, taking a slow breath. "If you're looking for an easy answer, you won't find it. This is bigger than that."

His gaze flickers, but his expression remains impassive. I can't tell if I've impressed him or simply irritated him. Maybe it's both. Either way, I can feel the tension settle around us like the aftermath of a storm.

He takes a step closer, his boots clicking against the floor with an assuredness that feels a little too much like a challenge.

"Let's see what you find, then," Callum says quietly, his voice smooth but edged with something like a dare. "But just remember, Sergeant, things aren't always as clear as we want them to be."

And just like that, the conversation shifts. The cool air in the room feels thicker now, heavier with the weight of something unspoken. I look down at my hands, the ink stains from the documents staining my fingertips, and I wonder if I've just become part of something far bigger than I anticipated. Something I'm not sure I can control.

The night stretches on, the hours slipping away as I dive into the recent string of fires. I sift through data, analyzing burn patterns, locations, and witness statements. But the deeper I dig, the more unsettled I feel. There's something strange here, something off. It's as if the pieces are all in place, but they don't fit together quite right. Like a jigsaw puzzle missing a crucial piece that you can't find no matter how hard you look.

I can't stop thinking about Callum's question. *Have you considered the possibility that the fires might be accidental?* It's a subtle thing, the way he said it—so casual, so offhand—but it lingers. Almost like he's trying to steer me in a direction I don't want to go.

I'm not sure why, but I can't shake the feeling that he knows something I don't. That somehow, I'm walking into a trap. The thought gnaws at me as I stare at the reports scattered across my desk. Each one has the same unnerving detail: a pattern that suggests intent. But what if the person behind these fires isn't just a criminal? What if they're someone with access, someone who knows how to make the flames behave?

I need answers. I need them fast.

The clock ticks on, but the world outside my window seems to have faded into oblivion. There's nothing but the weight of this investigation pressing against my ribs, and the nagging suspicion that maybe—just maybe—Callum is involved in ways I can't yet understand.

The next morning arrives with the same oppressive weight hanging in the air—thick with the sense that everything in my world has become just a little bit more complicated. I don't know if it's the dark circles under my eyes from hours of poring over reports, or the gnawing feeling that something's off, but it's like I've woken up to a different version of myself. There's a sharpness to my movements as I head into the station, an edge I didn't have before, and it's all thanks to Callum.

It's not like I'm jealous of him, or at least, I don't think I am. He's got the experience, the knowledge, and the expertise that I—at least on paper—can't match. He's the kind of investigator who has seen a thousand fires, each one an opportunity to untangle a mystery. And for some reason, I'm fixated on the idea that he might know more than he's letting on.

By the time I step into the station, I'm already dreading the moment our paths cross again. But as soon as I walk in, there he is—standing by the coffee machine with his arms crossed, eyes glued to his phone. It's the kind of pose that makes him look like he owns the place, and for a second, I consider turning around and walking back out the door.

But I don't. I'm not running from this. I'm not running from him.

"Sergeant Hughes," he says, not looking up, his voice smooth as always, like he's already a step ahead of me. "Busy night?"

I hesitate. It's almost a challenge, the way he phrases it. Almost like he knows exactly what I was doing until three a.m. and he's daring me to admit it. But I'm not here to back down.

"Couldn't sleep," I answer, forcing a smile that doesn't quite reach my eyes. "The reports were a little... intriguing."

That's putting it mildly. The more I go through the details, the more I'm convinced that something is happening here that we're missing. The fires—they're too clean, too precise. The pattern, the timing, the locations—there's no way it's just a series of unfortunate accidents. Someone is orchestrating this. But who?

"You're digging deeper than usual," he observes, finally looking up, his gaze piercing in a way that makes me feel like I'm under a microscope. "What exactly are you trying to prove, Sergeant?"

There it is again. That look. The one that makes my stomach flip and my fingers twitch with the urge to defend myself. I can't tell if it's genuine curiosity or just another way for him to test me, but I'm not about to give him the satisfaction of a flustered response.

"I'm just doing my job," I say, keeping my tone even, refusing to let the nerves creep in. "Someone needs to figure out who's behind this, and it's not like I'm going to let someone else do the work."

He leans against the counter, eyes narrowing slightly. "Someone else? You're the one in charge here, aren't you?" His words linger, dripping with a hint of something almost... sarcastic.

I bristle at the implication, but I manage to swallow the retort that rises to my lips. Instead, I let the silence stretch between us, watching as Callum taps his fingers against the edge of the coffee cup like he's thinking something over. It's almost like he's enjoying this little back-and-forth—this game we're playing.

"Have you considered the possibility," he says slowly, "that maybe you're overthinking this? Not everything needs to be a conspiracy."

I blink, caught off guard by the sudden shift in his tone. It's not like him to be so... casual about this. Callum doesn't strike me as the kind of person who throws out theories without reason. But then, maybe that's the point. Maybe he wants me to doubt myself.

But I won't. Not this time.

"I'm not overthinking anything," I respond firmly. "There's something here, and I'm going to find it."

He regards me for a moment, his gaze flicking to my lips as if he's trying to read between the lines, and then he straightens up. His expression hardens, and I swear, I can feel the temperature in the room drop a few degrees.

"Well," he says, his voice suddenly tight with something I can't quite place, "let's hope you're right. For your sake."

And then he's gone, striding out the door without another word, leaving me standing there, heart pounding in my chest. What was that? What did he mean by that last remark?

Shaking my head, I turn back to the stack of reports on my desk, trying to focus on the details again. But the nagging feeling that something isn't right refuses to let me go.

As the day wears on, I dig through the fire reports, cross-referencing them with my earlier findings. The patterns are there, sure, but it's the gaps that keep catching my eye. Small things, things that no one else might notice unless they were looking for them. A suspiciously perfect pattern of destruction. A series of locations that, at first glance, seem random, but when laid out on a map, suggest an uncanny level of premeditation.

The more I think about it, the more I realize that there's a structure to it all—a structure I'm not sure I've uncovered yet. But I'm getting closer. I can feel it. The hairs on the back of my neck stand up with each new discovery, but it's not just the thrill of the chase. It's a sense of dread creeping up on me, something deeper than just a case to solve.

By the time I leave the station, the sky outside is a dull gray, the promise of rain hanging in the air like a threat. I pull my jacket tighter around me, hoping that the storm doesn't follow me home. But I can't shake the feeling that the real storm is just beginning.

By the time I return home, the quiet of my apartment feels foreign, too still. The rain has started to fall, tapping against the window with the kind of persistence that sets my nerves on edge. The world outside is a blur of gray, each drop collecting in uneven lines down the glass like tears that have been forced to stay hidden. I kick off my boots, leave them by the door, and make my way to the small kitchen where I put the kettle on. I need something to ground me, something to focus on, so I don't fall into the trap of spiraling.

But my mind refuses to quiet. Instead, it picks apart every little interaction with Callum. His presence lingers in the corners of the room, a ghost I can't shake. That tone of his, the way he looks at me like a problem to solve, but never quite acknowledging me as an equal. It's infuriating. And yet, there's a part of me that wonders if he's seeing something I'm not. What if he's right? What if I am overthinking this?

The thought gnaws at me until I feel like I'm suffocating under the weight of it. Maybe it's time to take a break from the reports, just for a little while, and get some air. I grab my coat, pull it on without much thought, and step out into the rain. The streets are almost empty, save for the occasional car speeding by, its headlights slicing through the mist. It's quiet enough for me to think, but not loud enough to drown out the feeling of tension that's been coiling inside me since I first laid eyes on Callum.

I walk, letting my feet lead me without any real destination in mind, the steady rhythm of my steps matching the pulse of the rain. But as I turn a corner, something catches my eye—a figure standing under the dim glow of a streetlamp. It's Callum. His posture, relaxed, almost casual, is out of place in the storm, as if he's waiting for someone—or something. I pause, hidden in the shadows, watching as he glances around, his face hard to read in the half-light.

For a moment, I almost turn back, not wanting to intrude. But then, against my better judgment, I stay, curiosity pulling me closer. Why is he here? What's he doing out in the rain, so far from the station?

Then, it happens. A figure approaches him, slipping out from behind the alley like they've been waiting for him. The exchange is swift, too quick for me to make out any words, but I see enough to make my heart race. Callum's hand brushes something into the other person's palm—just a flash of silver, a glint of something sharp in the low light.

And then they disappear into the night.

I stand there, frozen, every nerve in my body screaming at me to go, to get out of sight before they notice me. But I can't. Not yet. I need to understand. I need to know what I just saw.

I take a slow step back, careful not to make a sound, and I start walking away, my heart pounding in my chest. The rain has picked up now, each drop heavier than the last, as if nature itself is trying to drown out the questions flooding my mind. What did I just witness? Why was Callum meeting with someone in secret? And what was it that he handed off so casually?

The walk back to my apartment feels longer this time, the air thick with uncertainty. I barely register the passing scenery, my mind too busy turning over the pieces of what I've just seen. But as I reach the entrance to my building, something stops me. The same figure—the one who met with Callum—is standing just inside the lobby, silhouetted against the flickering lights. My breath catches in my throat as I realize it's not just any person—it's someone I recognize.

It's one of the witnesses from the fire.

My pulse skips in my chest. What is this person doing here, in the building where I live? And more importantly, why hadn't I noticed them before? The witness, a man in his mid-thirties with dark eyes and a nervous energy, stares at me as I approach. There's a flicker of recognition in his gaze, like he's seen me too, but neither of us says a word. Not at first. I can feel the tension hanging between us, thick enough to slice through.

"Can I help you?" I ask, my voice steadier than I feel.

He hesitates, glancing over his shoulder as if to make sure no one else is watching. "I—uh—sorry, I just thought I might've dropped something," he says, his words fast, too rehearsed, like he's not used to lying but is doing a poor job of it.

I raise an eyebrow, sensing the lie hanging in the air like smoke. "Really? In the lobby?" I cross my arms, the instinct to probe rising up inside me. "I don't think you're looking for something."

He shifts uncomfortably, his fingers twitching by his side. For a moment, I wonder if he's going to bolt, but instead, he steps toward me, his voice dropping lower, almost to a whisper. "I'm not here to cause trouble. But you need to be careful, okay?"

The warning is clear, but it makes no sense. My mind spins as I try to process what he's saying. He's not giving me anything concrete, not a single clue to explain why he's standing here, or what he knows.

Before I can ask him anything else, the door slams open behind me with a deafening crash. I spin around, heart in my throat, but no one's there.

The man is gone, vanishing into thin air. The only sound is the rush of my own breath, the rain against the windows, and the cold, hard silence that's left in his wake.

My pulse races as I realize, with an icy clarity, that something is happening. And it's happening faster than I can keep up.

Chapter 3: Smoke and Shadows

The first time I caught him staring at me, I chalked it up to a slip of attention, something easily dismissed. But when it happened again, a chill brushed across my skin. The man in the corner of the room, hunched over his desk, eyes tracking my every movement—like a hawk waiting for a moment of weakness. It wasn't the look of a casual observer. It was different, somehow, like he was searching for something I couldn't see.

I had learned to ignore the oddities of this place—Old Town was a labyrinth of secrets—and most of its people were too entrenched in their own shadows to pay much attention to anything outside their narrow view. But this? This was unsettling. The old cases of arson that I'd been scouring through for weeks now suddenly felt like they were all pulling at my sleeve, each one whispering a bit louder, demanding my attention. Something was off about this city, and I'd just stumbled on the first thread.

His name was Detective Killian Grayson, and if you asked anyone in the precinct, they'd tell you he was a man obsessed with his work. A man who buried himself in the past like some people buried themselves in bottles of cheap whiskey. What they didn't tell you was how unnerving he was to be around. How his silence, like a heavy blanket, seemed to swallow any light in the room. He wasn't much to look at—dark hair, just the right amount of stubble, but it was the eyes that got you. Those eyes that seemed to be cataloguing every corner of your soul, drawing conclusions you couldn't understand. I tried to ignore it. Tried to convince myself that I had a job to do, and he was just another complication in a long line of them.

But something was happening, something I couldn't shake. His gaze followed me everywhere. Sometimes I'd turn to find him already looking, his lips twitching, like he'd been waiting for me to notice. It wasn't until the night I had enough and confronted him that things truly began to unravel.

I had been hunched over my desk for hours, digging through case after case of unsolved fires, when the distinct sound of his boots on the hardwood floor reached me. I glanced up, annoyed more than anything, only to meet his gaze. His expression was unreadable, but there was something sharp in his eyes, something that made my heart skip a beat. He leaned against the doorframe, arms crossed, his jaw clenched as though in some silent battle.

"I need to talk to you," I said, my voice a little more brittle than I wanted it to be. "Why are you always watching me?"

A smirk tugged at the corner of his lips, the kind that should've made my stomach flutter but only made my irritation grow. "Watching you? I'm just... observing," he said, stepping closer. "In this job, it's important to observe everything."

I stood up, a flash of anger rushing through me. "Observing me? Like I'm some kind of experiment? Is that what you're doing, Grayson? Trying to figure me out?"

He didn't flinch, didn't even move, but his eyes darkened with something I couldn't place. "I'm not trying to figure you out," he said softly, but the words carried weight, like they meant more than they should. "You're the one who's been trying to figure everything else out."

That stopped me. My mouth went dry. He had a point. I had been obsessively combing through the old arson cases, digging through files long buried, trying to make sense of patterns that seemed to lead nowhere. And yet, every time I thought I had a breakthrough, another dead-end would slap me in the face. Maybe I had become obsessed with the idea that there was something hidden in this city—something dark and dangerous that I had to uncover before it devoured me.

I crossed my arms, suddenly very aware of how small the room had become. The weight of his gaze pressed down on me. "What do you want from me, Grayson?" I demanded, though I wasn't entirely sure I wanted to hear the answer.

His smile returned, slow and deliberate, as though he knew exactly how uncomfortable he was making me. "Sometimes, the truth isn't what you expect," he said, his voice low and knowing. "Sometimes, the truth is exactly what you're not looking for."

I took a step back, my heart hammering in my chest. "What the hell does that mean?"

He pushed off the doorframe, taking a single step toward me, his presence suddenly overwhelming. "You've been looking in the wrong places," he said, his voice a whisper that seemed to hang in the air, heavy and thick. "The truth isn't buried in those old files, Alex. It's closer than you think."

I felt a shiver run down my spine, but I couldn't tear my eyes away from him. "You're saying I've been wasting my time?" I asked, my voice sharp.

He didn't answer right away, his eyes narrowing like he was sizing me up. And then he did something I didn't expect—he reached into his pocket and pulled out a crumpled piece of paper. He handed it to me without a word.

I unfolded it slowly, my eyes scanning the handwritten note. It was an address, scribbled hastily, and something else—a date. The ink was smudged, like it had been written in a hurry.

"What is this?" I asked, my voice trembling despite myself.

"Sometimes the past isn't dead," he said, his voice like gravel. "Sometimes it just waits."

I looked at him, the puzzle pieces falling into place in ways I wasn't prepared for. The city's unsolved arson cases, the smoke that still lingered in the air, the way everything felt too connected. I hadn't just been investigating fires—I had been chasing ghosts.

And for the first time in weeks, I didn't feel so alone in this. Grayson's gaze, sharp and filled with something I couldn't name, told me he knew exactly what I was walking into. And he wasn't letting me do it alone.

The following days were a blur, a strange cocktail of adrenaline and suspicion that kept me awake long after my usual hours. I found myself retracing every step I had taken in this investigation, the files, the old news clippings, the missing pieces that Grayson had hinted at but never fully explained. The address he'd handed me, scribbled so carelessly, was still folded in my pocket like a ticket to somewhere I wasn't sure I wanted to go. But there was no turning back now. The air in the office felt different, suffocating, as though the truth was hanging above me like a storm cloud, just waiting to burst.

I hadn't seen Grayson again after that strange exchange, though I felt his presence lurking just out of reach, always in the corner of my mind. Every time I walked past his desk, I expected him to be there, watching, waiting. But he wasn't. The silence that filled his absence made the hairs on my neck stand up, more unnerving than his presence ever had been.

It was as though he had slipped into the shadows completely, leaving only the remnants of his gaze behind. But the feeling lingered—heavy, pressing. I couldn't shake it.

The truth wasn't what I expected, he'd said. What did that even mean? Was he warning me? Or was he just trying to throw me off track, make me second-guess everything? I didn't have the answers, and frankly, I didn't think I was ever going to get them. But something in me—something stubborn and reckless—drove me forward. I was too deep in this mess now, and I wasn't about to turn around.

That night, I decided to follow the address. The whole city felt different at night, like a stranger you could almost trust. The streets I'd walked a thousand times seemed unfamiliar under the harsh glow of streetlights, the shadows stretching long and eerie as though something was watching me from the dark corners. I couldn't shake the feeling that I was being followed, but every time I glanced over my shoulder, there was no one. It was just the city, playing its tricks.

The address Grayson had given me led to an abandoned building on the outskirts of town, a crumbling old factory that looked like it had been forgotten by time itself. The windows were shattered, the brick walls covered in peeling paint and graffiti. It was the kind of place you didn't want to enter, not unless you had a death wish or a reason that was far more dangerous than curiosity.

I stood across the street for a moment, my heart thudding in my chest. Should I go in? Should I turn around and pretend like I'd never seen it? But the question hung in the air, unanswered. There was no going back now.

Taking a deep breath, I crossed the street, my boots clicking on the pavement like a countdown. The closer I got to the door, the more the hairs on the back of my neck stood on end. Every instinct in me screamed to run, to leave this place and forget I'd ever gotten involved. But I couldn't. I had made a promise to myself, and I wasn't about to break it.

The door was hanging open, just slightly ajar, like someone had left it that way on purpose. A chill ran through me, and I hesitated for a moment before pushing it open. The air inside was stale, thick with dust and the remnants of old machinery. The silence in the building was almost deafening, like the walls were holding their breath.

I stepped inside cautiously, my footsteps echoing in the emptiness. The faintest hint of smoke lingered in the air, the smell so faint that it might have been a trick of the mind. But I knew better. The scent of fire, of something burning, never really left a place. It clung to the walls, to the very bones of the building, like a memory that refused to fade.

I moved deeper into the space, my pulse racing in my ears. The floor creaked under my weight, the wood long rotted and fragile. The further I went, the more the shadows seemed to close in around me. And then, at the far end of the room, I saw it—a faint light, just a glimmer of something barely visible in the darkness.

I approached it cautiously, every instinct screaming at me to turn around, but I ignored it. The light was coming from behind a set of rusted metal doors, the kind you'd expect to find in a basement or an old cellar. I reached for the handle, the cold metal sending a shiver up my spine. But before I could turn it, a voice rang out from the darkness.

"Did you really think I'd let you come here alone?"

I froze, my breath catching in my throat. I knew that voice.

Grayson.

I spun around, my hand still on the door handle, but he was already there, leaning against the doorway, his eyes glinting in the dim light. There was no warmth in his gaze, only something darker, something I couldn't quite grasp.

"You," I said, a mixture of relief and frustration flooding my chest. "What the hell are you doing here?"

He took a step forward, his boots making no sound on the crumbling floor. "I told you, the truth isn't what you expect," he said again, his voice low and deliberate. "And now you're here, walking right into it."

I stared at him, my mind racing, trying to make sense of everything that had led me to this moment. "What is this place?" I asked, though I feared the answer.

His lips twitched, but he didn't smile. "It's where everything started. And it's where it will end."

I felt a tightness in my chest, the weight of his words settling over me like a shroud. There was no escaping this, no running. The truth was here, in this place, and Grayson? He was right in the middle of it.

His eyes stayed on me for a moment longer than comfortable, and I couldn't decide if I should be furious or just... confused. Something was happening, but I couldn't quite put it all together yet. He'd shown up like a shadow at the very place I'd been digging into for weeks, as if fate itself had decided to hand me the most cryptic clue imaginable. But the look in his eyes... there was something too calculated in the way he spoke. I knew that look—half amusement, half danger. He knew something, but he wasn't saying it. And that drove me crazy.

For a split second, I almost felt embarrassed, standing there like I was the one who didn't belong in this dank, abandoned place. But I'd come too far to retreat now. "You've been watching me for days," I said, my voice much sharper than I intended. "Following me around. Why? What's your game, Grayson?"

He took a step toward me, his eyes never leaving mine, the silence growing heavy between us. He was impossibly close now, close enough that I could hear his breath, the faintest scent of old leather and something darker—earthy, like smoke or rain-soaked asphalt. I wasn't sure if it was the air in the building or the tension between us, but the way his presence surrounded me, I was starting to feel like I was suffocating.

"I'm not playing a game," he said slowly, each word deliberate. "I'm trying to keep you from making a mistake."

I rolled my eyes, taking a step back, needing space, because my instinct was screaming at me to get away. "A mistake? What mistake? You've been lurking around like some mysterious ghost, feeding me cryptic nonsense. I'm trying to find answers, Grayson.

Real answers. And I'm not about to take advice from someone who can't even tell me the truth."

His lips twitched again, a hint of something unspoken in that smile. But this time, it was different—less patronizing, more... rueful. "You think the truth is going to be some neat little package, something you can wrap up with a bow at the end of the day?" He leaned in, his voice dropping lower. "What if the truth is uglier than you could ever imagine?"

I swallowed hard, not trusting myself to speak. A tightness coiled in my chest. His words were too close to something I'd been avoiding, something that clawed at me every time I opened the case files. I wasn't just investigating a string of arson cases anymore. I was getting too close to something dangerous, something that could destroy everything I thought I knew.

He saw my hesitation, the flicker of uncertainty crossing my face, and for a brief moment, I wondered if he was enjoying this, enjoying the power he had over me. But then I saw it—a shadow in his eyes, something fleeting but real. Was he trying to protect me? Or was he trying to keep me from uncovering something that wasn't meant to be found?

"I'm not afraid of the truth," I finally said, my voice steady, though I wasn't sure if I believed it. "You can't keep me from it."

He stared at me for a long moment, a strange tension in the air, before nodding slowly. "Fine. But understand this. What you're looking for—what you're digging into—it's bigger than you think. And the further you go, the more you'll be in danger. You're not prepared for this, Alex."

I flinched, though I didn't want to. It wasn't just his words; it was the way he said them, the gravity in his voice that made the air seem denser, like we were standing on the edge of something we couldn't pull back from.

"And you think you're prepared for it?" I challenged, my chin lifting, defiance creeping back in.

He didn't answer, but the way his eyes darkened sent an uncomfortable shiver through me. For a second, we stood in silence, the unspoken understanding hanging thick between us. And then, without another word, he turned and walked away. But not before saying something that made my stomach tighten with unease.

"You'll regret it," he called over his shoulder. "Sooner or later, you will."

I didn't know whether to call him a coward or a fool. Maybe both. He couldn't just leave me hanging like that, throwing out cryptic warnings and disappearing into the dark. But despite myself, a small part of me—an insidious little voice in the back of my mind—wondered if he was right. If I wasn't ready for whatever it was that I was about to uncover.

But I wasn't going to stop. I couldn't. I had come too far.

I followed the trail deeper into the building, my heart pounding in my chest, but every step forward felt heavier than the last. The walls seemed to close in around me, the shadows growing longer and darker with each passing moment. And then, I saw it.

A door. Small, tucked away in the corner of the room, hidden behind a pile of old crates and broken furniture. It was barely visible, but I knew it was the one. I could feel it in my bones. This was where the answers lay—where the truth would finally be revealed.

I reached for the handle, my breath shallow, my heart racing as the door creaked open with a sound that was far too loud in the silence.

Inside, the room was dark, the faint glow of a single light bulb hanging from the ceiling illuminating only part of the space. And in the center of the room... the sight that greeted me made my blood run cold.

A pile of old photographs, scattered across the floor like they had been thrown in a hurry. But it wasn't the photographs that made my stomach drop—it was the names written on the backs. Names I recognized. People who had been connected to the arson cases I'd been investigating. And one name, scrawled hastily on a torn piece of paper, made my breath catch in my throat.

My own.

Before I could process it, a sound behind me made me spin around. The door slammed shut.

And then, everything went black.

Chapter 4: A Spark of Fear

The fire was a monster. A ferocious thing, as if the very building it had chosen to devour had once insulted it, and now it wanted revenge. I was standing on the steps of Fenton Library, the air thick with smoke, when the first flicker of red-orange light illuminated the night sky. The smell of burning wood and scorched paper flooded my senses, curling around my lungs with a suffocating intensity. The library had stood for over a century, but tonight, it was being reduced to ashes in an unsettlingly short time.

I could feel the heat from where I stood, despite the fire trucks blocking most of the street. The firefighters were hustling with practiced urgency, but they looked like they were losing. The flames were spreading far too quickly for anyone's comfort, licking at the stained glass windows like a lover hungry for one last taste. It was all so sudden. I had been inside the library not even two hours ago, lingering over old manuscripts that smelled like dust and history, thinking about how the place might collapse under its own weight one day, like everything else. I never imagined it would happen tonight.

That was when I saw him—Callum.

I don't know how he got there or how long he had been standing in the shadows, but there he was, leaning against the stone wall of the building, his face pale under the glow of the fire. I hadn't expected to see him, not here, not now. His dark eyes were fixed on the chaos unfolding before us, the flames twisting in the night air like something alive. His jaw was tight, the line of his lips barely perceptible in the shadows. But there was no mistaking it—he was here, and the suddenness of his appearance sent a ripple through my already jittery nerves.

"Don't get too close," he called out without turning, his voice steady, but there was something underlying it—a crack of urgency, the faintest tremor beneath the surface. He still didn't look at me. His focus was locked on the fire, but I could sense his awareness of my every move. His presence unsettled me in a way I couldn't quite explain.

I didn't listen. I was already moving, stepping toward the edge of the scene, unable to tear my eyes away from the inferno that was claiming the library I loved. Every inch of me itched with the need to be closer, to understand, to see the damage that would be left behind. The fire was something more than just a disaster—it was a question, an unspoken riddle that demanded an answer. Why now? Why Fenton?

As I neared the perimeter, one of the firefighters barked at me to stay back, but I ignored him, brushing past with an air of defiance. I was so close to the flames I could feel the heat curling against my skin, and I took a sharp breath, trying not to choke on the acrid smoke that stung my eyes. I had to know.

That's when Callum grabbed me.

His fingers dug into my arm with a fierceness that sent a wave of panic through me. "Get away from here," he hissed, his voice low but filled with raw tension. His grip was unyielding, and I was certain he wasn't letting go until I did as he said.

"Let go of me!" I snapped, jerking my arm free from his hold. My heart raced in my chest, and for a moment, I felt trapped between him and the fire, both dangerous in their own right. But Callum's eyes—those dark, fathomless eyes—were locked on mine now, and something about the look in them made my breath hitch. His face was drawn tight, and his lips parted ever so slightly, as though he were about to say something.

I didn't want to read too much into the brief flash of something I saw in his eyes—something almost like fear—but it stopped me in my tracks. There was something deeper there, something I hadn't noticed before. I couldn't quite place it, but it was there, flickering between us like the flames behind him. The intensity in his gaze was almost too much to bear, and for a second, I wondered if he knew something I didn't. If there was more to this fire, more to him, than I had ever suspected.

But the moment was fleeting.

Before I could speak, before I could ask, before I could even process the thoughts racing through my head, he was pulling away, his face slipping back into its familiar, unreadable mask. The moment of vulnerability vanished, leaving me questioning whether it had been real at all or just a trick of the light.

"Don't stand too close," Callum said again, this time with a cold edge to his voice. His gaze didn't falter from mine, but he was already turning, his coat flaring out behind him as he moved away. The fire roared louder behind him, and I was left standing in the thickening smoke, the taste of ash in my mouth.

I wanted to call out to him, to demand he explain what I'd just seen, but something about the way he walked away stopped me. There was no time for answers, not now, not when the library—my library—was being consumed before our eyes. So, I stayed silent, my feet rooted to the pavement, my mind reeling.

But as I watched him disappear into the distance, I couldn't shake the feeling that the fire had been waiting for him. As if it had called him here, just as I had been called to it.

And something told me the answers I was seeking might be buried in the ashes.

The fire wasn't the only thing consuming the night. There was something in the air, a lingering heat that had nothing to do with the flames but everything to do with the tension that crackled between Callum and me. I stood there, a few feet away from the edge of the fire's reach, staring after him as he disappeared into the chaos, his silhouette barely visible through the thick smoke. A thousand questions swirled in my mind—questions I didn't even know how to ask.

It wasn't just the fire, or the strangeness of the night, or even the fact that something—someone—had set the entire scene in motion. No, it was the way Callum had touched me. The grip of his hand on my arm had been too intense, too desperate. I could still feel the warmth of his fingers on my skin, the sensation lingering as if he had marked me in some way. And when he had pulled me away, it wasn't just to keep me safe; there had been something more in it. There was an urgency in his touch, an intensity that wasn't about fire or danger. It was about something I couldn't name, something deeper and much harder to understand.

I rubbed my arm absentmindedly, where his hand had gripped me, feeling the phantom ache of his touch. And yet, my mind kept circling back to the look in his eyes. The flicker of fear. It had been there, sharp and sudden, like a crack in glass. I couldn't unsee it, couldn't stop thinking about it.

But there was no time for wondering. No time to unravel the mystery that was Callum, the man who seemed to arrive just in time to save the day, or at least to keep me from making a fool of myself. A loud crack from the direction of the library pulled me from my thoughts, and I turned just in time to see a part of the roof collapse, sending a plume of sparks into the air. The firefighters were still battling the blaze, but it felt like a losing game. The fire was too much, too fast, too wild to contain.

I should have left. I should have gone home, let them do their job and stand back while they fought the flames. But something kept me there, my feet unwilling to move. It was the same feeling I had when I was close to the library itself, a pull, an urge to uncover what had been hidden in the place I had spent so many hours. This fire felt like a message, and I wasn't about to walk away without understanding it. Without knowing who had sent it.

I glanced back at the shadows where Callum had vanished, my pulse quickening. The thought of him, of his unsettling presence, made my stomach twist with something that wasn't fear, but something else—something I couldn't quite identify. He was the kind of person who made you feel like you were drowning in a pool of your own thoughts, the kind who could look at you without speaking and make you believe he knew every last secret you'd ever had. That's the problem with people like Callum—they didn't let you forget how much you didn't know.

My eyes narrowed as I scanned the area. I had lost sight of him in the crowd, but I knew he hadn't gone far. There was something in the way he moved that kept him in the periphery of my vision. I didn't have to search for long. He was back—emerging from the side of the building with a fire chief in tow. I couldn't make out what they were talking about, but their body language was enough to tell me that Callum wasn't here just to watch the fire burn. He had a plan. He always did.

I moved closer, my curiosity sharper than my instinct for self-preservation. The air was thick with smoke, and it stung my eyes, making them water as I stood just behind the crowd of onlookers. I could hear bits and pieces of the conversation—fragments that meant nothing to me but felt important somehow.

"...too risky... can't risk another flare-up..."

"I know what I'm doing. Let me help."

"Help?" The fire chief's voice was skeptical, but I could hear the thread of concern underneath. "You sure about that, Mr. Callum?"

I moved a little closer, just enough to make out Callum's response. He was standing taller now, his posture straight, his demeanor cool. "I've been here before. I know how this works."

There was no mistaking the tension in his voice, and when I saw the way the fire chief looked at him—narrowing his eyes like he was seeing something he didn't entirely trust—I felt a chill crawl down my spine.

Callum wasn't just a man with a plan. He was someone who made people uncomfortable, someone whose presence made you wonder what kind of dangerous things you were missing. That, right there, was the kind of person who didn't show fear. Not to anyone.

Except he had shown it. Or at least, I thought he had. The way his eyes had locked with mine—there was something there. I wasn't imagining it.

Before I could approach them, before I could ask any of the questions that were now burning through me, I saw Callum turn sharply and begin moving toward the street. His eyes met mine for a split second, and without a word, he walked past me. His presence was like a shadow, wrapping around me, making the hairs on the back of my neck stand up.

I wanted to stop him, to ask him everything I had been holding back, but my feet stayed rooted to the ground, my mouth suddenly dry. He wasn't going to answer any of my questions. Not now. Not ever.

And then, just as quickly as he had come, he was gone again—disappearing into the dark streets beyond the fire's reach.

I stood there, alone in the smoke, my thoughts tangled, my heart still racing. The library burned, and with it, the pieces of a puzzle I wasn't sure I could solve. And I wasn't sure I wanted to.

The fire's sirens still echoed in the distance, a high-pitched scream that seemed to carve through the heavy, suffocating air. It should have been fading, but the closer I got to the heart of the chaos, the louder they became, cutting through the fog of my thoughts, making everything feel too sharp, too real. I tried to swallow, but the smoke, still thick and lingering, made it feel like my throat was closing. I needed to leave, to find a moment of clarity, but my feet felt like they were stuck in place. I kept replaying the way Callum had looked at me, that brief flash of vulnerability, and it gnawed at me with each passing second.

Was it fear? A crack in his calm, measured exterior? Or had I simply wanted it to be fear? The thought kept turning over in my mind, over and over, until I couldn't hold onto it anymore. What had been there—if anything—was gone now, replaced by the same stoic, almost cold mask he always wore. But I could still feel his touch, still feel the heat of it on my arm, searing through the fabric of my jacket, like it was a brand that left its mark no matter how far I walked.

I glanced around the street, as though someone might suddenly have the answers to all my questions. But there was no one to ask. The fire crew, organized chaos in motion, were huddled in their own world of equipment and urgency, their faces set in grim determination. I stepped back, away from the building and the confusion, trying to put some distance between myself and the shifting whirlwind of my thoughts.

That's when I saw it.

A figure standing just at the edge of the crowd, half-hidden behind the smoke, watching me. I blinked. No way. It was Callum again, his silhouette too familiar to be anyone else. He hadn't left, not really. He was just waiting, like a shadow, waiting for something—waiting for me, maybe. Or maybe he was waiting for the fire to finish what it had started.

My pulse quickened as I made my way toward him, my steps tentative, as though the ground might swallow me whole if I wasn't careful. As I drew closer, I could see the tension in his posture, the way he stood slightly hunched, like a predator, coiled and ready to spring at the slightest provocation. His eyes, dark and unreadable, flicked over me with an intensity that sent a shiver up my spine.

"You're still here," I said, my voice quieter than I intended, almost surprised to hear it. I didn't expect an answer, or at least, I didn't think I did, but he surprised me.

"I told you not to get too close," he muttered, almost to himself. His gaze never wavered from the fire, his jaw tight as if he was battling an internal war, one that I didn't want to think about too hard.

"You didn't tell me why," I replied, the words sharp and a little more insistent than I'd meant them to be. I didn't want him to know how much I had noticed, how much I had been trying to piece together from the flashes I'd seen in him. But I couldn't help it. His silence, his refusal to answer, was infuriating.

For a long moment, he didn't say anything. He just stood there, his eyes tracing the path of the flames, flickering in the night air. I could feel the weight of his gaze on me, though he wasn't looking at me directly. He was still calculating something, as if he was deciding whether to speak, whether to allow me in just a little more.

I couldn't stop myself from speaking again. "You're not going to tell me anything, are you?"

A faint, almost imperceptible smile tugged at the corner of his lips, though it was gone before I could fully grasp it. "I'm not in the habit of explaining myself to anyone," he said, his voice smooth but laced with something dark. It wasn't just dismissive—it was... protective. Like he was keeping something from me, something that he thought was better left untouched.

I felt my frustration rise, my body bristling with the urge to push him, to break through whatever it was he was keeping locked inside. "You're lying," I shot back, surprising even myself with the force behind the words. "This fire—this isn't just some accident. You know that, don't you?"

He didn't flinch. If anything, he seemed to brace himself, the tension in his body heightening, as if he knew exactly where this conversation was heading. "I don't lie," he said, his tone colder now, his eyes finally meeting mine, and I could see the steel beneath them. But there was something else, too. Something that flickered in those dark depths. "I don't have to explain myself to you. You'll figure it out in time."

I took a step forward, emboldened by something I couldn't quite place. "You want me to figure it out?" I asked, narrowing my eyes, daring him to admit it. "You want me to know something you're not telling me? Fine. Then answer me this—what is it you're really afraid of, Callum?"

His face, usually a mask of calm, shifted for the briefest moment. His jaw clenched, and I saw the flash of something in his eyes—something so raw and primal it made my stomach lurch. But before I could process it, he stepped back, his hand lifting in a swift motion that told me I had crossed a line.

"I told you to stay away," he repeated, this time quieter, more dangerous. There was something in his voice now that made me question whether I had pushed too far. And before I could react, he turned, disappearing into the crowd as quickly as he had appeared.

I stood there for a moment, my heart pounding in my chest, my mind racing. I hadn't expected that—any of it. Not the fear in his eyes, not the way he had seemed almost desperate to keep me from uncovering whatever it was he was hiding. And as the fire crackled behind me, swallowing everything in its path, I couldn't help but feel that it wasn't the only thing threatening to burn.

Chapter 5: A City Ablaze

The city was ablaze, though not in the way the firemen would have liked. It was a hunger—an insatiable thirst for something to burn. A passion that seethed under the skin of Oldtown like a fever. We all felt it, from the nervous cough of the town criers to the frantic clatter of heels on cobblestones. Fire had always been a presence in Oldtown—part of our rhythm, our heartbeat—but now it was something else. Something wrong. A dark tide that no one could hold back.

It wasn't just the infernos licking the sides of buildings, their tongues of red and orange staining the night sky. No, it was the undercurrent. The tension in the air. You could taste it in the sour bite of the smoke. People were no longer walking casually between the market stalls or pausing to admire the wares of the street vendors. There was a hasty urgency in their movements, a frantic hurry to get somewhere, anywhere, away from the madness that seemed to be spreading through every corner of the city. It was in the way the air felt heavier than it should, pressing down on your chest as you tried to breathe.

I'd always thought Oldtown was built on fire—a city carved from ash, with walls that could withstand the heat, but even those once sturdy bricks now seemed to tremble. Every step I took felt like I was walking in someone else's world. I had lived here all my life, but the faces seemed unfamiliar, the streets unrecognizable, like I was a stranger in my own home. The city that had once hummed with the rhythm of daily life now quivered on the brink of something darker. Something like madness.

And then there was Callum.

We had a complicated relationship, one that was less a friendship and more an ongoing battle of wills, though the battlefield was never clearly drawn. He was the kind of man who didn't do anything halfway. When he stepped into a room, it felt as though the air itself shifted to make space for him. His presence was heavy, commanding, and I could never quite tell if it was because of his raw intensity or his tendency to make every conversation feel like a duel.

Lately, however, that intensity had a new edge to it. I couldn't place it at first, but it was there. Lurking. Lurking in the way he always seemed to know more than he was saying, especially about the fires. I had learned to keep my thoughts to myself around him, to watch the way he shifted his weight when I asked questions, how his eyes narrowed just slightly before he offered some vague, half-hearted explanation.

But this was different. There was something in his silence that spoke volumes.

We had stood together, staring at the remnants of another burned-out warehouse. The heat from the flames had long since faded, leaving the scorched skeleton of the building behind. The smell of charred wood still clung to my clothes, but Callum seemed unaffected, as if the smoke had never reached him. I wasn't sure what bothered me more—the fact that he stood there, unmoved, or the way he seemed too comfortable with the ashes of a place I had once known.

"You know," I said, my voice tight, "every fire has been the same. All of them. The pattern, the timing, the method."

Callum's jaw tightened, his gaze fixed on the ruins before him. "It's just the way things go sometimes. Old buildings are dry. The wind picks up, and—"

"Don't," I cut him off, frustration bubbling in my chest. "That's not it. You've been here every time. Every. Single. Time. You know more about how these fires start than anyone. How do you explain that?"

He turned toward me, his face shadowed by the flickering flames, but there was something in his eyes that I couldn't decipher—something cold, something distant.

"You're imagining things, Elsa. It's just coincidence. Bad luck, that's all."

His words were smooth, almost too smooth. And it was that lack of hesitation that made the hairs on the back of my neck rise. I wasn't imagining things. There was something in the way he spoke, the way he brushed off the question like it was nothing.

But I couldn't get him to admit it. The silence between us stretched thin, taut like a wire ready to snap.

"I don't think you're telling me the whole truth," I muttered, stepping closer. The words spilled out before I could stop them, but there was no going back now.

"Maybe," he said softly, his voice like gravel scraping against stone. "But that doesn't mean you'll like the answer when you find it."

The words hung there, and for a brief moment, we both just stood there, staring at each other. The wind rustled through the charred remains of the building, sending ash spiraling into the air. The flames flickered, casting eerie shadows that made the city feel alive—like it was waiting, too.

I could feel the pulse of the city beneath my feet, vibrating through the cobblestones, and I wondered if I had been right all along. Maybe the fires were the least of our problems. Maybe it was the people—like Callum—who held the city's future in their hands, even if they didn't know it yet.

His voice broke the silence again, low and measured, as if weighing each word carefully. "The city isn't what you think it is, Elsa. It's been burned to the ground before, and it will be again. Some things don't change."

My breath caught in my throat as I stared at him. The firelight danced across his face, making him look like a stranger, someone I didn't recognize, someone with secrets of his own. And I wondered—no, I was certain—that his connection to this madness was deeper than he let on. But whether he was part of the fire or simply caught in its wake, I still couldn't tell.

The next few days bled together in a blur of smoke and heat. It felt as if the fires were spreading faster than anyone could contain them. And the city, once bustling with life, was now hushed, the usual noise muffled under a blanket of unease. I would walk the streets, keeping my head down, trying to blend into the crowd, but I always felt the weight of eyes on me—eyes that were no longer friendly, no longer curious. They were wary, suspicious, and I couldn't blame them.

Everyone was looking for a reason, a person to blame, and the city was already splitting into factions, each group pointing its fingers in a different direction. I heard whispers in the marketplace, voices rising in anger about the 'outsiders' who had come to Oldtown in the wake of the fires. They were the first ones accused, blamed for setting the flames as some sort of twisted revenge on the city that had welcomed them. But I wasn't so sure. There were too many inconsistencies, too many gaps in the story. And in the middle of it all, there was Callum, slipping in and out of the shadows, his presence more unsettling with each passing day.

I found myself following him more than I cared to admit, trying to make sense of the tension that pulsed between us like an electric current. It was in the way he looked at me when I asked questions—those dark eyes that seemed to see through me, like he knew something I didn't. It was in the little things: the way his hands would flex, the slight tension in his jaw whenever the topic of the fires came up. And there was that silence—the kind that stretched out, thick and heavy, between us, as though he was waiting for me to figure it out on my own.

One evening, as the sun dipped below the horizon, painting the sky in fiery hues, I found myself outside the tavern where Callum was known to frequent. The building was tucked away on a side street, dark and quiet, but tonight, there was an energy about it that I couldn't ignore. The door was cracked open, a dim light spilling into the street, and I could hear the low murmur of voices inside. I hesitated for a moment before pushing the door open, slipping inside like a shadow.

The atmosphere was different from the usual rowdy chaos of the tavern. The air was thick with tension, every conversation hushed, every glance wary. I spotted Callum at the bar, his back to me, leaning against the wood like he owned it. He hadn't seen me yet, and for a moment, I stood there, watching him. There was something about the way he held himself, the easy confidence in his posture that unsettled me. It wasn't just the way he moved or spoke—it was the way he made everything else seem irrelevant.

I approached slowly, feeling the weight of my footsteps as they echoed through the quiet room. When I was close enough, I dropped into the seat beside him without a word. He didn't look at me, didn't acknowledge my presence, but the slight shift in his shoulders told me he knew exactly who had joined him.

For a long moment, the silence stretched between us. The only sound was the clink of glasses and the soft murmur of conversations too low to catch. Finally, I couldn't take it anymore. "You're hiding something, Callum," I said, my voice barely above a whisper, but sharp enough to cut through the stillness.

He didn't flinch, didn't even glance at me. Instead, he took a slow sip from his glass, the amber liquid catching the light as he swirled it lazily. "I'm not hiding anything," he said, his tone as casual as ever, but there was a sharp edge to it now, something that told me I had touched a nerve.

I leaned in closer, my voice low, a thread of frustration creeping into it. "You're involved in this somehow. I can feel it. You know more than you're letting on."

This time, he finally turned to look at me, his eyes locking onto mine with an intensity that made my breath catch in my throat. His gaze was unreadable, the faintest flicker of something there and gone before I could name it. "You're wrong," he said, his voice low, almost too low. "I'm not involved. I'm just trying to keep my head down, same as you."

I wanted to believe him. I wanted to take him at his word, but I couldn't. Not when there was too much left unsaid, not when every word that came from his lips sounded like a carefully crafted lie. I had seen it in the way he reacted to the fires, in the way he held back when the conversation turned to the arsonist. The things he didn't say spoke louder than anything he did.

"You're a terrible liar, you know that?" I said, the words escaping before I could stop them. "You think I don't see it? The way you get all twitchy whenever the subject comes up? You can't hide it from me, Callum."

His lips twitched into a smile, but there was no humor in it. It was sharp, almost bitter. "I'm not trying to hide anything, Elsa. But if you really want to know the truth—if you're so damn desperate to figure it out—you're going to have to be prepared for what you might find."

I leaned back, my heart hammering in my chest. His words hung in the air, pregnant with promise, and for a brief, terrifying moment, I wasn't sure if I wanted to hear whatever truth he was holding back. But I couldn't stop myself. I couldn't walk away from it. "Tell me," I whispered. "What aren't you telling me?"

Callum's eyes softened just for a moment, something flickering behind them, and then he sighed. "You're not ready, Elsa. Not yet."

And just like that, the walls went back up. He was shut off, closed down. But this time, the silence wasn't uncomfortable—it was a challenge. A dare.

The fire was spreading, and so was the distance between us. But I couldn't turn away now, not when I was this close to the truth.

The fire raged through the night, a beast that refused to be tamed, its red glow reflecting off every surface, bathing the city in an unholy light. I had always believed that Oldtown was built to withstand such destruction, its cobbled streets and stone buildings thick with history. But now, as the flames danced in the distance, licking the sky, I realized how fragile this place really was. It was all so fragile.

The smell of smoke, thick and acrid, was everywhere. Even the air felt different—stale and choking, as though the city itself was suffocating. I'd walked these streets for years, knew every twist and turn, every hidden alley, but today, it felt like I was a stranger in my own home. The fires had done something to the people, too. Their eyes were wide with fear, their movements jerky, as if at any moment the city could collapse beneath them. The community I had once known, that shared look between neighbors and the casual greetings on the corners, was now replaced with distrust, suspicion, and a heavy silence that hung like a fog.

And still, there was Callum.

Every time I saw him, he seemed more distant, more wrapped in his own thoughts, always watching, always waiting. I could feel his presence even when he wasn't there. He had become a shadow in my life, slipping in and out of view, and yet I couldn't stop following him. Not literally, of course. But I watched from a distance, always aware of where he was, what he was doing. He had become my obsession, my puzzle, and for some reason I couldn't leave it unsolved.

It was on the fifth day after that last conversation, when the fires had grown closer, their heat so fierce it seemed as if the entire city might burst into flames at any second, that I found myself at his door. I had no intention of knocking, no intention of engaging him in more of the same game of cat and mouse we'd been playing. But something inside me—the same something that had driven me to seek answers in the first place—pushed me forward, until my knuckles were rapping against the door.

It creaked open after a long moment, and there he stood, his face half-lit by the low-burning lamp on the table behind him. His eyes, though, were dark, impenetrable, as though he had known I was coming.

"Elsa," he said, his voice flat, as though he were already tired of the conversation we were about to have.

I swallowed, gathering my resolve. "I need to know, Callum. I can't keep wondering."

His gaze flickered for a fraction of a second—just enough for me to catch it, but too quickly for him to mask it. "I don't know what you're talking about." His words were carefully chosen, but the tension in his voice betrayed him.

I stepped inside before he could shut the door, brushing past him with the ease of someone who had been here more times than they could count. "Don't lie to me. Not anymore. Not when this whole city is burning."

He closed the door with a soft click, his back pressed against it, his arms crossing in front of him like a wall. "And you think I have answers to that?"

"I think you know more than you're letting on. I think you've known it from the start," I said, my voice rising, sharp with frustration. The raw anger I had been holding in since the fires began spilled out, unfiltered. "You've been here every time, Callum. You know how the fires start. You know how they spread. You—"

"I don't know anything," he cut me off, his voice sharp, colder than I'd ever heard it. "And you need to stop looking for something that isn't there. It's not as simple as you think."

"I think you're hiding something," I said, stepping closer, my heart pounding in my chest. "I think you're hiding the truth."

The words were out before I could stop them, and I could see the way his jaw clenched, the muscles in his neck tightening. There was something different in him tonight. A flicker of something I couldn't quite name, a shift in the atmosphere that made the air feel suddenly thick with tension. It wasn't just the anger now—it was something deeper, something older, something that had been festering for far longer than I had realized.

He moved away from the door, his steps slow and deliberate, but the storm that had been brewing in his eyes was evident. "You don't want to know the truth, Elsa. Not the way I know it."

I frowned, narrowing my eyes. "What does that mean?"

He turned, his back to me now, his voice quieter but heavier. "It means you think you're ready for the truth. But there are things in this city—things that go beyond the fires. And they're not the kind of things that can be undone."

I took a step forward, unwilling to back down. "What are you saying? That you know something no one else does? That you've been hiding it all this time?"

Callum didn't answer immediately. Instead, he stepped toward the window, the low glow from the streetlamps casting long shadows over his face. His back was still to me, but I could feel the weight of his words pressing down on me like a vice.

"Why do you think they're spreading so fast?" he asked, his voice barely a whisper.

The question hung in the air like a challenge, daring me to answer. But I didn't know. I had no answers. Just the same burning questions, the same gut feeling that I was missing something important, something essential.

"I don't know," I said, the words coming out softer than I intended.

Callum turned, his gaze sharp, focused. "Because it's not just about the fires, Elsa. It's about who is lighting them—and why. And I think you're getting too close."

I froze, the blood in my veins running cold. "Who?" I whispered.

The words were already hanging on his lips, but then the sharp sound of shattering glass cut through the night. A crash. Then a scream.

It came from just outside the window. The voice was frantic, panicked. My heart skipped a beat. Something was happening. Something that had to do with all of this—something I wasn't prepared for.

"Get down," Callum barked, his tone suddenly urgent. But it was too late.

The fire had already come. And this time, it wasn't just in the city. It was here, at the doorstep.

Chapter 6: Sparks Fly

The hum of the station's fluorescent lights had long since become the soundtrack of my nights. They flickered in their usual rhythm, casting faint shadows across the cluttered countertops, the rows of coffee cups, and the stacks of paperwork. Outside, the night was still. If it wasn't for the occasional hum of a distant siren or the call of the crickets in the alleyway behind the building, it could have been the kind of silence that lingers too long, wrapping itself around your chest like a heavy blanket. But it was late, and the station had emptied out—everyone else had gone home, leaving just me and Callum to keep watch.

I could still feel the prickling tension from earlier, the way his eyes had narrowed when I spoke, like every word I said was a challenge he wasn't willing to let slide. Callum, with his stern jaw and the air of someone who didn't need to explain himself to anyone, had a way of making everything he said feel like a test. Maybe I had failed. Maybe I didn't care. But standing there now, with only the two of us left in the echoing space, I couldn't shake the feeling that something had shifted between us, even if I wasn't sure what that something was.

I was just reaching for my coffee cup, still lukewarm from hours ago, when the lights flickered. Then went out.

The sudden quiet in the dark was palpable, a thick fog that seemed to seep into the walls of the station. I couldn't hear anything—no hum of the machines, no faint rush of wind outside. Just... stillness. Absolute stillness.

"Great," I muttered to myself, reaching for the flashlight beneath the desk. "Perfect timing."

Callum's voice sliced through the darkness. "You're not afraid of the dark, are you?"

I smirked, hearing the challenge in his words even without the aid of light. "Afraid? I grew up in this town. If anything, the dark's afraid of me."

"Is that right?" His voice was closer now, and I could hear the smile in it, even without seeing it. I hesitated before answering, finding his proximity suddenly overwhelming. Something about the dark made everything seem sharper, heightened.

"Yeah, well, a few years in this place teaches you how to keep your head on straight. You should try it sometime."

He chuckled, low and almost dangerous. "I think I've got my own way of keeping my head on straight."

I couldn't help the laugh that escaped me. "Right. I'm sure you do."

The tension that had clung to us earlier was still there, but now it felt almost like a current, zipping through the space between us. I couldn't remember the last time I had been alone in this station with him. Alone with anyone, for that matter. It was strange.

And then, just like that, the air between us shifted.

In the dark, it was like the world fell away, leaving just the two of us with our unspoken words and shared history. Callum's voice was quieter now, almost vulnerable, like he wasn't used to letting his guard down, but didn't mind that I could see a crack in the armor.

"My dad used to take me out to the firehouse when I was a kid," he said, the words heavy with memory. "I used to sit on the counter, play with the knobs on the equipment, watch them get ready for calls. He never made a big deal out of it. Just... let me be there, you know?"

I felt my heart soften before I could stop it. The casual way he spoke, like the memory wasn't an ache, was a stark contrast to the tension that usually surrounded him.

"What happened?" I asked, the words slipping out before I could think about them. There was a rawness in his tone that made my chest ache.

Callum paused, and for a moment, I thought he wouldn't answer. But then his voice came again, barely above a whisper.

"He didn't make it out of a blaze one night. He was... caught in the collapse of a building. I was fourteen."

I swallowed. The weight of his words hung in the air like the smoke from a fire that hadn't quite gone out. My mind raced, piecing together the layers of a man who wore his scars like a badge, even if no one could see them beneath the cold exterior.

"God, Callum... I'm sorry."

His laugh was bitter. "Don't be. You didn't do it."

I didn't know what to say to that, so I didn't say anything at all. The room felt smaller now, the darkness pressing in, wrapping us in its cool, distant embrace. I could hear the soft shuffle of his shoes as he moved closer. Just a step or two. Just enough to close the distance.

"You're not the only one with baggage," he said, his words cutting through the silence. "Everyone's got something they're running from."

There was a tremor in his voice then, something that wasn't anger or frustration, but something far softer, far more dangerous. Something real.

Before I could respond, the lights flickered back on, harsh and jarring.

The room snapped back into focus, the familiar clamor of machines and desks and paperwork filling the space. It was like the world had hit rewind, and we were suddenly thrust back into the ordinary, the mundane, as if nothing had changed. The air between us was electric now, charged, and I couldn't tell if I wanted to lean in or pull back.

"Guess the power's back," I said, forcing a grin to cover the knot that had suddenly formed in my stomach.

Callum didn't answer right away, his gaze lingering on me, the flicker of something unreadable in his eyes. He took a deep breath and, for a moment, I thought he might say something. But he didn't. Instead, he turned, the air between us still crackling with the ghost of what we'd almost said.

And I couldn't help but feel that I had missed something important. Something that could have changed everything.

The sudden blast of fluorescent light hit me like a slap to the face, dragging me back into the world I knew, the world where everything had clear boundaries—lines you didn't cross, expectations you didn't shatter. Callum took a step back, his eyes still on me, as if we'd just shared something we couldn't name, something that lingered between us like smoke from an old fire, impossible to sweep away.

I cleared my throat. The moment was over. It had to be.

"Guess we're back to business," I said, the words a little too sharp, a little too forced. I tried to swallow the sudden dryness in my throat, as if that would somehow quell the pulse of something—I wasn't sure what—sizzling beneath my skin.

Callum nodded, but his gaze was still intense, like he hadn't quite left the space where we'd just been. I wanted to look away, but I couldn't. There was something magnetic in the way he stood, something that pulled at me even when I wished it wouldn't.

"So, uh, are we going to pretend that didn't just happen?" I asked, awkwardly shuffling some papers on the desk in front of me. Anything to stop the conversation from lingering where it didn't belong. I wasn't equipped to deal with the softness that had flashed through his eyes, with the vulnerability that had cracked his otherwise stoic demeanor.

Callum didn't answer right away. He didn't need to, because I knew. We weren't going to pretend. Not this time.

Instead, he turned away, running a hand through his hair. "No," he said, his voice rougher than usual. "I don't know what happened. But—"

He stopped, clearly unsure of how to finish the sentence.

"Well, we can't exactly go back to normal after that, can we?" I muttered, my mind racing to catch up with the strange current between us.

"Normal's overrated anyway," he muttered back, but there was something in his tone that made me wonder if he was talking about more than just our situation.

I didn't know why, but it irritated me. I had learned to rely on my understanding of normal, on what was expected, even in this unpredictable town. But in that one unexpected, silent moment, when the lights had gone out, when it had been just the two of us, something had shifted. And it didn't feel like something I could easily slide back into the box I'd kept it in before.

The stillness between us stretched on, neither of us speaking, both of us trapped in the silence of what could've been—and what wasn't. I glanced at the clock. It was almost time for my shift to end, and I had a half-formed plan to leave, to escape the weight of the night and its strange, heavy atmosphere.

But of course, things didn't go as planned.

The sudden blare of a siren outside shattered the tension, yanking me out of my thoughts. Callum was already on his feet, his face tightening into the professional mask I had come to expect from him. He moved quickly, grabbing his jacket, a grim line forming on his lips as he checked the time.

I stood too, following his lead. "Another fire?"

"Could be," he said, already heading for the door. "You coming?"

I wasn't sure why I hesitated, but I did. The last thing I wanted to do was get caught up in this firestorm of confusion I'd suddenly found myself in. But the adrenaline kicked in, the instinct to help, to be useful, overriding everything else.

"Yeah," I said, more firmly than I felt. "Let's go."

We were both outside before the sound of the sirens had fully faded, heading toward the fire trucks parked across the street. The chaos of the moment seemed to strip away all the weight of the earlier conversation, replacing it with the focus and urgency of the job at hand. There was no time for small talk, no room for the awkwardness that had been simmering between us.

Callum slid behind the wheel of the firetruck with the ease of someone who had done it a thousand times. I climbed in beside him, our knees brushing for the briefest second, and the heat flared up again, sharp and unwelcome. I was already breathing harder than I should've been, but I didn't let myself focus on that.

"Everything okay?" I asked, watching him as he checked the dashboard.

"Fine," he answered quickly, but there was something in his voice that made me doubt the simplicity of his response. His hands tightened around the wheel, and his jaw set in that familiar, hardened line.

"You don't look fine," I said, my tone softer now, though the words had slipped out before I could stop them.

Callum glanced over at me, his eyes narrowing. "You're not in my head, you don't get to decide if I'm fine or not."

I blinked, momentarily stunned by his sharpness. It felt like a slap, one that left a sting lingering far longer than it should've. But I couldn't help it; his reaction hurt, and I hated that I was the one who had caused it.

I opened my mouth to apologize, to say something, anything, that would smooth over the jagged edge of the moment, but before

I could, the truck jerked forward, and the sirens screamed once again.

It was a familiar chaos, one I had known for years, and for the next few minutes, there was no room for anything but the urgency of the situation. We worked like we always did—silent, focused, efficient—each of us playing our part without the need for much exchange. But I couldn't shake the feeling that something had shifted. And with every pull of the gearshift, every turn of the wheel, I felt that shift stretch between us, impossible to ignore.

The fire truck screeched to a halt in front of the building. The faint smell of smoke lingered in the air, a reminder that, no matter how far we tried to run from the heat of the past, it always had a way of catching up with us. The fire was contained, but I could still feel the electric hum of tension vibrating between us as I unbuckled my seatbelt.

Callum was already out of the truck, his feet hitting the pavement with that purposeful stride I had come to know all too well. I hesitated for a split second, watching him, that same pull twisting in my gut. The man wore his emotional armor better than anyone I'd ever known, and yet, there was something raw in his movements now, something unguarded.

I shook myself out of it. This wasn't the time. I followed him quickly, my boots thudding against the asphalt as I tried to catch up. The smoke from the fire was already starting to dissipate, leaving the cold night air to settle in its place. A shiver crept down my spine, but it had nothing to do with the temperature.

"Is it over?" I asked, more out of habit than any real concern. Callum had already dropped his jacket, grabbing for a hose to clean up the last traces of the fire.

"Yeah," he grunted, his face lit up with the glow of the flashing lights, but his eyes were focused on the ground, almost as if he was working through some internal problem rather than paying attention to the job in front of him.

I watched him for a beat longer than I intended, noticing the way his muscles tensed with every move, how he was always in control, always detached, as though the weight of the world was something he could carry without ever letting it break him.

"Well, that's a relief," I said, trying to inject some levity into the moment, though I wasn't sure it landed. Callum didn't respond, his focus unwavering as he worked the nozzle of the hose with quick, practiced movements. I bit my lip, wondering if he would talk to me again, if that odd moment between us earlier had been enough to change the way we interacted. Or maybe I'd been imagining things, caught in the darkness, thinking too much about a connection that didn't exist.

I glanced around the scene—nothing too serious. The fire had burned out in a few buildings, but there was no real damage, nothing permanent. A few firemen were still putting out the last embers, and the rest of the crew was finishing up paperwork. I turned to Callum, ready to ask him about the next move when I noticed that something was different in the way he stood. His shoulders were hunched, the usual precision in his movements gone.

"You good?" I asked, my voice quieter now, more cautious.

He paused, the hose hanging limply in his hand as he stared down at the ground. His expression was unreadable, distant. Then, he shifted slightly, as if he didn't want me to notice the way his jaw clenched.

"I'm fine," he said, his voice low, but there was a sharp edge to it.

I wanted to believe him. I really did. But something in his tone made the hairs on the back of my neck stand up.

"Callum," I started, taking a step closer. "You don't have to pretend—"

"I said I'm fine!" His voice cut through the air like a whip, and for the first time, there was nothing holding him back. His mask had cracked, revealing the exhaustion and frustration underneath.

I wasn't sure how to respond. Everything in me screamed to take a step back, to leave him to process whatever demons he was fighting. But something wouldn't let me go. I couldn't just walk away—not now, not after everything that had happened. I watched him, trying to make sense of the man standing in front of me, the man who wore his past like a weight around his neck, even though it was clear he didn't want anyone to know it.

"I don't need your pity," he muttered, still refusing to meet my gaze. "I don't need anyone feeling sorry for me."

I was silent for a long moment, the weight of his words settling over me. His bitterness—so raw, so unyielding—was enough to break anyone. But I wasn't just anyone.

"You think I feel sorry for you?" I asked, finally finding my voice. "No. I'm just trying to understand what you're going through. You don't get to push me away just because you're scared of what's underneath all that anger."

His head snapped up, his eyes flashing with something dangerous. "You have no idea what it's like," he spat, his breath coming faster now. "You don't know what it's like to lose someone—"

I froze.

To lose someone.

I wasn't sure what came over me in that moment, but it was like a switch had been flipped. Everything I had tried to keep buried—every fear, every regret—came crashing down around me. I stared at him, heart pounding, mouth dry. We had never really talked about our pasts, and I had never told him about my own struggles, about what I had lost and what I still carried. And now, suddenly, the distance between us was so much bigger than I had realized.

I opened my mouth to say something, but before I could speak, the radio crackled, cutting through the silence.

"Unit 42, we've got a situation. Potential hostage situation. Suspect armed."

Callum's face went pale. He turned to me, his eyes wide for the first time tonight.

"We have to go," he said, his voice tight, suddenly back to business. There was no time for anything else, no room for what had been said between us, no moment to breathe.

And just like that, the door to whatever might have been between us slammed shut again.

Chapter 7: The Firebug

The air hung heavy with the scent of smoke, a stubborn reminder of the fire that had already gutted part of Westville. I'd been here before, but this time, there was something different in the way it felt. Callum's figure was already cutting through the haze as I stood on the curb, my boots crunching against the wet pavement. It wasn't the usual dampness of a storm; no, this was something darker, something wrong. The kind of damp that clung to your skin long after the flames had been put out.

It wasn't just the smell of scorched wood that seemed to saturate the air. No, it was the undercurrent of tension, thick as tar, curling up around us as we surveyed the damage. The youth center, once a safe haven for the neighborhood kids, now resembled a hollowed-out shell, its windows shattered, the walls blackened with soot. You could feel the loss—the fire had taken more than bricks and mortar. It had taken a part of the community, a sense of safety.

And there he was, always one step ahead, Callum. His silhouette a sharp contrast against the backdrop of destruction. His jaw was clenched, eyes fixed on something only he could see, his entire body tense with purpose. I should've expected it, should've braced myself for what was to come. But when he turned and his eyes locked onto mine, a jolt ran through me—something sharp, almost painful. I hated how it felt, the way my heart did this ridiculous flutter in my chest, the way it flipped when I remembered that he was just as capable of destruction as the fire itself.

"Why are you here?" His voice was rough, like gravel scraping against stone, carrying a weight I could feel even before he spoke. His tone was sharp, but the question wasn't what stung the most. It was the way he said it, like he was questioning my every move, my very reason for standing there, as if I didn't belong.

"I'm here because the fire didn't start itself, Callum," I said, my voice tighter than I intended. "Because I'm not going to just stand around while you play hero and try to figure out who's setting these damn things."

He scowled, lips curling just enough to show the frustration building inside him. I wasn't sure if it was directed at me or just the situation, but I didn't really care. He was already walking toward me, the sound of his boots loud against the empty street. I held my ground, despite the unease creeping under my skin like some slow-acting poison. I wasn't about to let him intimidate me, not again.

"You've got a lot of questions," he muttered, voice low but cutting. His eyes flickered over me with that too-familiar judgment, the one that made me feel like he could see straight through me, right into the mess I was desperately trying to keep buried.

"You're damn right I do," I shot back. "And you're not giving me anything. What's going on, Callum? You've been on every scene, every fire. Don't tell me you're just trying to 'save the day' here. This is personal. You're too close to this."

He narrowed his eyes, and I could see the muscles in his jaw twitch, like he was holding back the words he wanted to throw at me. I wasn't afraid of the anger I could see brewing behind those eyes. What I was afraid of was the thought that I might be right. That there was something he wasn't telling me.

"I don't know what you're talking about," he said, the words clipped, each one sharp as a knife. "You think I'm responsible for this? You think I'm the one behind the fires?"

The accusation in his voice was too much to ignore. It was like a slap, even if it was veiled behind the facade of calm. And I snapped.

"Maybe I do," I spat. "Maybe you've got something to hide. I'm not an idiot, Callum. I can see it. You're here too often, too soon. Every damn time, you're the first one on the scene."

His eyes flashed with something—a flicker of something darker, and for the briefest second, I wondered if I had hit too close to the truth. Maybe I had. But before I could process that thought, he was turning away, his coat swirling around him like a shadow.

"Get out of here," he said, his voice cold and distant. "I'm done talking to you."

And just like that, he was gone. It wasn't just that he walked away—it was the finality of it, the way he shut me out, leaving nothing but the distant roar of sirens and the whispering flames. I stood there for a long time after he was gone, my chest tight with something I couldn't name.

The city felt different somehow. The edges were sharper, the shadows darker. Was he really involved in these fires? Was it possible, or was I just imagining things, pulling threads together that didn't belong?

I didn't know. But what I did know, standing in the ashes of another disaster, was that I couldn't shake the feeling that this was only just beginning. That something more sinister was lurking beneath the surface, and I was in the middle of it.

The hum of the city felt wrong that morning, as though it was holding its breath, waiting for something it knew was coming but couldn't quite name. Westville, once a neighborhood that hummed with the simple chaos of everyday life, now pulsed with an undercurrent of dread. The fire had gutted the heart of it, leaving only the charred remains of hope behind. I could almost hear the echoes of the children's laughter that had once filled the halls of the youth center, replaced now by the oppressive silence that hung in the air.

I watched the scene unfold through the cracked window of my car, the glass smeared with condensation from the early morning fog. Callum was already there, working his way around the remains of the building, his sharp profile cutting through the smoke like a man on a mission. And I couldn't help myself—I was drawn to him, to the magnetism that had always pulsed between us, even when I wished it wasn't there.

I parked a few blocks away, taking a moment to gather myself before stepping into the chaos. My pulse quickened as I reached for the door handle, my fingers brushing against the cool metal. I'd been here before, stood in this place where everything was just on the cusp of something dangerous. But this time, it felt different.

The moment my feet hit the ground, I spotted him, the way his broad shoulders seemed to draw in all the light around him. He was bent over the ashes, eyes scanning the wreckage like he was piecing together some puzzle that no one else could see. I approached cautiously, but it wasn't the distance between us that made me hesitate. It was the way he was looking at me.

Callum's eyes met mine as if he'd been expecting me all along, as if he knew exactly when I would show up, and what I would do next. His lips barely moved when he spoke, the words slipping out with the kind of intensity that made my throat dry. "You're here early."

"I'm not the one who shows up before the fire trucks," I shot back, crossing my arms. The edge to my voice wasn't entirely accidental; I couldn't help myself. His proximity—his presence—tugged at me in ways I didn't want to acknowledge.

His jaw tightened, the sharp line of it practically gleaming in the pale sunlight that managed to break through the smoky haze. "I've been investigating this fire," he said, his voice colder now. "And I'm trying to figure out who's behind it."

I didn't need him to explain it further; his eyes had already given it away. There was something else there—something deeper than the job. Something more personal.

"Who else has been investigating?" I asked, my tone lighter, but underneath the surface, I was watching him like a hawk. The way his gaze flicked away from mine for a split second told me everything I needed to know. He wasn't being completely upfront with me.

"I don't know what you're implying," Callum said, his voice a little too tight. He was playing the game of pretending like everything was fine, like we were strangers in a field of ashes, when we both knew it was much more complicated than that.

I tilted my head, leaning against the side of a nearby building, unwilling to break the eye contact. "The thing is, Callum, I think you're hiding something. Maybe it's not the fire. Maybe it's you."

The words fell between us like a grenade, and for a moment, the only thing that seemed to exist in the world was the weight of what I'd said. He froze, a muscle twitching in his neck, but he didn't respond immediately. Instead, he took a step closer, closing the space between us with an unsettling deliberateness.

"You think I'm involved?" His voice was low, almost a growl, the edge of danger sharp in his words. But there was something else, something I hadn't expected—a flicker of something almost vulnerable. I didn't know whether it was regret or anger, but it left me feeling unsteady, like I had touched something raw that I wasn't supposed to see.

"I didn't say that," I replied quickly, almost defensively. "But you're acting like it. You're too... interested. Too close."

He didn't back down, but there was a shift in his expression—something deeper than the simmering tension between us. "If I'm close to anything, it's trying to stop whoever is doing this before they burn down the whole city." His voice dropped to a whisper, and for a second, it almost sounded like a plea. "I'm trying to find the truth. But the more I dig, the more I feel like I'm being pulled into something that's bigger than me."

His words hung there, the weight of them pressing on me like an invisible force. I wanted to tell him it was all right, that we would figure it out together. But something told me he wasn't ready to share whatever this was, whatever darkness had wrapped its tendrils around him. I wasn't sure I was ready for it either.

"So, what's the next move?" I asked, trying to shift the conversation, to move away from the tension that was rising between us like a storm.

He hesitated before answering, his gaze moving toward the horizon, where the smoke still curled up into the sky, dark and foreboding. "I don't know. But I'm going to find out."

I nodded, but I couldn't shake the feeling that I wasn't just talking to a man who was investigating a string of fires. No, I was talking to someone who was fighting his own fire—one that could very well burn him alive. And whether or not he would let me close enough to help was the question that lingered between us.

The world around me seemed to pulse with the echo of Callum's departure, the space where he'd been standing now feeling impossibly empty. It was one of those rare moments when the hum of the city seemed muted, as if all the noise had been swallowed by the tension between us. I didn't even know why I was still standing there, but I couldn't seem to move. My feet were stuck to the ground, and my mind kept replaying the flicker of something I couldn't name in Callum's eyes before he'd turned and walked away. Was it guilt? Or something else entirely?

I leaned back against the crumbling wall of the youth center, my eyes fixed on the charred remnants of what used to be a place of joy. The morning fog had lifted, but the smoke from the fire still lingered, curling in the air like a slow, silent reminder that something was wrong here—something more than just a string of fires.

I didn't know why I felt this deep need to find the truth, to pry into the mess of secrets Callum was so carefully guarding. Maybe it was the way he had looked at me, his gaze laced with frustration and something darker—something like fear. Maybe it was the way I couldn't stop wondering if he was hiding something, something that could bring the whole city down in flames.

The distant sound of sirens reminded me that I couldn't linger too long. I pulled myself from the wall with a sharp exhale and started toward the scene, my mind a whirlwind of thoughts. I had to find out what Callum was hiding, or risk the fires claiming more lives. And if he wasn't the one behind it—then who was?

I crossed the street, the soles of my boots clicking against the pavement, and felt the weight of the question pressing against my chest with each step. It was impossible not to notice the way the other officers seemed to treat Callum like some kind of reluctant hero, as though he had the answers when no one else did. He was respected—maybe even feared—by the people in charge, and that made me uneasy. How could I be sure he wasn't involved if no one else was asking the same questions I was?

"Are you planning on standing there all day?" The voice was sharp, biting, and I turned to find Dan standing a few feet away. He was one of the few officers who didn't seem to have fallen under Callum's spell. He crossed his arms over his chest, his eyes scanning the remains of the building. "Or do you have a better idea than just gawking?"

I hadn't expected him to show up, but then again, I should've known. Dan had this habit of turning up when I least wanted him around. Still, I was grateful for the distraction. He wasn't as close to the case as Callum, but there was something about the way he carried himself—like he could smell a lie from miles away.

"Actually, yes," I replied, my tone sharper than I meant. "I'm going to get to the bottom of this. Someone's behind these fires, and I'm not just going to stand around pretending I don't know it."

Dan raised an eyebrow, his lips twitching into a half-smile. "Is that so? And what exactly do you think you'll find?"

"The truth," I said, the words coming out stronger than I intended. "There's more to this than what they're telling us. Callum knows more than he's letting on. He's been showing up too damn early, every time, and I'm not buying the 'good cop' routine anymore."

Dan's expression hardened, and for a split second, I thought he might call me out on it, tell me I was going too far. But instead, he just nodded slowly, the smile fading. "You're not the only one who's noticed. But you should be careful, okay? Some people... some things, they aren't what they seem. And Callum? He's not someone you want to mess with."

His words hung in the air like a warning, but I didn't flinch. Not now. Not when I was so close to something.

"Do you have any idea where he's gone?" I asked, my voice low. I didn't need to say it out loud for Dan to understand what I meant. I was trying to track down Callum again—if I could find him, I could get answers. If I could get him to talk, maybe I could finally make sense of the fire and whatever it was he was hiding.

Dan hesitated for just a moment, his gaze flicking to the ruins behind us before he sighed. "I've got a hunch, but I don't think it's going to be as simple as you think. Callum's got his own agenda, and you're not on the same page."

I nodded, feeling a knot tighten in my stomach. But I didn't back away. There was no turning back now, no way to unsee what I'd already discovered about Callum. I couldn't let it go. Not when everything I had been told felt like a string of lies.

I took a deep breath, steeling myself for whatever came next. My fingers brushed the edge of my phone, ready to make the call. "I need to find him. And this time, I'm not leaving until I get answers."

Dan moved in closer, his eyes flicking nervously around the wreckage of the building. "If you're going after Callum, you better be sure. There are things he's done that might just change your mind."

Before I could respond, the sound of an engine roaring to life cut through the tension. I turned just in time to see Callum's truck pull away from the scene, the tires kicking up dust as he sped down the road. My pulse spiked, and instinctively, I ran toward my car, desperate to follow.

"Wait!" Dan called after me, but I didn't stop.

I couldn't afford to. Not when the trail was still hot.

I slammed my foot down on the accelerator, the tires screeching as I followed Callum through the city streets, heart pounding. What was he running from? What was he hiding?

And just as I thought I might catch up, the sound of screeching brakes filled the air, followed by a single, piercing gunshot.

Everything inside me froze.

Chapter 8: Heat of the Moment

There are moments in life when the heat is unmistakable. When it creeps up on you like a sudden summer storm, unpredictable and unforgiving. I could feel it building as I watched Callum, his jaw clenched in that way that told me he was trying to maintain control. And me? Well, I was losing mine. The investigation had begun as something objective, something I could manage with a cool head. But now, standing in front of him, the lines between professional and personal had blurred so thoroughly that I couldn't see where one ended and the other began.

The feeling in the pit of my stomach wasn't hunger or fear; it was a dangerous cocktail of both. I had been digging for days, tracing the connections between the recent fires and a family that had been entangled in this town for generations. Callum's family. The Ashford name had a long history here, one of power and wealth, with shadows that stretched farther than anyone cared to acknowledge. Every fire seemed to draw a new line, a new thread, and somehow, every thread led back to them.

I'd taken my hunch, my gut feeling, and followed it to the archives. Hours of sifting through dusty records and half-burned newspapers, trying to unearth something—anything—that would give me a clue. And there it was. The Ashford estate had been involved in a fire almost a century ago, a fire that had leveled the original mansion. Not a coincidence, I told myself. Fires like this didn't just happen, not with this kind of precision. Someone was sending a message, and I was starting to think that message was meant for Callum.

I wasn't sure why I hadn't confronted him sooner, but something about his presence always unraveled my plans. There was a magnetism to him, an intensity that made it impossible to think straight. It wasn't just his eyes—though those damn eyes could burn through a person like a wildfire. It was the way he carried himself, as if he were a storm cloud with a silver lining, always on the edge of breaking but never quite letting go.

I found him at the bar, the place where everything started, where our paths first crossed. The old wood of the counter creaked under the weight of the day's tension, the air thick with the scent of bourbon and wood smoke. He was leaning against the counter, his sleeves rolled up, exposing tattoos I hadn't noticed before. Callum Ashford, always just out of reach, like a puzzle with too many missing pieces.

"Got a minute?" I asked, my voice more uncertain than I would have liked it to be. It came out sharper than I intended, but Callum didn't flinch. Instead, he straightened, giving me that crooked grin that I hated and adored all at once.

"For you? Always." His voice was low, laced with something I couldn't quite name.

I took a deep breath and slid onto the bar stool next to him. "I've been looking into the fires," I said, keeping my tone level, even as my heart started to race. I had to be careful. I couldn't let him know how much this was affecting me. Not yet.

His smile faded, just a fraction. "Still chasing ghosts?" he asked, a little too casual. But the edge in his voice was unmistakable. He knew exactly where I was going with this.

"I'm not chasing ghosts," I said, my gaze meeting his. "I'm chasing a pattern. A pattern that connects the fires, and it leads straight to your family."

For a moment, there was nothing but silence. Then, just as quickly as it appeared, the silence shattered with a laugh, a quick, dismissive laugh that didn't sit well with me.

"You think my family's behind this?" Callum's voice was tight, his words hanging in the air like smoke. He leaned back, crossing his arms over his chest, his posture defensive. "That's a hell of an accusation."

I held my ground, even though something in his eyes made my pulse jump. "The fires," I said, "they're too specific. Too calculated. The Ashford estate, the history of fire with your family... it's too much of a coincidence."

He shook his head, the laughter from earlier still dancing on his lips, but it didn't reach his eyes. "You're looking too hard, Amelia. You'll burn yourself out if you keep going down this road."

There it was. A warning. Maybe I should have taken it. But instead, I pressed on, leaning in just a little closer. "What are you hiding, Callum?" The words slipped out before I could stop them, sharp as glass, and I saw his jaw tighten, just the slightest twitch of a muscle beneath his skin.

"I'm not hiding anything," he said, and there was a crack in his voice. A break I hadn't expected. "You think you know everything, don't you? Think you can put the pieces together without knowing the bigger picture."

I wanted to push further, to demand more, but there was something in his tone, something in his eyes, that made me hesitate. For a second, the walls he'd so carefully built around himself seemed to crumble, and what I saw beneath them wasn't anger—it was fear. Fear that something was coming for him, for his family, and that no matter how hard he tried to outrun it, it would always catch up.

The air between us thickened, the weight of his vulnerability pressing down on me like the air before a storm. I wasn't sure if it was the heat of the moment or something deeper, but I suddenly realized I was no longer just chasing a story. I was chasing him. And that was a dangerous game to play.

"You're right," I said softly, breaking the silence. "I don't know the bigger picture. But maybe, just maybe, you'll let me in on it before it's too late."

He didn't answer at first. Instead, he reached for his drink, swirling it in his glass with a thoughtful expression, his gaze fixed somewhere beyond me. Then, without looking at me, he murmured, "Maybe I will."

And in that moment, I knew. The fire wasn't just outside. It was inside him too.

It was the kind of night that made you forget the world existed outside of this dim-lit room. A soft amber glow spilled from the hanging lights, casting long shadows across the worn wooden floors. The place had a charm, a rustic, homey feel that made you want to sink into the comfortable silence of it all, as though you could just forget the noise of the world outside. But there was no forgetting tonight. The air was electric, charged with a tension that hummed between us like a live wire.

Callum hadn't said much since our conversation, his face a mask of unreadable lines, though the moment I walked into the bar, I could feel his gaze on me, like heat radiating from a fire that I didn't want to get too close to. But I couldn't stay away. No matter how hard I tried, I couldn't shake the pull of it—the pull of him.

I ran my fingers over the rim of my glass, pretending to focus on the amber liquid inside, but all I could think about was the raw vulnerability that flickered in his eyes earlier. It was a rare thing, that look, one I hadn't expected. It made me wonder how much he was really hiding, and how much of it had to do with me.

He hadn't responded to my last question, the one about his family, and I'd given him space—space I was too eager to fill. It was funny, really. The way his deflections only seemed to draw me closer, like the harder he pushed away, the more I wanted to know. He didn't want to be questioned, and I hated that I wanted to do just that, over and over. The detective in me was itching for answers. But the part of me that was completely out of my depth—the part that could feel the pull of his silence, his strength—wanted to stay in that haze of tension, wanting more even when I knew it could burn me alive.

"Are you going to keep pretending you don't have a question?" His voice cut through the haze, sharp and familiar. There was a touch of amusement in it, but it was more resigned than playful. He must have known that the quiet would only last so long.

I glanced up, meeting his eyes. There it was again, that smoldering look, as if he could see straight through to the messy, tangled mess of thoughts in my head. "I don't know if I want to know the answer," I said, surprised by the honesty in my voice.

He chuckled, low and rich, and I felt it stir something inside me. "Is that so?" His smile was wry, like he knew exactly what I meant—and he didn't like it.

"You're a puzzle, Callum," I muttered, turning my gaze to the drink in front of me. I wasn't sure what I was even drinking anymore—couldn't taste it, couldn't care. "A riddle wrapped in a mystery. And every time I try to figure it out, I just get more tangled in it."

He didn't respond immediately, and for a long moment, the only sound was the soft clink of glasses and the low hum of conversations around us. Then, in a voice that was far too quiet for the noise of the bar, he said, "I'm not the only one hiding something, Amelia."

I froze. The words hit me with the weight of a storm cloud suddenly gathering above us. "What are you talking about?"

His eyes softened, just for a split second, before that familiar mask slid back into place. "You've got your own secrets. And you keep digging, but all you're doing is burying yourself deeper in them."

I opened my mouth to retort, but the words faltered on my tongue. There was something in the way he said it, as though he knew exactly what I was hiding. As though he saw through every layer of my carefully constructed walls.

"Don't." His hand shot out to stop me, his voice sharp, though there was no malice in it. "Don't pretend like you're some innocent bystander in this mess. We're both caught up in it. The fires. Your investigation. Me. You're not walking away from this untouched."

I swallowed hard, my throat suddenly dry. He was right, of course. I had never expected to be untouched. But I hadn't expected to be so tangled up in it all, either.

The fire had started out as something distant, something I could report on, a job that would keep my life predictable. But now? Now it was everything—burning around me, in me. And Callum was the kindling, whether I liked it or not.

"You think you know me?" I asked, the words slipping out before I could stop them. My voice was barely above a whisper, but it felt like I was shouting.

He leaned in closer, his presence overwhelming, that same, unshakable confidence that always made my heart race. "I don't need to know you, Amelia. I can see you. I see the way you're trying to keep control of everything. And I know what happens when people like you try to control things they can't."

I wasn't sure what hurt more—the fact that he was right or the way it made me feel like I was losing myself with every step I took closer to him. Every word he spoke was like a match to my skin, setting it on fire from the inside out.

"Maybe I don't want to lose control," I said, my voice so quiet now that it felt like I was confessing to myself as much as to him.

"Then stop pretending this is all just a case to you," he shot back, his gaze intense, and for a moment, I swore I could feel the heat from his eyes like the blaze of a fire threatening to consume me. "This isn't just a story, Amelia. It's real. And you're in it, whether you want to be or not."

I took a deep breath, trying to steady my racing pulse, but it didn't work. My heart was still pounding, faster now, with the kind of urgency that told me we were standing on the edge of something neither of us could stop.

"Tell me what you're not saying," I demanded, my fingers gripping the edge of the bar as if holding on would keep me grounded.

For a second, his eyes darkened, something raw flashing in them before he spoke, so quietly I almost missed it.

"I can't. Not yet."

The words lingered between us, an unspoken promise, or maybe a warning, I wasn't sure. But in that moment, I realized I wasn't the only one playing with fire. And Callum? He was the flame. And I? Well, I was getting burned.

I couldn't tell if the warmth creeping up my neck was from the bourbon or the electricity buzzing in the air between us. Probably a mix of both. Callum was still leaning in close, his breath warm against my skin, his presence filling every inch of space. The kind of closeness that should have been comforting. But all it did was make the walls I had carefully built around myself start to crack and tremble.

"Is this where you tell me I'm digging too deep?" I asked, trying to keep my tone light, even though my heart was threatening to pound out of my chest. The air felt thick, as though it was alive, watching us, waiting for something to happen. It was a sensation I knew too well—one that usually signaled danger.

Callum didn't move, didn't shift. For a moment, his eyes softened, just enough for me to see the truth in them. I didn't know what that truth was, not yet. But I felt it. The weight of it. The way it made me want to dig further, just to see what he was hiding.

His lips twitched, the faintest ghost of a smile. "You already know the answer to that," he murmured, and I could feel the shift in him, that guarded wall he was so good at hiding behind snapping back into place. "You don't need me to tell you what you're already figuring out."

I clenched my jaw to keep from saying what was really on my mind. The truth was, I wasn't sure what I was figuring out anymore. The investigation, the fires, the connection to his family—every lead was tangled in a knot I couldn't quite untangle. And then there was Callum. Every time I thought I had a handle on him, on what he wanted or what he was hiding, he shifted, slipping through my fingers like smoke.

"Then why don't you just tell me, Callum?" My voice had lost its bite, and I hated that. I hated how he made me feel off balance, like I was walking on the edge of something I wasn't prepared to fall into.

His expression hardened again, his eyes flickering with something darker. "You want the truth, Amelia?" he asked, his voice low, dangerous. "Fine. The truth is... you don't want it. Not really. Because once you know, there's no going back. Once you understand what's really going on, you can't just turn away. You're in this as much as I am."

I swallowed hard, my throat suddenly dry. I wasn't sure what scared me more—his words or the weight of them, the finality in his voice. What was he talking about? What was I missing?

But before I could press him further, a loud crash cut through the air, jolting both of us out of the moment. The sound of shattering glass, followed by frantic voices. I turned instinctively toward the noise, heart racing, but when I looked back at Callum, he was already moving—his expression now stone cold, a mask of composure that I was starting to despise.

"Stay here," he said, his voice like ice. "Don't move."

And before I could protest, he was already striding toward the commotion, leaving me behind, rooted to the spot like a fool.

I should have stayed. I should have listened to him. But something in me snapped. Maybe it was the frustration bubbling inside me, or maybe it was the fact that I was tired of feeling like I was always a step behind. I wasn't just a reporter anymore. I wasn't just investigating fires. I was in the middle of something far darker, something that felt as though it was swallowing me whole, and I had no intention of letting it go without a fight.

I pushed off the barstool and followed him, my heels clicking sharply against the floor as I moved toward the back of the bar. The noise grew louder, the frantic shouting clearer. When I rounded the corner, I froze.

Callum was standing there, facing a man I didn't recognize, his body tense and coiled, like a spring ready to snap. The man was tall, built like a wall, and the rage in his eyes was unmistakable. There was no mistaking the tension between them—it was personal. Whatever was going on here, I had just stepped into the middle of it.

"What the hell is going on?" I demanded, striding up to them, trying to make my presence known. The man's glare shifted toward me, but Callum didn't even blink. His face was unreadable, his jaw tight, but I could see the flicker of recognition in his eyes.

"This doesn't concern you, Amelia," Callum muttered, his voice sharp. There was no warmth in it, no care. Just the cold, harsh edge of someone who was used to being in control, even when he was clearly losing it.

"Don't tell me what concerns me," I shot back, my own frustration spilling over. "If you want to keep me out of this, you should've stayed out of my life in the first place."

Callum's eyes darkened, a muscle in his jaw twitching. But instead of arguing, he stepped toward the man, putting himself between us, as if trying to shield me from whatever was about to happen. "Get out of here, Jared. Before I make you."

The man, Jared, sneered. "You think you can keep me out of this, Callum? You think you can hide behind your family's name and pretend nothing's going on?" His voice was low, menacing, and I could see the vein in his neck bulging with the anger he was trying to control.

I took a step forward, ready to intervene, but before I could say anything, the door to the bar slammed open with a deafening crash. A rush of cold air poured in, and two more men stormed inside, their faces hard with intent. They weren't here for a drink. They weren't here for any reason other than to escalate whatever this was.

Everything froze in place.

The room seemed to narrow, the buzz of the bar dying away as the tension reached a fever pitch. Callum's eyes flickered between me and the men in the doorway, and for the first time since I'd met him, I saw something—something raw and unguarded. It was fear.

"Amelia," he said, his voice shaking slightly, just enough for me to catch it. "Get out of here. Now."

Before I could move, Jared took a step forward, and just like that, the world around us exploded into chaos.

Chapter 9: The Scent of Smoke

The evening air had grown thick with the scent of saltwater and smoke, curling into the quiet corners of the city as the sun dipped below the horizon. The evening was no longer the soft, golden promise of a perfect night, but something darker, more tense. A fog had settled in my mind, though not from the mist rising off the water. It was the kind of fog that only comes after you've been handed a secret you weren't meant to know. One that weighs you down, even if you want to pretend it doesn't.

I leaned against the railing of my apartment, looking out at the flickering lights of the marina. The world outside looked peaceful enough, but inside, nothing was at rest. The tip had come in an untraceable email, anonymous, as they always were. A string of words that cut through the night like a shard of glass. Someone close to Callum. They had no name, just a threat: "He's hiding something."

My fingers ran across the rough wood of the railing as I stared down at the water. It should have been a relief to have something tangible, something that could explain the strange behavior I had noticed in Callum over the last few days. But the problem was, I didn't know how to handle it. If I confronted him, it would feel like betrayal, like I didn't trust him. But if I didn't, what would that say about me? Was I willing to ignore something because it made my life easier?

I knew I had to confront him eventually, but I wasn't prepared for how quickly that moment came.

I found him in the kitchen later that night, his back to me as he leaned over the stove, the faint glow of the overhead light catching the sharp edges of his profile. His silhouette was the same as ever—tall, broad-shouldered, imposing—but there was something off about him tonight. Maybe it was the way he didn't turn when I walked in, or the tightness of his jaw, but it was as if I could feel the tension between us before it even had a chance to surface.

"Callum," I said, my voice quiet but deliberate, cutting through the low hum of the apartment. "We need to talk."

He didn't flinch, didn't even pause his stirring. The motion was slow and deliberate, almost mechanical, like he was trying to keep his mind busy, to block out the things he didn't want to hear. But I wasn't going to let this go. I had no choice.

"You've been avoiding me," I added, taking a step closer. "And I can't help but wonder why."

Finally, he turned, his dark eyes locking onto mine. There was nothing in them that resembled warmth, just a cold calculation that sent a shiver crawling up my spine. He sighed, long and deep, like he was resigning himself to something. I wanted to believe it was because he knew I was right. But the more I saw him, the less I understood him.

"What did you find?" His voice was low, almost flat, as if I hadn't even surprised him.

My heart skipped a beat. The tip hadn't mentioned anything about him knowing I was investigating. But his reaction? The way he stood a little straighter, his posture stiffening? He knew something. Maybe he knew everything.

"I..." I hesitated. The words I needed to say felt like they were stuck in my throat, wrapped in layers of doubt. "I got a tip. Someone close to you... is working against you."

His lips curled into something that could have been a smile—though I couldn't remember the last time I had seen one from him. It didn't reach his eyes.

"You've been reading too many tabloids, or maybe you've been talking to the wrong people," he said, his tone far too smooth, too rehearsed. It was like he was playing a role, hiding behind a mask I wasn't sure I could see through anymore.

"No, Callum," I pressed, my voice tight with frustration. "I know what I heard, what I saw. Someone's watching you. I want to know what's going on."

For a long moment, there was only the sound of the stirring spoon clinking against the side of the pot, the sizzle of whatever he was cooking filling the silence between us. His expression remained unreadable, but his eyes... those eyes that had once looked at me with a softness I could hardly believe in anymore—they were sharp, calculating, suspicious.

"I'm being watched," he finally said, the words slipping out in an almost inaudible whisper, so unlike him that it felt like someone else had spoken them. "Someone is trying to sabotage everything."

I leaned against the counter, my mind racing. "Sabotage?" I repeated. The word echoed in my head, bouncing off the walls like it had a life of its own. "By who?"

He set the spoon down with a sudden clatter, his jaw tight, the muscles in his neck bulging from the strain. "I don't know," he said, his voice now cold and clipped. "I don't have all the answers. But they're closer than I thought. And you..." He paused, looking at me with a sharpness that cut through the last remnants of any illusion I had left about him. "You need to stay out of it. It's too dangerous."

My breath caught in my throat. Stay out of it? After everything we had been through, after everything I had already uncovered? I could feel the distance between us widening, the gulf growing wider with every word he spoke. It was clear now—he wasn't being honest with me. The question wasn't just whether I believed him, but whether I still trusted him.

"Do you think I'm just going to let you push me away?" I shot back, my voice rising with the sharpness of my emotions. "You think I'm going to walk away from this? After everything?"

His eyes flickered with something unreadable, but his expression remained locked in that mask of indifference. "I don't need you involved," he said again, his voice as firm as a wall. "You don't understand what's at stake."

And just like that, the space between us felt like miles, the divide more than just physical. It was as if all the walls he had ever put up were back in place, stronger than ever before. And I—stubborn, frustrated, desperate to make sense of this mess—was standing on the other side of it, unsure whether I was trying to break through, or simply losing my way.

The smell of smoke, faint but unmistakable, lingered in the air as if to remind me of the fire that had only just begun to burn.

The night stretched on, tangled in its own shadows as I stood there, trying to decipher what exactly had just happened. Callum, who had once been so open with me, had become a stranger. His words, his mannerisms—everything about him felt like a puzzle that I couldn't quite solve. And yet, I was still standing there, frozen in place, wondering whether I had walked into something deeper than I had ever intended.

"I can't do this," I muttered to myself, the air feeling thick with the weight of his silence. I didn't know what I expected from him—a confession, maybe, or some shred of vulnerability—but instead, I got nothing but an impenetrable wall of deflection.

I turned to leave, but before I could make it halfway across the room, I heard him.

"I didn't ask for any of this." His voice, still low and distant, stopped me dead in my tracks.

I didn't look back immediately, though. I stood there, my hands clenched at my sides, fighting the urge to turn around, to face him head-on. But I couldn't. Not yet. Not with all the confusion swirling inside me. The trust I had given him was splintering, cracking in ways I hadn't even realized were possible.

He sighed, a long, tired exhale that made my heart ache. "I'm sorry. I didn't mean to push you away." His voice softened slightly, though it wasn't quite an apology. It wasn't the easy, soothing tone I'd grown accustomed to. This was different.

For the first time in days, I felt like I was seeing the real Callum, or at least, a version of him that wasn't so guarded. But even then, it didn't feel like enough. He wasn't offering me any real answers—just fragments of something I wasn't sure I could piece together.

I turned around slowly, locking eyes with him. His posture was still tense, like he was standing at the edge of a cliff, waiting for the wind to push him off. There was something raw in his gaze, a flicker of vulnerability I hadn't expected to see. But that moment of honesty, fleeting as it was, left me more uncertain than ever.

"Then tell me," I said, my voice catching slightly. "Tell me what's really going on. All of it. I can't help you if you don't let me in."

For a long time, he didn't answer. Instead, he stepped back from the stove, the smell of the simmering sauce still hanging in the air, a strange contrast to the tension in the room. His hand hovered near the kitchen counter, but he didn't seem to know what to do with it. He wasn't looking at me now, but I could still feel his eyes on me, assessing, weighing the situation.

"I didn't want you involved in this," he finally muttered, rubbing the back of his neck. "But here you are, in the middle of it anyway."

"Funny," I said, a bitter laugh escaping my lips before I could stop it. "I didn't ask for any of this either, Callum. But I'm not about to sit back and let you push me away. Not after everything."

The air between us was electric now, charged with something dangerous and unpredictable. I was walking a fine line, one that had shifted under my feet since the moment I'd walked into his life. My chest ached, a mix of frustration and something far more complicated bubbling to the surface. I wasn't sure if I was angry at him for shutting me out, or angry at myself for trusting him so easily. Maybe it was both.

"I'm not the person you think I am," he said, his voice hoarse now, the words dragging out like a confession. "And I've made a lot of enemies in the process. I don't want you anywhere near this. It's not just about me anymore—it's about you, too. You've seen things you shouldn't have. People are watching you."

The chill in his tone cut through me like a blade. Watching me? My head spun with the implications of his words. Someone had been keeping tabs on me. That small, sinister detail made the pit in my stomach grow deeper, colder.

"Who's watching me?" I demanded, stepping forward, my pulse quickening. "Who's trying to sabotage you? And why are you shutting me out instead of telling me everything?"

He swallowed hard, like the words were physically painful to say. "I'm not trying to push you away. I'm trying to protect you. It's bigger than you think. Bigger than either of us."

I didn't know how to respond to that. I wasn't sure if I was supposed to believe him or not. The entire conversation had taken such a twisted turn, I wasn't sure where to stand anymore.

"Protect me?" I repeated, incredulous. "From what? From you?"

Callum's jaw tightened at the accusation. "No," he said quickly, his voice low and tense. "From the people who want to destroy everything."

I didn't understand. None of this made sense. Callum, the man who had once been so open with me, now seemed like a stranger wrapped in layers of deceit. But something about his desperation, the way he was pleading without saying a word, made me falter.

"I don't know what to think anymore, Callum," I whispered, my voice wavering despite myself. "I don't know who you are anymore."

His eyes softened then, his gaze haunted, like he was seeing something in me he didn't want to confront.

"I know," he said quietly. "I know."

And just like that, the tension between us seemed to break, but it was replaced by something far more dangerous—an uncertainty that I couldn't shake. Because in the end, I had no idea whether I was helping him—or falling straight into a trap of my own making.

I woke the next morning to the sound of distant traffic, muffled by the stillness of the apartment. The air was thick with the smell of old coffee and something else—something burnt, but faint, like a memory lingering in the air. Callum's words echoed in my mind, unanswered and unresolved. Someone was watching us, or so he claimed. But who, and why? And most importantly—did I trust him enough to believe it?

I had no answers to those questions, but I knew one thing for sure: I couldn't shake the feeling that I was caught in something far darker than I had imagined.

I stepped into the shower, the hot water cascading down in a steady stream, trying to wash away the remnants of last night. But nothing felt clean. The walls of this city, the walls around Callum, all of it seemed to be closing in. I could feel it in the way my skin prickled with unease.

When I stepped out, I was no clearer than I had been before. I dressed in the first thing I could find—some faded jeans and a loose shirt. I didn't care about how I looked today. I didn't care about much at all, really. My mind kept circling back to him. To Callum.

I grabbed my phone, fingers hovering over the screen. I had to do something. If I didn't, the questions would consume me. I dialed his number, though I wasn't sure what I expected from the conversation. Maybe it would be easier this time, now that we had spoken openly, or at least as openly as he was willing to be. Or maybe he would shut me out entirely, and I'd be left trying to pick up the pieces of something I couldn't understand.

The phone rang once, twice, and then he answered.

"You're up early," he said, his voice low, raspy. It sounded tired, distant.

"I'm not sure if I should be," I replied, tapping my foot against the tile floor. "I have some questions."

"Are you sure you want answers?" The question came out clipped, like it had been rehearsed, but I could hear the hint of something else in his tone—something that made my chest tighten.

"Do you really want me to answer that?" I shot back, surprising myself with how sharp I sounded. But the more I thought about it, the more it seemed like the only option left. There was no going back now.

A long silence stretched between us, thick and unspoken. I could hear the quiet shuffle of movement on the other end of the line, the faint sound of him taking a breath, perhaps weighing whether or not to say what needed to be said.

"I never wanted you to get involved," he said finally, his voice softer now. "I thought I could handle it, but it's—complicated."

"Complicated doesn't even begin to cover it," I replied, feeling the frustration rise like bile in my throat. "This isn't just about you anymore, Callum. I've been dragged into something I don't even understand. And you're not exactly helping me figure it out."

He sighed heavily. "I know. I know. But it's not like I can just tell you everything."

"Why not?" I demanded. "You want me to trust you, but you're not giving me any reason to. You're keeping secrets, and they're not even your secrets to keep anymore."

There was a beat of silence before he spoke again, this time with a quiet resolve. "It's not about trust. It's about safety."

The words hit me like a slap. "Safety? What do you mean by that?"

But he didn't answer. Instead, there was the distinct sound of him putting the phone down, followed by muffled voices in the background. I heard a shift in the atmosphere—like something was happening, something I wasn't supposed to witness. My pulse quickened. My stomach dropped.

"Callum?" I called into the silence, but there was no response. I could feel my heart pounding in my chest, a drumbeat of fear that I couldn't shake. Was this another lie? Another way for him to push me away?

I could hear voices, distant but growing louder, though I couldn't make out what they were saying. Panic crept into my veins, making my hands tremble as I pulled the phone away from my ear. I waited, half-expecting him to pick up again, but the seconds ticked by with no answer.

Then the doorbell rang.

I jumped, my heart slamming against my ribcage. Who could be at the door? I wasn't expecting anyone, and the way everything had been unfolding, I didn't know if it was a good idea to let anyone in, let alone someone who might have answers. Or worse, someone who might want to stop me from finding the truth.

I grabbed the nearest thing to me—a half-empty bottle of wine—and crept toward the door, the sound of the bell ringing through the quiet apartment like an alarm. My hand shook as I reached for the handle, my mind a mess of possibilities, none of them good.

I opened the door.

Standing in front of me was a woman I didn't recognize. She was tall, with sharp features and a confidence that radiated off of her like a heat wave. Her eyes were dark, almost too dark, and they locked onto mine with an intensity that made me take a step back, instinctively.

"Are you..." she began, her voice smooth and cold, "...are you the one asking questions about Callum?"

I swallowed, trying to ignore the way my throat felt tight. "Who are you?" My voice didn't sound like my own. It was too high, too frantic.

She stepped forward, closing the distance between us with a calmness that made my skin crawl. "I think you've been asking the wrong questions. But I can help you with that."

I didn't have time to react. Before I could open my mouth, her hand shot out, pressing a small envelope into my palm. It was thin, unmarked, and as I touched it, I could feel the faintest pulse of heat radiating from it.

"This is your answer," she said softly. "But you won't like it."

The door slammed shut behind her before I could ask anything else. I was left standing there, the envelope burning through my fingers, my heart hammering in my chest.

Chapter 10: Hearts on Fire

The moment I step into the alleyway, my boots crunching against the damp cobblestones, the air thick with the scent of rain-soaked earth and a faint trace of gasoline, I feel the weight of the world press down on me. Or maybe it's just Callum, lurking in the shadows, his dark presence more unsettling than any storm.

"You're late," his voice cuts through the night, low and rough, like gravel being ground underfoot.

I glance over my shoulder, finding his silhouette framed by the dim light from the streetlamp above. Even in the hazy glow, there's no mistaking him—tall, broad-shouldered, and impossibly still. He seems to be one with the night, blending into its darkness as if he's always belonged there.

"I was held up," I say, stepping closer, my pulse quickening as I approach him. He's not the type to be merciful about my lateness, and he's certainly not the type to let a slip go unnoticed. But I've learned a few things in our time together. For one, I've learned that if there's one thing Callum's good at, it's pretending not to care.

He doesn't respond right away. Instead, his eyes narrow, and his lips press into a thin, unforgiving line. There's something in his gaze—something sharp and calculating—that makes me second-guess the confidence I'd worked up on the way here. I want to tell him we have a job to do, that we can't afford to be distracted. But when he looks at me like that, it's hard to remember anything but the burn of his stare.

"I've got a lead," he says, finally, his voice breaking the silence. "The kind that might actually lead somewhere this time."

I nod, even though I'm not sure what to make of it. We've chased dead ends for days, each clue fading into nothing. Callum's seen things I can't even imagine—he's done things that would make anyone else crumble. But beneath the hard, jagged edges of the man I'm forced to work with, there's a quiet desperation. It flickers in the moments when he thinks I'm not paying attention, the way his jaw tightens just a fraction, or how his hands ball into fists when he thinks no one is watching.

But tonight, as he steps out of the shadows, I see something else.

I don't know why it happens, but in that instant, I catch a glimpse of him—a man at war with himself, his defenses temporarily forgotten. The mask slips, just for a second, and in the unspoken exchange between us, I realize that whatever we're chasing, whatever this thing is between us, it's not just a job for him. It's personal.

I take a step forward, my heart suddenly pounding harder than I want it to. "What's going on, Callum?" The words leave my mouth before I can stop them, and as soon as they're out there, I wish I could pull them back.

He freezes, his dark eyes flicking to mine, and in that brief moment, I see something raw and exposed. But just as quickly, it's gone, and the familiar coolness returns. "Focus, Alex," he says, his tone suddenly all business. "You're here to help me with this, not to dig into my life. Got it?"

I don't flinch. Not this time. He's trying to put up a wall, but I can tell it's shaky—tired. Like a fortress made of sand, just waiting for the tide to wash it away. The trick is not to push too hard. Not yet.

"Fine," I mutter, shoving my hands into my coat pockets. "Let's get this over with, then."

The tension between us crackles, but neither of us says anything else as we head down the alley. I'm acutely aware of the way his presence seems to engulf everything around us. I can feel his every move, every breath. It's unsettling. Impossible to ignore.

Callum stops in front of an unmarked door, hidden behind a cluster of dumpsters. I've been here before, but never with him. It's a place where bad deals go down, where desperation and secrets breed in equal measure. And now, it's our only lead. We've got to see it through, no matter what.

He's already moving, the quiet authority in his movements impossible to miss. But when he turns to look at me, something flashes in his eyes, something that doesn't belong here. Something that sends a shiver down my spine.

"Stay close," he says, his voice just above a whisper.

I can feel my pulse leap at the proximity, the sudden closeness that makes my skin hum. I force myself to breathe, to focus. This is a job. It's always been a job.

But then his hand brushes mine, just a touch, just enough to make my head spin. His fingers linger for a fraction of a second longer than necessary before he pulls away.

I've known Callum long enough to know that every move he makes is calculated. But tonight, something feels different. It's not just the way he's holding himself, tight like a coiled spring. It's the way his eyes flicker to mine, like he's waiting for something—something I can't quite place. He's a man teetering on the edge, and I'm not sure if he's about to fall or if he's about to drag me down with him.

We enter the building, and the air is thick with the scent of mold and the faint tang of old cigarette smoke. It's dark, save for the few weak lights flickering overhead, casting shadows that stretch long and uncertain. We move through the halls in silence, our footsteps echoing too loudly in the emptiness.

I catch myself watching him, watching the way his jaw tightens with every step, the way his muscles tense under the strain of whatever he's holding back. There's something there, something more than the sharp edges he lets everyone else see. He's hiding something. I know it. And as much as I want to ignore the gnawing feeling in my gut, I can't.

I want to trust him. I want to believe that we're in this together, that whatever storm is brewing in him won't tear us apart. But I can't shake the sense that there's something lurking beneath the surface, something dark and dangerous.

And then, just as the tension between us is unbearable, he stops. Turns. Looks at me in a way that makes my heart skip.

Before I can react, he's kissing me. And it's everything—fury, need, and something far more dangerous. There's no space between us now, no time for hesitation. Just the collision of lips and breath, of hearts racing in time with each other, both of us too far gone to care about anything but the fire burning between us.

But even as I give into the kiss, I can't shake the nagging feeling that this isn't just about desire. That there's something more—something that could change everything.

The kiss lingers longer than it should, but neither of us pulls away, caught in the desperate urgency of it. It's like something fragile is shattering between us—some unspoken boundary, some invisible line we both knew was there but pretended didn't exist. I can feel the heat of Callum's body pressed against mine, his hands grasping my shoulders as though holding on for dear life. The frantic rhythm of his breath mirrors my own, each inhale and exhale more frantic than the last.

But even as I let myself sink into him, a nagging voice in the back of my mind refuses to quiet. It's not doubt, exactly, but something else. Something colder. A sense that there's more to this moment than either of us is willing to admit. That something is waiting just beneath the surface, and it's not just the passion that's burning through us. It's the things we've both chosen not to say.

His lips break away from mine with a soft gasp, but his forehead remains pressed to mine. There's a flicker of something in his eyes—something unreadable, impossible to decipher. He pulls back just enough to study me, his gaze intense, searching. I can't help but shiver, even though the air is thick with the remnants of the kiss.

"You shouldn't have done that," he says, his voice rougher than it was a moment ago.

I blink, stunned by the sudden shift. "Shouldn't have?" I repeat, a laugh escaping me despite the tension. "It's a little late for that, don't you think?"

He doesn't laugh with me, doesn't even look amused. Instead, his jaw tightens, and for a moment, I see the weight of something heavy in his expression—something I don't want to ask about, but the impulse is there, too strong to ignore.

"Trust me, Alex," he says, his voice low and clipped. "This isn't how this works."

I pull away from him then, physically and emotionally. The distance between us feels necessary now, like the air is too thick, too heavy, and I need space to breathe. But my chest still burns from where his body had pressed against mine, and my mind races as I try to make sense of everything that just happened. The chemistry between us was always undeniable, but this—this felt different. Felt dangerous. Like we were both teetering on the edge of something we couldn't stop.

I don't say anything at first, instead trying to force the words through the fog in my mind. There's a part of me that wants to demand answers, to ask what the hell just happened and why I feel like I've just been set on fire. But something about Callum's face—something in the tension that's suddenly thick between us—keeps me from doing it. He's shutting down. And I know better than to push too hard when he's like this.

"Fine," I say, settling for the words I know will get me nowhere. "I get it. We keep it professional."

His eyes flash, and for a second, I wonder if I've pushed him too far, if I've made a mistake. But then he just nods, an unreadable expression falling over his face.

"Good," he mutters. "We've got work to do."

I stare at him for a long moment, trying to figure out how to move past this—how to turn back the clock to before that kiss. But I can't. It's already out in the open, hanging in the air between us, lingering like the smoke of a fire that won't die down. The question now is whether we can move forward with it or if it's going to smolder and burn us both.

The sound of footsteps in the hallway interrupts my thoughts, and I instinctively reach for my gun, slipping it from its holster and holding it loosely at my side. Callum doesn't move, but his eyes flick toward the sound with a sharp, predatory focus that sends another jolt of unease through me.

He doesn't speak, but there's a shift in the air—his whole body coiled, ready for whatever's coming. I try to steady my breath, keeping my senses alert, and for a split second, I think I can feel his tension reach out and wrap itself around me, pulling me into his rhythm.

The door creaks open, and two figures step inside, their faces shadowed by the low light. I don't recognize either of them, but Callum's posture shifts just enough to tell me they're not strangers. The taller of the two—dark hair, sharp features—gives me a cursory glance before focusing entirely on Callum. The other, shorter man, watches me more closely, as though evaluating my worth.

"You're late," the tall one says, his voice calm but clipped, as though he's already tired of the game.

Callum steps forward, cutting off any further words. "Did you bring the intel?" he asks, his tone sharp and demanding, but I notice the way his hands are clenched into fists at his sides.

Whatever they're dealing with, it's not just business for him. It never is.

The shorter man, who's still watching me with that calculating look, shifts uncomfortably before handing over a small envelope. The tension in the room thickens as Callum takes it, tearing it open with practiced ease. He scans the contents quickly, his face unreadable. The words on the paper seem to set something off inside him, because suddenly he's all business again, every inch of him exuding that dangerous calm he's so good at.

But even as he turns his back on the men, dismissing them with a brief gesture, I can't shake the feeling that something is unraveling. The way Callum's posture has changed, the way his eyes don't meet mine as he speaks—it's like he's retreating into himself again, burying whatever it is that he's not willing to share.

And I know, deep down, that whatever's buried is about to surface. I just don't know if I'm ready to see it.

I feel the air thicken as I step into the small, dimly lit office, the walls closing in like a pressure cooker. Callum's still distant, despite the unspoken thing that passed between us moments ago. It's as though the weight of the world has descended upon him, and I'm just the unfortunate observer who's been pulled into the chaos.

I watch him work, his eyes scanning the folder in front of him with laser-like intensity. But he's not really reading it—his mind is elsewhere, tangled up in a mess of things he isn't about to share. I try to ignore the sudden pang of frustration in my chest. There's no denying that he's brilliant, but the walls he's built around himself could rival any fortress.

"So, what are we dealing with here?" I ask, trying to keep my voice light, easy. But I know better than anyone that when it comes to Callum, light doesn't work. Not when the storm inside him is this close to breaking free.

His eyes flick up to meet mine for a moment, and then just as quickly, they return to the paper in front of him. "Same as before," he mutters, "but bigger. More dangerous."

I raise an eyebrow, leaning against the edge of the desk. "Dangerous. Is that what you call it when someone's holding all the cards and you don't know the rules of the game?"

He doesn't answer, but the muscles in his jaw tense, and I know I've hit a nerve. This game, whatever it is, has become personal. For him, maybe for both of us. But he's too good at hiding it. Too good at pretending like it's just another job.

I swallow the words that threaten to spill out—words I know will push him farther away. I'm not sure what this is between us, but I'm certain of one thing: if I let myself believe that there's something deeper, something more than just this... partnership of necessity, I'm going to get burned. And yet, here I am, standing on the edge of that flame.

The silence between us stretches, thick with unspoken thoughts. There's no denying that the tension is palpable. The kiss we shared, the one that has been lingering like a ghost in the back of my mind, doesn't feel like the end of something—it feels like the beginning of something I can't yet understand.

"So," I start again, trying to break the ice that seems to have formed between us. "What's the play here?"

Callum looks up at me, his expression unreadable, and I wonder if he even knows how much control he has over this situation—how much of him is still within reach. But then, he shifts, a small muscle twitching beneath his eye, and the usual steely determination settles over him. "We go after the source. Get to the bottom of this, find out who's really pulling the strings."

I can feel my heart rate pick up as he speaks, the adrenaline from the chase pulsing through me. But there's something else in his words, something I can't place. I can't help but ask, even though I know I shouldn't.

"And what if we're too late?" I ask, my voice lower now, softer. "What if this is bigger than we thought? What if we're already in over our heads?"

Callum doesn't answer right away. He leans back in his chair, rubbing his eyes like he's trying to erase something from his mind. When he finally speaks, it's with the same blunt honesty that he always reserves for moments like this. "Then we deal with it. Like we always do."

I nod, but the unease in my stomach won't go away. Something is shifting, something I can't quite grasp, and I can feel it in every fiber of my being. But before I can say anything else, the sound of a phone ringing slices through the tension. I glance at the device on the desk, and Callum's eyes flick to it as well. For a brief moment, I see the ghost of something flicker across his face—something close to panic—but it's gone in the next breath, replaced by the usual indifference.

He picks up the phone without hesitation. His voice drops low, businesslike, as he speaks into the receiver. I can't hear the words clearly, but from the way his jaw tightens, I know it's bad. Worse than bad.

He mutters a string of profanities under his breath and slams the phone down, his hand still gripping the receiver like it might explode.

"Who was that?" I ask, cautiously stepping toward him. The change in him is palpable—something's happened, something that's thrown him off balance. And I can feel it, deep in my gut, that we're standing on the edge of something much bigger than I ever expected. Something that could rip us both apart.

"Trouble," he says, his voice rough, but not with anger—more like the weight of inevitability. "The kind we can't ignore anymore."

I don't press him, but the unease in my chest grows. The walls around Callum are getting taller, thicker, more impenetrable with each passing second. I reach out, just barely brushing my fingers against his arm, a tentative gesture—one that feels like it's teetering between comfort and something else entirely. But he doesn't flinch, doesn't pull away. He doesn't do anything.

Instead, he stands abruptly, his chair scraping against the floor in a harsh, jarring sound. "Get your things," he says, his voice flat and businesslike again. "We're moving out."

I blink, momentarily stunned by the shift in his tone. "What? Now?"

"Now." He doesn't look at me as he walks toward the door. "We don't have time to waste."

I don't move right away. A thousand questions race through my mind, but only one manages to surface.

"Where are we going?"

Callum turns to face me, his eyes hard, unreadable. "Somewhere they won't expect us."

But there's a flash of something in his gaze—something that's too quick for me to catch. And in that moment, I know he's hiding more than just his emotions. He's hiding something bigger. Something that could change everything.

Before I can respond, the lights flicker once, then twice. The room is plunged into darkness.

And then, just as suddenly as it had gone black, the door bursts open with a force that rattles the walls, a figure standing in the doorway. I can't make out the silhouette, but the unmistakable glint of a weapon catches the low light.

I freeze. Callum's already moved into position, his gun in hand, eyes narrowed, lips pressed into a thin line of determination. And as the figure steps forward, I realize that whatever this is—it's only just beginning.

Chapter 11: Scorched Earth

The hum of the fluorescent lights buzzed above me as I rifled through the files, each paper crackling like dry leaves under my fingertips. My eyes burned, but I didn't care. The heat from the fire that still smoldered in my memory was nothing compared to the white-hot ache in my chest. Another night, another pile of paperwork to sift through, each page as frustratingly silent as the last. But there had to be something—something buried deep in these reports that would make sense of it all.

The fire had started almost a week ago now, but the city still smelled of ash and desperation. You couldn't escape it, no matter how many candles you lit or how many windows you opened. It clung to the streets, to the air, to every surface, as if the flames had left their mark on the very soul of the place. And then there was the body count. Official reports said twelve. Unofficial whispers—like the kind that made it past closed doors and nervous glances—put the number at twenty, maybe thirty. It didn't matter, though, because the question was the same: who had set these fires, and why?

I slammed the folder shut, the sound echoing in the empty office like a challenge. The archives were supposed to be quiet, sterile, but tonight they felt oppressive, like the walls were closing in on me. I wiped a hand over my face, trying to brush away the fatigue and frustration. It didn't work. The more I read, the more I realized how little I actually knew. Everything felt like a puzzle piece, but none of the pieces fit.

"Are you still awake?" Callum's voice was soft, but there was a sharpness to it that told me he wasn't asking out of simple curiosity. His footsteps were light on the linoleum floor, but they carried the weight of something much heavier.

I glanced up from my desk, meeting his eyes for the briefest moment. He looked just as tired as I felt—dark circles under his eyes, his shoulders hunched in a way that told me he had been carrying this weight for longer than he was willing to admit. "Always," I replied, forcing a smile that didn't reach my eyes. "You know me better than that."

He hesitated before crossing the room and leaning against the desk. I noticed the way he placed his hands carefully on the surface, almost as though he were trying not to disturb the fragile air between us. It was funny, really—how a room full of dust and paper could suddenly feel like the most dangerous place in the world.

"Any luck?" he asked, his voice low, but there was an edge to it now. I wasn't sure if it was frustration or something else—something I couldn't quite put my finger on. We had been working together on this case for days, but the longer we stayed in each other's company, the more I wondered if we were really on the same side.

I shook my head, fingers curling around the edge of the folder I had just closed. "Nothing that makes sense," I muttered. "Everything's pointing to a single person, but I don't think that's right. The timing's off. Too convenient."

Callum raised an eyebrow, clearly not buying what I was saying. "Too convenient? You think someone's setting us up?"

I hesitated, the weight of his question pressing down on me like a vice. Could I trust him with what I was thinking? Could I trust anyone? I wasn't sure anymore. "I don't know, Callum," I admitted, my voice softer than usual. "But something feels wrong. Like we're missing a bigger picture. And the more I dig, the more I feel like we're not supposed to be looking here at all."

His gaze sharpened. "What do you mean by that?"

"I mean... it's like we're playing a game we don't understand," I said, voice barely a whisper now. "Like someone wants us to chase our tails, and we're too caught up in it to see we're being led in circles."

There was a long pause, the silence stretching between us like a taut wire. Then Callum straightened, his lips curling into a smile that was almost too quick, too knowing. "You really think someone's toying with us? That's bold."

I shrugged, unwilling to explain further, unwilling to let him see how much I doubted myself. "I don't know. But I'm not willing to just roll over and accept that we're out of leads."

He stood there, looking at me with a mixture of something that felt like admiration and something else—something far more dangerous. It made my stomach twist in a way I couldn't quite explain.

"Okay, then," he said finally, his tone changing, hardening. "I'll keep digging too. You're not alone in this, remember?"

I nodded, though I wasn't sure if it was his presence I found comforting or the possibility that he might know more than he was letting on. There was always a sense with Callum that he wasn't sharing the whole truth with me, and I was starting to wonder if that was the case now more than ever. He didn't trust me completely. He couldn't.

"I'm not alone," I repeated, but the words felt hollow in my mouth.

The fluorescent lights hummed again, louder now, almost deafening. But the quiet in the room—the kind of quiet that felt like a trap—was louder still.

The city had a way of swallowing the light, especially at night. It was as if the dark could creep into your bones, settle there, and refuse to leave. I was starting to think that was exactly how the fire had worked. It didn't just burn. It seeped into everything—the air, the people, the buildings—and, in some cases, it became a part of you. I was beginning to feel like one of the scorched remnants myself.

It had been three days since Callum and I had exchanged those quiet words in the office. Three days, and yet I hadn't been able to shake the feeling that everything was closing in around me. Not just the city or the fire. The investigation, the pressure, the way I couldn't escape the nagging feeling that we were chasing the wrong lead—it was all closing in.

"Why are you still here?" Callum's voice was the first thing I heard when I finally pulled myself from my pile of notes late the next evening. I glanced up, blinking in surprise at his sudden presence. He was standing in the doorway, shoulders drawn tight, his expression a mix of disbelief and something darker, something I couldn't quite place.

I stretched, feeling every muscle in my body protest. "Because, unlike you, I don't have the luxury of walking away when it gets hard."

He didn't laugh, but the faintest flicker of something moved across his face—something like regret or maybe guilt. I couldn't decide, and honestly, I didn't want to. He had a knack for being unreadable, and it was starting to grate on me. Not that I would ever say that out loud.

"I think we need to rethink our approach." His words were heavy, the suggestion hanging in the air like smoke, thick and suffocating. "We're chasing shadows, Della."

I crossed my arms, holding my ground. "That's a nice way of saying I've wasted the last three days, but I don't need your pity."

"It's not pity." His voice softened, and for the first time, I saw the hint of something—perhaps concern, perhaps something else I couldn't name. "I just think you're getting too close. To the case. To the fire. To me."

I stared at him, not knowing how to respond. The words felt like they had been a long time coming. He was right, of course. I had spent the past few days getting too close to everything, but I had to. The stakes were too high, and every piece of the puzzle felt like it was just out of reach.

"I'm not afraid to get close," I said, my voice sharper than I intended. "And neither are you, if you're being honest."

His eyes darkened, a flicker of something dangerous passing between us. But then he exhaled, the tension draining from his posture. "You're right. I'm not. But I also know that sometimes, getting too close means we end up in the fire ourselves."

I wanted to laugh. To tell him I'd been in the fire for years now, but I didn't. I couldn't. The truth was, he was right. I was in deeper than I had ever intended, and it wasn't just the fire that scared me anymore. It was everything else. Callum. My own lack of control. The fear that once this all ended, I would be left with nothing but ashes and regret.

I glanced back at my desk, my eyes moving over the scattered papers. "So, what? You think we walk away? Forget this ever happened?"

"No." He shook his head, his jaw tight. "I think we need to stop trying to force something that isn't there. Let's step back. Look at it from a different angle."

I wanted to argue. I wanted to keep pushing, to keep chasing down the pieces that didn't quite fit. But something about the way Callum was looking at me—the rawness in his eyes, the quiet intensity—made me pause. He was right. The pieces didn't fit. I had known that for days now, but it was easier to keep grinding away at something that felt familiar, even if it was wrong. It was safer.

"I don't know if I can just stop, Callum." The words slipped out before I could stop them. "I can't. Not when I know there's something here."

"You don't have to stop. Just—" He hesitated, then stepped closer, his presence too near for comfort. "Just let it breathe for a minute. You've been holding your breath this whole time. What if we just let everything go for a night?"

I couldn't help it. I laughed. It was a bitter sound, sharp and hollow. "I don't think either of us knows how to do that."

He smiled, but it was brief, like it wasn't supposed to be there at all. "No, we don't. But we need to. For a second. We need to stop pretending that everything's in our control."

I stared at him, unsure what to say. Everything in me screamed to keep fighting, to keep pushing, but that was getting me nowhere. "Maybe we're already too deep," I murmured. "Maybe the fire's already burned through everything, and we're just left standing in the ruins."

Callum didn't answer at first. He just looked at me, really looked at me, like he was seeing me for the first time. I didn't know what he saw, but it made the air between us feel thick with unspoken words.

Finally, he broke the silence. "Maybe. Or maybe we're just not looking in the right place."

There was something in his tone that made my heart skip. Maybe it was the way he said it, like he knew something I didn't. Or maybe it was the way he had always managed to make me doubt myself, even when I didn't want to. Either way, the words hit harder than I expected.

"Maybe," I repeated, but it didn't feel like a question anymore. It felt like a confession.

The night air in the city felt colder than it had in days, a bitter breeze cutting through the crack in the window as I sat, staring at the blank screen of my computer. The world was starting to feel like a fog—dense and suffocating. The longer I spent in the archives, the more I realized the truth I was chasing wasn't just elusive. It was a ghost, a shadow of something that had been buried so deep it no longer seemed to matter.

Callum hadn't left my side, not in any meaningful way. He had a quiet presence that never quite let me forget he was there, lurking in the periphery of every thought. I could feel his eyes on me even when he wasn't in the room, could feel the weight of his unspoken questions. We both knew we were tangled up in something too complex, too dangerous, but there was no going back now. The fire had already begun its work, leaving scorch marks across our lives. We were just trying to outrun it.

I hadn't spoken to him in hours, not since our last exchange about stepping back. He had gone, disappearing into the labyrinth of the city's crumbling streets, the kind of places where secrets festered in the cracks between buildings. I couldn't blame him for wanting to escape. I wasn't sure I knew how to live in a world that felt as burned as this one.

But I couldn't let go. Not yet.

I flicked through the files, my mind numb to the words on the page. It was like trying to assemble a map of a place you'd never seen, using landmarks that no longer existed. The clues didn't connect, and the gaps only grew wider.

"Why do you keep torturing yourself like this?" Callum's voice startled me, pulling me from the haze of exhaustion. He stood in the doorway, his posture still rigid, but something about the way he spoke made the walls feel thinner, more fragile.

"Maybe because I'm not ready to admit that everything I thought I knew was a lie." My words came out sharper than I intended, but I didn't apologize. Not this time. Not when everything was on the verge of shattering.

He took a step closer, his eyes scanning the room—my cluttered desk, the papers strewn in chaotic disarray. "You're not going to find the answers in these, Della," he said softly. "You're just going to drive yourself crazy trying."

"Maybe I already am," I muttered, leaning back in my chair. The room felt smaller somehow, like the walls were pressing in with the weight of unsaid things.

He leaned against the edge of my desk, his arms crossed, his gaze never leaving me. "Is that really what you think? That all of this—" He gestured vaguely at the files, the papers, the burn marks on my skin that hadn't yet healed "—doesn't matter?"

I didn't answer at first. His question hung in the air, thick and heavy, but I couldn't form the words. The fire hadn't just burned the city; it had singed away everything I thought I understood about it. And about myself. About us.

"I don't know," I finally said, my voice quieter. "I'm starting to wonder if I've been chasing the wrong thing."

Callum's eyes softened, a flicker of understanding crossing his face. "And what would you do if you knew the answer was right in front of you?"

I stood up abruptly, pacing across the small room. "If I knew the answer, then what? What do I do with it? How do I live with it?"

His voice followed me, slow and deliberate, like he was carefully choosing each word. "You don't live with it. You change it."

I froze, my back to him, staring out the window at the flickering lights in the distance. The city looked so peaceful from here, untouched by the chaos that had gripped it. I could almost convince myself everything was normal again. Almost.

"You can't change everything," I whispered. "You can't fix the past."

He was right there, right behind me, too close. His breath was warm against the back of my neck, his presence overwhelming.

"Maybe you can't fix everything. But you can stop the next fire from starting."

His words sunk in, too deep and too fast. I felt the ground beneath me shift. "Stop the next fire?"

I turned to face him, searching his eyes for something, anything that might explain the sudden change in tone, the shift in the air between us. There was a resolve in him now that hadn't been there before, a certain finality that made my stomach twist with the kind of unease I couldn't explain. "What do you mean?"

"Let's stop chasing shadows and start looking at the people who've been hiding in the light," Callum said, his voice steady. "Maybe it's time we start asking questions that no one wants to answer."

I swallowed hard. The weight of his words hit me all at once, too much to absorb in a single breath. My heart skipped a beat. "You think someone's been pulling the strings? From the beginning?"

He didn't say anything at first. He just looked at me, his expression unreadable. For a moment, I thought he might say something—something that would make everything clear. But he didn't. Instead, he turned away, walking toward the door without a second glance.

"Get some sleep," he said over his shoulder, his voice low. "We've got a long day ahead."

I stood there, the silence deafening as he left the room. But I didn't move. I couldn't. The pieces of the puzzle were starting to align, but not in a way I could understand. Not yet.

The cold wind howled through the cracks in the window, the night pressing in with the weight of a thousand unanswered questions. I felt like I was on the edge of something—something big, something dangerous—but I couldn't tell if it was a breakthrough or a trap.

And then I heard it.

The unmistakable sound of footsteps in the hall. Someone was outside. Watching.

Chapter 12: The Phantom Flame

The cold air wrapped around me like a forgotten memory as I stepped into the darkness of the abandoned warehouse. Its looming silhouette, hunched and decaying, had the smell of old oil and dust, the kind that clung to your skin and made your nose wrinkle. The faint clink of metal echoed in the cavernous space, like a hesitant heartbeat. Every footstep I took reverberated against the exposed concrete, the eerie silence hanging heavy in the air. My fingers twitched at my side, itching to grip the gun holstered at my waist, but I kept them still, steadying myself against the rising tide of anxiety.

Something was wrong, I could feel it deep in my bones. The hairs on the back of my neck stood up, a whisper of dread brushing against the edges of my thoughts. This place had the aura of a dead thing—forgotten and forsaken, but still clinging to life in some cruel, twisted way. My flashlight flickered as I moved further in, casting long, jagged shadows on the peeling walls. The remnants of old wooden crates, broken glass, and shredded tarps lay scattered across the floor, the detritus of a long-forgotten industry. But it wasn't the emptiness that bothered me—it was the feeling that I wasn't alone.

I stopped, heart pounding, listening. Nothing. I thought I heard something—footsteps, maybe? The faintest scrape of something against the ground. But it was gone in an instant, swallowed by the silence once more.

"Hello?" I called out, my voice strong despite the knot of unease tightening in my stomach. "Anyone here?"

No response. Of course, there wouldn't be. If this was going to be anything like the rest of this damn case, I'd be talking to shadows. But I wasn't about to back down now. I'd come too far to turn around.

The beam of my flashlight caught on something in the distance. A figure, hunched near one of the broken windows, obscured in the half-darkness. My heart jumped. This wasn't a shadow—this was a person.

I took a step forward, my instincts kicking in, adrenaline flooding my veins. "Stop right there!" I commanded, but the figure didn't move. My hand slid to the gun at my waist. "I said, stop."

For a long, tense moment, nothing happened. Then, slowly, the figure straightened, turning just enough to reveal the profile of a face I would recognize anywhere.

Eliot Rivers.

The bastard who had been slipping through our fingers for months. The one who knew more about the fires than anyone had been willing to admit. The arsonist? Possibly. Or perhaps the informant we never had. Either way, I wasn't going to let him walk away this time.

"I should have known you'd be here," I said, my voice low and steady despite the churn of anger rising inside me. "You've been hiding in the shadows all this time."

He smirked, his dark eyes glinting in the faint light. "You're getting closer, aren't you?" His voice was smooth, almost mocking. "A little too close for comfort."

I felt a chill creep down my spine. This wasn't just about the fires anymore. He knew something. He was playing a game, one I wasn't sure I could win. "What do you know about the fires?" I demanded. "Who's behind them? Tell me."

His lips twisted into a cruel smile, and for a moment, I thought I saw something flicker in his eyes—something darker, more dangerous. "You're not going to like the answer," he said, his tone almost too casual, like we were discussing the weather instead of lives being torn apart.

I didn't flinch. I couldn't afford to. "Try me."

Before he could respond, the sound of screeching tires echoed from the distance, sharp and jarring. My heart stuttered, and instinctively, I turned toward the entrance. There, pulling up in a cloud of dust and headlights blinding in the dim night, was a familiar black SUV.

Callum.

I should've been relieved. I wanted to be relieved. But something inside me—some darker part—tightened at the sight of him, my chest constricting with a tension I couldn't explain. I wanted to stay focused on Eliot, to keep my eyes locked on him, but my mind betrayed me, dragging my gaze back to the approaching vehicle.

The door slammed open, and Callum's tall, broad form emerged from the shadows, his jaw clenched tight, eyes flashing with barely contained fury. The moment our gazes locked, a spark of something dangerous flickered between us—a tension so thick, it was like a live wire thrumming in the air.

Eliot chuckled under his breath, and I felt the weight of his gaze move between the two of us. "Ah, the knight in shining armor," he mused, as Callum's footsteps rang out across the warehouse floor, his presence filling the space like a storm gathering speed. "This should be interesting."

"Step away from her, Rivers," Callum barked, his voice low and dangerous. It was a command, not a request. The heat radiating from him was impossible to ignore, but it wasn't just anger. There was something else there—something darker, something broken.

Eliot held up his hands in mock surrender, his smirk never faltering. "Is that how it's going to be? A little too much testosterone in the room, maybe?"

Callum didn't answer. He was too focused on me, his gaze sharp and unreadable, as though he was trying to piece together a puzzle I didn't have the answers to. I wanted to say something, to ease the tension between us, but the words got stuck in my throat, tangled with something I wasn't ready to confront.

The standoff hung in the air for a long, painful moment before Eliot finally broke the silence. "You want the truth, don't you?" His voice dropped lower, the playful edge gone. "Well, I can give it to you. But you won't like it."

Before I could respond, the distant sound of sirens began to wail, cutting through the stillness. Someone had called the cops. I should've been grateful for the backup, but something in my gut twisted at the timing. Callum's eyes flickered, a brief flash of something vulnerable crossing his face before his mask snapped back into place.

It wasn't over. Not by a long shot. And whatever secrets Eliot was keeping, whatever demons Callum was wrestling with, they were about to collide in ways none of us were ready for.

The sirens screamed louder, a stark contrast to the calm that had settled between Eliot, Callum, and me. The tension hung thick in the air, wrapping around us like a smothering blanket. I could hear Callum's harsh breathing, the way his chest rose and fell, but there was more there—something beneath the anger, a flicker of something dark that I wasn't sure I wanted to understand. He hadn't taken his eyes off me, and the weight of his gaze felt like a thousand unsaid things crashing into me all at once.

Eliot's smirk faded, but only for a second. He was playing us, baiting us, but for what, exactly? He knew something, that much was clear. He knew something about Callum, something that wasn't just about fire or destruction. It was personal.

"You've got one hell of a temper," Eliot said to Callum, his voice dripping with amusement, as if he were savoring the slow burn of the moment. "You sure you want to keep going down this road, man?"

Callum didn't respond, but I saw his hand twitch at his side, and for a brief, unsettling moment, I wondered if he was about to unleash whatever storm was brewing inside of him. I couldn't take my eyes off him, though I desperately tried to focus on the task at hand, on Eliot, on the damn case. But everything about this—this situation—was twisted, tangled, and making less sense by the second.

"I asked you a question," I said, my voice cutting through the thick silence. "What do you know? About the fires. About him."

Eliot's lips twitched into something resembling pity. "You really don't get it, do you?" He shook his head slowly. "You're so focused on the who, you haven't stopped to think about the why."

My stomach twisted, unease making my head spin. "The why? What the hell is that supposed to mean?"

Eliot chuckled, the sound low and dark, like the hum of a faraway storm. "You think this is about one person, one arsonist? Oh, sweetheart, it's bigger than that. Way bigger."

Before I could demand more answers, a loud bang echoed through the warehouse. The doors, the very same ones Callum had stormed through just moments ago, slammed open, and officers in uniform flooded the space. Their presence brought a sense of relief, but it was temporary—fleeting. It was clear we were losing control, and fast.

I shifted to take in the scene—Eliot had already disappeared into the shadows, slipping away with the grace of a phantom. My eyes darted between the officers, Callum, and the empty space where Eliot had been. But my mind kept circling back to one thing: whatever had just happened, it wasn't over.

I turned to Callum. The storm that had once been brewing in him now seemed to dissipate, replaced by a cold, calculating anger that I couldn't quite understand. There was something so raw, so unsettling about it, I couldn't breathe properly.

"Let me guess," I said, my voice shaking with frustration. "You've been holding something back, haven't you?"

He didn't respond immediately, his jaw tight, his gaze fixed somewhere past me. I could see the muscle in his neck twitch as he swallowed hard, his every movement taut with restraint. "This doesn't concern you," he finally muttered, and though his words were sharp, they held a tremor that betrayed him.

I pressed forward, refusing to back down. "It does concern me. All of it." The words tasted bitter in my mouth, but they were true. This entire mess, this case, it was personal. "What aren't you telling me, Callum?"

The flicker of vulnerability that had flashed in his eyes earlier was gone, replaced by something colder. Something that made my pulse quicken and my stomach drop.

"I told you already," he said, his voice tight, barely above a whisper. "It's not your fight."

I could feel the space between us closing, but at the same time, it felt like we were miles apart. The distance wasn't just physical; it was deeper than that. There was something Callum wasn't saying, and I could feel it pulling me under, like an undertow I couldn't escape.

"I'm not stupid, Callum," I said, stepping closer, not backing down this time. "I've been through this before. I know when someone's hiding something. So either tell me what's going on or get out of my way."

The silence between us was electric, thick with words left unsaid, each one hanging in the air, a weight neither of us was willing to lift. Callum opened his mouth, but before he could speak, something broke the tension. A flash of light, followed by a loud whoosh—a sound I knew all too well.

The arsonist had struck again.

The air was heavy with the acrid stench of gasoline, the telltale sign of a fire started with malicious intent. And then the unmistakable crackle of flames grew louder, filling the space with a horrifying soundtrack that made my chest tighten.

"Get out of here," Callum snapped, his hand grabbing mine, pulling me away from the flames that were rapidly consuming the corner of the warehouse.

"I'm not leaving you!" I shouted back, but my voice was drowned out by the roar of the fire, the heat from the flames licking at my skin.

"We're running out of time," Callum said, his voice hoarse, his grip on my hand unyielding. "You don't understand. This—it's not just about stopping the fires. It's about surviving them."

I tried to pull away, to make sense of his words, but the heat was rising too fast, and the smoke was thickening. The urgency in his voice cut through my foggy thoughts like a blade. Something in the way he said it—surviving them—sent a shiver down my spine.

I looked at him, eyes wide, and for the first time, I saw it. The raw fear he'd been hiding. The fear of something he couldn't control.

"I'm not going anywhere without you," I said, but even as I spoke, I knew we weren't running from just a fire anymore. Whatever we were facing, it was bigger than both of us—and neither of us had the answers. Not yet.

The smoke burned in my throat as the flames began their inevitable dance, licking the warehouse's beams with a greedy hunger. The heat surged, crawling under my skin, making every breath feel like it might be my last. Callum's grip tightened on my hand, pulling me away from the inferno's reach, but I couldn't shake the feeling that we were already too late—that we'd missed our chance.

"Get out!" he shouted over the crackling fire, his voice harsh, edged with something that wasn't just panic—it was the sound of a man trying desperately to outrun his own demons.

"I'm not leaving you behind," I snapped back, but the words felt hollow even as I said them. The fire was spreading faster than I could process, and the reality of our situation hit me hard. We were no longer just chasing an arsonist; we were in the thick of something far more dangerous, something we hadn't yet fully understood.

Callum turned to me then, his eyes wild, his jaw set in a hard line, and for the first time, I saw it—the raw, frantic fear that had been buried beneath all that controlled fury. It wasn't about saving people anymore. It wasn't even about stopping the fires. It was something personal, something that gripped him tighter than the flames themselves.

"I told you before," he said, his voice low and broken, "you don't know what you're dealing with."

I shook my head, refusing to back down. "I don't care what you think I know. I'm here, Callum. We are in this together." My heart pounded harder, faster, as if the very words might be the thing that kept us tethered to reality in the chaos around us.

He didn't respond immediately, his gaze flickering between me and the fire as if weighing some unspoken decision. And then, in one fluid motion, he shoved me toward the nearest exit. "Get out now!" His voice was commanding, like a shout from a man who had been pushed to his limits, a man who thought he was saving me from something far worse than the flames.

I dug in my heels, unwilling to move. "I'm not running. Not now."

"Then you'll die with me," he growled, his anger boiling over, but it was clear—he wasn't angry at me. No, it was something else. Himself.

A sound—a sudden thud—brought both our attention to the far side of the warehouse. I turned, heart in my throat, and saw a figure emerging from the haze of smoke. A man, tall and broad, his silhouette barely visible through the haze. But there was no mistaking him—Eliot Rivers.

I didn't need to ask how he'd gotten there. The answer was already written in the line of his shoulders, in the gleam of something predatory in his eyes. He'd known we'd be here. This had been his plan all along. The message he'd left for us—every fire, every clue—had been leading us to this very moment. He had been manipulating us from the start.

"What do you want, Eliot?" I said, trying to keep my voice steady, but the crack in it betrayed me.

He smirked, his eyes narrowing as he took a step forward, unfazed by the chaos surrounding him. "Don't play coy with me, Detective. You know exactly what I want."

The fire roared behind him, a living beast of heat and flame, but Eliot stood untouched, unaffected by the storm of destruction he had set in motion. The world felt like it had slowed down, the crackling of the fire and the rush of air between us all suddenly too much. It was hard to think, hard to breathe, as if the very atmosphere had turned against us.

"We've been chasing shadows, haven't we?" he said, his voice low, almost mocking. "But it's more than just fire, Detective. It's about the fear, the control. I thought you'd get it by now."

I could see the way Callum's body stiffened at Eliot's words. It was like a punch to the gut, a blow that hit somewhere deep—too deep to be ignored. His grip on my hand loosened, and for a brief, terrifying moment, I wondered if he was considering walking away. Or worse, letting me walk away. But then, just as quickly, his hand shot out, grabbing Eliot by the collar.

"You don't get to play games anymore," Callum snarled, his voice full of a venom I hadn't expected.

Eliot laughed, a dark, hollow sound that felt more like the rasp of a dead thing scraping against stone. "You think it's that easy? That you can just walk in here and take everything back? You have no idea what this is, Callum. No idea what you're really up against." He leaned in close, his lips curling in a wicked smile. "You think you're here to stop me? You're not even in control of your own fate."

The world felt like it was tilting, and I had to blink hard to stay grounded. There was something about Eliot's words—about the way he spoke to Callum—that sent a ripple through me. Something about him... it wasn't just about the fires anymore. It was about Callum.

"Enough games," I said, stepping forward, trying to break the tension before it tore us apart. "What do you want, Eliot?"

He looked me up and down, his expression unreadable. For a moment, he didn't say anything, just stared at me like he was trying to figure out if I was worth the effort. Then, he spoke, his voice lower this time, almost to himself. "I want you both to understand something. You're already too late. This isn't just about stopping fires, Detective. It's about starting something much bigger." His gaze flickered briefly toward Callum. "And I think he knows it, too."

Callum's face went pale, his jaw clenching tight as he stepped forward, positioning himself between me and Eliot. "If you think I'm going to let you manipulate us any longer—"

But before he could finish, a sudden explosion shook the very foundation of the building. The ground beneath us rumbled, sending shards of glass and debris flying through the air. For a split second, I couldn't breathe, couldn't hear, couldn't think. All

I could do was watch as the flames reached out like greedy hands, swallowing up everything in its path.

In that instant, a figure appeared in the distance—another figure, moving through the smoke, silhouetted in the glow of the fire. A flash of red hair caught my eye, and I knew immediately who it was.

I didn't have time to process it. The world around me exploded into chaos, and all I could do was run.

Chapter 13: A Trail of Ashes

The fire had been on everyone's lips for weeks. It was the kind of catastrophe that demanded attention—blazing through the city's old quarter like an unforgiving force, tearing apart history and homes without a shred of mercy. In the aftermath, the air had smelled like ash for days. Even now, a faint burnt scent clung to the edges of everything, a reminder that nothing, not even the sturdy brickwork of the city, was immune to the ravages of flames.

Callum and I stood in the cluttered office, surrounded by case files, paper scattered like a storm had passed through. The overhead light buzzed in a way that made my teeth ache, a low hum that echoed in the silence between us. My fingers lingered over a manila envelope, the corners frayed from years of neglect. Inside was something that made my heart skip: a series of photographs, yellowing at the edges, and beneath them, a file marked with a name that shouldn't have been there.

"Is this...?" I trailed off, unsure if I even wanted to finish the question.

Callum, who had been leaning against the desk, his arms crossed and jaw set in that familiar, brooding way, glanced at the file, his eyes narrowing as though something had just pricked at his mind. I could see the shift in him—the small tightening of his posture, the slight flare in his nostrils as if the air had suddenly thickened with something unspoken.

"Don't—" he began, but I'd already lifted the file from the stack, my fingers trembling just enough to make the paper rustle audibly in the stillness. I glanced at the top of the page, where the letters "C.A.L.L.U.M" were stamped, bold and unyielding, as if to make sure I knew who I was dealing with.

His name. In a case file tied to the fire.

"Callum," I said again, my voice quieter this time, like I was testing the weight of the word. The rest of the world fell away as I stared at him, trying to piece together the layers of mystery that were pulling us closer, tighter with each passing moment. The unspoken between us—what we were becoming—seemed to collide with the cold reality of what I was holding in my hands.

Callum's face didn't shift, but I could feel the rush of tension ripple through him. His gaze flickered to the window behind me, his eyes momentarily distracted by the city skyline, the sun dipping low and casting everything in shades of amber and violet. He was always like this when he didn't want to answer something—distant, retreating into the city as though the streets held the answers he refused to give.

I could feel the cold edge of the file against my palm, the thinness of the paper betraying how long it had been buried. I opened it, and the first photograph made my breath catch. It was a building—one that had been reduced to rubble during the fire. But this wasn't just any building. It was a place I knew well. A place Callum knew well.

"This is—" I stopped myself, blinking hard, trying to process the image. It was a church. A small, private place tucked in between two old brownstones on a side street. I had spent afternoons there as a child, my mother's soft whispers of prayer still echoing in my ears. Callum had been there too, though I wasn't sure I'd ever asked why. We hadn't discussed much of the past, especially not the things we'd shared before the city had burnt away some of its more tender memories.

The file had more. As I flipped through the pages, they weren't just photographs of buildings reduced to rubble. There were notes, scribbled quickly and then crossed out. Words like "suspect," "suspicious activity," and "unresolved." And then, buried deep at the bottom of the last page—two words that made the room feel like it had shrunk around me.

"Your involvement."

I didn't even know where to begin. I looked up at Callum, my mind racing, a thousand questions fighting for dominance. His eyes, usually so steady, were now flickering, and I couldn't read the emotion in them—too sharp, too guarded.

"I don't know what this means," I said, but my voice faltered.

He pushed away from the desk, walking across the room with an ease that only made the air around us feel heavier. I watched as his fingers drummed against the edge of the window, the glass cool beneath his touch, and for the first time, I noticed the tension in his shoulders—the way he carried something old, something heavy, that hadn't quite been released.

"You're right," he finally said, his voice quiet but carrying the weight of a thousand unspoken things. "You don't. But you will."

There was something in that sentence. A promise, a warning. I wasn't sure which one it was.

And then he turned to face me, his eyes dark with something I couldn't place. "You need to understand," he began, his voice low, the words taking on an edge that cut through the room. "I didn't just watch the fire. I wasn't just there as an observer. I was in it—knee-deep. The things that burned were never meant to be destroyed. And I couldn't stop it."

The truth hung between us, unspoken, lingering like the smoke from the flames that had once consumed our city.

The silence that followed Callum's words felt like it was made of something thicker than air—like it was pressing against me, urging me to say something. But nothing came to mind. No words, no questions that could make sense of what he had just confessed. The fire, I had known, had been devastating, but I never thought of it as anything but an accident. An unfortunate, horrific thing, yes, but an accident all the same. Yet, as I watched Callum standing there, the dim light playing over his sharp features, I understood. He hadn't merely watched it burn. He had been part of it.

It was a strange thing, that kind of revelation. The way a person you think you know—someone you've shared fleeting moments of laughter and quiet with—can suddenly become a stranger, cast in a new light. I'd always assumed Callum was a man who operated in the shadows, the one who stepped in when others didn't have the stomach for it. I never thought that the shadows he embraced might be darker than I'd imagined.

"I need to know what you mean," I finally said, my voice steady despite the knot in my stomach. "I need to know everything. Now."

He ran a hand through his hair, the movement sharp, almost agitated. "I didn't start the fire, if that's what you're thinking," he said, the words clipped, tight. "But I knew it was coming. And I couldn't stop it."

There it was. The first crack in the facade.

"Who's 'it,' Callum?" I asked, the question slipping out before I could stop it. "Who or what are we talking about? What do you know that you haven't told me?"

He turned away from me then, his back to me in a way that said there was something he wasn't willing to share. I knew that feeling all too well—the way the words caught, the secret things that refused to be released, buried deep within. But I also knew something else: whatever this was, it couldn't be solved without truth. Not the half-truths we'd been trading, not the comfortable lies we'd let slip through.

The city outside had gone quiet, as if it too were listening, waiting for him to speak.

"I don't know how much of this I can explain," he said, his voice barely above a whisper now. "There are things—things about the fire that go beyond anything either of us can control. But I'll try. I'll try to make it make sense."

I watched him for a moment, that familiar flicker of uncertainty in his eyes, like he was deciding whether to trust me with the pieces of a puzzle too jagged for anyone to piece together. But then he exhaled, long and slow, like he had been holding his breath for far too long.

"I'm not just some guy on the sidelines, watching things burn to the ground," he began, his tone sharp now, biting at the edges. "I have ties to the people who planned it. I didn't know how far it would go, but I knew it was coming. The fire—it wasn't random. It was engineered. Set. And it had a purpose."

My heart skipped a beat. "A purpose? What kind of purpose could a fire have?"

He turned to face me then, and his eyes were dark with something—something raw, something that hadn't seen the light of day in far too long. "It wasn't just to burn buildings, to hurt people. It was a message. And I think—no, I know—it's tied to me. I'm the key to it."

My breath hitched. The words hung between us like a storm waiting to break. He was right—this wasn't just a fire. This was something personal, something more complicated than I'd ever imagined. I had to swallow hard, trying to force the racing thoughts into order. I'd been so sure that we were just piecing together old clues. So sure that the truth was somewhere hidden in the archives, in forgotten files, in the remnants of a tragedy.

Now, standing there, listening to Callum, it was clear that the truth wasn't just buried in the ashes. It was tangled up with him.

"Why didn't you tell me any of this before?" I asked, my voice a little unsteady, though I wasn't sure if it was fear or something else entirely that made my throat tighten.

Callum ran a hand over his face, his jaw clenched. "Because I didn't want you to get involved. I didn't want you to know. This isn't just a case. It's not something that can be solved by looking through old papers or chasing down clues. It's dangerous. And I—" He stopped, his eyes flickering briefly to the door, as if to make sure no one had overheard. "I don't want you to get hurt."

I opened my mouth to protest, to tell him that I wasn't some delicate flower who needed protection, but the words stuck. He was right in a way I hated to admit. There was danger here, something much bigger than the petty crime and corruption I'd been used to uncovering in this city. The kind of danger that seemed to swallow whole lives without a second thought.

"I can handle it," I finally said, my voice firm, though I wasn't sure if I believed it myself. "I'm already involved. You don't get to push me away now, Callum."

He met my eyes then, and for a moment, there was something almost desperate in the way he looked at me. His lips parted as if he wanted to say something, but then he seemed to reconsider, his words getting tangled in his throat.

"Alright," he said finally, his voice low. "We'll do this together. But you have to promise me one thing."

"What?"

"Promise me that you won't let this consume you. This thing—this fire, these people—they're dangerous. And once you're in, there's no going back."

I looked at him, trying to read the weight in his gaze. Trying to understand the man who stood in front of me—not the one I thought I knew, but the one who was buried deep under all the shadows. I wanted to tell him I wasn't afraid. That I could handle anything. But the truth was, there was something about this mess, this fire, that felt like it was already pulling us under.

And the worst part? I wasn't sure if I cared.

The walk back to my place with Callum felt like a journey through a dark, twisting maze where every turn held a secret I wasn't sure I wanted to uncover. The city streets, once familiar and safe, now seemed cloaked in shadows that stretched a little too long, lingered a little too near. I could feel his presence beside me, quiet and intense, as though he was both there and somewhere far away, lost in his own thoughts. Every so often, our arms brushed, and each time I felt a flicker of something almost electric—an unspoken pull that had been simmering between us since we'd started this search.

When we reached my door, he stopped, his eyes scanning the street in a way that told me he was still watching, still expecting some shadow to slip out of the darkness. His gaze was sharp, unreadable, and yet when he looked back at me, there was something softer, something hesitant.

"I shouldn't stay," he murmured, his voice carrying the faintest hint of regret.

"Probably not," I replied, though my hand lingered on the door handle, and neither of us made a move to part. I let out a sigh, pressing my forehead to the cool metal of the door. "You really know how to make a girl's night complicated, don't you?"

A hint of a smile touched his lips. "Complicated is practically my middle name."

"And here I thought it was just a bad habit," I shot back, my voice light, though the weight of the night hung heavy between us.

He let out a quiet chuckle, and for a moment, we both just stood there, caught in a silence that was strangely comforting. But then, as if a switch had been flipped, his expression darkened, and he leaned closer, his voice a low murmur. "I'm serious, though. This isn't just some game. You have no idea what we're up against."

"Then tell me," I challenged, meeting his gaze. "Or are you planning to keep me in the dark forever?"

He opened his mouth as if to respond, but then he hesitated, his eyes flickering with a battle of thoughts he didn't want to voice. I waited, watching him, feeling the tension between us coil tighter with every passing second. And just when I thought he was going to turn away, he stepped closer, his hand reaching out to touch my arm, his fingers warm against my skin.

"There are people in this city who will do anything to protect their secrets," he said, his voice barely more than a whisper. "They're not just dangerous—they're ruthless. They don't care who gets hurt, and if you get too close..." He trailed off, the words catching in his throat.

"What about you?" I asked softly, the question slipping out before I could stop it. "Where do you fit into all of this?"

His gaze dropped, and for a long moment, he didn't respond. It was as if he was trying to find an answer he wasn't even sure of himself. But then he looked up, and I saw something raw and vulnerable in his eyes—something that made my heart ache in a way I couldn't quite explain.

"I don't know anymore," he admitted, his voice thick with an honesty that felt almost too heavy. "But I know one thing—I can't let them hurt you. Not because of me."

I swallowed, the intensity of his words sinking into my chest. "Then let me help you, Callum. Whatever this is, we can figure it out. Together."

For a moment, I thought he might actually agree, that he might finally let me in. But then he pulled away, his expression hardening as if he'd suddenly remembered some unbreakable rule. "Go inside. Lock your door. Don't open it for anyone, not even me. Just—trust me on this."

"Callum—"

"Promise me," he cut in, his voice firm, almost pleading. "Just this once. Do as I say."

I hesitated, but something in his gaze made me nod, the words catching in my throat. He held my gaze for a second longer, then turned and disappeared into the shadows without another word.

I watched him go, the weight of his warning pressing down on me like a stone. Once he was gone, the street felt eerily quiet, the silence almost oppressive. Reluctantly, I slipped inside, locking the door behind me, as instructed. But I couldn't shake the feeling that this was just the beginning—that whatever secrets Callum was hiding, they were bigger than anything I had anticipated.

The next morning, I found myself replaying the events of the night in my mind, picking apart his words and the tension that had hung between us like a loaded gun. I knew I couldn't let it go, not now, not after everything I'd seen and heard. And despite his warning, I had no intention of staying locked away like some passive witness.

I decided to start where any good investigator would—by tracing Callum's steps. If he wouldn't tell me the truth, I'd find it myself. I had just slipped on my coat and was reaching for my bag when I felt it—a prickle of unease, the sense that I wasn't alone. I froze, my heart pounding as I scanned the room, my eyes landing on a small, folded note resting on the kitchen counter.

I hadn't put it there.

The paper was crisp and clean, almost mocking in its simplicity. I walked over slowly, every nerve in my body on high alert, and unfolded it with trembling fingers. Scrawled in neat, slanted handwriting were just three words:

You're being watched.

A chill ran down my spine. The world seemed to close in around me, the walls too tight, the silence too loud. I turned, half-expecting to see someone lurking in the shadows, but there was nothing, just the empty apartment and the faint hum of the city outside.

The weight of the note settled over me, and for the first time, I felt the true scope of the danger Callum had warned me about. This wasn't just a mystery to solve; it was a threat that had already wormed its way into my life, wrapping its dark tendrils around me without my even realizing it.

Without thinking, I reached for my phone and dialed Callum's number. It rang once, twice, three times before going to voicemail. I left a short message, my voice barely above a whisper. "Callum, I need to talk to you. Someone's watching me. I found a note..." I trailed off, unsure if I should say more, if there was any point to sharing what I now knew was the truth: whatever this was, it had already found me.

I hung up and paced the apartment, the feeling of eyes on me refusing to fade. And then, as I reached the window, I saw it—a figure standing across the street, barely visible in the morning light. They were cloaked in a dark coat, a hat pulled low over their face, just enough to obscure their features. But there was no mistaking the way they stood, the way their gaze seemed fixed on my window.

I took a step back, my heart hammering in my chest as I tried to think. I could call for help, run, confront them. But before I could act, the figure turned and slipped away into the crowd, vanishing as quickly as they had appeared, leaving me with nothing but the lingering dread and the chilling certainty that my life had just been drawn into something I might not escape.

Chapter 14: The Inferno Within

It starts with the crackling hum of embers, an eerie, restless lullaby drifting through the window. I'm staring out at the city skyline, silhouetted in fiery ribbons of smoke that lick their way up into the night. For a moment, I'm mesmerized, caught in the perverse beauty of a city on fire. But the flames only flicker brighter, mocking me, as if they're aware of the trap closing in around us, and I can almost hear them whisper, *Run.*

But I don't. I just sit, steeling myself against the inevitable. I've known for days now—maybe longer—that the truth was coming. I just never thought it would sound like this. Callum's voice, low, unapologetic, shakes me from my trance.

"So, are you going to say anything?" he asks, each word falling heavy as a stone, laden with that biting blend of frustration and vulnerability he hides so well. A tone I've learned to understand like the back of my hand, and yet tonight it feels like a foreign language.

"What am I supposed to say?" I shoot back, my voice sharper than I'd intended, but he's standing there, looking at me like he's waiting for an apology—me, of all people. As if I should be the one trying to fix the pieces he's just shattered.

His gaze drops to his feet, and for a split second, the confident, composed Callum—the one who storms through boardrooms and commands attention without even trying—vanishes. I see the edge of his vulnerability, raw and flickering like those damned flames outside. "You could start by saying you understand," he mutters, though he knows that's a stretch. His hands are jammed into his pockets, and I can tell from the tension in his jaw that he's clinging to some semblance of control. Or maybe he's just bracing for the fallout.

"Understand?" I repeat, incredulous. "You think I should just sit here, understanding that the past three years have been one giant lie? That you've been lying?"

He flinches, just barely, but it's enough. I see it. "It wasn't—look, I didn't want it to be like this."

"Well, congratulations, Callum," I say, my tone dripping with sarcasm. "It's not like this. It's worse." My voice cracks at the end, betraying me, and I hate myself a little more for it.

He reaches for me then, a hesitant hand lifting as if he's not sure I'll let him touch me. And maybe I won't. But before I can decide, his hand drops back to his side, fingers curling and uncurling like he's lost even the nerve to try.

"I never wanted to hurt you, Lena," he says, his voice softening, like that might be enough. "I just thought...maybe if you didn't know, it would protect you."

"Protect me?" I laugh, bitterly. The irony tastes ashy in my mouth. "You think I needed protection from the truth? Or was it just easier to keep me in the dark while you ran around pretending to be someone else?"

There's a flash of anger in his eyes now, like he's tired of the fight. "Pretending? You think any of this was pretend?" he asks, his voice laced with a desperation that doesn't suit him. "I never pretended with you. But I knew...if you knew who I really was, it would end things before they even started."

"And maybe it should have!" My voice rises, carrying with it all the hurt and frustration I've bottled up over the years. "Maybe I deserved to know who I was falling for before I got in too deep."

His face falls, but he doesn't turn away. That's one thing about Callum—no matter how broken, how bruised, he never retreats. He'll stand there, soaked in his own mistakes, letting them stain him because he knows there's no clean way out. "Would it have made a difference?" he asks quietly.

"I don't know." I shake my head, my voice barely a whisper. "But at least I wouldn't be here wondering if I even know you at all."

We stand in silence, the words that could save us hovering just out of reach, while the city burns around us. The glow from the fires casts strange shadows across his face, and for a brief, terrifying moment, I see him differently. Darker. A stranger lurking behind a face I used to love.

Just then, the wail of sirens echoes through the streets below, sharp and relentless. The arsonist. He's been at it for weeks, hitting places that matter—to Callum, to me, to this whole damned city. There's a twisted logic to it, some kind of sick pattern I haven't yet unraveled, but I know it's only a matter of time before we're caught in the crossfire. Another trap, just waiting to snap shut.

"Lena." Callum's voice breaks through my thoughts, and there's something in his tone—something almost pleading—that sends a shiver down my spine. I turn to face him, bracing myself for whatever he's about to say.

"If you stay here...with me, I mean..." He trails off, but his meaning is clear. He's offering me a choice. A way out, if I want it. Maybe even a chance at freedom. But the thought of leaving him—leaving us—feels like a betrayal in itself.

"If I stay, Callum..." I start, my voice trembling, "how do I know you won't hurt me again?"

He looks away, his jaw clenched, but he doesn't answer. And I realize, in that moment, that there are no guarantees. Not with him. Not with this. But even so, the thought of walking away feels impossible, like trying to leave a part of myself behind.

The sirens grow louder, and I know our time is running out. I can feel the weight of my decision pressing down on me, a heavy, suffocating burden that makes it hard to breathe. But then he steps closer, his hand brushing against mine, and I feel a spark—a reminder of everything we once had, and everything we could still be.

"I won't ask you to trust me," he says, his voice barely above a whisper. "Not after everything. But I'm asking you to believe in us, Lena. Because if you don't..." He pauses, swallowing hard, as if the words are too painful to say. "If you don't, then all of this was for nothing."

His words hang in the air, a fragile thread connecting us, and for a moment, I'm tempted to believe him. To believe that maybe, somehow, we can still find a way through this mess. But as the flames rage outside, I know it's not that simple. And deep down, I wonder if I'll ever be able to trust him again.

The weight of Callum's words lingers, heavy and oppressive, settling into the cracks he's spent the past few years carefully keeping hidden from me. I can feel his eyes on me, but I refuse to meet his gaze, not when I'm still trying to process this tangled mess he's handed me with such reckless honesty.

Instead, I focus on the window, where the glow of the fires paints the night with hues of molten orange and angry red, transforming the cityscape into a twisted work of art. It's beautiful in a way that makes me sick to my stomach—a stark reminder of just how dangerous beauty can be. There's something almost poetic about it, that the world around us is unraveling in flames while Callum and I are doing the same right here in the suffocating darkness of his apartment.

"Do you think I planned this?" he finally asks, his voice quiet but firm, threading through the silence like a needle through fabric. "Do you think I wanted any of this?"

I let out a bitter laugh before I can stop myself. "That's the problem, Callum. I don't know what you wanted. I thought I did. But now?" I shake my head, feeling the sting of tears I refuse to shed. "Now, I don't even know who you are."

He winces, and for a moment, I see something break in his expression, something that makes me think he might actually feel remorse. But then, just as quickly, his face hardens again, retreating behind that impenetrable wall of his. Classic Callum. He's always been a master at keeping people at arm's length, revealing just enough to make you feel close without ever really letting you in.

"It wasn't supposed to be like this," he says, almost to himself. "I thought...maybe I could keep you separate from everything else. From the mess. From me."

I scoff, crossing my arms as I fix him with a glare. "And how did that work out for you, Callum? Did lying to me somehow make this whole thing easier for you?"

He takes a step forward, hands outstretched like he's pleading with me to understand, to see this from his perspective. But I can't. Not when my whole world feels like it's been doused in gasoline, with him holding the match.

"It wasn't a lie," he insists, his voice breaking on the last word. "Not the way you think."

"Oh, really?" I challenge, my tone laced with sarcasm. "Then why don't you enlighten me, Callum? Because from where I'm standing, it looks a whole lot like you were hiding the truth—maybe even from yourself."

There's a beat of silence, and for a moment, I think he's going to retreat again, disappear behind that unbreakable mask he wears so well. But then, to my surprise, he takes a deep breath, his gaze steady as he meets my eyes with a vulnerability I haven't seen from him in...well, maybe ever.

"I thought if you knew everything, you'd leave," he admits, his voice barely more than a whisper. "And I couldn't... I didn't want to lose you."

Something inside me softens, just a fraction, but I shove the feeling down, reminding myself of all the ways he's betrayed me.

"You think that makes it better? That because you were afraid of losing me, you had the right to lie to me?"

He sighs, running a hand through his hair, a gesture that would almost be endearing if I weren't so furious. "I know it doesn't excuse anything. But... I wasn't prepared for you, Lena. I didn't think I'd... that I'd fall for you like this."

The admission takes me by surprise, and despite my anger, I feel a pang of something I can't quite name. Hope, maybe. Or longing. But I push it aside, refusing to let him off the hook so easily.

"You're still missing the point," I say, my voice trembling. "It's not about whether or not you loved me, Callum. It's about trust. About honesty. How am I supposed to believe anything you say now, knowing that you've been hiding this...this part of yourself from me?"

He opens his mouth to respond, but before he can say anything, a loud crash echoes from somewhere outside, followed by the unmistakable sound of glass shattering. We both freeze, the tension in the air thickening as we realize just how close the fire must be.

"Lena," Callum says, his voice urgent. "We need to get out of here. Now."

I hesitate, torn between the instinct to run and the stubborn desire to stay, to confront him, to demand answers. But the heat outside is intensifying, and I know deep down that we don't have much time. Reluctantly, I nod, allowing him to take my hand as he leads me toward the door.

As we make our way down the stairs and out onto the street, the full extent of the devastation becomes clear. Flames dance along the edges of nearby buildings, casting an ominous glow over everything. The smell of smoke is thick in the air, acrid and suffocating, and I can feel the heat prickling against my skin as we hurry through the chaos.

We're halfway down the block when a familiar figure emerges from the shadows—a tall, imposing man with a twisted smile and a glint of malice in his eyes. My heart sinks as I realize who he is: Sebastian Hale, the arsonist who's been terrorizing the city for weeks. And he's here, right in front of us, watching with a look of satisfaction that makes my blood run cold.

"Well, well," Sebastian drawls, his voice dripping with mockery. "If it isn't the star-crossed lovers themselves. Enjoying the view?"

Callum tenses beside me, his hand tightening around mine as he takes a step forward, positioning himself between me and Sebastian. "What do you want, Sebastian?" he demands, his tone steady but laced with barely-contained fury.

Sebastian chuckles, a dark, menacing sound that sends a chill down my spine. "Isn't it obvious? I want to watch it all burn. And if you two get caught in the flames...well, that's just a bonus, isn't it?"

The words hang heavy in the air, a chilling reminder of just how dangerous this man is. I glance at Callum, my heart pounding as I realize the full extent of what we're up against. This isn't just some petty vendetta. This is a calculated, twisted game, and Sebastian is willing to destroy everything in his path to get what he wants.

Without thinking, I tighten my grip on Callum's hand, a silent plea for reassurance. He glances down at me, his expression softening for a brief moment before he turns back to face Sebastian, his jaw set with determination.

"You're not going to win, Sebastian," Callum says, his voice steady and unyielding. "No matter how many fires you set, no matter how much destruction you cause...you won't break us."

Sebastian's smile falters, just for an instant, and I feel a surge of hope, a flicker of defiance in the face of his cruelty. But then he steps closer, his gaze dark and predatory as he fixes his eyes on me.

"We'll see about that," he murmurs, his voice low and menacing. "After all...fire has a way of revealing the truth. And something tells me you two have plenty of secrets left to burn."

Sebastian's gaze lingers on me, predatory and amused, and I feel a pulse of anger rising, defiant in the face of his twisted glee. But as my hand tightens around Callum's, I catch the flicker of tension in his eyes, an unspoken warning. This isn't a game I can win with stubbornness alone, not with someone like Sebastian, who looks at people and sees nothing but pawns to be moved, to be sacrificed.

"So, what's your plan, Sebastian?" I ask, surprising even myself with the steadiness in my voice. "Burn the city to the ground and then what? Sit on the ashes and wait for someone to be impressed?"

He lets out a low, mocking laugh, the kind that makes the hairs on the back of my neck stand on end. "Oh, I have no interest in impressing anyone, Lena. You, of all people, should understand that sometimes...destruction is the only way to rebuild."

I exchange a quick, silent look with Callum, whose jaw is set in a hard line, his body tense beside me. This isn't the time to argue with a madman about the flaws in his logic, but the reality settles over me, thick as smoke—Sebastian isn't doing this for money, for power, or even for revenge. He's doing it for the sheer thrill, for the love of watching things unravel. And to someone like that, we're nothing more than kindling.

"Well, if you're going to bore us with the details of your philosophy, could you at least do it somewhere less likely to catch fire?" I say, feigning nonchalance. "All this heat can't be good for my skin."

Callum shoots me a sidelong glance, a glimmer of something like approval in his eyes, and I can tell he's fighting back a smile despite the tension. Sebastian, however, just narrows his eyes, his expression darkening.

"Charming as always," he says, his voice dripping with disdain. "But I wouldn't worry too much about the flames, Lena. You and your dear Callum here might not be around long enough to feel the effects."

There's a flash of metal in his hand, barely a glint in the firelight, but it's enough to make my heart pound. I grab Callum's arm instinctively, pulling him back as Sebastian steps forward, his gaze fixed on us with deadly intent. But Callum doesn't move, doesn't flinch—he just stands there, watching Sebastian with a quiet, steely determination that sends a shiver through me. He's calculating, assessing, and I realize with a sudden pang that Callum might be willing to take whatever's coming, as long as it keeps me safe.

But I can't just stand here, waiting for one of them to make the first move. Not when every instinct in me is screaming to fight, to survive. I take a slow, measured step back, keeping my eyes locked on Sebastian, hoping he won't notice the slight shift in my stance. But his gaze is fixed on Callum, and for a split second, I think we might have a chance. Until Sebastian's gaze shifts, zeroing in on me with an intensity that sends my heart racing.

"You know, Lena," he says, his voice low and taunting, "I almost feel sorry for you. Falling for a man who keeps secrets as well as Callum does...it must get lonely, living in the dark."

His words are a slap to the face, and I can feel the heat rising in my cheeks, but I refuse to give him the satisfaction of a reaction. Instead, I lift my chin, meeting his gaze head-on. "If loneliness is the price of survival, then I'd rather be alone."

A flicker of annoyance crosses his face, and I see his hand tighten on the metal object—a lighter, I realize, the small flame flickering dangerously close to his fingers. Callum's hand brushes against mine, a silent reassurance, and I can feel the tension radiating off him, ready to explode at the slightest provocation. But there's something else in his expression, too—a determination, a strength that I hadn't noticed before, like he's been waiting for this moment.

"Sebastian," Callum says, his voice calm but laced with steel. "You don't have to do this."

Sebastian's lips curl into a sneer, his gaze darting between us with an almost delighted malice. "Don't have to?" he repeats, mocking. "Callum, you of all people should know better. I don't do anything I have to do. I do what I want. What I enjoy. And right now…" His gaze shifts to me, his eyes gleaming with a dangerous, twisted glee. "Right now, I think I'd enjoy watching you two burn."

He flicks the lighter open, the flame springing to life, and my heart pounds in my chest, a wild, frantic beat that drowns out everything else. But Callum doesn't move, doesn't flinch, and I realize with a sickening jolt that he's got a plan. I just don't know what it is.

"What's the matter, Callum?" Sebastian taunts, the flame hovering dangerously close to a stack of papers on the ground, ready to ignite with the slightest flick of his wrist. "Afraid of a little heat?"

Callum's eyes narrow, his jaw clenched, but he remains perfectly still, his gaze fixed on Sebastian with an intensity that's almost unnerving. And then, just as Sebastian makes a move to toss the lighter onto the pile, Callum lunges forward, faster than I thought possible, his hand reaching out to grab the lighter from Sebastian's grasp.

For a moment, everything is chaos—the three of us struggling, grappling for control as the fire around us grows hotter, the smoke thicker, suffocating. I can barely see, barely breathe, but I refuse to let go, clinging to Callum's arm with a strength I didn't know I possessed.

"Lena, go!" Callum shouts, his voice strained, but I shake my head, refusing to leave him, not when I can feel the tension in his muscles, the desperation in his grip. I can't just abandon him, not like this.

But then, in a heartbeat, everything changes. There's a flash of movement, a blinding pain as something collides with my side, knocking me to the ground. I gasp, struggling to catch my breath, but all I can see is Callum, still locked in a deadly struggle with Sebastian, his face twisted with determination and fury.

And then, as if in slow motion, I see it—the lighter slipping from Sebastian's grasp, tumbling through the air, its small, deadly flame still flickering as it lands on the ground beside them. I reach out instinctively, my hand grasping for something, anything, but it's too late.

The flame catches, a spark turning into a blaze in an instant, and I feel the heat rising, scorching, as the fire spreads around us, consuming everything in its path. I struggle to my feet, coughing as the smoke fills my lungs, my eyes burning, but there's no escape, no way out.

I turn to Callum, my heart pounding, and I see the fear in his eyes, the raw, unguarded fear that tells me he knows exactly what's about to happen. He reaches for me, his hand outstretched, but before I can move, before I can reach him, a wall of flame erupts between us, separating us, trapping us in our own separate corners of hell.

And as I watch him through the fire, his face illuminated by the blaze, I feel a cold, paralyzing dread settle over me, a fear so deep it numbs me to everything else.

Because I know, in that moment, that this might be the last time I ever see him.

Chapter 15: Beneath the Embers

The smoke from that first fire clings to my memory as stubbornly as it clings to Callum's clothes. It's there, even if faint, whenever he walks into a room, slipping past the notes of cedar and rain on his skin. I'd ignored it for months, chalked it up to the occupational hazards of a man who's always putting himself at the scene. Yet tonight, as I sit hunched over these faded photos, its scent drifts around me like a ghost. The stench of ash, sharp and unwelcome, fills my senses again, and I swear I can almost taste the grit of it on my tongue. It's here, sprawled out across my tiny apartment floor, in the glow of a single lamp, that I finally let myself consider what I've been burying under hope and half-lies: the possibility that Callum isn't the man I thought he was.

That first fire was barely a blip in the news—an abandoned warehouse, no fatalities, hardly a story. A few charred beams, a smudge on the city skyline. But I remember every detail: the crackling heat on my face, the hiss of water as firefighters tamed the last of the embers. Callum had been there too, one of the first to arrive, stepping out of the darkness with a look so calm it bordered on reverence. I'd assumed it was professionalism, the quiet acceptance of a man hardened by years of dealing with flames and destruction. But now... maybe it was something else entirely. Maybe it was satisfaction.

I shake my head, scolding myself for even considering it. After all, I'd built an entire life on trust in him—blind, foolish trust maybe, but trust nonetheless. Even now, the memories I've been clutching so tightly come flooding back with stubborn loyalty. The way he laughed, rough around the edges but so open, his hand reaching to brush a stray hair from my face. The long, quiet nights where he let himself unravel just enough, revealing slivers of his past that he'd never talk about in daylight. A thousand reasons

I should believe in him, yet here I am, picking through files and holding them up to the faint, flickering candle of doubt.

And then I see it—a photograph, half-buried under a stack of grainy, black-and-white images of the warehouse ruins. I almost missed it. My fingers hover above it, tracing the lines of smoke and debris like they're delicate bones. In the foreground, there's a figure. It's the silhouette of a man, blurry but unmistakable, standing just beyond the perimeter tape. The streetlight catches him at an odd angle, throwing shadows that seem to twist and elongate across the cracked pavement. I blink, letting the image burn itself into my mind, as if holding it there might somehow make it disappear.

It's him. Callum.

My stomach clenches, twisting like a coiled rope, and I drop the photo as if it's burning my fingers. There's no denying it now. He was there, lurking on the edge of that first fire, long before he should have been. And he hadn't mentioned a thing about it. Not then, not now. Just stood there, watching the fire rage like he was taking it all in, learning something from the destruction.

The apartment feels too small, too quiet, the air thick and stagnant. I want to storm out, burst into the night and let the cold slap me back to my senses. But instead, I grab my phone, fingers numb as I type his name. There's no answer, just a hollow ring that drowns out the heartbeat pounding in my ears. I try again, pressing harder, as if that might compel him to pick up, to offer me some miraculous explanation, something that makes this whole thing dissolve like mist. But it's only the echo of my own desperation ringing back.

Finally, there's a shuffle on the other end, the rough scrape of fabric against the receiver. "What's wrong?" he says, his voice low, unsteady.

"What's wrong?" I repeat, voice barely above a whisper. I clench my fist, the nails digging into my palm, grounding me. "You need to come over, Callum. Now."

There's a pause, one that stretches so long I think he's hung up, but then he sighs, resigned, like he knew this was coming. "I'll be there in fifteen."

I don't know if I can wait that long. Time twists and stretches, tightening around me with each minute. I pace the room, the photos strewn across the floor like pieces of a puzzle I don't want to finish. And when there's a knock at my door, I practically jump, the tension snapping as I stumble toward it. Callum stands there, his face cast in shadows that seem darker than usual. I step back, letting him enter, watching the way he carefully closes the door behind him, each movement slow and measured.

"What's this about?" he asks, his gaze sliding from my face to the photos at my feet.

I cross my arms, swallowing the knot in my throat. "You tell me. How long have you been watching these fires, Callum?"

He meets my gaze, and for a moment, something flickers in his eyes—guilt, fear, regret. It's gone almost instantly, replaced by that careful, unreadable expression he wears so well. "I don't know what you mean," he says, but the lie is too thin, too weak to hold.

I step forward, daring him to lie to me again. "I found this." I hold up the photograph, fingers trembling. "You were there. At the first fire. Before it even made the news. How do you explain that?"

His face pales, and he takes a step back, like I've hit him. "It wasn't... it wasn't supposed to happen that way." His voice cracks, barely a whisper.

I force myself to stay steady, to ignore the way his words chip away at the foundation of everything I thought I knew. "So it did happen, then," I say, each word a stone in my throat.

He closes his eyes, running a hand through his hair, and when he looks at me again, I see a glimpse of the man I fell for—torn, uncertain, grasping at something he can't quite hold onto. "Yes," he says finally, the word heavy, final. "I was there. I started it."

The silence that follows is thick, suffocating, pressing in from every corner of the room. I don't want to believe him, but the truth is laid bare between us, sharp and undeniable. And as I look at him, I realize that I'm not sure which of us is more broken.

The room feels unbearably small now, with Callum standing there, his confession hanging thick in the air between us. He's looking at me with an expression I can't read, somewhere between apology and defiance. The man I thought I knew was supposed to look guilty, ashamed even, but here he is, shoulders back, face set as if daring me to throw the first stone. And as much as I want to be the righteous one here, I can feel my resolve wavering. There's still a part of me clinging to the idea that there must be some logical reason, some explanation that makes all of this... forgivable.

"Why?" I manage to ask, my voice barely more than a whisper. It's all I can do to stand there, to face him, the weight of betrayal pressing down on my chest. "Why would you do this?"

Callum lets out a long, shaky breath, rubbing the back of his neck, eyes fixed on a crack in the floor. He's stalling, searching for the right words, or maybe just waiting for me to break the silence for him. But I don't. I stand there, arms crossed, feeling every second stretch between us.

"It's not as simple as you think," he finally says, his voice low, like he's afraid the walls might hear. "I didn't want this. None of it was supposed to happen this way."

I scoff, the sound brittle, like glass cracking under pressure. "So it just... happened? You just happened to be there? Just happened to start a fire?"

He flinches, and for a moment, I think I see a flicker of regret in his eyes. But it's gone in an instant, replaced by that familiar, guarded look, the one he wears like armor. "You think I wanted to do this?" His voice is harsh, almost angry. "I didn't have a choice. Sometimes, things get out of control. You don't understand."

"Then make me understand," I say, hating the plea in my voice. I don't want to sound desperate, but I am. Desperate for answers, desperate to see some part of him that isn't coated in ash and lies. "Tell me why. Because right now, it looks like you've been playing me from the start."

He shakes his head, pacing the small space, his hands running through his hair in frustration. "You think this is some kind of game? That I enjoy this? The fires, the lies, pretending to be someone I'm not? You have no idea what it's like."

"Then tell me," I say, sharper now, daring him to answer me, to stop hiding behind half-truths and evasions. "Tell me what it's like. Because I'm done guessing."

Callum stops, turning to face me, his eyes dark and weary. "Do you remember what you told me the first night we met?" he asks, his voice softer now, almost hesitant. "About why you do this work?"

I nod, caught off guard by the question. I remember that night all too well—the smoky bar, the whiskey burning down my throat, the way he looked at me like I was something rare and precious. I'd told him about my father, about the fire that had torn through our old house, leaving nothing but charred remains. About how I'd felt so helpless, watching it all burn, and how I'd promised myself I'd never let that happen again. That's why I joined the force, why I dedicated my life to finding answers, to uncovering the truth behind every spark and flame.

He watches me, his gaze intense, and I can see a hint of something raw, something vulnerable. "That feeling," he says, his voice barely more than a whisper. "That helplessness. It never goes away, does it?"

I don't answer, can't answer, because somehow, he's hit on something I haven't even admitted to myself. The fear, the gnawing sense of powerlessness—it's always there, buried deep, but it's what drives me, keeps me going even when the answers seem impossible to find.

"That's what it's like for me," he says, his voice steady now, resolute. "Only worse. Because I'm not just trying to fight the fire. I'm trying to control it. To make it do what I want, to bend it to my will. But sometimes, it doesn't listen. Sometimes, it gets away from me."

The words hang in the air, and for a moment, I feel a pang of sympathy, an understanding that I don't want to admit. I know what it's like to feel trapped, to be driven by forces you can't fully control. But that doesn't excuse what he's done, the lives he's endangered, the trust he's shattered.

"So, what?" I ask, my voice sharper than I intend. "You're just some kind of... fire whisperer? Is that supposed to make me feel better? Because it doesn't. It just makes you sound like a madman."

He lets out a bitter laugh, running a hand through his hair. "Maybe I am. Maybe we both are. Because only a madman would believe he could control something as wild and destructive as fire. But that's the truth. It's in me, as much a part of me as my own skin."

I step back, a wave of anger washing over me. "And what about me? What was I? Just another part of the game? Another spark to keep you going?"

His eyes widen, and for a moment, I see real pain there, raw and unguarded. "You were never part of the game," he says, his voice breaking. "You were the one thing I thought I could keep separate, the one thing that was real."

"Real?" I laugh, the sound sharp and hollow. "You don't get to say that. Not after all the lies, the secrets. If this was real, you wouldn't have dragged me into this mess, wouldn't have made me question everything I thought I knew."

He reaches for me, his hand hovering inches from mine, but I step back, refusing to let him close that distance. I can't trust him anymore, can't let myself fall for the softness in his eyes, the warmth in his touch. Not when I know what he's capable of.

"Please," he says, his voice pleading. "I know I've made mistakes. But I need you to believe me, just this once. I'm not the monster you think I am."

I shake my head, the anger melting into a dull ache in my chest. "I don't know what to believe anymore. You've left me with nothing but questions, nothing but doubt. And I don't know if I can live like that."

Callum closes his eyes, a flicker of pain crossing his face, and for a moment, I almost feel sorry for him. Almost. But then I remember the fires, the lies, the betrayals, and the sympathy dies, replaced by a hard, cold resolve.

"Then I'll prove it to you," he says, his voice steady, determined. "I'll show you the truth, even if it costs me everything. Just... please, give me a chance."

I hesitate, caught between the man I thought I knew and the man standing before me now, a stranger with Callum's face, his voice. The choice hangs in the air, fragile as a spark in the wind. And as I look into his eyes, I feel the weight of it settling over me, an uneasy mix of hope and fear, trust and betrayal. The one thing I know for certain is that whatever happens next, there's no turning back.

I can't seem to stop staring at Callum, searching his face for any hint of the man I used to know. He's looking back at me with that same steely determination, the quiet, unyielding stare I once thought meant strength. Now it just feels like a mask, hiding secrets so twisted and deep that I wonder if I'll ever really know him.

I don't say anything for a moment, letting the silence coil around us, feeling the tension snap at my nerves. Callum shifts, his shoulders squared, as if he's ready for me to throw another accusation. He'd probably just take it, letting it bounce off that shield he's built up, the one I only now see has been there all along.

"You know, when I first met you," I finally say, "I thought you were the kind of man who could keep me safe." I bite my lip, hating how vulnerable I sound, but there's no taking it back. "Turns out I was wrong."

His jaw clenches, and for a second, I think I see a flash of pain in his eyes. But just as quickly, it's gone, replaced by that infuriatingly calm exterior. "I wanted to keep you safe," he says, voice so low I almost miss it. "That's all I've ever wanted."

"Then why keep lying to me?" I ask, my voice sharper than I intend. "If you wanted to protect me, maybe you could've started by telling me the truth. Or is that just not your style?"

He sighs, a sound that's heavy with something like regret, but it does nothing to soften the anger churning inside me. "I didn't want you to get caught up in this," he says. "The fires, the risks. I thought... I thought I could handle it alone."

I laugh, a brittle sound that echoes in the small room. "So, this was you protecting me? Keeping me safe by dragging me into a mess I didn't ask for?"

"Believe me, I tried to keep you out," he says, his voice taut, his fingers curling into fists. "But you just kept pushing. You couldn't let it go."

"Because I thought you were in danger," I shoot back. "Because I cared about you." The words taste bitter on my tongue, but I don't let them stop. "And you used that, didn't you? Played the part of the man who needed saving, all the while knowing exactly what you were doing."

He opens his mouth to argue, but I hold up a hand, stopping him. "You know what the worst part is? I still want to believe you. Even now, after everything, I'm sitting here trying to convince myself that there's some piece of you that's not a lie."

"Not everything was a lie," he says, his voice rough, breaking. "There's a reason I tried to keep you at arm's length, why I didn't want you looking too closely. I didn't want you to see... this side of me."

I raise an eyebrow, crossing my arms. "And which side is that, Callum? The one that sets fires for fun? Or the one that pulls people close just to manipulate them?"

His face tightens, and for a moment, I think he's about to walk out, to turn his back and leave me standing here in this mess he's created. But instead, he steps closer, his gaze fierce, intense. "You want the truth?" he says, voice barely more than a whisper. "Fine. I'll give it to you. But I don't think you're ready for it."

"Try me," I say, holding his gaze, refusing to let him intimidate me.

He takes a deep breath, his eyes searching mine, as if he's weighing some decision he's barely willing to make. "Do you remember that warehouse fire three years ago?" he asks, voice steady, careful.

I nod, feeling a chill creep up my spine. That fire had been one of the worst I'd ever seen, consuming half a block in a matter of hours, leaving nothing but smoldering rubble and twisted metal. There'd been talk of arson, rumors about insurance fraud, but no one was ever charged. I'd looked into it myself, combed through the evidence, but the trail had gone cold.

"That fire..." he hesitates, as if choosing his words carefully. "It wasn't an accident. It was... deliberate. And I was there."

The words hit me like a punch to the gut, and I stumble back, the ground seeming to tilt beneath me. "You were... you started it?"

He shakes his head. "No. I didn't start it. But I was there, watching. I knew what was going to happen, and I didn't stop it." His voice breaks, and he looks away, his face etched with something close to shame. "I thought I could control it, thought I could make it end cleanly. But it got out of hand. People got hurt."

I stare at him, my mind spinning, trying to make sense of what he's saying. "So you... you just let it burn? Watched it happen?"

He nods, his expression haunted. "I thought I could make it right, that if I kept control, no one would have to know. But it didn't work. And now... now it's happening all over again."

I feel a shiver run down my spine, my breath catching in my throat. "What do you mean?"

He looks at me, his gaze dark and serious. "There's something you don't know. Something I've been trying to keep from you, to protect you." He hesitates, then steps closer, his voice barely more than a whisper. "There's someone else out there, someone who's been setting these fires. And they're watching us, waiting. I think... I think they know about you."

I blink, the words sinking in like ice water. "What do you mean, they know about me?"

"They know you've been looking into the fires," he says, his voice tense, urgent. "They know you're close to finding out the truth. And they're not going to let that happen."

A chill runs through me, and I feel my pulse quicken, fear clawing its way up my throat. "So what? They're just going to... come after me?"

He nods, his face grim. "They've already tried once. That night you thought you were being followed? That wasn't an accident."

My heart races, a thousand thoughts swirling in my mind, each one darker than the last. "So what do we do?"

"We have to be smart," he says, his voice steady, his gaze unwavering. "I can't protect you if you're reckless, if you keep pushing like you have been. You need to trust me, let me handle this."

I shake my head, anger flaring up despite the fear twisting inside me. "Trust you? After everything you've lied about? You think I'm just going to sit back and let you handle it?"

He reaches for me, his hand brushing mine, sending a shock of warmth up my arm. "Please. I know I've made mistakes. But I'm the only one who knows how dangerous this is. If you don't let me help you, I don't know what they'll do."

For a moment, I waver, the fear in his eyes mirroring the panic gnawing at my insides. But just as quickly, a spark of defiance flickers to life. I've come too far, risked too much, to back down now. "Fine," I say, pulling my hand back, meeting his gaze with as much steel as I can muster. "But we do this my way. No more lies, no more half-truths. I want to know everything."

He hesitates, a hint of reluctance flickering in his eyes, but finally, he nods. "Alright," he says, his voice barely more than a whisper. "Everything."

We stand there, the weight of his promise settling over us like smoke, thick and suffocating. And as he holds my gaze, I feel a chill settle in the pit of my stomach, a dark, creeping sense of dread that tells me whatever truth he's about to reveal will change everything.

Then, from somewhere outside, the unmistakable sound of glass shattering splits the night.

Chapter 16: In Harm's Way

The acrid smell hit us before we reached the smoke, thick and rolling in dusky waves across the street. Callum's footsteps thundered beside me, matching my own in a mad, desperate rhythm. Flames curled against the roof of a building just a block over, embers like fireflies in the deepening dusk, casting eerie shadows that danced against the walls. Every part of me screamed to turn back, to retreat into the safety of dark alleys and quiet corners, but something stronger than fear—a fierce, gut-clenching need to be there, to do something—kept me pressing forward.

Callum was right behind me, his breaths shallow, his hand reaching instinctively toward my arm as if to keep me from running straight into the blaze. And, truthfully, if I thought it would help, I might have. "Slow down," he called, his voice taut with an urgency that held more than worry, something closer to frustration, or maybe the weight of too many things left unsaid. "This isn't your fight."

I whipped around, meeting his gaze under the flickering glow, and something fierce and wild sparked between us, a silent, mutual defiance that carried more heat than the fire behind me. "Maybe it isn't," I replied, brushing off the sting of his words, though I felt them settle heavily into my chest. "But someone has to be here, and right now, that someone's me."

For a heartbeat, he looked at me like he was about to argue, like he wanted nothing more than to push me back to safety, to hold me there in some bubble where nothing could touch me. But I could see it—maybe for the first time—his own exhaustion, his anger and frustration barely held in check. He held himself like a man at war, not just with the flames in front of him, but with everything and everyone around him. The look in his eyes made me wonder how many times he'd gone charging in just like this, only to come out feeling emptier than before.

We barely spoke as we moved toward the blaze, working with a strange synchronicity that surprised me. We threw ourselves into the thick of the battle, shouting orders and urging bystanders to clear out, making split-second decisions that held the weight of people's lives. My muscles ached, my lungs burned with the effort, and all I could think was, I have to keep going. Every time I caught a glimpse of Callum's face, hardened with determination, I felt the invisible tether that bound us—an unlikely alliance forged under fire.

When the worst of it was under control, we sank down onto the curb, a brittle silence falling between us. I wiped soot from my cheek, glancing sidelong at him, and for the first time, he didn't look back with that familiar, guarded intensity. He stared at the ground, and when he finally spoke, his voice was barely audible above the distant crackle of the dying flames.

"Fire's a strange thing," he murmured, almost to himself. "It'll take everything if you let it. People think they can control it, but...they're wrong."

I studied him, caught off guard by the rough vulnerability in his voice. There was a story there, buried beneath the ash and smoke, something old and raw. I wanted to press him, to peel back the layers of his carefully controlled demeanor, but some instinct told me to hold back. Instead, I gave him the space to talk, letting silence fill the gaps.

After a long pause, he continued, his eyes still fixed on the ground. "Once, a long time ago, I trusted someone. I thought they'd never... Well, I thought wrong. They'd built this whole world around me, made me feel like I was the only one they'd ever protect." He let out a sharp, bitter laugh that felt like a shard of glass. "Turns out, that trust was just something they needed to get what they wanted. And once they got it..." His voice trailed off, leaving me to imagine the rest.

I watched him carefully, feeling an ache that wasn't quite mine, a pain that I recognized nonetheless. "You think I'm like that?" I asked softly, realizing as the words left my mouth that they held a question I hadn't known I wanted answered.

He glanced at me then, his gaze intense, searching. "I don't know," he admitted, his voice edged with a weariness that felt too old for a man his age. "I just know what it feels like to trust someone, to believe in them, and then..." He looked away, his jaw clenched. "Let's just say it makes you question things. Everyone, really."

The vulnerability in his voice cracked something open inside me, a thread of sympathy wrapped in a wary understanding. I wasn't ready to let go of my own suspicions, not entirely, but I could see now that Callum's armor wasn't just a defense; it was the fragile shell of someone who'd been broken and pieced back together, one jagged shard at a time. For a moment, the weight of our shared silence felt heavier than the smoke that clung to us.

After what felt like an eternity, I reached over, brushing soot from his hand in a small, tentative gesture. "I'm not them," I said simply. I meant it, every word. Whatever he saw in my eyes, it was enough to make him nod, the barest hint of a reluctant, guarded smile ghosting across his face.

"We'll see," he replied, his tone a little lighter, as if he didn't quite believe me, but was willing to pretend for now.

As we sat there on the edge of the curb, watching the smoldering remains of the fire, I felt a tentative peace settle over us, a fragile truce in the midst of the chaos. I knew better than to hope it would last—Callum's trust was a thin, fragile line, one that could snap with the slightest misstep. But for now, as the last wisps of smoke faded into the night, I let myself believe that maybe, just maybe, we could find our way through this—together.

The night stretched on, heavy and quiet, a blanket of uneasy silence settled over the street. Embers still glowed in the blackened frame of the building, their warm light catching in Callum's eyes as he studied the wreckage. He'd retreated back into that familiar hard shell, the one I'd grown accustomed to, where every line of his face was sharp with the determination of someone who would rather grit his teeth through the worst than admit to feeling any part of it.

"So, what's your plan?" I asked, breaking the silence that had begun to feel more like a wall than a reprieve.

"Plan?" he echoed, raising an eyebrow, but I could see the faintest smirk lurking just behind his mask.

"Right, the brilliant investigator with no plan." I leaned back against the curb, letting my tone dip into something closer to teasing. "I don't believe that for a second."

He huffed out a laugh, the sound rough and reluctant, as if it had snuck past his guard. "Maybe I'm not that brilliant," he muttered, though his eyes sparkled with a defiant gleam, one that dared me to challenge him on it.

I glanced over, unable to resist the bait. "Says the man who single-handedly evacuated half the neighborhood and talked down a panicking shop owner in the same breath? Sorry, but you're not getting away with that kind of false modesty around me."

A flicker of something softer passed over his face, and for a moment, I thought I'd struck a nerve. But he only shook his head, giving a rueful grin that was so unlike his usual guarded expression that it caught me off guard.

"Fine," he said, voice low but steady. "You want to know the plan? It's to get out of this mess with as few burns as possible." He shrugged, as though the very thought of real vulnerability might weigh him down. "Trouble is, some things...they don't just burn. They leave marks that don't ever really fade."

I stayed quiet, the words hanging heavy in the air between us, and for the first time, I realized that his cynicism wasn't just a shield. It was the armor of someone who'd fought wars on invisible fronts, who had watched the people he trusted slip away like sand through his fingers. And maybe it wasn't just the fire that had brought us here, sitting side by side with nothing but our own ragged edges laid bare.

"You don't think it's worth trying again?" I asked, my voice barely more than a whisper.

He looked at me, really looked, his gaze so intense it was almost a physical force. "That's the problem," he said quietly. "Sometimes you want to believe it's worth it, even when everything inside you is screaming not to. But people aren't always what they seem, and by the time you figure it out..." His voice trailed off, leaving the words half-spoken, like a secret he couldn't bring himself to say.

I opened my mouth, searching for something—anything—that might pierce through that wall he'd built around himself, but before I could speak, a noise cut through the silence. It was faint, barely there, but Callum's attention snapped to it immediately. He tilted his head, listening, every line of his body tense as he scanned the shadows that clung to the edge of the street.

"What is it?" I whispered, my heart pounding as I tried to follow his gaze.

He held up a hand, signaling for silence, his expression sharpening as he stood, moving with the quiet, fluid motion of someone who'd been trained to notice even the smallest disturbances. And there it was again—a rustle, the scrape of footsteps on concrete, the barely perceptible shift of movement in the dark.

"Stay here," he murmured, his voice so low that I almost missed it. Without waiting for my response, he slipped into the shadows, leaving me alone on the curb with nothing but the distant, fading warmth of the fire and the cold weight of fear settling in my stomach.

For a long, agonizing moment, I waited, my eyes straining to see any sign of him. The street felt different now, empty and menacing in a way that made the hair on the back of my neck stand up. And just when I thought I couldn't bear the silence any longer, I saw him—a figure moving quickly but carefully, his outline sharp against the dim glow from a nearby streetlamp. He stopped just a few yards away, his gaze fixed on something in the shadows.

"Show yourself," he demanded, his voice steady, controlled, like he was more annoyed than afraid. The bravado was pure Callum, a bluff as good as any he'd ever pulled. But there was an edge in his voice, a tension that I couldn't ignore.

To my surprise, there was a response—a low chuckle, soft and mocking, coming from the darkness. "Impressive, Callum. Didn't think you'd catch on so quickly."

The voice was smooth, with a dangerous, almost taunting lilt that sent a shiver down my spine. Callum's posture stiffened, his hands clenched into fists at his sides, and I felt my own pulse quicken as I watched him.

"You're not supposed to be here," Callum replied, his voice tight.

The shadowy figure stepped forward, revealing a man in a dark coat, his face partially obscured but his smirk clear enough. There was something predatory in his stance, an air of quiet menace that sent my instincts screaming.

"Oh, come on," the man said, his tone dripping with feigned disappointment. "Surely you didn't think I'd stay away forever. You and I—we have unfinished business, don't we?"

Callum's jaw tightened, but he kept his gaze steady, unflinching. "You're not as clever as you think, Marcus," he said coolly, his voice laced with a bitterness that I'd never heard from him before. "If you were, you'd know how this is going to end."

Marcus's smirk widened, his eyes glinting with something cruel. "Oh, I know exactly how it'll end. But it doesn't matter, does it? Because in the meantime, I'm here, and there's nothing you can do to change that."

A tense silence fell over us, so thick I could almost feel it pressing down, suffocating. Callum held Marcus's gaze, his expression unreadable, but I could see the tension in his shoulders, the barely-contained fury simmering beneath his calm exterior.

Finally, Marcus gave a mocking shrug, turning away with a nonchalant wave of his hand. "See you around, Callum," he said, his voice dripping with the promise of more to come.

As he disappeared into the shadows, Callum's stance softened, the hard edge of his expression slipping just enough for me to see the exhaustion underneath. When he turned back to me, his face was a mask, but I could feel the weight of everything he wasn't saying pressing down between us.

"Come on," he muttered, gesturing for me to follow. "It's not safe here."

And as I fell into step beside him, I realized, with a sinking feeling, that whatever we were dealing with was far from over.

The fire raged with an intensity that felt almost personal, like a furious beast determined to take everything in its path. Its hungry tendrils clawed at the sky, and the acrid scent of burning timber stung my lungs, filling the air with a thick haze. I could barely see through it, my heart pounding against my chest as I moved closer, Callum's silhouette always a step ahead of me, his movements fluid and practiced. He was a man made for this, a soldier in a war against the unpredictable. But I couldn't shake the feeling that something else was gnawing at him, that the fire we were battling wasn't the only thing consuming him.

We had arrived too late, or perhaps it was too soon, depending on how you looked at it. The flames had already taken the majority of the building, and what remained was nothing but skeletons of charred wood, hunks of metal warped by heat. Callum's jaw was clenched as he scanned the perimeter, his eyes sharp, unyielding. He was in control, or at least he appeared to be. But there was a tremor in his hands when he reached for his radio, his voice betraying nothing but the raw command he'd mastered over the years.

I stayed close behind him, feeling the weight of each decision hanging over us. It was a familiar sensation, one I had lived with for too long. The unspoken truth that no one could be trusted—not completely, not ever. Not even Callum. Especially not him.

"Stay sharp," he muttered under his breath, though I wasn't sure if the warning was for me or for himself.

"Always," I replied, forcing a calmness I didn't feel. We moved further into the wreckage, our footsteps muffled by the crumbling debris. His eyes flicked back to me once, briefly, before he went to assess the damage near the building's entry. But his glance lingered longer than it should have. There was something in his gaze, something dark and heavy, like a storm waiting to break.

I took a deep breath, ignoring the burn in my chest, and followed him. The heat of the flames on my skin was nothing compared to the tension crackling between us. It was as if the fire, instead of purging, was stirring up something deeper, something we couldn't control.

Minutes passed in silence, each one heavier than the last. Finally, Callum stopped, his back stiff, and I could see the moment when he made the decision to tell me something—something important.

"I wasn't always like this," he said, his voice low, carrying the weight of a thousand unsaid words. "I trusted once. Maybe too much."

I watched him carefully, not sure what to make of the vulnerability creeping into his tone. He had never spoken of his past, not in any meaningful way. Not even when we'd been close enough for secrets to feel natural.

"What happened?" I asked, barely whispering the words. My voice felt distant, like a stranger's.

His eyes flickered to mine, and for a fleeting moment, I saw the man beneath the stoic exterior. The façade he'd spent years building, layer by layer, had begun to crack. "A betrayal. Someone I trusted more than anyone... they turned on me. Left me with nothing but a lie."

His words hung in the air, heavy and unyielding. I could see the cracks forming, like the fragile foundation of a house built on sand. His gaze never wavered, though his jaw tightened, his body tense with a mixture of fury and grief. It was a look I'd seen before, in the eyes of those who had been broken by the very people they thought they could trust.

I didn't respond immediately. What could I say to that? I had my own walls, my own scars, but none of them seemed as deep as what he was carrying. I could feel my own breath catch in my throat as I tried to piece together the fragments of his past.

"You're afraid of me," I said at last, the realization creeping through me like a slow-burning fuse. "Afraid I'll do the same."

He didn't answer at first. Instead, he turned back toward the ruins, his back to me, as though the weight of his confession was too much to bear in the light of day. "It's not just you. It's everything... everyone."

His voice cracked on the last word, and in that instant, something inside me shifted. I had never seen him this raw, this open. And I wasn't sure what to do with it. I had always prided myself on my ability to see through people, to read the subtle shifts in their expression, the hidden meanings behind their words. But this... this was different. Callum was a man wrapped in layers of pain, his eyes shadowed with things he had never told anyone. And now, I had the feeling that I was standing at the edge of a precipice, one that could swallow us both whole.

"You don't have to trust me," I said softly, my words careful. "But I'm not them, Callum. I'm not going to hurt you."

He stiffened, his back still to me, but I saw the brief clench of his fists, as though he was fighting against something darker than the fire that still raged behind us. Then, without warning, he turned to face me, his eyes locking with mine in a way that felt almost too intense, too intimate. His gaze flicked to my lips for a fraction of a second before returning to my eyes.

"What if you do?" he whispered, the question heavy between us, hanging like a specter.

And then, before I could respond, the world shifted beneath my feet. A distant explosion rang out, the ground trembling with the force of it, and the fire suddenly roared louder, spreading faster, more violently than before.

Callum's expression hardened, the moment between us shattered in an instant. His hand shot out to grab mine, pulling me toward the safety of the nearby alleyway, and for the first time, I didn't question the urgency in his touch. The world outside was burning. And whatever was waiting for us in the flames, whatever was hidden beneath the smoke, was something we had yet to face.

Chapter 17: An Unexpected Witness

The air in the dimly lit room was thick with the scent of stale coffee and something more elusive, something darker that clung to the walls as if it had always been there, waiting. The small table between Callum and me felt like a vast chasm, though the space was crowded with tension. I could feel it in the taut set of his jaw, the way his eyes flitted over the man who had just walked in—the so-called "witness" whose timing couldn't have been more convenient. I wasn't sure what had brought him here, but I didn't believe in coincidences, not in this mess. Not anymore.

Callum's hands rested, almost rigidly, on the table, the fingers flexing as if to steady himself against the pull of something unknown. His gaze never fully settled on the witness, though it was hard to miss the way his shoulders tensed as the man spoke. "You say you have information," Callum's voice was low, clipped. He didn't trust him. I didn't blame him. Neither did I, not entirely, but the whisper of hope that maybe—just maybe—this man could help was too alluring to ignore.

"I saw him," the witness insisted, the words coming out in a rapid, breathless rush, as if the very act of speaking might cause him to disappear. "I saw him that night, and I saw the woman with him."

The mention of a woman brought a flicker of something in Callum's eyes—a flash of recognition—or maybe something darker, something that made my chest tighten in a way that had nothing to do with the airless room. It didn't take a seasoned investigator to know that the story had holes, but there was something about the way he spoke. Desperation, maybe. Guilt. Or just fear.

"Who?" I pressed, leaning forward, my fingers curling around the edge of the table, instinctively searching for some kind of solid ground. My heart raced as I tried to ignore the small voice in my head that urged caution, that whispered to keep my distance.

The witness looked between us, shifting uneasily in his seat. He couldn't decide if we were on the same side or if he was about to walk into a trap. "A woman. Dark hair, pretty... with a scar across her cheek. You know her."

I froze. The room shifted, blurred for a moment, like I'd stepped out of time. There was a name that danced on the tip of my tongue, but I couldn't make it out. It hovered in the space between us, like a ghost too familiar to be forgotten but too elusive to grasp. Callum's expression hardened, the mask of composure slipping for a moment as the room seemed to close in on him.

"Who is she?" I repeated, more insistent now, my pulse quickening, desperate to break through his wall of silence.

But Callum's eyes, dark and unreadable, met mine. He didn't respond. Not yet.

"Her name was... Carla." The witness's voice was shaky, uncertain. It was clear he wasn't used to dealing with people who didn't trust him, people who didn't want to believe. The name hung in the air between us, a taut string pulled so tight it could snap at any moment.

Carla. The name landed with the force of a thousand blows, and in that moment, the world tilted ever so slightly. I knew it. I knew exactly who he was talking about. I'd only heard the name in passing before, whispered in the back corners of rooms where no one was supposed to listen, linked to a part of Callum's past he rarely spoke of. But it had always been there, lurking—just beneath the surface of whatever calm he tried to present to the world.

Callum's fingers twitched, and I saw the muscles in his jaw tighten. His body language screamed discomfort, something raw and untapped, and yet he still hadn't moved, hadn't reacted to the name. Not the way I would have expected. Not the way I had hoped he would.

"Who was she to you?" I asked, my voice barely above a whisper, but the words felt like they thundered through the room, vibrating against the air.

Callum stood abruptly, the chair scraping sharply against the floor, its sound so loud I almost flinched. His gaze was colder than I had ever seen it, harder than steel, and yet I could sense the cracks beneath the surface. "I don't know what you think you're doing, but it's not going to help you," he said, his voice tight, almost too controlled. "There's nothing there, Violet."

But there was. There was something there. I could feel it in my bones. And for reasons I didn't understand, for reasons I didn't want to face, it was pulling me toward him, deeper into this mess that was his life, his secrets, his past.

"You need to talk to me," I pressed, standing up slowly, my gaze never leaving his. "This could be the key we've been looking for, Callum. I know you don't want to dredge this up, but it's not about what you want anymore. It's about getting you out of this. Out of everything that's been following you for all these years."

He glanced at the witness, who had gone silent, watching the two of us like a spectator to something far more dangerous than he could understand. Then Callum turned his back on me, his voice cutting through the air with an edge that made me pause.

"I don't need your help. I never did."

I could feel my heart sinking, the words I'd meant to say dying in my throat. But I couldn't back down now. Something inside of me was screaming that I couldn't walk away. Not this time. Not with everything I'd learned, everything I'd uncovered, everything I'd put on the line to help him—help us.

I took a breath, steadied myself, and closed the distance between us, my steps measured, deliberate. "I'm in this, Callum.

I'm in too deep to walk away now. Whether you want me here or not, I'm not leaving. Not until we get to the truth."

The silence that followed was thick, suffocating even, and for the first time, I wasn't sure who I was trying to convince. Him? Or myself?

The door slammed shut behind us, the sound echoing through the narrow hallway like a warning. Callum's footsteps were heavy on the cracked tiles, each one a silent drumbeat in the rhythm of his withdrawal. I knew I should have stepped back, should have let him retreat into his fortress of silence. It was easier that way. For both of us.

But the words were already spilling out of me before I could stop them. "You can't just shut me out, Callum."

His shoulders stiffened at the sound of my voice, and I could almost see the familiar wall go up, piece by piece. The mask, the careful indifference, it all fell back into place like a suit of armor. "I'm not shutting you out," he said, the words tight and controlled, but I heard the undercurrent of something else there—something darker, something far more fragile. "I'm trying to keep you safe."

"Safe?" I repeated, my voice a little too sharp. "You think keeping me in the dark about all of this is keeping me safe?"

His eyes flashed, and I felt the air between us thicken. "It's not about you. It's about—" He stopped himself, visibly biting back something, some truth, some unspoken burden that had been sitting on his chest for far too long.

I took a step toward him, the space between us suddenly feeling smaller, more intimate, even though I knew that was the last thing he wanted. "You don't get to say it's not about me, Callum. I'm in this with you now. Whether you like it or not."

He turned, his jaw clenched so tightly that I half-expected him to snap his teeth together. "This is my mess. And I don't want you to get dragged into it. It's dangerous."

My heart thudded in my chest at the finality in his tone. I could hear the unsaid words loud and clear: Leave now. While you still can. But the thing was, I couldn't leave. I hadn't just stepped into this storm—I had walked straight into its eye, and now I was caught, spinning with everything I hadn't known I was capable of. I couldn't pull myself out now without ripping the fabric of everything we'd built.

"And what about you?" I asked, my voice quieter now, almost gentle. "What do you think this is doing to you? Pushing everyone away isn't going to fix anything."

He ran a hand through his hair, the tension in his shoulders spilling over, but there was no breaking him. Not yet. "I'm not asking for your help. I didn't ask you to get involved, Violet."

There it was. The words I'd been waiting for. Not the ones I'd hoped for, but the ones I'd feared. He hadn't asked for me.

I shook my head, trying to breathe through the sting of that truth, the bitter taste of it settling on my tongue. "I didn't ask for this either. But here we are."

I was running on fumes—tired, worn, and still carrying the weight of everything that had happened since the first moment I stepped into his world. I knew I was stubborn, that I often pushed too hard. But this... this felt like more than stubbornness. It felt like survival.

There was no easy way to explain it, but somewhere between the sharp words, the late-night calls, and the tension that had coiled itself around us, something had shifted. I wasn't sure when it happened, but I'd crossed a line. And now, every moment I spent with him felt like I was being pulled deeper into the current, caught between the need to know, the fear of what I might discover, and the impossibility of walking away.

His eyes softened for a split second, and I could see it—the flicker of something that wasn't just pain, but vulnerability. The very thing he hated to show. And yet it was there, threading through the hardness, the walls that kept everyone at arm's length.

"You don't have to stay, you know," he murmured, his voice barely above a whisper.

But I knew better than to believe that. I knew better than to think that this was about a choice. It wasn't about whether I could leave or not. I was already too far gone.

"I'm not going anywhere," I said firmly, my resolve tightening in my chest like a band. "And neither are you. Not until we figure this out."

The silence stretched out between us, uncomfortable and thick, until I could almost hear the sound of the world falling apart in the distance. Maybe it wasn't just Callum who was holding everything together. Maybe, just maybe, it was me. I had no illusions that I was the hero of this story. But I was here, I was present, and for the first time in a long while, I wasn't about to let go.

He gave a sharp, frustrated exhale, his hands shoved deep into his pockets, his gaze flicking back toward the door. "You should've walked away a long time ago, Violet. This isn't a game. It's not some... project for you to fix."

"I know," I replied softly, moving to stand beside him. "I never said it was. But you don't get to decide what I do with my life, Callum."

He turned toward me then, his expression still guarded, but I could see the conflict warring in his eyes. His lips parted, like he was going to argue, but instead, he exhaled sharply, as if releasing the breath he'd been holding in for days, maybe even weeks.

"Just... just be careful," he muttered, his voice rougher than I expected. "This isn't something you can just walk away from."

"I don't want to walk away," I said, the words slipping out before I could stop them.

I regretted them the instant they left my mouth. Because I could see his face harden again, the mask coming down once more, the distance growing in an instant. But there was something else in his eyes too. Something I couldn't quite place.

"Good," he said quietly. "Because this isn't over. Not by a long shot."

I didn't ask him what he meant. I already knew the answer. This was just the beginning.

The room had never felt smaller, not even the first time I stepped into it. And yet, as we stood there in the oppressive silence, the walls seemed to close in, squeezing the air out of me until I could hardly breathe. Callum was no longer just a man I was trying to help; he had become a puzzle, a maze with too many walls, too many dead ends. And yet, no matter how many times I hit a wall, I kept looking for another way through.

We stood in the dimly lit hallway, the sound of our footsteps too loud in the otherwise quiet apartment. His posture was rigid, a thousand miles away, and I had to remind myself that even though he wasn't saying anything, I wasn't alone in this. Not completely.

"You don't get to do that," I finally said, my voice a little steadier than I felt. "You don't get to shut me out and expect me to just leave."

"I never expected you to leave," he said, his voice rough, almost too soft, like he was choosing his words with care. "But I expected you to understand why you should."

His gaze was distant, his focus on something far past me, some place only he could see. He wasn't speaking to me anymore. He was speaking to the ghosts that followed him, the ones that lingered in the corners of the room, in the spaces between his words. The ones I wasn't sure I even wanted to know about.

"You think I don't get it?" I pressed, feeling my frustration burn hotter. "That's what you think of me? You think I don't understand what this is doing to you?"

Callum ran a hand through his hair, his movements sharp and frustrated. "It's not just about me, Violet. You have no idea what you're dealing with."

"I've got a pretty good idea," I said, leaning in slightly, my voice firm. "I might not know the whole picture, but I'm trying to help. You don't get to push me away like this."

He turned on me then, a sudden shift in his stance. "I'm not pushing you away, Violet. I'm protecting you."

I wasn't sure whether to laugh or cry. Protection. That's what this was all about? After everything that had happened, everything I'd seen, everything I'd learned? "You're not protecting me, Callum. You're keeping me in the dark. You're keeping us both trapped in this... this... mess."

There was a beat of silence, then a sharp, bitter laugh escaped him. "I didn't ask for any of this."

I wasn't sure what stung more—his words or the brokenness I saw in his eyes. "I know," I said quietly, finally lowering my voice. "But here we are. And I'm not going anywhere."

The room felt smaller still. My chest ached with the weight of everything left unsaid. And yet, in the space between us, something shifted again. I wasn't sure if it was a step forward or just another misstep, but I could feel the tension crackling in the air. He was so close to the edge, and I had no idea whether I was about to drag him over it or help him find his footing again.

He exhaled, shaking his head slowly. "You think you know what this is, Violet. But I don't think you do. Not really."

I caught the flicker of something in his eyes. A vulnerability, maybe, or something darker. A warning. But even as he spoke, the words felt more like a plea than a command.

"I think you underestimate me," I said, my voice quieter now, but sure. "But I'm not backing off. Not this time."

He didn't respond right away. Instead, he turned, walking over to the small window overlooking the city. I could see his reflection in the glass, the way the light caught the angles of his face, the hardness of his jaw. For a moment, I thought he was going to say something, but then his shoulders slumped, just enough to make me realize how exhausted he really was.

"You don't get it," he repeated, softer this time, as though the words were meant for himself as much as for me. "There's a price to all of this. A cost I can't let you pay."

I couldn't keep still any longer. My heart beat so loudly in my chest, I could almost feel it pounding in my ears. I walked toward him slowly, uncertain of what I was doing but unable to stop myself. "You can't decide that for me," I said, just a breath away from him now. "I'll decide what I'm willing to risk. Not you. Not anyone."

Callum turned then, and his eyes met mine with a clarity that made my chest tighten. "You think you're strong enough for this?" His words weren't cruel, but they felt like a challenge. A test.

I didn't hesitate. "I don't know," I admitted, my voice quieter now. "But I'm going to find out."

His gaze softened just a little, a flicker of something that could have been relief, or maybe just the sheer weight of everything that had been unsaid between us. But the moment was fleeting. Gone as quickly as it came.

Then the silence stretched again, thicker this time. Neither of us spoke for what felt like an eternity. But the longer we stood there, the clearer it became. This wasn't just about solving the case anymore. It was about something bigger, something that had been brewing between us since the first moment I stepped into his life.

And maybe, just maybe, it was the one thing neither of us knew how to handle.

Finally, I spoke again, my voice low but insistent. "You're not going through this alone. Not anymore."

Callum's eyes held mine for a long moment, and I saw the shift, the way his walls began to crack just enough to let something else—something real—seep through. He took a step back, his expression unreadable. But as he moved, I felt it. The world wasn't going to stop spinning, not yet.

There was a soft knock on the door, and before either of us could react, the door creaked open slightly. A figure stood in the doorway, their face obscured in shadow.

And before I could ask who it was, a single sentence cut through the air, as sharp and clear as glass:

"I know what you're looking for."

Chapter 18: The Fire Line

The air was thick with the acrid scent of smoke as I pulled my jacket tighter around my shoulders, squinting through the haze that clung to the streets like a veil of smoke. It seemed as if the whole city was holding its breath, waiting for the next fire to start, for the next warning to arrive, for something—anything—to ignite. The sounds of sirens were more constant than ever, wailing in the distance, echoing off the buildings that loomed like silent sentinels in the dim glow of streetlights. Callum and I had been assigned to the worst-hit sector tonight, and I could already feel the weight of it pressing in on me. The kind of weight that made your skin tight and your pulse beat in time with the flashing red lights.

We didn't speak much as we walked the patrol route, our footsteps the only sound on the quiet streets. I could feel Callum beside me, the faint shift of his weight as he walked, his presence almost too close. Too familiar. It wasn't like I didn't appreciate him as a partner—he was quick, sharp, and didn't hesitate when things got dicey. But something had shifted between us lately. I couldn't tell if it was the fires or something else, something quieter, but there was an undeniable tension in the air when we were together. Maybe it was the fact that we hadn't talked about the night I caught him looking at me like I was something more than just his partner. Maybe it was the fact that I hadn't brought it up, too.

"Someone's been busy," Callum murmured, his voice low, eyes scanning the darkened corners of the street. I followed his gaze, taking in the faint smell of burnt wood that still clung to the buildings we passed. The shadows seemed deeper tonight, the edges of the city far too close, far too dangerous. The arsonist was no longer just a rumor.

"We should've gotten ahead of this," I muttered, my eyes narrowing as I looked up at the sky, where thick, swirling clouds hung ominously. Another storm was coming. Another fire, too.

"We still might," he replied, glancing at me quickly. His eyes flickered, but his face remained unreadable. I knew him well enough to recognize the subtle shift in his expression, the tightness around his jaw. He wasn't just talking about the fire; he was talking about something else.

Before I could respond, the distant crackle of a radio interrupted the uneasy silence. It was the kind of noise that made the hairs on the back of my neck stand up. A crackling voice followed, too garbled to understand, but enough to make my pulse quicken.

"Get to the south side," the dispatcher's voice barked, finally clearing through the static. "We've got reports of movement near the old mill."

I shot a glance at Callum. The old mill had been abandoned for years, a dilapidated structure that had once been the beating heart of this part of the city. Now, it was nothing but a skeleton, its walls crumbling under the weight of time and neglect. But lately, it had become the perfect hiding place for anyone with bad intentions.

"We're close," I said, already reaching for the radio.

Callum nodded, and we both adjusted our grips on our gear. The air felt thicker now, as though the city itself was preparing for something.

The streets grew quieter as we made our way toward the south side. The occasional crack of broken glass or the shuffle of footsteps echoed between the buildings, but nothing that screamed danger—not yet. Still, there was something unsettling in the quiet. A kind of waiting, like the calm before the storm.

We reached the mill in silence, the imposing silhouette of the building casting long shadows across the alleyway. A cool breeze whispered past, but it wasn't enough to clear the thick atmosphere that hung in the air.

"Keep your eyes peeled," Callum said, his voice a notch lower, his eyes scanning the building ahead of us. I could feel his focus shift, sharpening, but there was something else there—something more than the usual vigilance. It was like he was on edge, as though he knew something I didn't. Something he wasn't telling me.

My heart skipped a beat. "You alright?"

His gaze flickered toward me, a flicker of something—guilt, maybe?—before he shook his head and stepped forward, signaling for me to follow.

We circled the building, keeping to the shadows, the wind carrying with it the scent of charred remains. But there was nothing there. Not at first.

The sound of movement came from the back of the mill, faint at first, and then louder, more distinct. Someone was there.

Callum motioned for me to stay back, and I barely resisted the urge to argue. He was in charge for a reason, but something about the way he held himself tonight made my instincts flare. This wasn't just a routine patrol. Something was different.

The figure emerged from the shadows, moving swiftly, almost too quickly. I froze.

It wasn't a firebug. No, this person was different—masked, their body language familiar. The moment they stepped into the light, I saw it, the warning written in their posture. I had to swallow the lump that formed in my throat when I noticed the gleam of recognition in Callum's eyes.

"Stop what you're doing," the figure said, their voice muffled by the mask, but there was a sharpness in it, an edge. "Or things are going to get worse."

For the first time in months, I saw Callum falter. A brief, fleeting expression passed across his face before he masked it, but it was enough to make my pulse race. He knew this person. And I didn't.

The air thickened, not with smoke, but with the weight of the unknown.

The masked figure stood in front of us, their stance rigid, each movement calculated, deliberate. The kind of precision that made me pause, make sure every muscle in my body was alert. I swallowed hard, trying to shake off the suffocating feeling that clung to me now that we were face to face with someone who had clearly expected us, prepared for us. It wasn't just the warning that made my heart race—it was Callum's reaction. I had seen that flicker in his eyes, the way they narrowed for just a split second, a brief recognition before he buried it beneath his usual cool exterior. It was the kind of thing you couldn't fake.

The figure tilted their head slightly, like they were studying us, watching our every move. The mask they wore was black, slick, almost theatrical, with only small slits for eyes. I could see the faint glimmer of moonlight reflecting off the edges of it, but nothing about the way they stood suggested they were going anywhere soon.

"Stop what you're doing," the figure repeated, their voice just enough to send a chill down my spine. "Or this ends badly for you."

I glanced at Callum. I didn't have to say anything. I could feel the tension radiating off him, almost palpable, like an electric current in the air between us. His jaw was set, his expression unreadable, but there was something in the way his shoulders had tensed that made me wonder how far he was willing to go to protect whatever secret was tucked away in the deepest parts of him.

"You're going to have to be more specific," I finally said, stepping forward slightly. My voice didn't waver, but I could feel my heart pounding in my chest, adrenaline shooting through me like a drug. I'd had my share of confrontations, but this—this was different. There was a layer to this situation that I wasn't seeing, something underneath the words, something hidden behind the mask. And I had no idea what it was.

The figure remained still, their hands hidden under the dark folds of their jacket. The silence between us stretched, thick and uncomfortable, and I was almost certain I could hear Callum's heart beating faster, though his expression hadn't changed. He was good at this—staying calm, staying detached—but I could tell he was teetering on the edge, like a rubber band stretched too tight.

"What is it you're after?" Callum finally spoke, his voice low but firm. It wasn't a question—it was a demand. And even though he hadn't raised his voice, it felt like a challenge.

The figure seemed to consider this for a moment, their masked face betraying nothing. "The investigation," they said, dragging out the words with deliberate slowness. "It's bigger than you realize. You should let it go."

I felt the shift in the air, the weight of the warning sinking in. There was no mistaking it now. This wasn't just about a couple of fires. This wasn't about a random arsonist. This was something personal, something deeper.

Callum's gaze flickered back to me, his eyes darting so briefly in my direction that I almost missed it. But I saw it. The tension, the worry—hell, even fear—flickered behind his eyes. I didn't know him to be afraid of much. But this? This had him rattled.

"I don't think we're going anywhere," I said, taking a step forward, my voice far steadier than I felt.

The figure's posture stiffened at my words, but they didn't move. Instead, they reached into their jacket, pulling out something small and sleek. For a moment, my mind raced through a thousand possibilities—weapon, device, another mask, something more dangerous—but what they pulled out made my stomach drop. A lighter. A flicker of flame caught the edge of the night, casting an eerie glow on the masked figure's face, making their eyes seem darker, colder.

Callum stiffened beside me, his fingers twitching as though he wanted to react, but something held him back. I could almost see the internal struggle, the clash between his professional instinct and something else—something personal. It was like he was holding his breath, waiting for a decision to be made. But what decision? And more importantly, whose decision was he waiting for?

I glanced back at the figure, the lighter now fully alight in their hand, the flame dancing precariously close to their fingers. It felt symbolic in a way, like a cruel reminder that we were playing with fire, both literally and figuratively.

"You think you can stop this?" the figure said, voice dripping with something like pity. "You think you can control what's coming?"

A cold shiver crept up my spine. I didn't like the sound of that. The way the words lingered in the air made my stomach twist, and I couldn't help but wonder if I'd just stepped into something much darker than I had anticipated.

"Who are you?" I asked, my voice more forceful now. There had been enough ambiguity, enough games. I needed answers.

The figure didn't answer immediately, letting the silence drag on, thick and suffocating. The flame from the lighter flickered again, casting long, wavering shadows on the pavement. Finally, they spoke, their voice so soft, so quiet, it was almost lost in the wind.

"You don't want to know," they said, as if the knowledge itself could burn us.

It was then that Callum shifted.

He wasn't fast, but his reaction was so measured, so precise, it made my heart lurch. His hand moved almost imperceptibly toward his belt, where his weapon was holstered. He wasn't reaching for it, not yet, but the gesture didn't escape me. It was like a silent promise—if it came to it, he would act.

And for the first time that night, I understood.

Callum was in this, all the way in. Whether he had a hand in it or just knew more than he was letting on, I couldn't say. But I knew then that I wasn't just walking into danger alone. I wasn't the only one who was tangled in this web.

I didn't know what was worse—the fact that Callum hadn't said a word, or the fact that I was certain he knew more than he was letting on. The masked figure had melted back into the shadows, leaving only the faint smell of smoke and a disquieting promise hanging in the air. I should have felt relieved that we were still standing, that the confrontation hadn't escalated into something worse. But the silence that settled between us, thick and suffocating, was more unnerving than anything that had happened so far.

Callum didn't look at me. He didn't have to. His every muscle was still tensed, as though he was bracing for something more than just the threat we'd just faced. I'd seen that posture before—when something was off, when he was trying to keep it together. But this time, I wasn't going to let it slide. Not again.

"We're not letting this go, are we?" I asked, trying to keep my voice steady, but it came out sharper than I intended.

He turned toward me then, his expression a careful mask of professionalism. "We don't have a choice," he said, his voice too calm, too controlled, as if he was afraid of letting anything slip. His eyes darted to the darkness behind me, then back at the street. "We need to get moving."

That was it. No explanation. No reassurance. And no apology for whatever had just passed between him and that figure.

"What was that about, Callum?" I asked, the words slipping out before I could stop them. "You knew that person, didn't you?"

He froze. Just for a second. The faintest flicker of surprise—or was it guilt?—crossed his face before he schooled it back into impassivity. I didn't care about the details. What mattered was that I knew him well enough to recognize the lie in his silence.

His jaw tightened. "It's complicated."

"Well, don't leave me hanging, then," I shot back, crossing my arms, despite the tension that hummed in the air. "You don't get to just leave that there."

He hesitated for a moment longer, and I could see the wheels turning in his head. He was trying to weigh his options, probably trying to figure out how much he could say without tipping his hand. It wasn't a good sign.

Finally, he exhaled, running a hand through his hair. "It's not what you think."

I couldn't help it. The sarcasm slipped out, almost involuntarily. "Right. Because there's always some hidden layer of the story, isn't there? That's what this job's all about, isn't it?"

His lips quirked for a brief moment—just enough to remind me that he still had a sense of humor buried deep under the armor he wore. But the look in his eyes, the wariness that had crept in, told me that whatever he wasn't saying was dangerous. It was personal.

"Look," Callum started again, his tone softer this time. "I'm not trying to keep things from you, okay? But there are things—things I'm not ready to explain."

I swallowed the frustration that rose up, clawing at my throat. "You think you're the only one who's dealing with this? You think I'm not out here risking my neck, too?"

His eyes flashed, but instead of the usual deflection, there was something else there—a flicker of regret, maybe. Or was it something else?

"I never said that," he muttered, the words almost lost in the wind that rustled through the alleyway. "But you need to know this—it's not just about fires anymore. There's more going on than you realize."

That stopped me dead in my tracks. I was about to demand an explanation, to press him for more details, but something in the urgency of his voice made me pause. Whatever was happening, it was bigger than both of us.

"More?" I asked, my voice barely above a whisper. "What do you mean by more?"

Before Callum could answer, the sound of footsteps echoed from behind us. Quick. Steady. Familiar. My heart skipped a beat, and I instinctively reached for the radio at my waist, but Callum grabbed my wrist before I could do anything.

"No," he said, his voice firm. "We can't let anyone else know we're here."

I turned to face him, my pulse quickening, a cold fear creeping into my bones. "What do you mean? We've already been seen. The whole damn neighborhood probably knows we're here by now."

He shook his head. "It's not that simple."

I could hear the footsteps drawing nearer, their rhythm slow, deliberate. I could feel the weight of every second as it dragged on. There was something different about the way the air felt now—thick with tension, charged with an energy I couldn't place. Every instinct I had screamed that we were about to be caught in something far worse than we'd expected.

"Callum, what the hell is going on?" I demanded, my grip tightening around the handle of my baton. "Tell me."

Before he could respond, a voice cut through the stillness. Low. Calm. But unmistakable.

"You're making a mistake."

I turned to find a figure standing at the far end of the alley, their silhouette barely visible against the streetlights. The voice was familiar, too familiar, and it made my stomach drop.

The figure stepped into the light, revealing a face I hadn't seen in years. A face I never thought I'd see again.

"Tyler?" I breathed, my voice cracking despite myself.

He didn't respond at first. Just stood there, his expression unreadable, his eyes locked on me like he was seeing something he hadn't expected.

"This is the part where you tell me why you're involved in all of this," I said, my heart thudding in my chest. My mind was spinning, trying to piece it all together, but it wasn't adding up. Not yet.

Tyler didn't move. He didn't have to. His presence was enough to make everything else fade into the background. His silence told me everything.

And in that silence, everything I thought I knew was suddenly in question.

Chapter 19: The Spark Between Us

The room was stifling, heavy with the weight of unspoken words and unacknowledged tension. I could feel the heat radiating off the hardwood floors beneath my bare feet, the air thick with the mingling scents of fresh-cut lavender and the woodsy musk of old books. It was a strange thing, how a single room could feel so alive with possibility. The light from the setting sun slanted through the windows, casting long shadows across the walls. I was alone for the first time in days, the house oddly quiet without Callum's footsteps echoing through it.

And yet, there was an unsettling presence that lingered in the corners of the room, like a storm cloud waiting to burst. Callum. I could feel him as if he were still here, just beyond the reach of my thoughts.

I'd spent too many nights imagining how this might play out between us. How the walls we'd built, brick by brick, would eventually crumble. Every glance we shared, every word that passed between us, only seemed to strengthen the invisible thread that tethered us together. But even in the thick of it, I knew better than to let my guard down. Too much had happened. Too many things remained unsaid.

The door creaked open behind me, and my breath caught in my throat. I didn't need to turn around to know who it was. The air shifted, the very temperature of the room changing as he stepped inside. His presence was like a spark, igniting the very air around us.

"Didn't think I'd find you here," his voice was low, rough, as though he'd been carrying something heavier than he let on.

I bit back a sigh, my fingers tightening around the glass in my hand, the cool liquid inside doing little to steady my nerves. "And where did you think I'd be?"

He didn't answer right away. I could hear the sound of his boots scraping softly against the floor as he approached. His presence was so overwhelming, so all-consuming, it was as if the walls were closing in around me. I'd gotten used to the distance between us, but now, with him here—so close, yet so far—it felt like the entire universe had compressed into this one room, and the weight of everything hung in the balance.

"You've been avoiding me," he said finally, his words like a challenge.

I couldn't help the half-laugh that escaped me, though it was more bitter than amused. "I wouldn't call it avoiding," I said, turning around to face him. "I just...needed some space."

He was standing too close, close enough that I could smell the faint trace of his cologne, mixed with the scent of rain that seemed to cling to his clothes. His eyes, dark and unreadable, locked onto mine with the same intensity they always did. A challenge, yes. But also something deeper. Something...unspoken.

"I thought you were done with me," he continued, his voice softer now, tinged with something like uncertainty.

"I am," I replied without thinking. But then I paused, my gaze falling to the floor before I met his again. "I was."

He took a step closer, and the heat between us doubled. "And now?"

The world seemed to hold its breath. In that moment, I wanted to scream. To push him away. But I couldn't. Not when every inch of me was drawn toward him, as if the very atoms of my body had been programmed to pull toward him. "Now..." I trailed off, not trusting myself to speak. I didn't know what was happening between us, only that I couldn't pretend it didn't exist anymore.

His hand moved, slow and deliberate, until it was resting on my wrist, just above the curve of my hand. His touch was warm, and it felt as though the contact alone could burn me. I flinched, not in fear, but in recognition of how much I had been avoiding this moment. How much I had been avoiding him.

"You don't have to keep running from this," he said, his voice softer than before, as if he were sharing a secret meant only for me.

I swallowed hard, my pulse quickening in my throat. "Maybe I do," I murmured, though the words felt hollow, like they didn't belong to me.

His other hand came up, brushing a strand of hair from my face with an ease that made me dizzy. "We can't keep pretending we're fine," he whispered.

I could feel his breath against my skin, warm and intoxicating. It was a dangerous thing, this proximity. It made everything else fade to the background—the anger, the mistrust, the things we couldn't say. All that remained was this raw, desperate pull between us.

And then it happened. I didn't see it coming, not until his lips were on mine, and the world tilted on its axis. His kiss was urgent, hungry, but there was something more there—something tender, like he was trying to communicate everything he hadn't been able to say in the years we'd known each other.

I felt it in every nerve, every inch of my skin, every breath that was shared between us. It was everything I'd been avoiding, everything I'd tried so hard not to feel. And yet, in that moment, it was impossible to deny.

His hand slid to the back of my neck, pulling me closer as though he couldn't get enough, as though he was trying to pull me into him, piece by piece. I responded without thinking, my fingers threading through his hair, tugging him closer. The kiss deepened, messy and desperate, and my mind went quiet for the first time in weeks.

For a moment, everything else ceased to exist. There were no secrets, no lies, no unfinished conversations. Only the press of his lips against mine, the heat of his body against mine, the undeniable feeling that this—this moment, this connection—was beyond anything either of us had bargained for.

But even as I lost myself in him, I knew. I knew there were shadows in his eyes, ghosts from the past that would always be there, lurking just beneath the surface. And no matter how much I wanted to give myself to him completely, part of me wondered if the foundation we were building this on would collapse the moment the truth came to light.

His kiss was like wildfire, igniting every part of me that had been buried under years of restraint, hidden fears, and unsaid words. I had been so careful, so determined to maintain control, but in the space between us, control became a distant memory. I let myself fall, deeper than I'd intended, as though my entire life had been leading up to this reckless moment.

He was an enigma, wrapped in silence and sharp edges, and I was, perhaps, the only one who could see it. Or at least, that was how it felt. But in that kiss, all the walls I had painstakingly built around myself crumbled. There was no room for reservations, no space for the doubts that had once kept me up at night. His hands were steady, strong, a silent promise that he wasn't going anywhere, even if he didn't say the words.

When we finally pulled away, breathless and desperate for air, I couldn't look at him. Not at first. My chest heaved, my heart pounding in my ears, and my fingers still tingled from where he had touched me. The silence between us was heavy, almost oppressive. He was standing too close, and I could feel the heat of his body radiating toward mine, but it was different now, in the aftermath of what we had just shared.

"What are we doing, Callum?" My voice was hoarse, and I hated that it wavered, betraying the part of me that still wanted to believe that this was just a fleeting moment. A mistake, perhaps. But I couldn't look away from him.

He didn't answer right away. Instead, his fingers brushed my cheek, as though memorizing the feel of me, as if this moment, this connection, might disappear at any second. "I don't know," he finally admitted, his voice rougher than I'd ever heard it. "But I can't walk away from it."

I blinked up at him, surprised by the raw honesty in his words. It wasn't what I expected—hell, it wasn't anything like what I thought I would hear. I had half-anticipated the typical guarded response, the half-hearted reassurance that he wasn't ready for this, or worse, the dreaded excuse that it was just a temporary lapse in judgment. But his confession caught me off guard. It was a slap of cold reality to a mind that had been running in circles, looking for any reason to make sense of this madness.

"I didn't ask for this," I said quietly, my voice trembling even though I had no intention of letting him see how deeply his words had rattled me.

He gave a single, almost bitter laugh, and his thumb traced the line of my jaw, sending an involuntary shiver down my spine. "No one ever does. But that doesn't mean it isn't real."

I swallowed hard, the words he spoke piercing through me in ways I wasn't prepared for. Real. The word echoed in my mind, settling there like a truth I hadn't been ready to face.

"I'm not looking for... whatever this is," I tried, but the words felt wrong as soon as they left my lips. I wasn't sure if I was trying to convince him or myself. "We can't just pretend this changes anything."

For a moment, there was a quiet understanding between us, as though he saw through the cracks in my defenses. "You're right," he said softly. "It changes nothing."

And yet, as those words hung in the air, I felt the undeniable shift, the weight of what had just happened between us, and I knew—deep down—that it was a lie. The tension, the connection, the intensity of everything that had come before it—it was all still here, like an unspoken promise lingering in the space between us.

He stepped back, breaking the spell that had bound us together, though I could feel his gaze on me, still watching, still waiting for something. I wasn't sure what exactly, but it felt like he was giving me space to breathe, to think, to make sense of the chaos that was swirling inside my chest.

I ran a hand through my hair, trying to steady my racing thoughts. "What now?" The question slipped out before I could stop it. What did we do now? Was there a way back from this? Or had we already crossed a line that couldn't be uncrossed?

He didn't answer right away, his gaze drifting to the floor as though contemplating his next words. "I don't know," he said, finally meeting my eyes again. "But I'm not letting this go. Not yet."

I stared at him, caught between disbelief and something else—something I couldn't quite name. The truth of the situation was slipping through my fingers, elusive and terrifying, and I was suddenly aware of how small the space between us felt now. How it was no longer filled with tension, but with something else. Something both thrilling and dangerous.

"I'm not sure I can trust you," I confessed, my voice barely a whisper, but it felt like the most honest thing I had said all night.

He nodded, his expression softening. "I know. I don't blame you for that." He paused, his gaze dark and unreadable, as though searching for the right words to explain himself. "But I'm not asking for your trust. Not yet."

It felt like the ground beneath me was shifting, the foundation of everything I thought I knew crumbling at an alarming rate. Callum, the man I had come to know in pieces, the man whose presence I couldn't seem to escape, was here, vulnerable in a way I had never expected him to be. It was both a relief and a curse. Because the truth was, I wasn't sure if I could afford to trust him, either. And yet, a part of me knew that the more I fought it, the more I found myself falling into whatever this was.

The silence stretched between us again, a strange comfort settling in the space we had created. I couldn't figure out if it was peace or the calm before the storm. But for now, it was enough. Just enough to keep me from turning away. Just enough to keep me from looking back.

The night stretched on in a haze of questions I didn't know how to ask. We sat there in the quiet, the soft flicker of candlelight casting warm pools of gold across the room, yet the air between us remained unnervingly cold. I had thought, at one point, that this kind of silence would be comforting, maybe even familiar. But now, it felt like a threat, a slow countdown to something neither of us was ready to face.

Callum was leaning back against the chair, his gaze fixed somewhere beyond me, distant and guarded. It was the same posture he took when he wanted to appear untouchable, unreachable. The coolness he wore like armor made my stomach churn with something I couldn't quite name—frustration? Fear? Or was it that inexplicable ache, the one that was becoming so familiar, the one that made me want to press forward, even when every instinct told me to pull back?

"So, what now?" I asked, breaking the silence that had begun to smother us.

Callum's eyes flicked toward me, sharp and assessing. His lips pressed together, his jaw tight. He seemed to be wrestling with something, and for a moment, I wondered if he was as lost as I was in this endless dance we'd somehow found ourselves in.

"What do you mean?" His voice was careful, like he wasn't sure how much truth he could afford to give.

I leaned forward, my hands clasped together on my lap. "I mean... what happens after this? After everything we just... did?" I gestured between us, at the space that still pulsed with energy, with something unresolved. "You can't pretend it didn't happen, Callum."

He ran a hand through his hair, a gesture so familiar it felt like an invitation to settle into whatever strange reality we were now occupying. "I'm not pretending it didn't happen. But I'm also not pretending it fixes anything."

I snorted, a sound that was equal parts disbelief and frustration. "You know, that's the most honest thing you've said in days. I was starting to think I was the only one pretending." I let the words hang between us, daring him to respond, daring him to break through the wall he kept building between us.

His expression hardened, but there was something vulnerable there too, a flicker behind his eyes that told me he wasn't as immune to this as he wanted to appear. "I never asked for any of this," he said quietly, as if the confession were more for him than for me. "But I'm not sure how to stop it, either."

I felt a knot tighten in my stomach at his words, at the weight they carried. Part of me wanted to tell him to walk away, to cut the ties before they grew even more tangled. But the other part—the part that had been buried under years of caution and restraint—wanted to do the opposite. I wanted to move closer, to reach for him and pull him into whatever this was between us.

"You're not the only one," I said, my voice softer now, the sharpness fading in favor of something deeper, something more raw. "I didn't ask for this either. But I'm not sure I want to walk away, either."

He was looking at me again, really looking at me, as though he were seeing me for the first time. The air between us seemed to shift again, crackling with the weight of that unspoken understanding. I was afraid of what that meant. Afraid of what it would lead to.

"You think this is just about what happened tonight?" His voice was rough, his eyes searching mine. "It's not. It's about everything. All of it. The years, the lies, the things we've both kept hidden. You can't just wipe that away."

I leaned back in my chair, letting his words sink in. "I know that." My voice was small, almost apologetic. "But how do we fix it? How do we move forward with all of this... baggage?"

He didn't answer right away, his gaze dropping to the floor, like he was thinking, calculating the risks of everything he was about to say. "We don't," he finally muttered. "Not until the truth comes out."

The weight of those words landed with a thud between us, heavy and final. The truth. The thing we had both been dancing around, pretending it wasn't there. My heart skipped a beat at the thought of it—what truth? What had he been keeping from me?

The silence stretched on, unbearable now, as though the room itself was holding its breath. I wanted to press him, to demand answers, to make him tell me exactly what he was hiding. But the more I thought about it, the more I realized that it wasn't just his truth I was afraid of. It was mine, too.

"So, we just keep pretending until the truth comes out?" I asked, my voice barely above a whisper.

He met my eyes then, and for the briefest of moments, I saw something raw there—vulnerability, regret, maybe even fear. "Maybe it's better this way," he said, though the words didn't sound like something he believed. "Maybe we wait until we're ready."

But we both knew it wasn't just a matter of being "ready." We'd never be ready. The truth would come crashing down on us like a storm, and when it did, I wasn't sure if there would be anything left of us to pick up afterward.

I could feel my pulse quicken as my mind raced. I needed to know what he was hiding. I needed to understand why this was so complicated, so tangled in shadows.

"I don't think we have that luxury," I finally said, my voice steady despite the chaos in my head. "We can't keep pretending, Callum. Not when everything feels like it's falling apart."

He pushed himself to his feet abruptly, his hands balling into fists at his sides. "I'm not pretending," he said, his tone sharp, his jaw clenched. "You don't understand—"

Before he could finish, the door slammed open, cutting him off. Both of us froze, the silence shattered.

I looked toward the doorway, my breath catching in my throat as a figure stood silhouetted in the frame, blocking the light from the hallway. My heart raced as I realized who it was, and a cold shiver ran down my spine.

This wasn't just a moment between Callum and me anymore.

Chapter 20: Ashes to Ashes

The air was colder than usual that morning, but it wasn't the temperature that made my skin prickle with unease. It was something subtler, something that had nothing to do with the crispness in the breeze or the thin layer of frost on the windows. It was him, or rather, the absence of him. Callum was there—of course he was—but it was like the spaces between us had grown wider, more difficult to bridge. I could feel it in the way he didn't meet my eyes, the way his voice had become flat, almost mechanical. It wasn't like him. But then again, nothing felt the same anymore.

I poured myself a cup of coffee, watching the steam rise in delicate spirals, and tried to ignore the ache gnawing at my insides. I should have been used to the silence by now. It wasn't the first time things had shifted between us, but this time it felt different. More final. More deliberate. The problem was, I had no idea why.

The apartment was too quiet, too still, and I couldn't decide if it was a blessing or a curse. Callum had disappeared into the living room, probably to bury himself in work or distractions or whatever it was he did when he wanted to avoid me. I didn't know anymore. I tried not to listen to the ticking of the clock on the wall, but it was impossible to ignore. Time was moving, and I was stuck—stuck in this haze of uncertainty and unresolved tension.

I slid onto the couch and flipped open my case file, but my mind wouldn't cooperate. I could feel his presence in the next room, and it was like the weight of it pressed down on my chest. I needed to focus. I needed to finish this case. But no matter how many times I read the same paragraphs, no matter how many notes I scribbled in the margins, everything kept circling back to him. To us. To the thing I was too afraid to face.

I pressed my fingers to my temples, trying to push away the thoughts that had settled there, as stubborn and unwelcome as cobwebs. The case was simple, at least on the surface. A missing person, a few leads, a lot of dead ends. But every time I followed a thread, I kept hearing echoes of our last conversation—his words, laced with bitterness and frustration. He was shutting down. And I didn't know how to reach him.

A knock at the door jerked me from my spiraling thoughts, and I opened it to find our neighbor standing on the other side. "Hey, I'm not interrupting anything, am I?" she asked, her voice light, but there was an edge to it. I'd never been good at reading people, but even I could tell she was more curious than concerned.

"No, of course not," I said quickly, stepping aside to let her in. "What's up?"

"I've been meaning to ask—have you seen Callum around lately?" She glanced behind me into the apartment, her eyes scanning for any sign of him.

I froze. My stomach twisted with something cold and unfamiliar. "Uh, yeah. He's here. Just in the other room."

She raised an eyebrow. "He hasn't been around much lately. We were supposed to grab dinner last week, but he cancelled at the last minute. He's been... acting a little off."

I swallowed hard, trying to hide the way my heart had started to race. I'd known it. I'd known something was wrong. "He's fine," I said, forcing the words out through a tight throat. "Just busy with work."

The neighbor didn't look convinced, but she didn't press. "Okay. Well, I just wanted to check. If you see him, tell him I'm still waiting on that dinner invite. He's always so mysterious, you know?"

I nodded, smiling tightly. "Will do."

She left with a friendly wave, but I could feel the weight of her words hanging in the air. Mysterious. That was one way to put it. Another way was closed off, unreachable, a man who no longer seemed to care. I closed the door, leaning against it as a shudder passed through me.

It was then that I realized the truth I'd been avoiding. He was pulling away. Slowly, methodically, until I wouldn't even know how to reach him anymore. And I had no idea why. No idea how to fix it.

I went back to the couch, but the case file no longer held my attention. Instead, I found myself staring at the empty space where Callum had been the night before. The night we'd shared something that felt real. Something that made me believe, just for a moment, that maybe this wasn't just some fleeting connection between two broken people. But that was yesterday. Today, there was nothing but distance.

I ran my fingers through my hair, frustrated, desperate for answers I didn't have. Should I confront him? Should I ask him what was going on? The words felt like they'd stick in my throat, too sharp and too raw to say aloud. But I couldn't keep pretending I didn't feel the strain between us. Every minute spent in silence was another minute that drove us further apart. And I wasn't sure how much longer I could stand it.

The problem was, I couldn't tell if I was afraid of losing him or afraid of what would happen if I actually got the truth. What if the truth was that he didn't want this? What if I was just another complication in his already messy life, someone he was only pretending to care about because it was easier than facing whatever had really been eating away at him?

I ran my hands over my face, exhausted by the weight of it all. My phone buzzed on the coffee table, and I reached for it with a sigh, hoping for something that could distract me from the chaos of my thoughts. But it wasn't a case update. It wasn't a message from a friend. It was a text from Callum. Simple. Brief.

"We need to talk."

And just like that, my world tilted again.

The text buzzed again in my hand, an insistent reminder of everything I was trying to avoid. We need to talk. His words were a cold slap, more final than the stillness in the apartment. There was no question in them, no softness, just a blunt statement that left my heart suspended in the air like a broken kite. I stared at the screen, my finger hovering above the reply button, but I couldn't bring myself to type anything. What was there to say? What could I possibly say that wouldn't make things worse?

I tossed the phone aside, the sound of it clattering against the table breaking the heavy silence. My mind raced, spiraling with possibilities, none of them pleasant. I could feel my breath coming in shallow bursts, like I was holding it in, waiting for something—anything—that would give me the courage to face whatever came next. But there was nothing. No words, no action, just the hollow echo of my own uncertainty.

I looked at the door to the living room. He was still in there, the same man who had shared my space, my bed, the night before—only now, he seemed like a stranger. And for the first time in months, the idea of walking into that room made me hesitate. What was I supposed to say? "I'm here, don't shut me out"? Or was it better to stay silent, to pretend that I wasn't slowly unraveling inside?

The weight of it all pressed down on me, making it hard to breathe. I could feel the pulse of the city beyond the windows—traffic, people, life moving as if it had no idea that mine was coming apart at the seams. I wanted to lose myself in that noise, to escape from this oppressive atmosphere that seemed to have settled in the corners of every room. But I couldn't. I wasn't sure I knew how anymore.

I grabbed my coat from the back of the chair, the soft fabric a fleeting comfort as I pulled it on. Maybe a walk would clear my head. Maybe if I moved, I could push the weight of this feeling off my shoulders for just a little while. The city was still waking up, the streets slick from rain, the air fresh with the scent of wet pavement. It was a world I could lose myself in, where no one cared about the tangled mess I'd become.

I stepped outside, the chill biting at my skin as I walked down the block. My feet hit the pavement with an easy rhythm, each step a distraction from the thoughts clawing at my mind. I could feel my pulse steadied by the familiar beat of the world around me. For a moment, it was just me and the city, and everything felt like it might still be okay.

But then, the text buzzed again. A different message this time. Can we meet? It was him, and the desperation behind those words, even without an exclamation point, made my heart drop.

I stopped in my tracks, the weight of his request pulling me back into the gravity of my own confusion. Did he know I was avoiding him? Could he feel the space growing between us, the crack in our connection? I glanced up, momentarily disoriented by the tall buildings around me. The crowd moved past, unaware of the internal war unfolding in my chest. I should have known better than to think I could escape by walking away.

The reality was inescapable. Callum wasn't just pulling away. He was retreating, locking himself up behind some wall I couldn't scale, and I had no idea what had caused the shift. If I had only been brave enough to ask last night, to demand answers instead of letting things go unsaid. But the fear of the truth, of hearing something I couldn't take back, had paralyzed me.

I turned around and started heading back toward the apartment. Each step felt heavier than the last, as though I was walking against a current I couldn't fight. The world outside hadn't changed, but everything in my life felt unrecognizable.

When I got back, Callum was still in the living room, sitting in the same place, his back to me. He hadn't moved. I lingered in the hallway for a moment, just listening to the sound of his breathing, trying to gauge what kind of mood he was in, if he was ready for whatever conversation was inevitable. But he didn't give me anything. His stillness was deafening.

I stood there, rooted to the spot, until the silence grew too thick to bear. I finally walked into the room, my steps slow but deliberate. He didn't look up when I entered, his gaze fixed on the empty space in front of him. I swallowed, fighting the wave of nerves threatening to swallow me whole.

"I got your message," I said, my voice steady but betraying the anxiety twisting in my gut.

He didn't respond right away, and for a moment, I thought he hadn't heard me. But then, slowly, he shifted, his shoulders stiffening as if he were preparing for a fight. He turned to face me, but his eyes avoided mine, staring instead at some invisible spot on the floor.

"We need to talk," he repeated, but this time, it wasn't a request. It was a declaration.

My heart beat faster, my chest tight with the weight of what was to come. I wanted to argue, to demand some explanation for the way things had been between us, but instead, I nodded. I had no idea what he was about to say, but the truth had a way of sneaking up on you, whether you were ready or not.

"I'm listening," I said, my voice firmer than I felt.

Callum hesitated for a moment, then leaned forward, his elbows on his knees, his hands clenched into fists. "I don't think this is working."

The words hit me like a punch. I could feel my heart stutter, then stumble, and for a second, I didn't know what to say. I wasn't prepared for this. I hadn't been ready for the weight of his words to feel like a judgment, a verdict.

"I—I don't understand," I stammered, the crack in my voice betraying me.

He finally met my eyes, but there was no warmth there, only cold distance. "I can't do this anymore."

The words still hung between us like smoke, heavy and choking. I could feel my lungs filling with something thick—something that wasn't air. My gaze locked on Callum, but he was a thousand miles away. He might as well have been standing on the other side of the world. He could have said anything. He could have told me he was just scared, just trying to figure things out. But instead, he said what I feared most. I can't do this anymore.

I opened my mouth, but nothing came out. My throat was too tight, the words stuck behind the pressure building in my chest. I had a million things I wanted to say—arguments, explanations, pleas—but they all dissolved into silence, leaving me as empty as the room around us. I could hear his breath, shallow but steady, as if he were bracing for the storm he knew was coming.

I shook my head, my hands trembling at my sides. "What do you mean?" The question was weak, pathetic, like I was somehow hoping he'd take it back. Like this was just another one of his moods, and once we got through it, everything would be fine. But I knew, deep down, that wasn't the case.

Callum's eyes flickered to mine, but he quickly looked away again, focusing on some point just beyond my shoulder. It was the look of someone who had already made up their mind, who had long ago stopped listening to anything I had to say. And that realization hit harder than anything he could have said.

"I mean it," he said, his voice low, almost too quiet to hear. But I caught it—every word. "This—whatever this is—it's not working. It hasn't been for a while."

I swallowed, trying to keep the lump in my throat from choking me. He sounded so calm, so certain. And that certainty was like a slap. I wanted to scream, to beg him to look at me, to see me. But I didn't. Instead, I stood there, paralyzed, my mind racing for something to hold onto, some part of him I could cling to and make him see reason.

"You're just... shutting me out," I said, my voice cracking, though I tried to hold it steady. "I don't even know what I did."

Callum's face was a mask, emotion carefully hidden behind a wall of indifference. It wasn't like him. He had never been this way—remote, distant. I had always known him to be the kind of man who felt everything, who wore his heart on his sleeve even when he didn't want to. But now? Now, he looked like a stranger, and the words coming out of his mouth only pushed us further apart.

"You didn't do anything," he muttered, his hand rubbing the back of his neck in that familiar gesture I had once found endearing. But now, it only made me ache. "It's just... it's just that things change. People change. We change."

I stared at him, a bitter laugh bubbling up in my chest that I immediately regretted. "Is that it? You've just decided we've changed? That's all?"

Callum's jaw tightened, and he stood up, pacing the floor like a caged animal. "No, it's not that simple. You're not hearing me. I've been trying to make this work. Trying to make us work. But I'm not... I'm not the person you think I am."

I took a step toward him, my breath catching in my throat as the gap between us seemed to grow. I wasn't sure if it was the space between us physically or the distance that had already settled in my heart. "Then tell me what you are. Who you really are."

His eyes flashed with something that looked dangerously close to frustration, but there was no anger in his voice when he answered. Instead, there was a quiet resignation that cut deeper than any shout could. "I don't even know anymore. I'm not the man I was when we started this... whatever this was."

I took another step, closer now, desperate for something—anything that might bridge the chasm he was creating between us. "Callum... don't do this."

He stopped pacing and turned to face me, his eyes dark and unreadable. He looked like he was at war with himself, and I was the collateral damage.

"I'm sorry," he said, his voice soft but firm. "I wish I could give you more, but I can't. I'm not the right person for you."

His words hit me like a blow to the chest. I took a shaky breath, trying to process what he was saying, but nothing made sense. This wasn't the man I had trusted, the man I had come to rely on. And yet, somehow, here he was, telling me he couldn't be what I needed.

The silence stretched between us, long and suffocating, until I couldn't stand it anymore. "So that's it?" My voice was sharp now, each word like a dagger. "You're just going to walk away without a fight? Without even giving me a chance to—"

"I'm not walking away, not in the way you think," he interrupted, his voice rough. "But I can't keep doing this. Not when we're both just pretending everything's fine. I can't lie to you. Not anymore."

I stared at him, my mind reeling. Pretending? Was that all we had been doing? I thought about the nights we spent talking, laughing, sharing everything and nothing at all. And I thought about the spaces that had started to open between us, small at first but growing wider every day. Had I been blind to it? Had I been pretending too?

Callum's eyes softened, and for a fleeting moment, I thought he might reach for me. But then the moment passed, and the distance between us remained, unbridgeable.

"I never wanted to hurt you," he said, his voice barely above a whisper. "But I think I already have."

I shook my head, fighting the tears that burned the back of my eyes. I didn't want to cry. Not now. Not in front of him. But I could feel the weight of everything he'd just said crashing down on me, and the sting was unbearable.

"I don't even know what this is anymore," I muttered, more to myself than to him.

Callum's expression softened, just for a moment, as though he wanted to say something, but then his phone buzzed. He glanced at the screen, his jaw tightening again. Without looking up, he murmured, "I need to take this."

I stood frozen, my chest tight, the room closing in on me. But just as he turned away to answer the call, his words echoed in my mind, sharp and cold.

"I think we've both been pretending... for far too long."

And just like that, the doorbell rang.

Chapter 21: A Dangerous Obsession

The wind picked up as I stood on the balcony, watching the sky fade from soft violet to a bruised orange. The air was thick with the scent of impending rain, and I could feel it, like a weight pressing down on my chest. I'd gotten good at noticing the little things lately—the way Callum would glance over his shoulder as though someone were always watching him, the way he'd get lost in thought at the oddest moments, as though his mind had wandered to places I couldn't follow. I wasn't a fool, and I'd never been one to turn a blind eye. But what I was beginning to uncover about him... I wasn't sure I was ready for.

Callum was like an old house—beautiful on the outside, with every pane of glass spotless and every brick laid just so, but when you really looked, you could see the cracks. You could hear the creak of the foundation, the faint echo of something long buried. His eyes, which once held the warmth of a fire that could melt anyone's heart, now seemed distant, as if the flames had turned cold. I knew something was wrong. I just hadn't known how deep it went.

It had started with small things. A nervous habit, a slight twitch of his hand when he thought I wasn't looking, the way he would snap at me over nothing. Then, there were the nights. The nights when he'd disappear into the woods behind the house, without a word, without even a glance my way. I knew it wasn't just some restless desire for solitude—Callum wasn't that kind of man. No, there was something darker, something he wasn't telling me.

The first time I'd pressed him, his answer had been easy, dismissive. "I just need some air," he'd said, with a tight smile that didn't reach his eyes. But I knew better now. There was something else hidden behind that smile, something buried so deep I wasn't sure it would ever see the light of day.

It wasn't until I found the journal that the pieces began to align. I had no intention of snooping, no desire to invade his privacy. But when I saw it—tucked beneath a stack of old papers, half-hidden in the drawer of his office—it was like a magnet pulling me closer. The leather-bound cover was soft, worn from years of use, and the gold lettering on the spine had long since faded. But when I opened it, the words inside were as clear as a bell.

Each entry was more fragmented than the last, but the pattern was unmistakable. Descriptions of fire, of darkened skies and choking smoke. Of a life he hadn't shared with me, a past I wasn't even sure I wanted to understand. But the more I read, the more I knew: Callum had been tied to the fires in ways I couldn't yet comprehend. The truth was unraveling like an old sweater, each thread more dangerous than the last.

I had to confront him. There was no choice anymore. The weight of the secrets was too heavy, too much to bear.

It was late, the house quiet except for the hum of the refrigerator and the distant sounds of the storm beginning to roll in. I found him in the study, sitting at the desk, his back to me. His broad shoulders were hunched, tense, as though waiting for something. Or perhaps dreading it.

"Callum," I said softly, trying to keep my voice steady, trying to ignore the way my pulse had quickened. "We need to talk."

He didn't turn around. The only acknowledgment of my presence was the slight tightening of his jaw. His silence spoke louder than any words could have.

"I found it," I continued, my voice firm now, though my hands were trembling. "The journal. I know what's been happening. I know what you're hiding."

There was a long pause, and I could hear the rain starting to fall in sheets against the windows. The sound was deafening, like a drumbeat marking the minutes as they dragged on.

When he finally spoke, his voice was low, thick with something I couldn't quite place. "You don't know what you're asking, Emma. You don't know what you're getting yourself into."

I took a step closer, my heart thumping in my chest. "Then tell me. I deserve to know, Callum. I'm not some... stranger. Not anymore."

His hands clenched into fists on the desk, his knuckles turning white. He still didn't look at me. "You're right. You deserve to know. But it's not something I can explain in a few words. It's..." He trailed off, as though the rest of the sentence was too much to bear.

My breath caught in my throat. "What is it? What happened? What aren't you telling me?"

He finally turned, his eyes dark and heavy with something like regret, or perhaps guilt. "I've been a fool to think I could outrun it," he said, his voice barely above a whisper. "A fool to think you wouldn't find out. But it's too late now."

There was a chill in the air now, a sudden shift in the room that made my skin prickle. The tension between us was palpable, thick and suffocating. I could see it in the way his eyes darted around, like he was looking for an escape, like he was trying to find some way out of this conversation without having to face what lay beneath the surface.

"Callum..." I whispered, my voice cracking with the weight of my emotions. "I love you. Whatever it is, we can figure it out together."

For the first time since this all started, I saw a flicker of something vulnerable in his eyes. But it was quickly masked, replaced by that hardened resolve I'd come to know all too well.

"You shouldn't have come here, Emma. You shouldn't have pried into things that don't concern you."

And in that moment, I realized: this wasn't just about fire. It wasn't just about the past he was running from. It was about something much darker. Something that could burn everything to the ground, including us.

The silence stretched between us like a chasm, deep and cold. His words—so close, yet so unreachable—lingered in the air, buzzing like static on a radio. I was dizzy with it, this sense that something was slipping through my fingers, something I couldn't quite grasp, no matter how hard I tried.

"I shouldn't have pried," I said, my voice thinner than I intended, the words tasting bitter. The hurt was bubbling up now, thick and ugly, and I hated that I couldn't keep it from showing. "You don't have to tell me, Callum. But don't pretend I'm not already involved. Don't pretend this doesn't affect me."

For a moment, his face softened, just the tiniest bit, but it was fleeting. Gone in the blink of an eye, as though he couldn't afford to let anything real slip through the cracks, as if real emotions were the very thing threatening to unravel him. I wanted to reach for him, wanted to shake him out of this haze he'd wrapped himself in, but there was a wall between us now—an invisible wall that neither of us knew how to dismantle.

"I never meant for you to get tangled up in this," he muttered, the words so quiet I almost didn't catch them. He stared at the desk, his fingers moving over the edges of the wood as though trying to ground himself. "I thought... I thought I could keep it separate. Keep you safe."

The idea of safety seemed laughable now, considering the storm outside—both literal and metaphorical. The world was swirling with rain, each drop crashing against the windows as if nature itself had decided to share its fury. The power of it, the chaos of it, mirrored the chaos inside me. I felt as though the wind was pressing in on us, carrying with it the scent of ash and smoke, the kind that burned the back of your throat and coated your lungs.

"You can't keep me safe from something you won't even acknowledge," I said, the sharpness of my own words surprising me. I hadn't intended to sound so cruel, but it was the truth. And sometimes, the truth stung.

Callum's hands dropped to his lap, his fingers clenched tight enough that his knuckles went white. He was trembling, just slightly, but I noticed. He was never like this—never so fragile, so... broken. It felt like there was a piece of him being chipped away, bit by bit, and he didn't know how to stop it.

"You don't understand," he muttered, his voice thick with emotion. "I can't just tell you. I can't. It's—there's no way to explain it, no easy way to make you understand why I did what I did. The fire... it's not just a thing. It's... it's a part of me, Emma."

The words hit me like a slap. My heart was pounding, the heat of it rushing to my face. "What do you mean, it's a part of you?"

For the first time in what felt like days, his eyes met mine fully—no more avoiding, no more turning away. His gaze was raw, a mixture of pain and guilt that made my stomach twist. And then, he spoke.

"I started the fire," he said quietly, the weight of those words hanging between us like smoke. "I was the one who—"

"No," I interrupted, the word bursting from me before I could stop it. "No. That's not possible. Callum, you're not... You're not the kind of person who—"

"I was, Emma," he said, his voice almost lost in the crackle of the storm. "I was exactly that person. I still am. I thought I could outrun it. I thought I could be something else, but it's always there. The fire—" He stopped, his breath shaky, as though the very memory was choking him. "The fire followed me."

It took everything I had not to reach for him, not to close the distance between us, but I stayed where I was, rooted to the spot. There was a sick feeling in my stomach now, a strange mixture of disbelief and dread, but underneath it, a deeper ache for him. For the man I thought I knew, the one who had seemed so sure of himself, so unshakable.

"You didn't—" I started, but he cut me off.

"I did," he said, his voice harder now, the sorrow in it replaced by something more dangerous—more desperate. "You have to understand, Emma. I didn't want it to happen, but it did. I didn't choose it. But in the end, I let it happen. I let the fire consume everything it touched. People. Homes. And I couldn't stop it. I couldn't stop myself."

His words were a confession, each one heavier than the last, and I could feel them sinking into me like stones, one after another, dragging me down into the murky depths of what was now our reality.

"Why?" I whispered, because I needed to know. I needed to understand why he hadn't told me before. Why he had chosen to hide this from me, from everyone. "Why didn't you tell me?"

He looked at me then, his face crumpled with shame, and for a long moment, I thought he wouldn't answer. But then, in a voice so quiet it felt like it came from somewhere deep within him, he spoke again.

"Because I didn't want to ruin you. I didn't want to bring you into this mess, into this darkness. I thought if I kept you away, if I kept you safe, you wouldn't see what I really am. What I've done."

The words stung, but I couldn't let them. I couldn't let myself fall into that pit of self-pity that seemed to beckon, because I knew this wasn't about me. This was about him, and whatever it was that haunted him.

But I couldn't walk away. Not now, not when the pieces were finally beginning to fit together.

"Callum..." I began, but he shook his head, as though he couldn't bear to hear the words he knew were coming.

"Don't, Emma. Please. You don't want to know the rest."

His eyes were dark now, shadowed with things I couldn't untangle. The storm raged outside, but it felt like there was another storm inside the room—one far more dangerous. Callum stood rigid, like a statue carved from stone, his gaze pinned to the floor. For a moment, I thought I could hear the crackling of fire in the silence between us, the way it burned everything in its path, leaving only ash and ruin behind.

"Don't say that, Callum," I said, my voice trembling, barely above a whisper. "I need to know. I need you to tell me."

He shook his head, his hands tightly gripping the edge of the desk, his knuckles turning white. The anger that had flared in him moments ago was gone now, replaced by something else—something quieter, deeper, almost like a final surrender.

"You don't understand," he said again, his voice barely audible, but filled with such anguish that it seemed to cut through the room. "I can't let you in. Not anymore. Not after everything."

I wanted to scream at him, wanted to shake him and demand he tell me what was happening, what had happened to him. But I knew he wasn't capable of it—not the way I needed him to be. There was something locked inside of him, a part of him that refused to break free, that resisted whatever bond had formed between us.

"Why didn't you ever tell me about the fire?" I asked, my voice wavering despite my best efforts to hold it steady. "Why keep it all hidden?"

A long pause followed, and for a moment, I thought he wouldn't answer. His eyes were haunted, like he was fighting with something inside of him, trying to keep it at bay. He finally exhaled, the sound rough and painful, and the weight of his words settled over me like a shroud.

"Because it's not just the fire, Emma," he said, his voice low, almost breaking. "It's what came after it. The people I left behind. The lives I destroyed. The choices I made."

I felt my breath catch in my throat, the pieces clicking into place in a way I hadn't fully expected. This wasn't just about some tragic accident; this was something deliberate. Something that had been years in the making.

"You're telling me you... you caused it?" The words felt foreign, wrong, coming out of my mouth. How could this man—the man I had come to trust, the man I thought I knew—be capable of such a thing?

His head dropped, his shoulders slumped as though the weight of his own guilt was too much to bear. The silence stretched again, and I could feel the air between us growing thicker, heavier.

"I didn't want to," he said, the words breaking like fragile glass. "But I had no choice. I thought I could stop it. I thought I could control it. But the fire—it doesn't just destroy, Emma. It leaves things behind. It makes you do things you never thought you could. It makes you... it makes you a different person."

I stepped closer, but the gap between us felt wider now, as though the truth had created an insurmountable divide. My heart ached for him, for the man who had been consumed by something so dark, so relentless. But at the same time, the hurt, the betrayal—I couldn't ignore that either.

"Callum," I whispered, reaching out, my fingers brushing his arm. "What happened after? What did you do?"

His body tensed at my touch, like he couldn't bear the closeness, but he didn't pull away. His gaze was distant, his face unreadable.

"It's not just about what I did," he said slowly, like he was weighing each word. "It's about what I couldn't stop. The fire... it didn't just take the things I loved. It took me too. And now... now I'm not sure who I am anymore."

The words hung between us, unresolved and fragile, like they could shatter at any moment. I wanted to push further, to ask him more, to demand the full truth. But I could see it—the fear in his eyes, the weight of a past that was far too heavy for either of us to carry. It was clear now: Callum was holding on by a thread, and whatever had happened in the past, whatever he had done, was not something he was willing to share—not yet.

"Callum," I started again, but he interrupted me, his voice suddenly firm, as though bracing for something terrible.

"You need to leave, Emma," he said, the words cutting through the air like a blade. "It's not safe here. Not for you."

I recoiled, my chest tightening with confusion and hurt. "What do you mean, it's not safe? Callum, I—"

"You don't understand. You don't know who's still out there, who's still hunting me." His voice cracked as he said it, and I could see the vulnerability that was barely hidden behind his tough exterior. But it didn't make the words any less terrifying. "I never wanted you involved in this. But now that you know—now that you're so close—I can't protect you anymore."

The storm outside had picked up again, the wind howling and the rain hammering against the windows. Inside, the room felt like it was closing in on us, the weight of his words pressing on my chest, making it harder to breathe.

"You're not making any sense," I said, my voice shaking despite my best effort to stay calm. "Who's hunting you? What's going on, Callum?"

He took a step back, his eyes wide, and for the first time, I saw genuine fear in them—raw, unfiltered terror.

"I don't have time to explain," he said, his voice low and desperate. "But you need to leave. Now."

I shook my head, the panic rising inside of me, but before I could argue, I heard a noise—a faint sound, like a footstep just outside the door. My heart stuttered in my chest as I looked at Callum. His face had gone pale, his jaw tight.

"Get out of here, Emma," he whispered urgently, his voice almost a plea.

The door creaked again, and this time, I didn't wait. I turned to leave, but the moment I stepped away, I saw it. A shadow moving outside the glass, its outline barely visible in the storm. And in that instant, I knew: whatever Callum had been hiding, whatever secrets he'd kept, they were about to find their way inside.

Chapter 22: Into the Inferno

The smoke was a thick, suffocating blanket, the kind that presses down on your chest and fills your lungs with the taste of ash. I could barely see through the haze, but I didn't need to. I could feel Callum's presence, sharp and undeniable, cutting through the chaos around us. His hands were steady on the steering wheel, his jaw set tight as we sped down the rain-slicked streets, the flashing red lights of the fire trucks reflecting in the puddles. He wasn't speaking, and I wasn't sure if it was because words failed him or if he simply didn't want to acknowledge me.

Either way, the silence felt unbearable.

When he slammed the car into park and leaped out, I followed, instinctively trailing behind him. The heat from the flames reached us long before we got close enough to see them licking the sides of the building, their hungry dance devouring the old bricks, the timeworn windows, the memories held within the stone. It was a landmark. A place that held a story of its own—one that Callum had told me about, more than once, in those quiet moments when the world outside was still. I didn't know what it meant to him. I wasn't sure I wanted to know, but I couldn't ignore the way his body tensed when he spotted the first responders trying to contain the blaze.

I was about to ask him what he was thinking, but the question died in my throat. He was already moving, shoving past firemen, his eyes wild, as though he could will the flames into submission just by sheer force of will. There was a desperation in his every step, a frantic energy that unsettled me more than the heat from the fire.

"Callum!" I called after him, my voice barely audible over the crackling of burning wood and the screeching of alarms.

He didn't look back.

I wasn't sure if I should be following him. A thousand thoughts raced through my mind, each one louder than the last, none of them more comforting than the next. I had known Callum to be intense, sure, focused in a way that bordered on obsessive when it came to things he cared about, but this—this was something else entirely.

As we neared the building, I could see it clearly now: the familiar structure, the weathered facade that had once stood tall and proud now reduced to nothing more than a burning skeleton. A ghost of the past, disappearing before our eyes.

I caught up to Callum just as he reached the yellow tape cordoning off the area. The firemen were shouting at him to stop, their voices swallowed by the flames. But Callum wasn't listening. He was moving with the kind of determination I had only seen in people driven by a singular, unshakable purpose. It wasn't until one of the officers grabbed his arm that I saw it—the unfiltered rage in his eyes.

"Let me go," Callum's voice was low, almost calm, but there was an edge to it that made the officer take a step back, hand still clutching his arm. I could see the muscles in Callum's jaw twitch, his grip tightening on the firefighter's wrist until the man flinched.

I was about to intervene, to say something—anything—that might pull him back to reality when he broke free and moved toward the flames. My heart stopped, panic seizing me as I realized that whatever he was doing, wherever he was going, it was a path I wasn't sure I could follow.

"Callum, stop!"

My words had no effect. He was already too far into the smoke to hear me.

I hesitated for a moment, torn between staying where I was and rushing in after him. I could feel the heat from the fire gnawing at my skin, but the idea of letting him go alone was unbearable. Without another thought, I followed.

The flames roared, their heat unbearable as I neared the building. The air was thick with smoke, and I could barely make out Callum's silhouette ahead of me, still pushing through the chaos, moving with a sense of urgency that left me breathless. He was too close to the inferno. Too close to the thing that could consume him if he wasn't careful.

I reached out for his arm, yanking him back just as he reached the edge of the building. His eyes flicked to me, wild and unrecognizable for a moment, and then the fury in his gaze softened.

"What are you doing?" I gasped, my voice raw.

His chest rose and fell with the same frantic rhythm as his breath. "I have to get inside. I have to find him."

I stared at him, trying to make sense of the words that had just slipped from his lips. "Find who?"

He didn't answer. Instead, he just jerked away, moving deeper into the haze, his figure growing more blurred with each step.

I had to think fast, but the words I needed to say—those I had no idea how to form. Because in that moment, the truth hit me like a ton of bricks.

I wasn't just following him through the smoke. I was chasing a ghost, too, and neither of us were going to walk out of here unscathed.

The fire crackled and snarled as if it were alive, hungry for something far more than just wood and stone. The heat slammed against me like a physical force, making my skin feel tight, my breath shallow. But even amid the chaos, I couldn't tear my eyes away from Callum. He was a blur of motion, darting around firemen and police officers, his expression one I couldn't quite decipher. He wasn't scared, not the way someone with sense would be. He was... furious. Desperate. His movements were erratic, frantic, but there was a single-minded purpose in everything he did. He wasn't just trying to stop the fire; he was trying to outrun something.

I stayed close, just a few steps behind, trying to keep pace with him while also navigating the crushing heat and smoke. My lungs burned, but I couldn't make myself stop. He hadn't stopped, so neither could I.

"Callum!" I shouted, but my voice was swallowed by the wind whipping around us, by the roar of the flames and the crackling of burning timbers. His name felt lost in the chaos, almost as if the fire itself were devouring it.

He didn't hear me. Or if he did, he didn't care. I could see the way his hands flexed at his sides, his jaw clenched, his eyes locked onto the building with a fierceness that made my pulse race. I couldn't help but wonder if he saw something that no one else could. Or if there was something inside that he was willing to risk everything for.

We reached the base of the old building, its structure sagging beneath the weight of the flames, the timbers cracking like the bones of some ancient creature. My eyes stung, my throat thick with the bitter taste of smoke, but Callum moved forward, undeterred, as if he had made up his mind a long time ago that nothing—least of all a raging fire—would stop him from what he came here to do.

He turned to me, his eyes locking with mine for the briefest moment before he gestured toward the entrance. "Stay here," he ordered, his voice rough, urgent. "This isn't a place for you."

I shook my head, stubbornness flaring in my chest. "No. I'm not staying behind."

For a second, I thought he might argue, but he didn't. His lips pressed into a tight line, and then he turned back toward the wreckage, pulling a heavy fireman's coat from one of the nearest crew members and tossing it in my direction.

"Put that on," he said, not even looking at me. "You'll need it."

I caught the coat mid-air, but I didn't need it. I didn't care about the coat. I cared about the way Callum was moving, as if he was walking into a storm with no intention of turning back. There was no hesitation in his steps, no doubt in his actions. It was like he had already made peace with whatever he was going to find inside—or maybe, whatever he was running from.

"Callum!" I called again, this time more frantic, my heart skipping in my chest as I watched him slip past the barrier the firefighters had set up, his silhouette swallowed by the smoke. "Wait!"

But he didn't.

I ran after him, slipping past the same barricade, dodging the flashlights and fire hoses as the firemen yelled at me to stop. But my focus was on Callum. Only him. I needed to understand what was happening. I needed to know what was driving him, what was pulling him into the heart of the inferno.

The heat intensified as I drew closer, making the air shimmer in front of me, distorting everything. My body screamed for relief, for fresh air, for anything but the thick, burning atmosphere around me. But I kept going, my feet moving on their own, drawn by the pull of something I couldn't define.

I found him again at the edge of the building, standing in front of a crumbling doorway, his hands braced on the stone frame as he stared into the shadows beyond. He was motionless for a long time, the flickering light from the flames casting wild shadows on his face, making it hard to read his expression. But I could see the tension in his shoulders, the clench of his fists, the way his breath came faster, as if he were preparing for something.

"I told you to stay back," he muttered, not looking at me.

"I'm not going anywhere," I said, my voice sharp despite the fear clawing at my throat. "What are you looking for, Callum? What's inside there?"

He swallowed hard, and for the first time since I had met him, I saw a crack in the armor he always wore. A hesitation. A flicker of something raw and human.

"I'm not looking for anything," he said quietly. "I'm looking for someone."

His words hit me like a slap.

"Who?" I whispered, a chill creeping up my spine. But even as I asked, I knew the answer would be something I didn't want to hear.

He closed his eyes, his breath shaky. "My brother."

The confession hung in the air like the smoke, thick and suffocating. His brother? He'd never mentioned a brother. Not once.

I took a step closer, my heart thudding louder in my chest. "But your brother—"

"Don't," he cut me off, his voice hoarse. "Just don't. You don't understand."

I didn't understand. But suddenly, the frantic energy, the rage, the desperation in him—it all made sense. He wasn't just fighting a fire. He was fighting a ghost. And in that moment, I realized I had no idea who Callum really was, or what haunted him. But I couldn't turn away now. Whatever was inside that burning wreckage—whatever was pulling him into the flames—was now pulling me, too. And for better or worse, I was going to see it through.

The sound of the flames roaring was deafening, but it wasn't the heat or the chaos that kept me rooted to the spot. It was Callum, standing at the edge of the building, his face half-hidden in the shadows, his posture stiff with something that looked like both resolve and dread. The air was thick with smoke, and every breath

I took tasted like the remnants of burned memories. I was close enough to reach out, to pull him away from whatever he thought he needed to find in that burning ruin, but I didn't move. I couldn't.

His words hung in the air like the remnants of something lost, a ghost of a time I couldn't understand. "My brother," he'd said, his voice so quiet, so raw, that it pierced through everything else. The smoke, the fire, the sirens—all of it blurred into the background as I tried to piece together the fragments of his confession.

"I don't understand," I whispered, the words barely escaping my throat. I wanted to reach for him, to pull him into the safety of the chaos outside, but my legs felt like lead. Every step felt heavier than the last. "You've never mentioned him."

Callum didn't answer right away. His eyes, those familiar gray eyes that always seemed so certain, were clouded with something darker. Something I couldn't place. For a brief moment, I thought he might not say anything more, that he would shut me out the way he always did when the past crept too close to the surface. But then, as if the words had been choking him for years, he spoke.

"Because I never wanted to," he said, his voice thick. "Because I thought I could bury it. Thought I could bury him."

I didn't know how to respond to that. What do you say when someone admits to burying something—or someone—alive in their past? I opened my mouth, but nothing came out. The weight of the moment settled over me, thick and suffocating, like the smoke curling around us.

The fire seemed to grow louder, more urgent, as if it were a living thing demanding attention. And yet, all I could hear was Callum's quiet admission. His brother. A piece of his life I had never known existed. A piece he clearly wasn't ready to confront, let alone share.

"I have to find him," he muttered, the words coming out in a breathless rush. "I thought I could just walk away from it all, but I was wrong. He's still here. He's still inside."

"Callum," I started, reaching for him, but he flinched away, as if my touch would burn him more than the fire already was. "You can't go in there. It's too dangerous."

But he was already moving, stepping closer to the edge of the burning doorway. His hand hovered over the charred frame, as if he were about to reach inside, to pull something—someone—out of the wreckage.

"Stop," I said, my voice rising in panic. My heart was beating too fast, a drum of fear pounding in my chest. "Please."

He didn't respond, not with words. Instead, he pushed forward, his body a dark silhouette against the flames. I tried to move toward him, but the heat was too much. It pushed me back, forcing me to stop. My hands shook, and my thoughts scattered in every direction. Was I supposed to let him do this? Was I supposed to stand by and watch him disappear into the fire, chasing a ghost that might have never existed?

I wasn't sure what terrified me more—the idea that Callum was chasing something from his past, or the possibility that he might never come back. I knew this wasn't just about his brother. This was about something much deeper, something buried beneath the surface, hidden from everyone, even me. And no matter how much I wanted to drag him away from the flames, I knew I wasn't the one who could save him.

The fire was growing. The heat was unbearable, licking at my skin, making every breath feel like a struggle. But Callum—Callum was a man possessed. His eyes were locked on that doorway, his every move a statement of purpose. Whatever this was, it had nothing to do with me. It wasn't about us. It never had been.

I could hear him calling out now, his voice hoarse, his words lost to the crackling of the fire. "Nate!" he shouted. "Nate, where are you?"

My pulse raced as I took a step forward, my feet moving before I could think. I couldn't stay here. Not while he was in there, risking everything for a past I didn't understand.

But then the ground beneath my feet shifted. A crack, deep and violent, split the pavement, followed by a roar that made my heart stop. The building was groaning, as if it were about to collapse in on itself. I froze, staring at Callum, who hadn't heard it. He hadn't even turned around.

My breath caught as the first flames licked at the foundation of the building, a deep red-orange that spread like a fever. A part of me—maybe the part that was still holding on to the man I thought I knew—wanted to yell at him to come back, to leave this place and never look back. But the other part of me, the part that had been following him through this hell, knew that there was no turning back for him.

There was something in that fire, something that kept him going forward even as the rest of us scrambled to save ourselves.

"Callum!" I shouted again, my voice now desperate.

But before I could take another step, the sound of cracking wood echoed through the night. The building was collapsing. And Callum was still inside.

I didn't know whether to scream or run. I didn't know whether to hope or to fear that I had just watched the last of him disappear into the flames.

Then, just as quickly as it started, everything went silent.

Chapter 23: Burned Bridges

The city had a way of swallowing up its secrets. I was beginning to understand that—how it hummed beneath the surface like a restless tide, always threatening to rise and drown you if you didn't tread carefully. Walking through the narrow streets, each step felt heavier, the cobblestones beneath my boots a constant reminder of the choices I'd made and the ones yet to come. It wasn't the kind of place you came to escape; it was the kind that dragged you deeper into its web, until you were so tangled you didn't know which direction was up anymore.

I pulled my coat tighter around me, the brisk autumn air biting at my skin as I made my way to the diner on the corner. The neon sign flickered weakly overhead, buzzing like it was about to give up entirely. I should have been more cautious, but there was something magnetic about it, something about the way the place had been a constant fixture in Callum's life. Even now, after he'd shut me out, I still couldn't quite let go of that thread. I kept thinking that maybe I'd find some clue, some flicker of truth that would explain why everything had unraveled so suddenly. Why the man I'd come to trust with my heart was so desperate to push me away.

The bell above the door jingled as I stepped inside, the warmth of the place wrapping around me like an old, familiar blanket. The air smelled of greasy fries and burnt coffee, a scent that should have been comforting in its predictability, but it only made my stomach twist. The booth at the back was where Callum used to sit—at least, that's where I always imagined he'd be, waiting for me with a half-grin and a story that seemed to always make me laugh, no matter how bad the day had been. But there was no Callum now. Just an old man hunched over his coffee at the counter, his face hidden beneath the brim of his cap.

I was looking for someone else, though. Someone who could answer questions I couldn't bring myself to ask Callum.

"Charlie!" The voice was rough, like it had been sanded down by years of whiskey and regret. I turned to see an older man approach, his posture a little stooped but his eyes sharp, reflecting something familiar in their depths. This was Benny, a man whose name I'd heard a dozen times in stories Callum had shared—each one wrapped in the warm, easy laughter of an old friendship. Benny was a firefighter, retired now, but still holding onto the past as though it were the only thing left that made him feel useful.

"Sit down," he said, gesturing toward the booth, his hands trembling slightly as he slid into the seat across from me. His eyes flickered toward the door before settling back on me. "You got that look. The one that says you're here for more than just coffee."

I hesitated, unsure of how to begin. He wasn't the kind of man you could talk to about something light. And the question burning on the tip of my tongue wasn't going to be any easier.

"Callum... He's shut me out." The words came out harsher than I'd meant, a little too sharp, as if I were testing them on the air before I dared to believe them myself.

Benny raised an eyebrow, his gaze shifting from me to the window, his fingers tapping out a quiet rhythm against the chipped mug in front of him. He was silent for a long moment, which only made my heart beat faster. People who knew Callum, people who had been through the fire with him, they had a way of taking their time. There were layers in their silences, like walls being built brick by brick.

"You should've known it'd come to this," Benny said finally, his voice low. "Callum's the kind of man who pushes people away before they get too close. Always has been. Thought you'd seen it by now."

I swallowed, feeling the sting of his words in places I wasn't prepared to touch. "I thought I could be different," I said, half to myself, half to him. "I thought... he wanted to be different with me."

Benny's eyes softened just a fraction, but it was enough to make my chest ache. He leaned forward, lowering his voice so no one else in the diner could overhear. "There are things about Callum you don't know. Things he doesn't want you to know. And maybe that's the biggest lie he's been telling you—that you could get close enough to know the truth. He's got a past, Charlie, one that doesn't fit with the picture he's painted for you. It's a mess. And it's one he can't let anyone else clean up."

I felt a chill run through me, as if the walls of the diner had suddenly drawn in closer, squeezing the air out of my lungs. I wanted to press him, to ask what exactly he meant, but Benny was already shaking his head, his eyes distant, his mind clearly back in places I wasn't sure I wanted to follow.

"You'll hear it all in time," he muttered, his hand reaching for his coffee again, as if the conversation had already moved beyond me. "Callum will tell you when he's ready. But it won't be today, and it sure as hell won't be because of anything I say."

I watched him for a moment, my mind reeling. He wasn't offering me any answers, just fragments. And those fragments felt like a puzzle I wasn't sure I was prepared to solve. There were pieces of Callum I hadn't seen, parts of him that were kept carefully hidden behind the walls of the man I thought I knew. But Benny's words felt like a warning. A warning I couldn't ignore.

I finished my coffee in silence, the words hanging between us like a thick fog. The weight of everything—Callum, the investigation, this city—was pressing down on me, and for a moment, it was hard to breathe.

By the time I left Benny's, the weight of his words had settled on me like a storm cloud, its dark presence hovering over everything. It didn't help that the day had gone from gray to downright bleak, a relentless drizzle turning the streets into slick rivers. My boots splashed through puddles as I made my way to the car, the scent of damp asphalt rising like an omen. I didn't have a plan, not really. I didn't even know if I wanted to keep looking for Callum, to keep digging into the mess he'd made of our connection, or if I should just walk away.

But walking away was the one thing I couldn't do. The investigation, the one thing I'd promised myself I wouldn't let slip through my fingers, still lingered at the back of my mind like a long-forgotten melody that refused to fade. I thought about the files still scattered across my desk, the ones that held the answers I was searching for. In those papers, I could almost hear the truth calling to me, like a voice I couldn't ignore. Callum had locked himself away from me, but the case—well, it didn't care about my feelings. The case would keep moving forward, whether I liked it or not. And if I was being honest with myself, I wasn't sure I was ready to give up on it.

Sliding into the driver's seat, I turned the key, the engine rumbling to life in protest against the damp chill. I glanced at my phone, half-expecting to see a message from Callum, maybe some explanation, a crack in the wall he'd so carefully built. But there was nothing. Only a message from work, a reminder of the next meeting I had to attend. Great. Just what I needed. As I drove, the city blurred past me, the headlights of oncoming cars streaking across my windshield like forgotten dreams.

By the time I arrived at my apartment, it felt like the whole world had taken on a sharper edge. The lights in my building flickered as I entered, the smell of Chinese takeout lingering in the hallway. It was always the same—too many delivery drivers, too many people trying to escape the reality of their own lives. But as I reached my door, something stopped me.

It was a sound—soft, barely audible, but there. A rustling behind the door, like paper shuffling, the kind of noise you make when you're searching for something you've misplaced. A chill ran up my spine. I reached for the doorknob slowly, my fingers brushing against the cold metal. I didn't know why I hesitated, but I did. I had this nagging feeling that something wasn't right. With one swift motion, I opened the door, and my heart nearly stopped.

Sitting at my kitchen table, looking far too at ease for someone who didn't belong there, was Callum.

I froze in the doorway, staring at him, my pulse quickening. He hadn't even looked up when I entered, his gaze focused instead on a stack of papers in front of him. The sharp line of his jaw, the way he held himself, exuded an authority I couldn't ignore. But his presence—unexpected, unwelcome—sank into my chest like a stone. I wasn't sure if I wanted to smack him or kiss him.

"Callum?" The word came out before I could stop it, rough and accusatory. He didn't react at first, his fingers tracing the edge of a file as though he had all the time in the world. I took a step forward, waiting for him to acknowledge me, but when he didn't, my patience snapped.

"Why are you here?" I asked again, my voice sharper now. "You disappear without a word, shut me out like I don't matter, and now you're just going to waltz back in here like nothing happened?"

His gaze finally lifted, locking onto mine with an intensity that sent an involuntary shiver down my spine. "I wasn't sure you'd want me to explain," he said, his voice low, rough. "You didn't exactly leave the door open."

I scoffed, hands on my hips, watching him like he was a puzzle I wasn't sure I cared to solve anymore. "You think you get to decide when I'm ready for an explanation? You think I'm just going to sit back and take it while you play your little game?"

Callum's lips twisted into a rueful smile, one that didn't quite reach his eyes. "It's not a game, Charlie. It never was." He leaned back in his chair, the quiet tension between us palpable. "I never meant to hurt you. But some things... they aren't meant to be shared. Not with anyone."

I felt the weight of those words settle in my stomach like a stone, a heavy truth I wasn't sure I wanted to carry. "I'm not asking for your secrets, Callum. I'm asking for you to be real with me. I'm asking for you to stop treating me like I'm some kind of obstacle in your life that you need to shove aside every time things get difficult."

He looked away for a moment, his jaw clenching, and I could see the flicker of something inside him—guilt, frustration, maybe even regret. But before I could say anything else, he spoke again, his voice softer this time. "You don't know what this place does to people. What it does to me." He sighed, rubbing his hands over his face. "I came here because I... I needed to make sure you were safe. The investigation you're working on, it's bigger than you think. It's more dangerous than you can imagine."

I blinked, trying to process his words, but they didn't make sense. "What do you mean? What are you talking about?"

Callum's eyes hardened as he stood up, his body language tense. "There are things going on behind the scenes, Charlie. Things you're not ready to face. You think it's just a simple investigation, but it's not. It's a damn powder keg, and you're standing too close to the fuse."

I could feel the ground shifting beneath me, like I was suddenly standing on the edge of something dark and uncertain. My heart pounded, not with anger, but with a growing sense of fear—fear that everything I thought I knew about Callum, about this city, was a lie. And the worst part? I wasn't sure I was ready to hear the truth.

The quiet that filled my apartment after Callum's departure was like the calm before a storm—suffocating, heavy, and uncomfortably thick. I stood there, staring at the door where he'd just been, trying to piece together the fragments of our conversation. Each word he'd said, every evasive glance, felt like a puzzle I wasn't sure I wanted to solve anymore. Part of me was angry, a bitter resentment bubbling up from the pit of my stomach. How dare he walk in here after weeks of silence, spewing cryptic warnings and walking away like it was all on his terms?

But then there was that other part of me. The part that had always been drawn to him, even when I knew I shouldn't be. That part, the one that hadn't quite given up on the idea of Callum—of who I thought he was—was the one that made me pause. His warning. The way his eyes had hardened when he said it, as though there was something bigger at play here. Was I just another pawn in his world, or was there something more? Something dangerous?

I shook my head, trying to clear the thoughts from my mind. The investigation—the reason I had been in this mess in the first place—was still at the forefront of my thoughts. It didn't matter that Callum was hiding something, that he was pulling away. The truth was still out there, and I wasn't about to let him—or anyone—derail me.

My phone buzzed, pulling me from my spiral. I glanced at the screen, the name flashing in bold letters: Benny. I should have known he'd be the next one to check in. Callum wasn't the only one who had eyes and ears in this city.

"Charlie," Benny's voice was gruff, but there was something else there, something softer. "You're still at it, aren't you?"

"Still at what?" I asked, trying to mask the tension in my voice, but failing.

"The investigation. I know it's hard. But I gotta tell you, there are things you don't know. People you don't know." He paused, letting the weight of his words sink in. "You need to be careful, Charlie. It's not just about the case anymore."

His warning sat in the pit of my stomach like a stone, just like Callum's. I didn't like it, but I didn't have the luxury of ignoring it either. "What are you trying to say, Benny?" I asked, frustration creeping into my voice. "I'm already in it. I've got people on the inside. I'm not walking away."

There was a long silence on the other end, and I could hear the rustling of paper before Benny spoke again. "I know you're tough, kid. But this... this is beyond tough. It's dirty. And if you keep digging, you might not like what you find."

I gritted my teeth, the anger flaring again. "I've been this deep before, Benny. You don't get to tell me when to stop."

He sighed, a deep, resigned sound that made me pause. "I'm not telling you to stop. But I'm telling you to be careful. There's something you haven't seen yet. Something that's been right in front of you the whole time."

I wanted to scream, to throw my phone across the room, to tell him to stop being so cryptic. But I held myself back. "If you know something, Benny, then say it. Don't just feed me these vague warnings."

"I can't," he muttered, his voice tight. "But someone will. Soon enough." He hung up before I could respond, leaving me standing there, the weight of his words pressing down on me like a physical force.

I was done with people hiding things from me. But Benny's warning had struck a chord, the kind that left a bitter taste in my mouth. I didn't know who to trust anymore—Callum had made that clear. And now, Benny? Was I really that naive? Was everyone in this town playing a game I wasn't equipped to win?

The next day, I found myself back at the diner, alone this time. The usual buzz of conversation filled the air, but my mind was a million miles away. I needed something, anything, to prove that I wasn't completely off track. The man who'd been sitting in the corner the other day had left, and in his place was a young woman with dark, tired eyes who kept glancing nervously at the door, as though she was waiting for someone.

I didn't recognize her, but she didn't seem out of place either—just another soul trying to blend into the backdrop of a city that never let you forget you didn't belong. I was halfway through my coffee when she stood up abruptly, her chair scraping against the floor with a screech that caught my attention. She hurried toward the exit, her pace quickening as she reached the door.

Something about her—about the way she moved—pulled at my curiosity. Without thinking, I stood and followed her, my heart racing as I pushed through the door behind her. She was almost at the corner of the block when I caught up, my breath fogging in the cold air.

"Hey," I called out, my voice shaky from the sudden rush of adrenaline. "Are you okay?"

She froze, her back stiffening. Slowly, she turned to face me, her eyes wide, her face pale. She looked around, as though checking for an escape route, before taking a cautious step back. "I didn't—I wasn't—" Her voice trembled, and I saw her hands shake as she gripped the strap of her bag. "You shouldn't be here."

The words hung between us, thick with warning. I didn't know her, and she clearly didn't want me around. But something in the way she said it—the urgency, the fear—made the hairs on the back of my neck stand up.

I opened my mouth to ask more, but before I could speak, there was a sharp sound behind us. A low, menacing hum of an engine, the unmistakable roar of a motorcycle.

I didn't need to turn around to know that someone was coming. The air seemed to freeze, the streetlights casting long shadows as the bike drew closer.

The woman's face turned even paler, her eyes wide with terror. She started to back away, but there was nowhere for her to go. And I— I couldn't bring myself to move.

Chapter 24: The Arsonist Revealed

I could feel the weight of the silence pressing down on me, a dense, suffocating thing that curled around my chest like the smoke from the fires we'd been chasing for weeks. It was just the two of us now—me, perched on the edge of the couch, trying to swallow the sour taste of disbelief that seemed to stick to my tongue, and Callum, standing by the window, his profile half-lit by the weak glow of a lamp that had seen better days. The kind of light that could make a person's face look a thousand years older than it really was.

The room was still, but the air hummed with tension, crackling like a live wire. I kept replaying the words in my head, as if that might make them make sense. "It was him."

Callum's voice had been hoarse when he said it, like he wasn't quite sure whether to believe it himself. I couldn't blame him. I still didn't believe it. But the file on the table, the police report, the photographs of the fires—it all pointed to one person. A man from Callum's past. A name I'd never thought I'd hear in this context.

Daniel Hayes.

Even the sound of the name felt like an insult, a betrayal to my ears. I hadn't known much about Daniel Hayes beyond the vague mention of him as Callum's old business partner, a man who had once been a friend before the split. But the fact that he was the one behind the fires—intentional, calculated destruction aimed at Callum's empire—felt like a punch to the gut. And yet, there was something else gnawing at me, an uncomfortable feeling lodged deep in my stomach. I hadn't expected this.

Callum was pacing now, his boots tapping against the worn hardwood floor in an erratic rhythm. The fire from the night before still flickered in his eyes, but there was something darker, more haunted behind them. The kind of look I'd seen in soldiers who'd come home from war, faces battered by the things they had to leave behind. He had trusted Daniel. And that trust, it seemed, had burned just as fiercely as the buildings that had crumbled to ash.

"Are you sure?" My voice came out before I could stop it. "Are you absolutely sure it's him?"

Callum stopped pacing, his eyes fixing on me with a sharpness that made my heart flutter. "I'm sure. I've seen that pattern before. The method. The timing. It's him, Mia. I—I never thought he'd go this far." His hand ran through his hair, tugging at the strands like he wanted to rip something apart. "I thought I knew him. Hell, I thought I knew him better than anyone."

I swallowed hard, looking down at my hands, trying to steady my breath. Callum's betrayal was sharp, and it was personal. But as much as I wanted to be angry, I couldn't ignore the vulnerability in his voice. It was the sound of a man who had lost more than just a business partner—he had lost a part of himself.

"But why? Why would he do this?" I asked, leaning forward, the question tumbling from my lips before I could catch it. "What could he possibly have to gain from destroying your life?"

Callum's jaw clenched, and I could see the muscles in his neck tightening. He moved to the window again, but this time he didn't look out. Instead, his gaze turned inward, like he was sorting through a collection of memories, trying to piece them together into something that made sense.

"He was always the one who thought bigger," he muttered. "I was the steady one, the one who kept things grounded. Daniel always thought the world was just waiting to be conquered." His voice dropped lower. "And when I decided to walk away—when I chose to leave everything behind for a life that felt real—he couldn't handle it. He didn't understand. To him, I was giving up. And in his eyes, I became weak."

I could see the way the words stung him, even as he spoke them. Like a wound that had never fully healed, just waiting for something to tear it open again.

"And this... this is his way of showing me what happens when you walk away from something bigger than yourself," Callum continued, his voice thick with the weight of regret. "A man like Daniel... he doesn't forgive easily. He doesn't forget."

I felt the sting of something in my chest—was it sympathy? Pity? Anger? Maybe all three. But it was tangled up with the knowledge that, for all the animosity between Callum and Daniel, there was a history there. A history that was more complicated than simple betrayal.

"And you?" I asked softly. "What are you going to do now, Callum?"

He didn't answer right away. Instead, he stared out the window, eyes distant, his mind still caught in a thousand unspoken thoughts. His shoulders were tight, stiff with a kind of anger I hadn't seen in him before. This wasn't just about revenge—it was about a part of himself he'd lost, a part that had been taken from him by someone he had trusted implicitly.

"I don't know yet," he said finally, his voice barely above a whisper. "But I'll figure it out. I always do."

There was a finality in his words, a certainty that told me he was already plotting his next move. The thing about Callum, I'd learned, was that he didn't just react to the world—he controlled it. And whatever plan he had in mind, whatever course of action he was setting in motion, it was going to be as calculated and ruthless as everything else he did.

I leaned back into the couch, feeling the soft give of the fabric beneath me. There was nothing left to say. Not yet. Not until we had answers. But in the silence that hung between us, I couldn't help but feel the cold tendrils of unease winding their way through my chest. Whatever was coming, I knew it would change everything. And nothing, not even Callum's steely resolve, could stop that.

The sun had barely risen, casting a muted, golden hue over the city's skyline, but the heaviness in the air was unmistakable. The last remnants of the night's tension hung like a thick fog, too oppressive to shake off. I could still feel Callum's words, sharp and jagged, bouncing around in my mind. They clung to me in ways I didn't know how to shed, like the weight of a ghost that refused to leave.

I needed to do something, anything to pull myself out of the haze that had settled over me. But the only thing that kept circling in my thoughts was the look on Callum's face when he admitted it. When he said Daniel had been behind the fires. When he spoke of betrayal, of a partnership turned into something darker. That raw vulnerability, those cracks in the walls he'd spent years building around himself—those were the things I couldn't stop thinking about.

I found myself standing in front of the apartment door, my hand hovering over the doorknob, feeling more than a little absurd for not being able to open it. I was just going to go in. I had to. I knew I couldn't let the silence stretch any longer between us, no matter how thick and suffocating it had become. But still, I hesitated, because I knew that beyond this door, the truth would be waiting to greet me in full force.

I pushed the door open.

He was sitting at the kitchen counter, his hands wrapped around a mug of coffee, the steam rising in lazy spirals. Callum hadn't been much of a coffee drinker, but these past few days, it seemed like he couldn't get enough. His eyes were distant, like he was looking at something beyond the surface of the room, some far-off place where his thoughts were tangled and twisted. His jaw was tense, the stubble on his face sharper than it should have been for a man who'd just woken up.

I stood there, watching him for a moment, not sure how to approach the space between us. The air felt brittle, like a thread stretched too thin. "Are you planning to sit here all day?" I asked, my voice a little louder than I meant it to be.

He didn't react immediately. The mug stayed steady in his hands, but I saw a flicker in his eyes that told me he hadn't been as lost in thought as he'd appeared. Finally, he spoke, his voice flat, weary. "What's the point of anything else?"

I winced at the heaviness of his words, but I wasn't about to let him wallow in that silence any longer. "You're not going to find the answers sitting here," I said, stepping further into the kitchen, the click of my boots on the floor sharp in the quiet room. "If you want to do something about this, you have to get up. You have to—"

"Do what, Mia?" he snapped, his eyes cutting to me, dark and stormy. "What do you want me to do? Go after him? Find him and beg for forgiveness?" He let out a short laugh, but it was humorless, bitter. "I don't even know where to start."

I didn't know what to say to that. What could I say? There was no way to take back what had been done. No way to fix it. And if I was being honest, I wasn't even sure I wanted to tell him what I was thinking—what I was starting to suspect. The truth was gnawing at me, sharp and uncomfortable. Daniel Hayes wasn't just some distant figure from Callum's past. He was someone who had once been so close that it made me sick to think of the betrayal in those terms. But now, there was something else I had to acknowledge.

I had been wrong about Callum.

Not in the sense that he'd done anything to deserve this, not in the sense that he had brought this on himself. No, he was the victim here, no question about it. But the way he had treated me, the way he'd kept so many of his past emotions locked away behind that mask of controlled indifference—well, I'd never really seen the full picture until now. And that was the most unsettling part.

I wasn't sure whether to be angry with him or sad for him.

"I don't know what you want me to do," I said, keeping my voice calm, careful. "But we can't just sit here and do nothing. You can't keep going in circles like this."

Callum's eyes softened for the briefest of moments, and for a second, I thought he might agree with me. But instead, he took a slow breath, setting the mug down with deliberate slowness, as if trying to force himself to stay grounded. "And what do you suggest? We start knocking on doors? Start asking people if they know where Daniel's hiding?"

"I suggest you stop letting him win." The words were out before I could stop them. I hadn't meant to be harsh, but the truth was, I was tired of watching him spiral. He had been a rock for so long, and I was starting to see cracks in that foundation. But I knew that if I let him wallow, if I let him stay like this, we'd both be stuck in the same place forever.

For a moment, the air between us thickened. The tension felt like it could snap at any second, but then Callum's gaze flickered to me, something raw and vulnerable in his eyes that hadn't been there before.

"I'm not sure I know how to fight this," he admitted quietly, his voice barely a whisper. "I don't even know how to forgive him."

I couldn't help the sympathy that welled up inside me. It was easy to think of Callum as this unbreakable force—this man who had everything together, who made decisions with a steady hand and unwavering purpose. But standing there, his walls crumbling away, it became painfully clear that he wasn't invincible. And I wasn't sure what I could do to help him.

"You don't have to forgive him right now," I said, my voice softening. "You just need to decide what you want next. And I'm with you. Whatever you choose."

I wasn't sure I believed those words completely—wasn't sure if I was prepared to walk into the fire with him, to face whatever darkness Daniel might throw our way. But for the first time since I'd known Callum, I could see that we were on the same side. And that, at least, was something.

The sound of rain outside seemed to match the heavy silence inside, soft and unrelenting, like the rhythm of an unwelcome thought that refused to let go. I could hear it pattering against the windows, a steady beat that only seemed to amplify the tension between us. Callum hadn't moved for what felt like hours, and I wasn't sure if it was exhaustion or something else keeping him rooted in place. The quiet had taken on a thickness, a weight, as if the room itself was holding its breath, waiting for something—anything—to break the spell.

I should've left, given him the space I knew he needed, but I couldn't. Not yet. Not when there was still so much unsaid between us, so much left to uncover. The words hung in the air like smoke, invisible but impossible to ignore.

"Callum, talk to me," I said softly, leaning against the counter, my voice nearly drowned out by the rhythmic sound of the rain. "Please. I don't know what's going on inside your head, but you can't just keep shutting me out."

He didn't look at me. Instead, his gaze was fixed on the darkened streets outside, where the city lights blurred in the rain-soaked glass. His shoulders were hunched, his posture defeated in a way that made something sharp twist inside me. I knew better than to push him too hard, but there was a part of me that couldn't stand the quiet anymore.

"I don't know how to explain it," he finally muttered, his voice raw, jagged. "I don't know what you want from me."

I took a step forward, the floor creaking beneath my feet, as if the house itself was reluctant to disturb the fragile calm that had settled over us. "I don't want anything, Callum. I just want to understand." I paused, waiting for a response that didn't come. "This whole thing... It's eating at you. I can see it. And I'm not going anywhere until you let me in."

His head turned slowly, and for the first time in days, his eyes met mine—not with the usual guarded distance, but with something else. It was raw, unfiltered, like I was seeing him for the first time, not as the man who'd built an empire or the one who kept everyone at arm's length, but as someone who had been hurt, who had loved and lost and was now standing at the edge of it all, uncertain of where to go next.

"You want to know why I haven't told you everything?" His words were laced with bitterness, the edge of a wound he hadn't been willing to face. "I haven't because I'm ashamed. I should've known better. I should've seen it coming."

My heart ached at the vulnerability in his voice, a sound that was so unlike him it nearly knocked the breath out of me. I took another step closer, closing the distance between us, but still, I waited. I could tell there was more—he was holding something back, some deeper truth he wasn't ready to share.

"Daniel... He wasn't always like this," he continued, his voice dropping lower as if speaking too loudly might shatter the fragile truth. "We were partners. Partners in everything. We had dreams, Mia. We were going to take the world by storm, and I—" He stopped himself, running a hand through his hair, his face contorted in frustration. "I thought I could trust him. I thought we were brothers, in every sense of the word. But somewhere along the way, I lost sight of who he really was."

I could feel the weight of his words, the unspoken regret in the way he looked at me. I wanted to reach out, to comfort him, but I knew better. Callum wasn't the kind of man who liked to be coddled, especially not when it came to something as personal as this. Still, the thought of his past, the man he'd once trusted as a brother, being the one to bring all this destruction down on him, left me feeling cold.

"What happened?" I asked, my voice barely above a whisper.

His gaze drifted back to the window, to the rain that now seemed to be falling harder, the world outside as turbulent as the storm inside him. "He got jealous. He didn't want to share anymore. The business, the power. He thought I was holding him back." He let out a breath, almost a laugh, but it was hollow. "I thought he was just frustrated, you know? That it was just growing pains. But I didn't realize... he was already plotting, already pulling strings behind my back."

There it was again—the rawness of his words. The confession. I could hear it in the way he spoke about it, that sense of disbelief that anyone could betray someone so deeply, so thoroughly. And yet, here I was, hearing it from him, the man who had stood tall, never showing cracks to the world, always keeping everything under control. But now, he was bare, unshielded, and I wasn't sure whether to admire him for it or pity him.

"So you think he planned all this?" I asked, my voice steadier than I felt. "The fires? Everything?"

He nodded slowly, his hands tightening into fists. "He was careful. He knew how to cover his tracks, how to make it look like an accident. But the thing is, Mia—there's one thing I never told anyone. One thing I kept from everyone, including myself."

My stomach tightened, a strange mix of dread and curiosity twisting within me. "What is it?"

Callum's eyes locked with mine, his expression unreadable. For a long moment, he didn't say a word, and I thought maybe he wasn't going to tell me after all. But then, with a look that felt like a dare, he finally spoke.

"Daniel didn't just want to take my business. He wanted to take me down, completely. And to do that, he needed to hurt the people I cared about. And you, Mia... you were never part of the plan." His lips twitched, a faint, rueful smile crossing his face. "But now that you're here, I think he's going to make sure you are."

A chill shot through me, colder than the rain outside, and for a split second, I couldn't breathe. Before I could gather my thoughts, the sound of footsteps echoed from the hallway, the sharp click of heels against the hardwood floor.

The door swung open, and I froze.

Standing there, with a smirk that could have frozen the air around her, was someone I never expected to see again.

Chapter 25: Heart of the Fire

The coffee was cold, but I drank it anyway, letting the bitter taste scorch my throat. It didn't matter. Nothing mattered much at that moment, except the quiet hum of the overhead lights and the way my fingers trembled, the sensation a reminder of the storm inside me that refused to subside.

Callum was pacing, his sharp movements sending ripples through the otherwise still room. I watched him, a part of me aching for the man I thought I knew, the one who had once made me laugh, who knew all the right things to say when the world felt too heavy to carry. The one who had made me believe in us, even when I was sure I shouldn't.

Now, that man was lost somewhere behind the walls he had built, walls that I had been stupid enough to think I could tear down.

"You don't get it, do you?" His voice was tight, strained with the weight of things unsaid. "It's not just about the fire. It never was."

I swallowed hard, my pulse quickening. "Then what was it about, Callum?" My voice was steady, despite the chaos inside me. "You've been hiding behind lies for months. I don't know who you are anymore."

He stopped in front of me, too close, the air between us thick with unsaid apologies and accusations. His eyes, those eyes I once thought I understood so well, were guarded now, unreadable. The flicker of something—regret, anger, shame—passed through them, but it was gone before I could grasp it.

"I never meant for you to get caught up in this," he said, his voice low, almost a whisper. "It was never supposed to be like this."

I laughed, a sharp sound that felt foreign to my own ears. "No? So what was it supposed to be like? A little danger, a little thrill, and then a neat little bow at the end?"

I could see it now, the way his jaw clenched, the way his body stiffened. The familiar defense mechanism I had come to expect when he was backed into a corner. He was retreating again.

"You don't understand," he repeated, stepping back as if he could physically distance himself from the truth.

And I didn't. Not completely. Not yet. But I was starting to. The arsonist was in custody, the immediate danger was over, and the city had begun to breathe again. But we were both still suffocating in our own ways. I had lived with secrets for so long that I had almost forgotten what it was like to live without them. To be completely open, without fear or hesitation. But Callum—his secrets weren't just his to keep anymore, not when they had dragged me into this mess.

I set the coffee cup down with a thud, my fingers slick with sweat. "Then help me understand, Callum. Help me understand how I'm supposed to forgive you for the lies, for everything. For using me like I was some...some pawn in your game."

His eyes narrowed, but there was no anger in them. Only pain. "I never meant for it to go that far," he murmured, his voice so quiet that for a moment, I thought I might have imagined it. But I hadn't. I knew better than that.

I stepped back, the floor cool beneath my bare feet. My head spun with everything we had been through, the emotions, the betrayals, the lies we had told ourselves in order to survive.

"You didn't mean for it to go this far?" I asked, incredulous. "You didn't mean for the fires to burn, for people to die?"

The words stung, sharper than I had intended. But they were out now, and I couldn't take them back.

His expression twisted, and for a moment, I saw the man beneath the walls. The one who had once cared about me more than anything. The one who had once trusted me.

"I'm not proud of what happened," he said, his voice breaking in a way that made my chest tighten. "I never wanted anyone to get hurt. But the truth is... I didn't have a choice. Not then."

It was the first time he had admitted that to me, and though the admission didn't change anything, it left me with a strange sense of vulnerability. He had been fighting a battle that I hadn't even known existed. A battle that had taken everything from him—everything we had built.

"I know you didn't," I whispered, the words barely escaping my lips. "I just wish you had trusted me. I wish you had told me before everything got so...so out of control."

He reached for me then, his hand hovering inches from my arm, the weight of his hesitation heavier than the distance between us. "I couldn't," he said. "I couldn't bring you into this, not when it was already too late."

I stepped back, suddenly feeling small, as if all the anger, all the heartbreak, had shrunk me down to nothing. "But it wasn't too late, Callum. Not until you decided it was."

The silence that followed was deafening, and in that silence, I felt the full weight of everything we had become—or perhaps, everything we had failed to become. I wasn't sure which one hurt more.

I closed my eyes, willing the tears back, feeling the jagged edge of something hard and unforgiving settle in my chest. I had to make a choice. We both did. And neither of us had the answers.

When I opened my eyes again, he was standing there, his expression softening, as if he had found the courage to say what had been left unspoken for too long. "I never stopped loving you," he murmured. "Not once."

And for a moment, just a moment, I let myself believe him.

The city had quieted, the smoke of the fire only a lingering memory in the crisp morning air. The windows of my apartment were cracked open, the faint scent of rain mingling with the smells of burnt wood and charred earth. I wanted to feel something—a sense of relief, maybe—but instead, I only felt the void left behind after the storm. The tension was still there, like a thread ready to snap if touched, and it wasn't just the aftermath of the fire that lingered in the air. It was the wreckage between Callum and me.

I turned to look at him. He had retreated to the far corner of the room, leaning against the doorframe as if the weight of his own body was the only thing holding him upright. He was trying—God, how he was trying—but the silence between us had become a chasm too wide to bridge with words alone.

"I'm not asking you to forgive me," Callum said, his voice gravelly, as if the hours of arguing had scraped his throat raw. "I just need you to understand that I never meant for any of this to happen. Not to you, not to anyone."

His eyes were full of remorse, but I couldn't bring myself to look at him. Not directly. Instead, I focused on the cracked vase on the shelf behind him, the one that had always been a symbol of imperfection in the midst of everything else. It had been a gift—a terrible, misguided gift from someone I had once trusted, but it had survived countless falls, chipped edges, and moments of forgetfulness. It was an odd metaphor, and I knew it.

"You say that, but it doesn't change anything," I replied, my voice low but steady. "It doesn't change the fact that I had no idea who you really were. That you lied to me from the start."

Callum pushed himself off the doorframe, his movements slow but deliberate. "I didn't lie to you. I just... I didn't tell you everything. I didn't think you needed to know. I was protecting you."

"Protecting me?" I scoffed, finally meeting his gaze, the fire of anger flashing back to life in my chest. "By keeping me in the dark about everything? By making me believe that we were on the same page when we were miles apart?"

His face softened. "I should have told you. I should have trusted you. But the truth is, I was scared. I was scared that if you knew—if you knew what I was really involved in—you'd walk away. And I didn't want that."

The confession landed between us like a stone dropped into still water, and I felt my resolve weaken, just a little. Because despite the hurt, despite the tangled mess of betrayal, a part of me still understood that fear. That fear of being rejected, of exposing the ugly parts of yourself to someone you cared about. It wasn't an excuse, but it was human.

"I don't know what to do with that, Callum." I rubbed my forehead, trying to chase away the ache that had settled there. "I don't know if I can forgive you. I don't know if I can trust you again after everything."

He took a step closer, and I could feel the heat of his body, the intensity of his gaze. "I don't want forgiveness," he said softly. "I just want a chance to prove that I can be the man you thought I was. The man I want to be."

It was too much. The weight of it pressed down on me, suffocating in its sincerity. "I can't carry that for you, Callum," I said, my voice breaking. "I can't fix you. I can't fix what's broken between us."

His expression hardened, but there was still a flicker of something—hope? Regret? I couldn't tell. "I'm not asking you to fix me," he said, his voice a touch sharper now. "I'm asking you to give me a chance to fix us."

The words hung there in the air, a fragile thing that could either shatter or take root. I wasn't sure which way it would go. All I knew was that my heart was a battlefield, and I wasn't sure who had the strength to fight anymore.

"You can't fix what's already been destroyed," I whispered, though a part of me wanted to believe him. Wanted to believe that somehow we could rise from the ashes of this, but that part of me felt like a distant memory. "I don't even know what I'm supposed to be anymore. The woman who believed in you? Or the woman who doesn't even recognize the man standing in front of her?"

For a long moment, Callum said nothing. His eyes held mine, and I could see the depth of the struggle within him, the anger at himself and the desire to make it right. It was a quiet war, but it was there, waging between us.

"I can't undo what I've done," he finally said, his voice tight with frustration. "But I'm not asking you to forget either. I just need you to understand that I'm willing to do whatever it takes. And if that's not enough... then at least I'll know I tried."

The admission, raw and unguarded, struck me with an unexpected force. He was laying it all on the table, every bit of himself exposed for me to either take or walk away from. And for a moment, I found myself at a crossroads. The path ahead was unclear, shrouded in uncertainty, but the path behind was lined with too many broken things to turn back now.

"So, what now?" I asked, my voice barely more than a whisper.

Callum took another step forward, but this time, I didn't flinch. There was no more running from this. No more pretending that we weren't standing on the edge of something that might either break us or force us to rebuild.

"We start over," he said, his voice steady now. "One step at a time. And we see if there's anything left worth saving."

I nodded, though the weight of his words pressed down on me. One step at a time. That sounded like both a promise and a warning. And I wasn't sure if I was strong enough to take that first step.

I couldn't breathe. I stood there, the silence between us stretched so thin I could almost hear the fabric of the universe tearing at the seams. The weight of Callum's words hung in the air like smoke, thick and choking, and despite my best efforts to remain composed, something inside me was unraveling.

His voice had gone quiet, as if testing the space between us, afraid of disrupting whatever fragile connection had been formed. "You think I want you to fix this?" His eyes were dark, a storm raging behind them that I didn't have the strength to navigate. "I'm not asking for redemption. Hell, I'm not asking for forgiveness. All I'm asking for is a chance to prove I can be what you need. To be the person I should've been from the start."

I shook my head, unable to form words. Part of me wanted to take his hand, to let the familiarity of his touch ground me, but I knew better. Nothing felt familiar anymore. Not the fire we'd just survived, not the wreckage of our relationship, not even the taste of his lips on mine—sweet and painful all at once. The memories we had, the ones that had once seemed unshakable, felt like sand slipping through my fingers.

"You think one conversation is going to fix this?" I forced the words out, though they were thick in my throat. "After everything? After all the lies and deceit, you think I can just snap my fingers and pretend like none of it happened?"

Callum didn't move, but there was a shift in him, a subtle tightening in his jaw. "No. I don't think it'll be that easy," he said, his voice low, as though trying to explain something to himself as much as to me. "But I can't undo what I've done. I can only move forward. And if you're not with me on that, then... then I'll carry this alone."

I wasn't sure which hurt more: the weight of his admission or the realization that the distance between us was no longer just emotional. It was physical, too. I could feel the space growing, spreading like an inevitable tidal wave that would sweep us both under, and yet, despite everything, I couldn't quite let go.

"You've been carrying it alone for a long time, haven't you?" I asked, finally giving in to the frustration that had been building in my chest. "That's what this was, right? You've been pushing me away so you didn't have to share the burden. Because sharing means trusting, and you can't even do that, can you? Not with me."

The words cut through the tension like a knife. I had meant to throw them away, to dismiss them as the frustration of the moment, but as soon as they left my mouth, I knew they were true. That was the crux of everything. Callum hadn't trusted me—had never trusted me—and now, everything we had was crumbling beneath that simple truth.

His eyes flickered with something like shame, but it was gone before I could decide if I had imagined it. "You're right," he admitted, his voice strained. "I was scared. Scared of losing you, scared of dragging you into something you weren't prepared for. I thought—"

"You thought you could handle it alone?" I interrupted, feeling a heat rise in me that I hadn't known I still had. "You thought you could control everything, including me?"

Callum winced, as though my words stung more than he'd expected. I wasn't sure why I felt this strange sense of satisfaction in it—maybe because it meant he wasn't entirely the unshakable man I had come to see him as. Maybe because it meant that, beneath it all, he had been just as human as I was.

"I don't have control over anything anymore," he muttered, a bitter laugh escaping him. "I lost that the moment I made those choices. But I'm still here, and I'm still willing to fight for this, for you." His gaze softened for a moment, but his next words were sharper, more urgent. "But you have to decide, right here, right now, if you want to be part of that fight."

His challenge hung in the air, demanding an answer. And for the first time in what felt like forever, I realized how little I had to offer in return. My heart was a battlefield, scattered with the remnants of trust, love, and rage. I wanted to scream, to demand he fix everything in an instant, but I knew that wasn't fair. Not when I didn't even know how to fix myself.

"Do I want to fight for us?" The question reverberated in my chest, but I couldn't answer it. Not yet.

Suddenly, a knock at the door broke through the tension, sharp and loud, and for a moment, I thought I might have imagined it. But then it came again, quicker this time, like someone desperate to be heard.

I looked at Callum, confusion flickering across his features. He was about to say something, but before the words left his mouth, the door swung open.

Standing in the doorway was a figure I hadn't seen in months. A figure that hadn't crossed my mind in what felt like years.

Ben.

I froze, my heart stopping for the briefest of seconds, as if time had decided to pause its relentless march forward. Ben was standing there, a dark bruise on his jaw, his shirt disheveled, but his eyes were alive with something unspoken. His gaze flickered from me to Callum, and then back to me, as if weighing some invisible truth that neither of us could see.

"I need to talk to you," he said, his voice low but intense. "Both of you."

And in that moment, I knew that nothing would ever be the same again.

Chapter 26: Rising from the Ashes

The air still smells like smoke, even though the fire's been out for hours. It clings to the ruins like a second skin, a reminder of everything we've lost. The city is alive around me, bustling with the usual noise—cars honking, children laughing, people shouting, but it feels distant, as though I'm watching life through a window that's slightly fogged. The sirens from earlier have long since faded into the distance, but I can still hear them in my mind, the wail of something far more primal, a warning that we ignored until it was too late.

I should feel relief, but it's as if my body is still waiting for the impact that never comes. It's like standing on the edge of a cliff and knowing you should jump, but something—someone—is holding you back. My feet don't want to move, but I'm frozen in place, caught between the wreckage of my past and the promise of a future I can't quite bring myself to embrace. I wish I could look at Callum and see the man I thought I knew, the one with the unshakable confidence, the one who built his life on control and precision. Instead, all I see is the man with the haunted eyes, the one who has spent too long buried in regret.

He stands a few feet away from me, hands shoved deep into the pockets of his jacket. The familiar scent of his cologne, earthy and rich, drifts towards me on the breeze, mingling with the sharp tang of smoke. It's not enough to mask the rawness in his voice when he speaks. "I never meant for things to turn out like this," he says, the words coming out slow, as if he's testing each one before he lets it fall. "I didn't know how to—"

I cut him off, my own voice harsher than I intend. "How to what? Fix it? You could've tried, Callum. You could've tried a hell of a lot sooner."

He looks at me, and there's something in his gaze—something dark and tender that makes me want to look away but forces me to meet it head-on. "I know. I failed you." His words are almost a whisper, but they carry the weight of years.

I swallow hard. The urge to push him away is strong, but there's a part of me, buried deep, that wants to reach out and pull him closer. "And what do you want me to do with that? Say 'It's okay' and move on? Pretend that everything's fine?"

"I don't know," he admits, his voice cracked. "I don't even know if that would make a difference, but I need you to know I'm sorry. And I'm not asking for forgiveness. Not yet. But I'm asking for the chance to—" He stops himself, his throat working as if the words are stuck.

I take a step forward, despite myself. There's something raw in his silence, something that feels like a thread pulling me closer. "The chance to what?"

"To make it right," he says simply, his eyes not leaving mine. "I've spent so long thinking I could fix everything by doing it alone, by holding people at arm's length. But I was wrong. And now... now I don't know how to fix it. Not alone."

His words hit me harder than I expect, and the sting of tears catches in the back of my throat. But I won't let them fall—not now, not here. Not when everything still feels too fragile, too uncertain. "We're both standing in the ruins of our mistakes, Callum," I say quietly, my voice trembling despite my best efforts. "I don't even know what rebuilding looks like. Do you?"

There's a long pause. His expression shifts, flickering between determination and vulnerability. "I think rebuilding starts with truth. With facing what we've broken and deciding if it's worth fixing."

The silence stretches between us, the weight of his words settling like dust in the air. I know he's right. I know I've been hiding behind my own walls, pretending that I could move on without ever confronting what happened. But facing him now—seeing the man who's been so afraid to love, so afraid of the past—there's a part of me that feels like the walls are cracking.

I take a deep breath, and for the first time in what feels like forever, I let myself really look at him. Not the man I thought I knew, not the one who seemed impervious to anything that could hurt him, but the man who's standing before me now. The one who looks like he's come through a storm and doesn't know how to stop the rain from falling. The one who's asking for something that terrifies me.

"You're asking me to forgive you," I say softly, the words tasting like ash in my mouth.

"I'm asking you to trust me again," he corrects, his voice barely a whisper. "I'm asking you to let me prove that I can be the man you need."

The world feels like it's spinning too fast and too slow at the same time. My heart is a battlefield, torn between the desire to hold on to something that might be broken beyond repair and the desperate hope that maybe—just maybe—there's a way forward. It's not the love I thought we had, the one built on safety and certainty. But it might be something more real. More raw. More human.

"Trust," I repeat, the word hanging between us like a fragile thread. "How do you expect me to trust you when you've shown me nothing but how easily you can walk away?"

Callum steps forward, his hand reaching out like a plea. "Because I'm not walking away now. I'm not asking you to forget. I'm asking you to take a chance. On me. On us. One last time."

The air between us shifts, and I know—just know—that this is the moment where everything changes. Whether we can rise from the ashes or be consumed by them, only time will tell. But for the first time in a long while, I'm willing to see where this fragile, uncertain path might lead.

I wish I could say there was some grand revelation, some moment of clarity when I made my decision. But the truth is, the only thing that felt clear was the weight of the silence between us. It wasn't just the space around us, though it felt wide and hollow, as if even the city had decided to hold its breath. It was the silence inside of me, the part of me that had always been too afraid to speak the words I knew were waiting there, buried deep under layers of doubt and fear. And now, for the first time in a long time, I wanted to hear them out loud.

Callum's hand is still outstretched, hovering just a fraction of an inch away from me, and I have to fight the urge to reach for it, to take that first step towards him. Instead, I look at him, really look at him, the way I should have all those months ago, before we let things fester and crumble into the ashes we're standing in now. His eyes, dark and earnest, are fixed on me, searching for something—an answer, maybe, or just the recognition that I'm still here, still willing to stand beside him in whatever this mess is we've made.

"Don't do that," I say suddenly, my voice cutting through the stillness. He blinks, startled, but I press on, frustrated. "Don't make this something it's not. You're not asking me to rebuild. You're asking me to forgive you. You want me to just... erase it. Forget all the times you walked away, all the ways you shut me out, and act like none of it matters anymore. But it does, Callum. It all matters."

His jaw tightens, but he doesn't look away. There's something fierce in the way he holds my gaze now, something like determination, or maybe desperation, I'm not sure. "I'm not asking you to forget. I'm asking you to see me for who I am now, not the man I was then. I've changed. I've had to change. But I can't do it alone."

"Who are you trying to convince?" I ask, incredulous. "Me? Or yourself?"

He doesn't answer right away. Instead, he looks down at the ground for a moment, his fingers flexing, like he's trying to work through some internal struggle. I can see it in his posture, the way his shoulders are slightly hunched, the tension in his neck. He's fighting something, something that's gnawing at him, but I can't figure out what. He's been doing that for as long as I've known him—fighting battles that no one else can see, carrying burdens no one else knows about.

"I'm not asking you to fix me," he says finally, his voice hoarse. "But I need you to see me. I'm not the same man who walked away from you before. I swear to you, I'm not. And I don't expect you to trust me right away, but I need you to try. I need you to let me show you that I can be someone you want to stay for."

I don't know what to say to that. I could tell him I've heard those words before, that they sound nice, but they're hollow, empty promises that only ever end in disappointment. I could tell him that I've been picking up the pieces of my life for so long, alone, that I'm not sure I even remember how to let someone else in anymore. But I don't. Instead, I find myself taking that first step, the one I didn't want to take. It's slow at first, tentative, but before I can stop myself, I've crossed the distance between us. His breath catches when I finally take his hand, and it's warm, real, a pulse of life I didn't think I would feel again.

For a long moment, neither of us speaks. We stand there, hands clasped, two people who have both been through hell and come out the other side a little bit broken, but still here. And that's something. Maybe it's enough. I want to believe it is.

"Callum," I say quietly, pulling him out of the silence. "I can't promise you anything. I can't promise that I'll forgive you, or that I'll even know how to trust you again. But what I can promise is that I won't let us burn down without trying. I won't walk away without giving this one last chance."

He exhales, like he's been holding his breath, and I feel the shift in him, the moment where he lets the walls fall. "That's all I'm asking for," he says, his voice so soft it almost breaks. "Just one last chance."

I nod, the weight of the words hanging between us, thick and heavy. "One last chance. But it's not just on you, Callum. It's on both of us. We both have to do the work. We both have to figure out how to make this right."

"Then we will," he promises, the resolve in his voice strong and steady. "We'll figure it out. Together."

And for the first time in what feels like forever, I let myself believe it. Maybe it's foolish, maybe it's a risk, but isn't that what life is? A collection of chances, of moments that slip through our fingers unless we're brave enough to hold on?

I squeeze his hand, the warmth of it grounding me in this fragile, uncertain moment. It's not perfect, nothing ever is, but it's something real. It's something we can build on, if we're willing to try.

The city continues to hum around us, indifferent to our small, fragile moment in time. But for us, this is everything. A new beginning, born from the wreckage of everything we thought we knew. And maybe, just maybe, that's how we find our way back to each other.

There are moments in life that seem to stretch, to hang in the air like a delicate thread, and this is one of them. The warmth of Callum's hand still lingers in mine, though the world around us has moved on, indifferent. I can feel my heart thumping like a drum, each beat a question, a hesitant step forward into a future that feels as uncertain as the ground beneath my feet. But the truth is, for the first time in what feels like forever, I'm not afraid. Not of him, not of me. I'm just... here.

I let go of his hand, unwilling to break the fragile moment we've just created. It's the kind of thing you want to hold on to, like a favorite book with a torn cover that still holds a story worth reading. "What now?" I ask, my voice almost a whisper, but sharp with the need to know. Because, in this silence, anything feels possible. Too possible, maybe.

His eyes meet mine, and there's an honesty in them that scares me. "Now, we rebuild." The words sound simple, but I can hear the weight behind them, the years of mistakes, the time that has passed between us, the loss. It's not just a promise; it's a choice, and one that neither of us can walk away from now.

"You really think we can do that?" I ask, still doubtful but more hopeful than I've allowed myself to be in a long time.

"I think we have to," he says, the resolve in his voice settling like a weight on both of our shoulders. "What's the alternative? To keep running from everything that's broken? To pretend like we're not standing here, in the middle of all this mess?"

I know he's right. There's no easy way out. There's no escaping the truth that we've both hurt each other, that we've both been the ones to pull away when things got too difficult. But somewhere in the rubble of everything we've done to each other, there's something worth saving. I feel it in my bones, like a quiet hum in the air.

"I don't know how to fix this," I admit, the vulnerability slipping out before I can stop it. "I don't know where to start."

He steps closer, his presence steady, like the calm in the eye of the storm. "We start with today. With this moment. We figure it out together. One piece at a time."

I wish I could believe him fully, but the walls I've built are still there, invisible but solid. I look at him—really look at him—and see the cracks, the way his jaw clenches, the way he's trying so hard to keep his distance, even though he's standing right in front of me. And then I realize something. The distance isn't just between us. It's between him and the man he wants to be. The man I need him to be.

"I don't know if I can forgive you," I say, the words a confession, not an accusation. "I'm not sure I can ever forget what happened. But maybe... maybe I can try."

He doesn't flinch, doesn't pull away. Instead, he nods slowly, accepting the weight of my words, even if they cut deeper than any silence we've shared. "I'll take whatever you can give me. I'm not asking for everything. Not yet. I just want a chance to prove that I can be what you need."

It's quiet again, the kind of quiet that's heavy, as if the air itself is holding its breath. We're both standing on the edge of something—something big and terrifying and full of possibility. I know I should walk away, that I should protect myself from the potential pain of more disappointment, more heartbreak. But I don't. Instead, I stand there, letting him see me, letting myself see him, and I choose to stay.

"I don't know how to move forward from here," I say, my voice barely a murmur. "But I want to try. I want to know if we can be more than the wreckage we left behind."

A flash of relief passes across his face, so brief I almost miss it. "I want that too. More than anything." His voice cracks slightly, and for the first time, I see the fragility behind the man who has always been so composed, so sure of himself.

I take a deep breath, pushing the doubts back into the corners of my mind. "Okay. We try. But no promises."

"No promises," he repeats, as if it's a vow. "But we'll take it one step at a time."

For a moment, we just stand there, side by side, the air thick with everything unsaid, everything we've been afraid to acknowledge. And then, almost instinctively, I look up at him, searching his face for something, anything that tells me he's telling the truth. I see it there, buried beneath the layers of guilt and regret—something softer, something that wasn't there before.

"Do you trust me?" I ask, the question falling from my lips before I can stop it.

His eyes soften, and for a second, I think he might say something easy, something that fits the moment. But instead, he looks at me, really looks at me, and says, "Not yet. But I'm willing to try."

I nod, the words settling in my chest like a weight I didn't know I was carrying. "Okay. I'll try too. I won't lie and say it'll be easy, but I'll try."

Callum reaches for me then, slowly, cautiously, as if testing the waters. His hand brushes mine, a tentative touch, and I don't pull away. Instead, I let it linger, the sensation of his skin on mine a small, delicate thing, like the first sign of spring after a long, cold winter.

And then—just as I'm starting to think that maybe, just maybe, we're making progress—a distant sound shatters the quiet, like an explosion, loud and sudden. My heart lurches in my chest, my instincts screaming for me to react, to move. I turn toward the source of the noise, panic bubbling up inside me, and in that instant, I realize that nothing, nothing in our lives, is ever truly safe from the chaos we've let slip through our fingers.

I squeeze Callum's hand tighter, my pulse racing. "What was that?"

Chapter 27: Under the Embers

The wind had changed its tune that morning, a soft whisper creeping in through the open window. It carried with it the scent of salt and the faintest trace of rain, a promise that the world beyond these walls hadn't yet given up on its own rhythm. I lingered by the window, watching the first signs of light stretch lazily across the sky. The streets below me remained quiet, still caught in that post-dawn hush, as if they, too, were waiting for something to break the silence.

I hadn't slept well. It wasn't the kind of rest that came easily after a thousand restless thoughts churned in your head all night. No, my sleep had been fractured, interrupted by flashes of faces, voices, and then... Callum. His face kept appearing, uninvited, in the dark corners of my mind. The way his eyes had softened when he spoke of his past, the rawness in his voice when he had let his guard down—everything he had shown me kept circling back, taunting me like a memory I couldn't shake. It wasn't just him that haunted me, though. It was the question that hovered over everything, that gnawing uncertainty. Was I supposed to trust him? Or had he been playing me from the beginning?

The thought of it made my chest tighten, but I pushed it aside. The past had become a collection of moments that no longer made sense. A web of lies and truths tangled together, each one pulling me further from the life I had once known. There were remnants, yes, little fragments of my past life that I could cling to—snatches of conversations, old photographs I refused to throw away, the smell of my mother's perfume that seemed to linger in the corners of my memories. But the more I searched for solid ground, the more it slipped through my fingers.

I sighed, closing the window and stepping away from the ledge, only to find myself caught in a mirror across the room. The reflection that stared back was a stranger. Her eyes were darker than I remembered, shadows clinging to the edges like some unfinished story. Her lips were set in a firm line, her posture too rigid for comfort. She looked like someone who had seen too much, lived too much, and lost too much. The woman staring back at me wasn't the same girl who had once believed in things like love, trust, and safety. She was something else now—someone hardened, yet somehow still searching for an answer that never came.

I tugged my sweater tighter around me, not for warmth, but for the illusion of comfort. I had always been good at pretending. But today, the act felt hollow.

The day unfolded like any other, but my mind refused to stay tethered to the ordinary. Each step I took seemed too heavy, as if the weight of unanswered questions pressed down on me. I couldn't help but think of Callum, his smile, his temper, the way his hands had clenched when I asked about his past. There was a side to him that I couldn't ignore, a side that had called out to something deep inside me—something I couldn't name but knew was there.

I walked through the small town like I had a hundred times before, but today, the world felt alien. The chatter of the café patrons, the soft clink of spoons against cups, the hurried footsteps on the cobblestone streets—it all seemed so distant. I found myself moving through it all like a shadow, never quite touching anything, never quite belonging.

And then, just as I was about to step back into the quiet of my apartment, I saw him.

Callum.

He was standing across the street, his posture casual but the lines of tension in his shoulders unmistakable. There was no mistaking that he was waiting for something, or perhaps someone. I froze for a moment, my breath catching in my throat, and before I could think better of it, my feet were moving toward him.

His head snapped in my direction the second I took a step, and for a moment, everything else disappeared. The noise, the people, the weight of the questions in my mind—they all vanished, leaving just the two of us standing there. His eyes searched mine with a hunger I couldn't quite place. I stopped a few feet from him, unsure of what to say. What could I say? All I had was a storm of conflicting emotions that I didn't know how to tame.

"I didn't expect to see you here," he said, his voice low, rougher than usual.

I nodded, swallowing the lump that had risen in my throat. "I didn't expect to see you either."

There was an awkward pause, the kind that seemed to stretch longer than necessary, both of us standing there, two strangers bound by something unspoken. I could feel the tension crackling between us, thick enough to touch. He looked different today—softer, almost vulnerable, like the weight of the world was pulling him down just as it had been pulling me.

"You've been thinking about it," he said, breaking the silence.

It wasn't a question, but a statement. I could hear the knowing in his voice. I didn't need to ask how he knew. Of course, he knew. We were both haunted by the same thing.

"Maybe," I said, and my voice came out sharper than I intended. "Maybe I'm just tired of not having answers."

His eyes flickered, and for a moment, I thought I saw something like regret in them. But it was gone so quickly that I wasn't sure if I had imagined it.

"Sometimes the answers come when you're ready for them," he said, stepping closer.

"Or maybe they come when it's too late," I muttered under my breath, but he heard me.

"I'm not asking for your forgiveness," he said softly, his voice low, as if the weight of the words hung between us. "I'm just asking for a chance to explain."

Explain. The word echoed in my head. My heart pounded in my chest, a mixture of longing and fear rising in my throat. What was I supposed to do with that?

The sun had climbed higher in the sky by the time I found myself standing in the small café, my fingers curling around the warm cup in front of me. The steam curled up in lazy spirals, drifting toward the ceiling like it, too, was searching for answers. The table before me felt too large for the small space between us, and I wondered how two people could share so much silence without cracking beneath its weight. Callum sat across from me, his fingers tapping an idle rhythm against his cup, eyes focused on something far beyond the cracked window. Maybe he was pretending not to notice the way my heart beat faster with every passing second, or maybe, like me, he was trying to force the moment into something it wasn't ready to be.

"I didn't think you'd actually show up," I said, breaking the stillness, my voice sounding too loud in the otherwise hushed room.

His lips quirked into something resembling a smile, but it didn't quite reach his eyes. "What did you expect?" he asked, leaning back in his chair, the casualness of his posture at odds with the storm I could feel gathering around us.

"I don't know," I said, unable to keep the edge out of my voice. "Maybe you'd keep pretending everything's fine, that we're fine."

His gaze sharpened then, his shoulders tightening, but he said nothing. The pause between us stretched long enough that it felt like the weight of the world was sitting in that moment, on my shoulders, on his. I was used to being alone in the quiet of my thoughts, but this—this silence between us—felt like an invasion.

He was still a stranger, no matter how many times we had crossed paths, no matter how many secrets he'd entrusted me with. I wasn't sure if I could call him a friend, let alone anything else.

"I came to apologize," Callum said suddenly, as though reading the thoughts I had tried to hide behind the walls I'd built. His voice had softened, but there was something in it that made me stiffen. "I haven't been fair to you."

"You haven't been fair to anyone," I muttered, staring down into my cup. It was like a reflex now, the way the words slipped out without me even thinking about them.

He didn't flinch, didn't argue. Instead, there was just that quiet moment where the air seemed to hold its breath.

"I've been running," he said, and the words felt heavier than any apology he could offer. "For so long, I've been running from things I didn't want to face, things I thought I could outrun. And now... I realize I was only running from myself."

I met his gaze then, and for the first time in days, I saw something in him that wasn't a mask, wasn't a carefully constructed lie. There was no bravado, no arrogance—just exhaustion. And in that moment, a part of me wanted to reach across the table and pull him back from the edge he was standing on.

"You're not the only one who's been running," I said, the words coming out sharper than I intended. My pulse was still hammering, the weight of everything unspoken pressing down on me. "Maybe we all are, in our own way."

The smile he gave me then was rueful, tinged with the kind of bitterness that felt all too familiar. "Maybe we are," he said, his voice low, almost a whisper. "But it doesn't change the fact that I've hurt you, and for that, I'm sorry."

I wasn't sure if I should believe him. In fact, I wasn't sure if I wanted to. There was too much at stake, too much confusion in the air between us for any apology to feel like it could change anything.

But something about the rawness of his admission shifted something inside me. I hated how much it made me ache for answers, for closure, for whatever it was I was still chasing.

"Why now?" I asked, finally meeting his eyes again, my voice trembling slightly. "Why after everything?"

Callum's fingers drummed against the ceramic of his cup again, his gaze flickering between my face and the empty space beside us. "Because I'm tired," he said simply. "Tired of pretending that I've got it all figured out, that I know exactly what's happening. But the truth is, I don't. I don't know what I'm supposed to do next, and that terrifies me."

I could feel my breath catch in my chest at the vulnerability in his voice, something I hadn't expected. But then, it all came rushing back—everything that had come before this moment, the lies, the betrayals. How many times had I let someone apologize only to watch them do it again? How many times had I stood in someone's shadow, waiting for them to come clean, only to be disappointed when they never did?

"I'm not asking you to fix me," he continued, voice rough. "I just... I need you to know that I'm not the person I've shown you. I never meant to drag you into all this mess, but now that you're here, I don't want to keep pretending."

I swallowed, the weight of his words settling heavily in my chest. There was a flicker of something deep within me—a part of me that wanted to believe him, to believe that somewhere under the layers of secrecy and fear, there was still something real. But I wasn't sure if I could afford to trust him again. I wasn't sure if I could trust myself.

"You can't just say things like that and expect everything to go back to normal," I said, my voice low, almost trembling with the force of my own doubts. "You can't undo the past with a few words."

"I don't want to undo it," he said quickly, his tone suddenly more urgent. "But I want to try to make it right. Even if it's too late for that, I at least want to stop running from it."

For a long moment, we sat in silence, the weight of his confession hanging in the air like a fragile thread. I wanted to reach out to him, wanted to say something to fill the emptiness between us, but I didn't trust myself to speak the words. Maybe because, deep down, I knew they would change everything.

And I wasn't ready for that. Not yet.

The café was quieter now, the soft hum of voices a mere background to the tension pulsing between us. I could feel the weight of every word that hung between us, each one heavier than the last. Callum was still watching me, his gaze a steady pressure I couldn't escape. It was as if he could see the doubts racing through my mind, the battle I was waging inside my chest.

"I don't know how to do this," I said, the words spilling out before I could stop them. I wanted to be strong, to stand my ground and keep the distance between us that I knew was necessary. But there was something in the way he looked at me, something in the raw honesty of his eyes that made it hard to remember why I should be running from him in the first place. "I don't know how to trust you again."

His mouth tightened, the muscles in his jaw flexing as though he were trying to hold back something. He leaned forward slightly, and I felt the shift in the air, the unspoken invitation to dive deeper into the mess we'd made.

"I know I don't deserve your trust," he said quietly. "I can't undo the damage, but I want to prove to you that I'm not the person I was before. I want to be someone you can trust again." His voice faltered, just a fraction, but it was enough to make me wonder if maybe, just maybe, he was telling the truth.

I met his gaze, my breath catching in my throat. The familiar ache in my chest swelled again—how many times had I told myself to move on, to forget about him, to let go of everything that had once felt so real? How many times had I pushed him away only to find that the space between us was never as wide as I thought? And yet, there was still a part of me that was terrified to take a step closer, terrified of what might happen if I let myself believe.

"So what now?" I asked, my voice quieter than I meant it to be. "We pretend like everything is fine and forget about the fact that we've both been lying to each other? Or do we keep going around in circles, talking about what we could've been if we hadn't—"

I stopped myself, the words burning in my throat. I had almost said it. Almost reminded him of everything that had come before, the wreckage we'd both caused. The lies, the games, the way he had disappeared on me, only to reappear like nothing had changed.

"You think I don't know?" His voice was sharp now, his expression hardening for the first time since we sat down. "You think I haven't been beating myself up over every damn thing I did? Every lie I told? You think I don't wish I could go back and change everything?"

I didn't respond. I couldn't. The truth was, I was still so lost in this tangled mess of emotions that it was hard to see which way was up. My heart and my mind were at war, one telling me to walk away and never look back, the other begging me to take a leap of faith, to believe that maybe—just maybe—there was something worth saving.

I took a shaky breath, trying to ground myself in the reality of this moment. He was right about one thing: I couldn't keep pretending that everything had been okay. We both knew better than that.

"Then why didn't you say something sooner?" I asked, my voice catching in my throat. "Why didn't you stop this before it got out of hand?"

Callum closed his eyes, running a hand through his hair, his frustration palpable. "Because I didn't know how," he admitted, his voice raw. "I thought if I kept going, if I just pushed through, things would fix themselves. But they didn't. And now I'm here, trying to clean up a mess I made."

It was the honesty in his words, the vulnerability that he hadn't shown before, that made my chest tighten with something that wasn't anger or resentment. It was something else. Something that felt like hope, but fragile and unsure. The same kind of hope I'd once let myself believe in, only to have it burned away.

"Callum," I started, but before I could say anything else, the door to the café opened with a sharp jingle, cutting through the tension like a knife. The air around us shifted, the atmosphere suddenly charged with something that had nothing to do with us.

I turned my head instinctively, my body going on alert. A man walked into the café, tall and broad-shouldered, his dark coat a stark contrast against the brightness outside. His eyes scanned the room, quickly landing on us. Something in his gaze made my stomach tighten, a flash of recognition shooting through me before I could fully register why.

"Who is that?" I asked before I could stop myself, my voice barely above a whisper.

Callum's expression darkened. His jaw clenched, his body stiffening. "Someone I thought I'd left behind," he said through gritted teeth.

The man was moving toward us now, his footsteps deliberate, steady. My pulse quickened. The moment he crossed the threshold of the café, I felt the room close in around us, as if the walls themselves were inching inward. It was the same kind of feeling I'd had just before everything had gone wrong the first time, the same kind of fear that had made me doubt every decision I'd ever made.

"Callum," the man's voice rang out, low and authoritative. "I think we need to talk."

And just like that, everything changed.

The man's eyes flicked briefly to me, but his focus remained on Callum. I couldn't help but notice the way Callum's expression hardened at the sound of his voice, the tension in his shoulders like a warning. Something was happening, something neither of them had expected, and I had the sinking feeling that it was about to pull us all into the fire again.

The air crackled with unspoken words, heavy and dangerous, as I sat frozen, unable to look away.

Chapter 28: Flickers of Hope

The air in the office felt heavier than usual, thick with the scent of stale coffee and the faint remnants of a thunderstorm that had passed through earlier, leaving behind the smell of damp pavement. The rain had stopped, but the coolness lingered, creeping through the cracked window as if it were trying to remind us that the world outside was still turning, even if we weren't.

Callum sat across from me, leaning forward, his brow furrowed in concentration as he scrolled through the evidence on the screen. His shirt, untucked and a little wrinkled, clung to his shoulders in a way that was distracting, though I tried not to let my attention stray. He wasn't wearing his usual mask of indifference—no, tonight was different. His eyes, usually sharp and guarded, seemed almost... tired. We'd both been burning the candle at both ends for weeks, but there was something more in the way he held himself tonight. It was as if the walls he'd erected had begun to crack, and the truth of it—of everything—was slowly seeping out. Or maybe it was just the exhaustion playing tricks on me.

I cleared my throat, forcing myself to focus. There was no time to second-guess, no room for anything but this case.

"The lead," I said, my voice steady despite the flutter of uncertainty that was making my stomach churn. "It doesn't make sense. How could he have been so close to the investigation, and we never noticed?"

Callum didn't answer right away, and for a moment, I wondered if he had even heard me. But then his eyes flicked to mine, the silence between us stretching just a bit too long. "People are good at hiding things," he said finally, his voice low, like he was speaking more to himself than to me. "Maybe we weren't looking hard enough."

I bit back the instinct to snap, to remind him that he was the one who'd told me to trust the process, trust the investigation, trust him. But something stopped me. Maybe it was the way his jaw clenched, or the tightness in his shoulders that seemed to speak louder than his words. It was as if he, too, was carrying the weight of something unspoken, something that had been buried just beneath the surface.

"Do you think he's involved?" I asked, unable to keep the doubt out of my voice.

Callum didn't look at me when he answered. "I think it's too soon to make that call. But the pieces fit. Just... not perfectly."

I sighed, rubbing my temples, trying to push through the headache that had been building for days. The case was wearing me down, and I could feel the tension creeping into my bones. The more we uncovered, the more questions arose, each one more complicated than the last. It was like trying to untangle a knot that only seemed to get tighter with every pull.

I stood up abruptly, pacing the small room, the soft tap of my heels on the hardwood floor the only sound in the otherwise quiet space. "We can't afford to make mistakes, Callum. Not now. We're this close—this close—to finding out who's behind all of this. And if we're wrong—"

"You're not wrong." His voice, sharp and low, cut through my sentence, and I froze mid-step. His gaze met mine, his expression unreadable, but there was something in it—something that almost felt like reassurance. Almost.

I swallowed the lump in my throat, my mouth suddenly dry. "You don't know that. We don't know anything for certain yet. There's too much at stake."

I could see the flicker in his eyes, the fleeting flash of something—anger, frustration, regret. But then, just as quickly, it was gone, replaced by that familiar mask of calm detachment.

"There's always too much at stake," he said, his voice soft, almost wistful. "But we don't have the luxury of playing it safe anymore. We follow the leads. We trust the process. And we get answers. One way or another."

I didn't respond. What was there to say? It felt like we were standing at the edge of a cliff, and the slightest misstep would send us tumbling into the unknown. And yet, despite the fear gnawing at the edges of my thoughts, there was a part of me—small and hesitant—that wanted to believe. To trust.

We worked in silence for a while, the sound of our breathing the only noise that filled the room. I felt the weight of the hours pressing down on me, my eyes straining against the glow of the computer screen as I scanned through the new information we had uncovered. It was the same sense of urgency that had pushed us both forward for weeks, but tonight, it felt different.

The flicker of hope, the smallest spark, had ignited between us. Maybe it was the quiet understanding in his voice, or the way his hand brushed against mine as we reached for the same file. But something had shifted. And it was both exhilarating and terrifying.

"I think," I said quietly, almost to myself, "that we're on the right track."

Callum didn't answer at first, but I could see the way his jaw tightened, the way his fingers flexed against the edge of the table. He was still holding back, still keeping parts of himself locked away, but the flicker of something—something more than just a professional distance—was there.

Maybe, just maybe, there was hope for us after all.

The night air felt oddly still as I walked down the narrow alley behind the office, the sharp scent of wet asphalt clinging to everything like a second skin. It was one of those evenings when the world seemed to hold its breath, as though waiting for something to happen, something that would finally shatter the silence. I pulled my jacket tighter around me, wishing I could do the same with my thoughts. The city buzzed on the edges of my consciousness, distant and faint, like a memory that couldn't quite come into focus. It was a welcome distraction from the gnawing worry that had taken up residence in my chest ever since the lead came through.

Callum was still in the office, hunched over the desk, eyes trained on the latest piece of the puzzle. His focus was almost unnerving—his entire being absorbed in the task, to the point where I almost wondered if he had forgotten I was there. That used to bother me. But tonight, it didn't. In fact, it felt almost... comforting. The familiarity of our routine, the shared purpose between us, was grounding. For the first time in weeks, I didn't feel like I was drowning in questions, drowning in the weight of uncertainty.

But that didn't mean the doubts had disappeared. They lingered, crawling just beneath the surface. Could we really trust this new lead? Was it a coincidence, or was it the breakthrough we'd been waiting for? And, perhaps more haunting, was Callum as invested in the truth as I was, or was this just another case to him, another puzzle to solve, another distraction from whatever it was that had been eating at him for months?

I stopped near the back entrance of the building, looking up at the dark windows, knowing full well that Callum's was the only one still glowing. There was a sense of finality in that, like he was the last one left in a place that had long since given up. I had no idea how much longer I could do this—how much longer I could walk the fine line between hope and suspicion, between the person I once knew and the man who was sitting alone in that office, solving mysteries like it was the only thing that kept him alive.

A movement caught my eye, and I glanced up to see a figure walking toward me. I almost didn't recognize her at first—Carla, a reporter who'd shown up at the scene one night, her eyes flashing with that typical mixture of curiosity and determination that made her so damn relentless. She had a knack for showing up when I least expected it, her wide smile disarming even the most guarded of individuals. I'd never understood why she and I had never quite clicked. There was something about her energy that always felt just a little too much. But tonight, as she approached, I felt a flicker of something akin to gratitude.

"I figured I'd find you here," Carla said, her voice light but knowing. "Hard at work, aren't you? Or should I say... still at work?"

I forced a smile, pushing aside the discomfort that always came when I interacted with her. "What brings you by, Carla? Come to dig up some dirt?"

She laughed, a genuine sound that rang through the night like a bell. "You're welcome, you know. You're welcome for the tip that put you on the right track." She eyed me, her gaze sharp. "Though, I can't help but notice the subtle shift in your demeanor. Something's changed, hasn't it?"

I stiffened at the implication, her words cutting just a little too close to the truth. There was a shift. A subtle one, but it was there. And I hated the fact that she could see it, even if she didn't quite know what she was looking at.

"We're making progress," I said, trying to sound casual, but I could feel my voice wavering ever so slightly.

Carla didn't buy it. "Progress? Or are you just getting closer to something you're not ready to confront?"

Her words hit harder than I expected, and for a moment, I just stared at her, unsure of how to respond. I'd never been good at hiding my emotions, and right now, I wasn't sure what I was supposed to feel—relief that we were finally on the verge of an answer, or fear that the truth would be too much to handle once we found it.

"I don't know what you mean," I said, my tone colder than I intended.

Carla gave a little shrug, her expression thoughtful. "You will. Soon enough."

I could feel the shift in the air around us. It wasn't just the case weighing on my shoulders anymore. It was something more. Something between us. I'd been working with Callum for so long, driven by the need to close the case, that I hadn't stopped to consider the quiet tensions that had been building. And now, with each passing day, each new lead, those tensions seemed to be coiling tighter, like a spring ready to snap.

"You know," Carla said, her voice softer now, "there's one thing I've learned in this business. People don't just change overnight. They don't just wake up and decide to be different. Especially not someone like Callum."

The name hung between us, charged and raw. She didn't have to say anything more for me to understand exactly what she meant. Callum had been distant lately, withdrawn, keeping parts of himself locked away, as if he were afraid of letting anyone close enough to see what was really going on inside his head. And as much as I tried to convince myself that it was just the pressure of the case, the closer we got to the truth, the more his walls seemed to grow, not shrink.

"Goodnight, Carla," I said, cutting her off before she could say anything else.

She smiled again, that knowing look in her eyes. "Take care of yourself, you hear? Whatever you think is happening between you two, it's not as simple as it looks."

I didn't have the strength to argue with her. Instead, I turned and made my way back to the office, the weight of her words pressing heavily on me. Would I be able to handle the truth? Would I be able to handle what I might find in the end, both in the case and in the man who had become so much more than just a partner in this investigation?

I wasn't sure I was ready to answer that. Not yet. But there was no turning back now.

The office was quieter now, the hum of the city outside nearly drowned out by the hum of the fluorescent lights overhead. I hadn't realized how much I craved silence until I stepped back inside, a heavy sense of finality in the air. Callum was sitting in his usual chair, leaning over the stack of papers like he could will the answers to jump off the page and into his hands. The shadows beneath his eyes spoke of nights spent chasing ghosts, and I couldn't help but wonder if that was all we were—two ghosts, moving in a world that was no longer ours, running toward a truth that would change everything.

I hesitated at the door, watching him for a moment longer. Part of me wanted to speak, wanted to bridge the distance that had been growing between us, but another part of me held back. What was the point in hoping that things could go back to what they were before? That part of me was gone now, buried beneath the weight of everything we'd learned. And maybe that was for the best. People don't come back from what we'd been through. Not without scars.

But then, without warning, Callum looked up, and our eyes met. For a second, time seemed to freeze, the tension between us thick enough to cut with a knife. I wasn't sure who moved first—him or me—but before I knew it, I was walking toward him, the sound of my footsteps loud in the stillness.

"Anything?" I asked, my voice softer than I intended, betraying the nerves I'd been trying to keep hidden.

He didn't answer right away, just flipped through the files in front of him, his fingers moving with deliberate slowness. The silence stretched between us, thick and oppressive. But when he finally spoke, there was something different in his voice, a hint of something I couldn't quite place.

"We're close," he said, his gaze flicking back to me briefly. "Closer than I thought we'd be. I think we're about to find out who's been pulling the strings."

The words sent a ripple of unease through me, like a gust of wind on a calm night, just enough to make the hairs on the back of my neck stand up.

"And when we do," I said, my voice tight with uncertainty, "what happens then?"

He leaned back in his chair, his eyes studying me with a quiet intensity. "We finish it. One way or another."

I wanted to say something, to push back, but the words wouldn't come. Instead, I just nodded and sank into the chair next to him, feeling the weight of the hours we'd spent chasing this case, chasing this truth, pressing down on me all at once. The room felt smaller, somehow, the air heavier as we sat there in silence, each of us lost in our own thoughts.

I couldn't help but wonder—how much of this was about the case, and how much of it was about us?

There was a shift, something subtle that had been growing between us for days now. Callum wasn't just a colleague anymore. He hadn't been for a while. But I couldn't decide whether that made everything more complicated or more simple. And as much as I wanted to pretend I had it all figured out, I was as lost as I'd ever been.

Minutes passed, or maybe it was hours. The clock on the wall ticked steadily on, marking the passing of time in a way that felt completely irrelevant. All that mattered was this moment, the space between us, and the flicker of uncertainty that still hung in the air.

Finally, I couldn't stand it anymore. "Are we really ready for this?" I asked, my voice barely above a whisper.

Callum's gaze flicked to mine, and for a brief moment, I thought I saw a glimmer of something—vulnerability, maybe, or regret. But then it was gone, buried beneath that familiar mask of his.

"We don't have a choice," he said, his voice low and steady. "We finish this, and we move on."

I stared at him, trying to read his expression, trying to figure out if he meant more than just the case. But there was nothing in his eyes but resolve. And maybe that was the problem. He was ready to move on. But I wasn't so sure I was.

The door to the office creaked open, and we both turned, instinctively falling back into our professional roles as if nothing had changed. The figure in the doorway was familiar, though it took me a moment to place her—Detective Larkin, the lead investigator from the department who'd been running point on a separate, but related, case. Her expression was tight, her eyes dark with the kind of news no one ever wants to hear.

"We've got a problem," she said, her voice clipped, and for a moment, I thought I saw a flicker of fear in her eyes. But that was impossible, right? Fear wasn't something you saw in the eyes of people like Larkin.

"What happened?" Callum asked, his tone sharp, all traces of weariness gone.

Larkin didn't answer right away. She stepped into the room, closing the door behind her with a soft thud. "I ran the name through the system. The new lead. It's not a coincidence. Someone's been feeding information to the suspect."

I felt the blood drain from my face. "What do you mean?"

She hesitated, then pulled a piece of paper from her folder and handed it to Callum. He took it without a word, his face going unreadable as he scanned it.

"Someone from inside the department," Larkin continued, her voice low, almost as if she were afraid of being overheard. "I don't know who yet, but they've been working against us from the inside."

My mind raced. Betrayal? In our own ranks? This was more than a simple leak. This was something darker, something deeper.

"Who?" I asked, my voice shaking. "Who's behind this?"

Larkin's lips parted, and for a split second, I thought she was about to say the name we'd all been waiting for. But she stopped, her gaze shifting toward Callum. Something passed between them in that brief, charged moment—something I couldn't name, something I didn't want to know.

"Not yet," Callum said, his voice cold. "But we're getting closer. We'll figure this out."

I wanted to believe him. But in that moment, something twisted in my gut, something that told me we weren't ready for what was coming next.

And as the clock ticked on, I realized that none of us might be.

Chapter 29: Shattered Promises

The air smelled of smoke and something fouler, something that clung to the back of my throat like regret. The fire had been raging for hours, consuming everything in its path, its flames licking the edges of what was once a thriving, industrious warehouse. The acrid scent of charred wood and melted plastic made my stomach twist, even though I'd seen it all before. This time, though, it felt different. It felt personal. There was no escaping the irony—the destruction of evidence was almost as calculated as it was brutal. The fire had devoured not only the building but the fragile hope that had been flickering in the pit of my stomach for the past few weeks. All our leads, all the painstaking work we'd put in, reduced to ash in the space of a few hours.

The charred remnants of what had once been a complex labyrinth of files, photographs, and witness statements lay scattered before me, the fire's aftertaste still hanging in the air. The fire trucks had left their blackened tire tracks across the wet pavement, their presence an unfortunate reminder that this was the third time in the last month we'd been dealt this blow. "You think it's deliberate?" I asked, though the answer was as clear as the smoke curling in the air.

Callum was silent beside me, his eyes trained on the rubble, his hand gripping his phone with enough pressure that I thought it might snap in his palm. It didn't. But the tension radiating off him might as well have been a physical thing, thick enough to cut through.

"Arson. No doubt in my mind," he finally muttered, his voice low and hard, like it was wrapped in a layer of steel. He didn't look at me when he spoke, his gaze locked on the scene, his lips barely moving. But I saw the way his jaw clenched, the subtle tightening of his neck muscles that told me he was just as torn up about this as

I was. He'd been the one to push hardest on this case—no surprise there. Callum always did. His stubbornness was legendary, and as much as it irritated me at times, I knew it was the very thing that kept him fighting. But tonight, it felt more like a curse than a blessing. Every time he thought we were close to a breakthrough, the universe seemed hell-bent on proving him wrong.

"I don't get it," I said, my words barely above a whisper. I wasn't talking to him, not really. I was talking to the fire, to the pieces of this nightmare that I couldn't quite put together. "If they're trying to stop us from finding the truth... why keep letting us get so far? Why not just bury us in the first place?"

Callum's eyes shifted then, flicking over to me briefly, the coolness in them betraying a flicker of something deeper—something like frustration, or maybe resignation. He gave a low, frustrated chuckle, one that didn't quite sound like amusement. "Because they want us to chase it. Want us to feel like we're close. It's the game, Emma. They're playing with us, dangling it in front of our faces like a carrot."

I nodded slowly, trying to swallow the lump that had formed in my throat. That made sense, in a twisted sort of way. But knowing why didn't make it any easier.

"I hate this," I murmured, more to myself than to him. The fire had just taken everything we had—our progress, our hopes, the pieces that felt like they were starting to fit.

Callum didn't say anything to that. Instead, he took a long, measured breath, like he was searching for a way to steady himself. He had that distant look on his face now, the one that always came before he started pushing us harder, faster, more relentlessly.

"We're not backing off," he finally said. The words were steel.

I didn't even think to protest, not this time. We were too far in for that. We didn't know who was behind this or why, but we knew one thing: they wanted us to stop. And we weren't about to give them that satisfaction.

I shifted my weight, my boots grinding into the cracked pavement as I glanced at the firemen still working, dousing the last of the embers. Their efforts felt like a joke—how could they put out something that seemed so determined to burn everything to the ground? But then again, it wasn't their job to stop the fire that was burning inside us.

I pushed past the scent of ash and the burn in my eyes, willing myself to focus. "We need to hit them back, Callum. Find a way to get ahead of this." My voice sounded sharper than I felt, and for a moment, I wondered if I believed it, or if I was just saying the words out of sheer desperation. But Callum's face had hardened, and that was all the motivation I needed.

"Right," he said, his lips pressing into a thin line. "I'll pull in more resources. We'll find something they missed."

The promise hung between us, a silent understanding. We had no choice but to keep moving forward. There was no going back now.

Still, the gnawing sense of dread at the back of my mind refused to let go. The more we fought, the more it felt like the truth was slipping through our fingers. The pieces were never quite right, never quite enough to make the whole picture clear. There was something—or someone—out there pulling strings we couldn't see, orchestrating this twisted dance we were stumbling through.

I shook my head, trying to clear it. "Do you ever wonder… if this is all for nothing?"

He didn't flinch at the question, didn't try to placate me. Instead, he just looked at me for a long beat, his eyes dark with some unspoken understanding. The firelight flickered across his face, casting sharp shadows that made him look more haunted than I'd ever seen him.

"Yeah," he said softly. "All the time."

The night crept in slowly, dragging with it a cold that had no business being here this late in the year. I pulled my jacket tighter around me, the fabric barely shielding me from the bone-deep chill as we stood in the shadow of the smoldering wreckage. The fire had consumed everything, but still, I couldn't shake the feeling that there was more to find, some piece of the puzzle that had escaped the flames.

Callum, of course, wasn't looking at the charred remains of the building the way I was. He wasn't looking for anything beyond the next step, his eyes scanning the crowd of firefighters and police officers, their movements efficient, practiced. The glow of the remaining embers made his profile seem harder, more chiseled, as though the fire had sculpted him into something sharper, a man shaped by the flames rather than diminished by them.

"Everything's gone, you know," I muttered, half to myself. My voice cracked in the silence, an echo of frustration that had been building for days. I could almost taste it in the air now, the sharp tang of defeat.

He glanced at me, his face impassive, unreadable, but there was something in the way his brow furrowed—something I hadn't seen before. "Don't do that," he said, voice low, but somehow, it carried. "Don't let the fire win."

I knew what he meant. I did. But the truth was that it was hard not to feel like everything we were doing—every lead we chased, every new question we asked—was pointless. Like we were fighting against a tide that only grew stronger the more we struggled. There was no manual for this, no guide to tell us how to fight an enemy who stayed hidden in the shadows, striking only when we thought we were safe.

"I'm not going to let it win," I said, although I didn't quite believe it. "But it's hard to keep fighting when you can't even see the damn enemy."

There was a pause, and for a moment, I thought he might say something else, something to lighten the weight that seemed to be pressing down on both of us. But instead, Callum just nodded, his eyes drifting back to the fire. He didn't offer words of reassurance. He didn't need to. I knew him well enough by now to understand that he didn't believe in empty promises.

And maybe, just maybe, that was what I needed. Not someone to tell me everything was going to be okay, but someone who would keep walking forward with me, even when the ground beneath us was nothing but ash and ruin.

The silence between us stretched, thick and uncomfortable. The fire trucks had finally cleared out, the last of their sirens fading into the night, but the smell of burning lingered. It wasn't just the smell of wood or paper or plastic, but something older, more primal—the scent of destruction, of things being undone, and it clung to the air like a warning.

"Do you think we're getting closer?" I asked suddenly, the words tumbling out before I could stop them. It felt like the right question to ask, even though the answer was almost too obvious to bear.

Callum didn't answer immediately. Instead, he took a slow breath, his gaze sweeping over the aftermath of the fire. His eyes were dark, distant, and for a second, I wondered if he was going to tell me what I didn't want to hear. That we were chasing shadows, that the truth was as elusive as the smoke rising from the ruins. But then, with a grunt of frustration, he turned to face me.

"Closer? Maybe," he said, his tone rough, like he hadn't meant to speak the words aloud. "But it doesn't feel like it."

I met his eyes, my stomach twisting with a strange mix of anxiety and something else—something I couldn't quite name. Callum didn't get rattled. Ever. Not in front of me, not in front of anyone. But I could see it in the way his jaw tightened and his shoulders stiffened. The weight of this case was starting to press down on him, too.

"Well, then what?" I shot back, sharper than I'd meant. "What do we do when we're not closer? When every step forward just pulls us deeper into this mess?"

He looked at me for a long moment, and I could feel the shift in the air between us, the tension thickening until it was almost unbearable. But instead of answering, Callum did something he hadn't done in a long time—he reached for me, pulling me in by the wrist with an urgency that caught me off guard.

I stumbled a step forward, my heart hammering in my chest, but it wasn't fear that made it race. No, it was something else, something I hadn't let myself acknowledge in far too long.

"Emma," he said, his voice quieter now, like the storm inside him was slowly passing. "This isn't just about the case anymore. It's not just about finding the truth."

I stared up at him, my breath caught in my throat, unsure of what he was saying. The words hung between us, charged with an energy I couldn't quite explain, but it wasn't the kind of energy that belonged here, not in the aftermath of a fire, not in the middle of a case that had already consumed too much of us.

"What do you mean?" I whispered, my voice barely audible.

He didn't answer immediately. Instead, he let go of my wrist, his fingers brushing mine in a way that felt like both an apology and a promise. His expression softened, but only for a second—long enough for me to catch the glimmer of something unspoken behind his eyes.

"I mean... we're in this together," he said finally. "All the way."

And just like that, the last shred of doubt I'd been carrying about this case, about him, about us—it evaporated. It didn't matter how far this went or how much more we'd have to endure. Whatever came next, we were in it together. And that—at least for tonight—was enough to keep me moving forward.

The first rays of morning filtered through the haze of smoke still lingering in the air, casting a weak light over the wreckage of what had once been the center of our investigation. The embers were nearly extinguished, but the faint glow of destruction was still alive, simmering under the surface, as though the fire might choose to resurface at any moment. It felt like the kind of day where nothing would ever feel right again, where the weight of what we'd lost—of what we were still losing—was too heavy to carry.

I pushed my hands deeper into the pockets of my coat, trying to force some warmth into my chilled fingers, but it didn't help. I was beyond cold now. Cold from the fire, yes, but also cold from the realization that we were standing at the edge of something bigger than we had ever anticipated. Something that had the power to consume everything in its path.

Callum was quieter than usual, which, given the situation, was saying something. His eyes remained fixed on the smoldering building, but his mind was far away, spinning, recalculating. I could almost hear the gears turning in his head, trying to figure out how to piece together the wreckage, how to make sense of the chaos.

"Do you ever think we're just... out of our depth?" I asked, my voice breaking the silence between us.

He didn't look at me immediately. His jaw tensed, and for a brief second, I wondered if he'd heard me at all. I'd never asked him a question like that before, and I wasn't sure if it was even fair to. But the frustration was spilling out of me, the constant rush of dead ends and lost time wearing me thin.

"We've been out of our depth since day one," he said finally, his voice rough but not unkind. "You know that. The only difference now is that we're starting to see just how deep it goes."

I blinked, the gravity of his words settling in. The truth of it was, I hadn't thought about it that way. I'd been so wrapped up in the details, in each individual fire, each new clue, each dead-end, that I hadn't allowed myself to step back and see the bigger picture. We weren't just fighting a case. We were fighting something far larger than either of us had anticipated. And that realization... it felt like the floor had just dropped out from under me.

"What if it's too much, Callum?" The words spilled out before I could stop them, the vulnerability there raw and unmasked. "What if it's bigger than we are? What if we're not strong enough to—"

"Don't," he interrupted, his voice sharp, like he was slicing through the air between us. He turned toward me, his expression softened, but the resolve in his eyes was still burning brightly. "Don't do that. Don't let them win by making you doubt yourself."

I was taken aback, not by the intensity of his words, but by the sudden shift in his tone, the way he seemed to square his shoulders against the weight of the world. For a second, I saw something new in him—something deeper, more vulnerable, perhaps, than I'd ever seen. And it caught me off guard.

"I wasn't doubting myself," I said, though I knew he could see through me. "I was doubting everything else. Us. The case. I don't even know what we're fighting for anymore."

He stepped closer, the distance between us suddenly shrinking, and for a fleeting moment, it felt like the world had paused, like the noise and confusion of the investigation, of the endless night, had disappeared entirely. He looked at me, really looked at me, and for the first time since we'd started this, I felt like he was seeing me, not just as the woman beside him in the investigation, but as someone who was just as lost and unsure as he was.

"We fight for the truth," he said quietly, his voice low enough that I could hear the weight of the promise in it. "That's all we have left."

I swallowed hard, the knot in my throat threatening to choke me, but I refused to give into it. We couldn't afford to be weak, not now. Not with the fire still burning inside us, both literal and figurative.

"You think we'll find it?" I asked, my voice smaller than I intended. My eyes searched his, hoping for some kind of reassurance, some glimmer of the certainty he always seemed to carry with him. But his gaze was just as uncertain as mine, a storm of doubt raging beneath the surface.

"I hope so," he said, and I couldn't tell if he was answering my question or his own. But the truth was, hope wasn't enough. Not anymore.

The sound of footsteps broke through the fragile silence between us, and I turned to see a figure approaching—one of the officers we'd been working with. He was walking briskly, his face tight with something I couldn't quite place, but it was clear from the look on his face that he had news.

"We've got a lead," the officer said, his voice sharp and low. "But you're not going to like it."

I exchanged a glance with Callum, and without a word, we followed the officer, our footsteps crunching over the gravel and ash. My heart raced in my chest, the uncertainty pressing down harder than ever. What could possibly be worse than this?

As we reached the back of the warehouse, the officer stopped, his eyes darting around nervously before he leaned in close, his voice barely above a whisper.

"We found something. A note. It's addressed to you."

The words hit me like a physical blow. My pulse jumped, and I felt the blood drain from my face. The officer handed me a small, folded piece of paper, its edges singed but still legible.

I unfolded it slowly, the weight of the moment crushing down on me with each breath I took.

It was simple, almost mocking in its brevity.

"Stop digging. You won't like what you find."

And beneath it, there was a single, jagged line drawn through the paper, as though someone had slashed it with a knife.

I looked up at Callum, my throat tight with the realization that we had crossed a line. Whatever game we were playing, it was no longer just a case. We had become part of something much darker.

The question wasn't just about finding the truth anymore. The question was whether we'd survive it.

Chapter 30: Ashes of Yesterday

The air tasted of smoke again, clinging to my clothes, my hair, to the very core of my lungs, as if I would never be rid of it. Every step I took felt like wading through a haze of memories—none of them good, all of them burnt beyond recognition. The fire trucks had long since stopped their incessant wailing, their red lights no longer casting shadows on the cracked pavement, but the smell of charred wood and the bitter tang of regret still swirled around the empty street. The city felt abandoned, as if it, too, had given up.

I tried not to let my hands shake as I dusted ash from the collar of my jacket, but my fingers betrayed me. How could they not? I had watched it all burn again, every building that had once stood with pride now reduced to smoldering skeletons, like the twisted remnants of a life I'd hoped for. A life that felt as fragile and fleeting as the smoke rising into the dark sky.

Callum's voice broke through the silence, low and rough. "We can't keep doing this." He stepped into my line of sight, his dark eyes heavy with the weight of the night's loss, but it wasn't just the fire he carried—it was something else, something I didn't want to face.

I didn't want to look at him. Not like this. Not when I felt like a stranger in my own skin. I could feel his presence like an electric charge, something between us that had never been there before, something cold and dangerous. The air around us hummed with it, thick with tension. A tension that started long before the fires.

"Don't," I said, not trusting myself to speak any louder. My voice was weak, cracking like the shattered glass that littered the ground at our feet. "You don't get to make this about us."

He flinched, but I didn't look at him. I couldn't. If I did, I was afraid the walls I'd built around my heart would crumble completely. And in this moment, I needed them. The truth was,

I was scared. Of him. Of me. Of what we had let slip through our fingers. Of everything that had led us here, to this point of no return.

"Is that what you think?" he asked, his voice softening, but there was a sharpness there too, a trace of something I couldn't name. "That this is just about us?"

I finally met his gaze, and the world seemed to stop for a second. His face was shadowed in the dim light, the lines of stress and exhaustion etched deeper than before. His jaw was clenched, his lips pressed into a thin line that made me want to say something, anything, to make it go away. To make the ache that had settled in my chest disappear.

But I didn't. I couldn't. "You think I'm worried about you?" I asked, my voice rising with something that felt dangerously close to bitterness. "I'm worried about the people who died tonight. About the ones who'll keep dying until we stop this. This isn't about us. It never was."

His eyes darkened, and he took a step toward me, closing the space between us like it was nothing. It was too much. Too close. My breath caught in my throat, and for a moment, I thought I might collapse under the weight of everything that was left unsaid. "Don't pretend like you're not running from something," he said quietly, his words almost a whisper. "You've been running for months. Running from me. From this."

I flinched, my stomach twisting. He was right, of course. I had been running. Not just from him, but from the parts of myself I wasn't ready to confront. The parts of me that felt just as burned as the city. The parts that had been scarred by the choices I made, by the secrets I kept.

"Don't," I repeated, but this time, I wasn't sure if I was talking to him or to myself.

Callum's eyes softened, but his hands—his strong, steady hands—came to rest on my shoulders, grounding me. My heart thudded painfully in my chest as I tried to focus on anything but the way his touch made the world feel a little less fractured. "We need to talk, Quinn. We need to figure out what's happening before it gets worse. Before we both do something we can't undo."

I looked away, but I couldn't escape the truth in his words. I could feel the pull of them, drawing me in, forcing me to confront everything I'd been running from. My heart ached with the weight of it, but I refused to let him see it.

"You think I don't know that?" I shot back, suddenly furious, though I wasn't sure if I was mad at him or at myself. "You think I don't know we're running out of time? Out of chances?"

His grip on me tightened, his voice harder now, but there was a crack in it—vulnerable, as if he too was struggling to keep it together. "Then stop running."

I didn't have an answer for that. Because I knew he was right, but I wasn't ready to stop. Not yet. Maybe not ever.

The silence between us stretched, thick and suffocating. The night seemed to hold its breath, waiting for something to give. And in that moment, I wondered if we both were waiting for the same thing—to either break or be fixed. Neither option felt like a victory.

The silence between us stretched into something suffocating. Callum's hand still hovered near my shoulder, as though afraid to make the first move, afraid that touching me would be an admission of the things we both feared but wouldn't say aloud. His breath was warm against my ear, his presence like a magnet pulling me closer even as my instincts screamed to stay away.

I stepped back, just enough to break the tension, but not enough to lose him entirely. The space between us had grown too large in the last few months, but I wasn't sure how to close it without everything around us—everything we had—cracking wide open. "I don't need you to fix this," I said, the words sharp, though I couldn't tell if I meant them.

Callum didn't flinch, his gaze steady and unwavering. "I'm not trying to fix you, Quinn. I'm just trying to find a way out of this mess. Together." His voice was low, the rough edges softened by something almost too vulnerable to acknowledge. His eyes held mine, and for a brief, foolish second, I thought I might just let myself believe him.

I shook my head. "It's too late for that. You can't just—" My voice faltered, and I turned away, fists clenching at my sides. "We've already lost so much. I can't—"

His footsteps followed me, quick and determined. I didn't turn around as I felt his presence just behind me, hovering like a shadow. "I know you're scared. But you don't have to do this alone. Not again."

My chest ached, a deep, gnawing feeling I couldn't shake. Was I scared? Yes, terrified. But I wasn't sure if it was of the fires consuming our city, or the fire that had once burned so brightly between us. The one I had tried so hard to extinguish but couldn't seem to get rid of.

I bit my lip, frustration and fear bubbling up in equal measure. "I don't know what you want from me anymore, Callum. What are we even doing here? Is this about the case or us?" The question hung between us, unanswered.

His silence seemed to stretch on for far too long. When he finally spoke, his voice cracked slightly, as if his resolve was slipping, "Maybe it's both. But if we don't deal with us, Quinn, then what's the point? What's the point in solving this case if we can't even look at each other without pretending like we're not falling apart?"

That hit harder than I expected. The weight of his words, the blunt truth of them, knocked the air from my lungs. We had been pretending, hadn't we? Pretending like we could do this—this job, this... whatever we were—without facing the fact that it was all unraveling. Like the arsonist's fires, it wasn't just the buildings burning; it was everything around us.

I turned to face him then, my mouth dry, my heart hammering in my chest. "What if we can't fix it? What if it's already gone too far?"

Callum stepped closer, his hands at his sides, his expression torn. "Then we find a way to fix what we can, before it burns us all to the ground."

The sincerity in his eyes almost made me believe him. But the doubt still lingered, festering like a wound that wouldn't heal. "You think I don't want that? You think I don't want to stop running and just... trust that things can be okay again?"

"Then why don't you?"

I laughed bitterly, turning my back on him once more, though I could feel the heat of his gaze on my skin. "Because it's easier to run. It always has been."

I heard his sharp intake of breath, but he didn't argue. Not immediately. Instead, I felt the weight of his gaze shift, and I knew he was calculating something—an angle, a way to reach me. Maybe it was the detective in him, but I was already too far gone for that kind of logic.

The last few months had been an exercise in survival, both of the city and myself. Each night felt like a countdown, the fires growing ever closer, the tension stretching tighter with every moment we failed to catch the arsonist. The press was losing patience, the public was growing restless, and somewhere, deep down, I knew it was only a matter of time before the truth came to light—the truth about the fire, and about what we had become.

"I'm not asking for trust, Quinn," Callum said, his voice low, as though the weight of the words mattered more than he was letting on. "I'm asking for a chance. To fix this. Together."

I swallowed hard. "I don't know if I can give you that. Not right now."

His eyes softened, but there was a flicker of something else there. Maybe it was regret. Maybe it was anger. I couldn't tell. But there was something undeniably raw in his expression, something that made the walls around me tremble.

"Then what do you want?" he asked, his tone almost a plea, though I knew he was trying not to sound desperate. But that was the thing about Callum—he never let himself show too much, never let himself get too close. And yet, somehow, with every word he said, every question he asked, I felt like he was peeling me open, layer by painful layer.

I wanted to lie. I wanted to say I knew what I wanted. But I didn't. Not anymore.

"I don't know," I finally admitted, my voice barely above a whisper. "I don't know what I want. I only know that I can't keep doing this."

And in that moment, I knew I was as lost as the city around us, consumed by flames and uncertainty, and I couldn't tell if there was a way out. Or if I even wanted to find one.

The weight of my own silence pressed against me, suffocating any thought that might have offered an escape. I stood there, just out of reach of Callum's touch, as the night enveloped us, thick with the scent of burned wood and the faint hum of distant sirens. It was as if the city itself had become a reflection of everything that had gone wrong—everything we had failed to fix. I wanted to walk away, wanted to tell him that there was no point in continuing this conversation. But something in his gaze anchored me, even as I fought to stay afloat in the flood of emotion he stirred.

"Quinn," he murmured, stepping closer again, his voice low and steady, like he was trying to keep the storm in check. "If we don't do something now—if we don't start facing what's happening between us—then we might not get another chance."

I took a deep breath, trying to steady my pulse, but the words felt foreign, trapped somewhere between my chest and my throat. He was right, of course. The thing was, it wasn't just about him or me anymore—it was about the city, about the fires that threatened to consume everything, every hope and every dream we had built together. I could feel the tremor in my hands as I clenched them into fists, my nails biting into my palms.

"You don't get to pull me into this, Callum," I said, a bite to my words that was as much a defense mechanism as it was a rejection. "You don't get to make it about us when there are people out there who need answers."

His expression shifted, a mix of frustration and something softer, something that tugged at the edges of my resolve. "You think I don't know that? You think I don't know how many lives are on the line?" He closed the distance between us, his voice rising, just barely, with the weight of the truth. "But how many more are we willing to lose before we face what's right in front of us?"

I flinched. His words, raw and honest, felt like a punch to the gut. There was truth in them—too much truth. But that didn't mean I was ready to swallow it whole. "I'm not some case to solve, Callum," I said, though the ache in my chest told a different story. "I'm not some... some puzzle for you to fix. I'm not ready to let you back in."

His jaw clenched, and for a moment, I thought he might argue. But he didn't. Instead, he stood there, eyes searching mine like he was trying to read a map of every fracture between us. It wasn't fair, this feeling of being torn between two opposing forces: the woman I was, the detective who had been taught to solve problems with precision and logic, and the woman I had been with him. The woman I didn't know if I could ever be again.

"You don't have to be ready," he said, his voice rough, like the words were hard for him to say. "I'll wait. But we don't have time to wait on this case. You've seen it. The fire... it's just the beginning."

I shook my head, the weight of the truth pressing down on me. "I don't need you to wait for me." I turned, feeling the sting of tears I refused to acknowledge. "I don't need you to save me."

His fingers brushed the back of my arm before I could pull away, a soft touch that made my breath catch. I refused to turn around, didn't want him to see the crack in my armor, but I felt the heat of his presence behind me, steady and unwavering. "I'm not trying to save you. I'm trying to help you save everyone else. But I can't do that if you keep pushing me away."

I inhaled sharply, unwilling to acknowledge the shift that was happening, unwilling to admit that part of me was listening. "What if I can't do this anymore?" The words slipped out, raw and unguarded, and I immediately regretted them.

Callum's hand, still on my arm, tightened just slightly. It wasn't a question; it was a lifeline. "You can," he said simply. "You've always been stronger than you think. Stronger than I ever gave you credit for."

There it was, that vulnerability I had tried so hard to ignore. That flicker of warmth that reminded me of what we once had—before the distance grew too wide, before the fire became more than just a metaphor. But I couldn't let it go. Not yet. Not when everything was still burning, inside and out.

"I'm not sure I believe you," I said, my voice barely above a whisper, as I pulled away from him once more, my feet taking me down the darkened street, away from the ruins and away from him.

"Then make me prove it," he called after me, his voice reaching me even as I moved further into the shadows of the night.

I didn't turn back. But the sound of his voice lingered, like a promise, or maybe a threat. Either way, I knew I had already made my choice. We were running out of time—not just to stop the arsonist, but to stop ourselves from falling apart. And I wasn't sure we had what it took to keep it together.

The wind shifted suddenly, whipping through the empty street, and something about the way it carried the scent of smoke made my heart skip a beat. There was a noise ahead of me—soft, barely perceptible—but I recognized it for what it was. Footsteps. Heavy ones. Someone was following me.

I stopped dead in my tracks, my hand instinctively going to the gun at my side, but before I could turn around, I heard a voice. Familiar. Dangerous.

"Did you think you could run forever?"

I froze, every muscle tensing. My heart pounded against my ribs as the world around me seemed to hold its breath. And then, just as quickly as the words had been spoken, everything went black.

Chapter 31: The Breaking Point

The storm had come in the night, fierce and sudden, as though the heavens themselves had conspired to reflect the chaos brewing in my chest. The rain lashed against the windows with a rhythmic insistence, each drop a drumbeat in the background of the thick silence that had settled between Callum and me. The house felt too big now, each room echoing with the ghosts of laughter, of whispered secrets shared in the early mornings, of promises made and never broken. And yet, here we were, two strangers, bound by a betrayal neither of us could have predicted, each of us trapped in a world that no longer made sense.

Callum hadn't said a word since the discovery. His face, usually so animated, had become a mask of numb disbelief. It was as if the very fabric of his being had been stretched too thin and now threatened to unravel. I couldn't blame him, of course. If anything, I understood all too well the devastation that had settled in his bones, in his posture, in the way he refused to look me in the eye. The betrayal wasn't just a personal one—it had shaken him to his core, a deep, violent rupture of everything he had believed in.

It was hard to say which part of it hurt the most—the fact that we had been so wrong, or the realization that the person responsible was someone who had stood by our side from the beginning, someone who had been in the very heart of our most trusted circle. The shock was still too raw, too fresh, to fully comprehend. Each time I replayed the events in my head, trying to make sense of it, the pieces never quite fit together. And yet, here we were, on the precipice of something neither of us was prepared for.

I had tried to talk to Callum, tried to break through the suffocating wall of his silence, but each attempt had only made him retreat further into himself. He spent his days locked away in his study, buried in papers and files, as if searching for a way to prove that we were wrong, that there had been some mistake. But there was no mistake. The evidence was damning, clear as day. And I couldn't escape the sickening truth that it had been right in front of us the whole time.

It was in the little things, the subtle signs we had overlooked. The way they always seemed to know just enough to steer us in the wrong direction. The odd coincidences that had seemed harmless at the time. The way their assurances had felt too smooth, too practiced, like a mask worn just a little too long. I hated myself for not seeing it sooner, for trusting them as implicitly as I had. But what was worse—what made the betrayal sting like acid—was that Callum had trusted them too.

That thought made me hesitate, my breath catching in my throat. He hadn't said it, but I knew he was questioning everything now. The way his hand tightened on the edge of his coffee cup that morning, the flicker of guilt that passed over his face when he met my gaze. He was blaming himself, and maybe I was too, in my quieter moments. How had we been so blind?

I closed my eyes and leaned against the cool stone of the fireplace, letting the faint smell of wood and soot ground me. I could hear the distant rumble of thunder, but it did little to ease the ache in my chest. I wanted to fix this, wanted to reach out to Callum, but something inside me was frozen, caught between a longing for his touch and a fear that it would only make the rupture deeper. What was left between us now? Could we still be what we once were, or had everything changed beyond repair?

The door to the study creaked open, and I straightened, my pulse quickening. Callum stepped into the room, his eyes shadowed and distant, his features unreadable. For a long moment, neither of us spoke. The only sound was the crackle of the fire, the wind howling just outside the window. He looked as if he hadn't slept in days, his hair tousled, his jaw clenched tight, but still, he was here, in the same room as me, and that was something I clung to with the last vestiges of hope.

"I've been thinking," he said, his voice low, like it was hard for him to get the words out.

"About what?" I asked, the word slipping out before I could stop it. I hated how strained it sounded, like we were strangers again, stumbling through a conversation we weren't ready for.

"About everything." He ran a hand through his hair, the movement slow, deliberate. "About... about how we got here."

There was a bitterness in his tone now, something sharp and bitter that hadn't been there before. It made my stomach tighten. I swallowed, trying to ignore the lump that had formed in my throat. I didn't know if I could bear hearing him say the things I feared the most—that this was it, that we were done.

But Callum didn't give me that. Instead, he stepped closer, his eyes meeting mine with a fierce intensity that left no room for escape. "We trusted them, you know?" His voice cracked, and the raw pain in it hit me like a physical blow.

I nodded, the weight of his words settling over me. There was no need to say more. The betrayal was not just about the facts we had uncovered, not just about the lies, but about the slow erosion of trust, the thing that had once held us together. The truth was, I didn't know if I could survive without it, and I wasn't sure if Callum could either. But I couldn't bring myself to say that out loud—not when everything between us felt so fragile, so fractured.

"I don't know what to do now," I whispered, the confession slipping from my lips before I had a chance to stop it. "I don't know how to fix this."

Callum stared at me for a long moment, and when he spoke again, his voice was quiet, almost detached. "Maybe it can't be fixed."

The words hung between us, heavy and unyielding, and for the first time in days, I didn't know how to breathe.

I didn't know how long I had been standing there, staring at the flickering shadows on the walls, but when I finally turned away, I was surprised to find that the storm outside had abated. The wind had dulled to a soft murmur, and the sky had shifted from a bruised grey to something softer, almost forgiving. But the calm did nothing to ease the knots in my chest. Everything felt hollow—like I was walking through a world that was slowly unraveling around me, a place that had once been so full of color and sound but now stood muted, stripped of the vibrancy I had known.

Callum had retreated again. I had known he would. But there was a distance between us now that was different—less about the physical space and more about something intangible, like an invisible barrier woven out of threads of silence and unspoken words. I should have gone to him, should have tried to bridge the gap that had grown so wide between us, but I couldn't make myself move. What could I say? How could I fix this when it felt like everything I touched turned to dust?

I wandered aimlessly through the house, my mind a swirl of fragmented thoughts, each one sharper than the last. In the kitchen, I ran my fingers over the countertop, feeling the cool smoothness beneath my fingertips. It was a silly, pointless gesture, but it grounded me in a way that nothing else had. As if, in some small way, I was still in control of something. The stillness was suffocating, though. The kind that sinks into your bones, that makes you question the very air you breathe.

I hated the silence. It clung to the space around me, heavy and thick, the absence of Callum's voice a constant reminder of how everything had changed. He had been so full of life, so full of that strange, captivating energy that drew everyone in. Now, his presence felt like a ghost—there, but not really. I hadn't realized until that moment just how much I had depended on him to be the one who made everything make sense. Now, without him, the pieces scattered like shards of glass, sharp and jagged and impossible to piece together.

I moved to the window, parting the curtains just enough to peek outside. The garden, once so carefully tended to, now looked wild—untamed, as though nature had finally rebelled against the order we had tried to impose on it. I supposed it was fitting. What had we ever been, if not a bit of well-ordered chaos pretending to be something more? It wasn't lost on me that I had ignored the signs, just as the garden had been left to overgrow. It had all seemed so small, so insignificant, until it was too late to fix it.

I let the curtain fall back into place with a soft sigh. The house felt cold now, in a way that had nothing to do with the temperature. I could still hear the creaking of the floorboards upstairs, the faintest sound of Callum's footsteps as he paced in his own private hell. I hated that I couldn't reach him, hated that I didn't know what to say to make it better. Was there even anything left to salvage? Was this the end of something that had once felt so certain, so unshakable?

The sound of a door opening interrupted my thoughts, and I froze, my heart jumping into my throat. It wasn't like I expected to hear anything at all. Maybe I had imagined it, the footsteps, the creaking, but then I heard it again—the sound of Callum descending the stairs. A slow, deliberate sound. Each step seemed weighted, like he was carrying something heavy, something that pressed down on him from all sides.

I turned, half expecting to see him standing there in the doorway, but when I glanced up, I found that the room was empty. The silence was still there, filling the space in a way that felt suffocating. It was almost worse when he wasn't there, his absence more present than his presence.

I shook my head, willing the thoughts to stop. I couldn't do this. I couldn't fall apart, not now. Not when we were already hanging by a thread.

With a deep breath, I moved toward the door. I had to see him. I had to say something—anything. The alternative was worse: letting this tension, this disconnection, fester between us like an open wound. And maybe that was what scared me the most. Because if I didn't say anything, if I didn't take that step, what would become of us? Would we simply slip into nothingness, becoming strangers to each other, our once-shared memories fading into the past like shadows in the dark?

I found him in the library, standing by the window, his back to me. The way he stood there, so still, so distant, made my heart ache. It was like he had become a part of the room, part of the landscape—frozen in time, locked away in a place where nothing could reach him. I hesitated, my hand resting on the doorframe, unsure whether to speak or to leave him in his isolation.

He turned slowly, his gaze locking with mine, and I saw the storm still raging in his eyes. It was a different storm now—one that was darker, more dangerous. I couldn't decide whether I was afraid of the look in his eyes, or whether I was more afraid of the fact that I recognized it. The weight of everything we had just discovered—the betrayal, the lies, the shattered trust—it hung between us, a tangible thing.

"Don't," he said quietly, his voice rough and strained. It was as though he could read my thoughts, as though he knew the words I had been preparing to say.

But I didn't stop. I couldn't. "I'm sorry," I whispered, though it didn't feel like enough. It never would be.

Callum's lips twitched, and for a fleeting moment, I thought I saw a flicker of something—anger, maybe, or frustration—but it was gone before I could make sense of it. "Sorry," he repeated, his voice thick with emotion. "You think that's going to fix this?"

I took a step forward, my heart pounding in my chest. I didn't have the answers. I didn't know how to fix anything. But I was here. And somehow, that had to count for something. "No," I said, "but maybe it's a start."

For a long time, neither of us spoke. The air between us crackled with the tension, thick and suffocating, but it was there. That small spark of something, still alive, still flickering. And maybe, just maybe, that was all we needed to begin again.

It wasn't until later that night that I realized the sound I'd been listening for—the creak of footsteps, the sigh of someone standing in the hallway—wasn't Callum at all. It was me. I was the one lingering just out of reach, unsure of where to place my next step. The air in the house was thick, almost suffocating, with something ancient and unspoken, like the walls were holding their breath, waiting for us to make some kind of reckoning. Every time I thought I could breathe, it was as though the house pressed in harder, the silence louder.

I wanted to ask him what he was thinking, but there was no way I could phrase it. How do you ask someone what's going on inside their head when you know they're just as confused as you? How do you open the door to a conversation that might tear everything apart? My fingertips brushed the edge of the banister, the wood smooth but strangely cold beneath my touch. I was at the edge, staring down a precipice, and I didn't know which way to jump.

I moved through the darkened hallway, my feet muffled by the thick carpet, each step dragging me further into the void. There was something comforting in the quiet of the night, the kind of silence that stretches between two people who don't know how to speak to each other anymore. But that comfort had its own cost. The longer

I waited, the more I feared that we'd drift apart entirely—that our hearts would simply refuse to find their way back to each other.

When I reached the study, I found the door ajar. The faint glow of the desk lamp spilled into the hallway, the only light in the house that seemed alive. Callum sat at the desk, his back turned to me, fingers tapping restlessly against the wood. He looked as if he were trying to write, trying to do something that could anchor him to the present, but the paper in front of him remained blank.

I stood there for a long moment, hesitant, unsure whether to make my presence known or slip quietly away. He hadn't said much in the past hours, and each word that had come out of his mouth had been laced with a kind of despair I couldn't quite place. I didn't know if I was supposed to wait for him to talk first or force the conversation myself.

It felt like I was waiting for some kind of sign, something that would tell me how to proceed. But there was no sign. Just me, and the weight of everything that had come before.

"Callum," I said, the name a fragile thing on my tongue, like it was a thread pulling me closer to him. His shoulders stiffened, and for a moment, I thought he might pretend he hadn't heard me. But then he turned, slowly, his eyes catching mine with a kind of rawness that stopped me cold.

"I don't know what to do with this," he muttered, a half-laugh escaping him as he ran a hand through his hair. "How do you fix something like this, Liv?"

I didn't have an answer. If I did, I'd have said it already. I took a step closer, my pulse quickening, unsure if I should offer comfort or distance, reassurance or a moment of silence. "I don't know either," I whispered. "I just know we can't keep pretending like everything's okay when it isn't."

The way he looked at me then... it wasn't just pain. There was something deeper, something I couldn't quite name. It was like he was fighting a war inside, and I was caught right in the middle of it. "It's not that simple," he said, voice rougher than before. "We don't just move on from this. It's... too much."

"I know," I replied, my voice barely a murmur. "But staying in this place where we don't talk, where we just... pretend it doesn't hurt—" I stopped myself, taking a steadying breath. The words felt too raw, too exposed. "That's not living. And we both deserve more than that."

There was a flicker in his eyes, a moment where I thought he might reach for me, but instead, he pushed back from the desk. The chair scraped against the floor, the sound louder than I expected. He stood and walked toward the window, his back to me again, staring out into the darkness like he was searching for something he couldn't find.

I stood frozen, helpless in my desire to help him, knowing that no matter how badly I wanted to make things right, I couldn't. I couldn't fix what had been broken, and I couldn't make him feel something he wasn't ready to feel. And yet, I stayed. I stayed because even in the silence, there was a part of me that refused to believe we were beyond saving.

When Callum spoke again, his voice was barely audible, his words heavy with emotion. "What if we can't come back from this? What if this—what's between us—has already been lost?"

I could feel my heart fracture under the weight of his words, but I refused to let him see how much it affected me. I took a deep breath, forcing myself to stay steady. "We don't know that," I said, my voice firm, but inside, I was shaking. "We can't just give up."

He turned then, and for the first time in hours, he looked at me like he was really seeing me. The distance between us felt insurmountable, and yet, I didn't move. I stood there, waiting, unsure if I was offering him my heart or my resignation.

"I don't want to give up," he said, his voice quiet but desperate. "But I don't know how to trust anymore."

There it was. The unspoken truth that hung between us like an immovable object. The trust was shattered, cracked beyond repair, and I didn't know how to put it back together. But we had to try, didn't we? Wasn't that the only way forward?

I took a tentative step toward him, and he didn't move away, but his body was rigid, like he was bracing for something. For me, for himself. I reached out, my hand trembling, but before I could touch him, the sound of the doorbell rang through the house, sharp and sudden, cutting through the thick tension between us.

We both froze, and for a moment, neither of us moved. Then Callum's eyes shifted to mine, something unreadable passing across his face. "You expecting someone?" he asked, his voice tight.

"No," I said, a chill running down my spine. Whoever it was, they weren't welcome.

I didn't need to ask who it could be. Neither of us did.

And then, before we could even decide what to do next, the door creaked open, and a voice we both recognized too well called out from the hallway.

Chapter 32: The Final Inferno

The night air clung to my skin, thick with the bitter scent of burnt wood and metal. The sirens had long since stopped their wail, leaving the city to settle into a suffocating silence, broken only by the occasional crackle of embers stubbornly refusing to die. Callum stood a few feet away, his hands shoved deep into the pockets of his leather jacket, his jaw tight enough to crack. He looked like someone who had lived through a thousand storms and come out drenched, but still standing. I'd always admired that about him—his resilience—but tonight, it felt like there was something different about him, something that didn't belong.

"You sure about this?" he asked, his voice low and tight, like a drawn bowstring.

I didn't need to ask what he meant. The arsonist we'd been chasing for months was close, dangerously close, and I could feel it in my bones. Every instinct screamed at me to turn and walk away, to leave it to the authorities and let them handle the rest. But I couldn't. Not when it was my city burning, not when it was our lives being shredded by someone too cowardly to face the truth.

"I'm sure," I replied, my voice steady despite the panic clawing at my ribs. "I'm not letting him get away this time."

Callum's gaze flicked over me, sharp and calculating, as though weighing whether he should argue or just let me do what I was so damn determined to do. He didn't argue. Instead, he exhaled, a puff of breath that seemed to carry with it every ounce of frustration and hope he'd ever felt in the face of failure. We both knew that one misstep, one second too long of hesitation, and this would all end in flames.

We moved in silence, the glow of the distant fire lighting up the street like the angry eye of some sleeping beast. Every step seemed to echo louder than the last, my boots tapping on the cracked pavement like a countdown to something inevitable. I'd heard the stories. A city devoured by flames, a face that would haunt your dreams long after the smoke had cleared. But I never thought it would come to this. Not like this.

The cold bit at my face, but I barely felt it. My mind was too consumed with what lay ahead, with the fire, with the man who had left a trail of destruction behind him. We were close now, just a few blocks away, and I could feel the weight of it—could feel the pounding of my heart in my ears as we approached the old warehouse that had become the center of the investigation.

It was the kind of place where bad things happened. The kind of place where good people went to disappear.

"Ready?" Callum asked, his voice barely above a whisper.

I nodded, my fingers curling around the handle of the gun at my side, though I didn't feel any safer with it there. Nothing would make me feel safe tonight. Not the gun. Not Callum's presence. Not the city that seemed to pulse with the rhythm of its own impending destruction.

We crept forward, every shadow in the alleyway stretching out like a threat. My eyes darted around, scanning every corner, every doorway, every movement in the periphery. Nothing moved. But there was something in the air, something electric, something that made the hairs on the back of my neck stand up straight.

"Stay close," Callum muttered, taking the lead as we neared the warehouse's rusted metal doors.

I followed, trying to keep my breathing steady despite the panic that wanted to claw its way up my throat. We reached the entrance, and Callum gave the door a firm push. It creaked open, the sound too loud for my liking. The inside was dark, the kind of dark where you couldn't even see your own hand in front of your face. But we weren't here to look at the walls.

The air smelled of stale tobacco and gasoline, the pungent odor of something that had been left to rot. A single light flickered overhead, casting sickly shadows across the floor. There was no one waiting for us. No grand confrontation, no trap waiting to spring. Just the deep, unsettling quiet of a place long abandoned.

"Nothing's ever easy with you, is it?" I muttered under my breath.

Callum didn't answer, his eyes scanning the room like a hawk, every inch of him poised for action. I could see the way his muscles tensed, the way his body prepared for whatever was coming next, and I knew that if we were going to make it out of this alive, we had to stay sharp.

The sound of something shifting from the far corner of the room made us both freeze. It was almost imperceptible, but it was there. Like the sound of a whisper just out of reach.

"Got him," Callum hissed, his hand darting toward me, pulling me back into the shadows.

Before I could ask what he meant, the world exploded. A flash of movement, a spark, and then the sound of a match striking. The stench of kerosene filled the air as a fire flared to life in the far corner.

I stumbled backward, my heart racing, as Callum swore under his breath. The flames leapt higher, licking at the exposed beams above us, casting everything in a red, oppressive glow. My eyes darted to Callum, his jaw clenched, his hands outstretched, as though trying to will the fire into submission.

"This is it," I said, my voice shaking despite myself. "This is what he's been leading us to."

"We don't have time to be scared," Callum replied, his voice steady. "We end this now."

We both turned toward the blaze, knowing there was no turning back.

The fire was rising like an angry beast, its flames licking at the metal beams overhead, twisting and curling with a life of their own. The heat pressed against my skin, threatening to swallow me whole, but I couldn't tear my gaze away from the chaos unfolding before me. I could hear the crackle of the flames, the sound of them devouring everything in their path. The warehouse, once a hulking mass of rust and disuse, was now a stage for something darker than I'd ever imagined.

Callum's hand was steady at my back, guiding me as we moved further into the room, closer to the source of the fire. I could feel the tension in his grip—strong, protective, and yet strained. We'd been through hell together, but this? This was different. This was the endgame.

"You're not thinking of running in there, are you?" I asked, my voice coming out sharper than I intended. I could hear the panic beneath my words, but I couldn't stop it.

Callum glanced at me, his eyes flashing with something I couldn't quite place. His expression was unreadable, but there was something in the tightness of his jaw that made me think he wasn't going to answer.

"Stay close," was all he said, his voice low, commanding. There was an edge to it now, one that made me want to argue, but I didn't.

There wasn't time for that.

I swallowed my nerves and followed him, my heart thumping against my chest like it might break free and run. The warehouse was eerily quiet except for the roaring fire. No footsteps, no other voices. It was just us and the arsonist. And yet, even though we were so close, I had the feeling we weren't alone. Something about this place—the shadows that clung to every surface, the way the air felt too thick, too full of secrets—told me the arsonist was watching us.

"Are you sure we're not walking into a trap?" I asked, trying to keep my voice steady. I could feel the tension crackling in the air between us, as if the world itself was holding its breath.

Callum didn't answer immediately, his focus unwavering as he scanned the area around us. There was a flicker in his eyes, something that almost resembled hesitation, but it was gone in an instant.

"No time to second-guess," he said, his voice a low rumble. "We need to get to the back. I think he's there."

"Great," I muttered, my nerves fraying at the edges. "Just what I wanted to hear."

I knew better than to argue, though. We were both past the point of reasoning. There was no going back now.

The fire seemed to pulse, as though it had a mind of its own. The heat intensified as we neared the back of the warehouse, the smoke swirling thick around us, choking the air. Every breath felt like it was pulling me deeper into a haze of panic, but I shoved it aside. There was no time to be afraid—not now, not when we were so close. I could feel the weight of Callum's gaze on me, even though he didn't look at me directly. He was scanning the shadows, the corners, the space between us and the fire.

"I don't like this," I muttered, my voice tight with unease.

"Neither do I," Callum replied, his voice clipped. He wasn't just worried; he was bracing himself. For what, exactly, I wasn't sure. But I didn't have to ask. I knew that this was the part where everything could go wrong.

And just as the words left my mouth, I saw him.

A figure, tall and cloaked in the dark corners of the warehouse, moving with the deliberate grace of someone who had done this too many times before. The arsonist.

He stepped into the flickering light, his face hidden beneath the shadows of his hood. His presence was suffocating—like he belonged to the smoke and the flames. His eyes, cold and unfeeling, flicked toward us, a flash of recognition passing between us. But there was no fear in those eyes. No remorse. Just a sick, twisted satisfaction.

"You think you've won?" he sneered, his voice low, like the hiss of a snake.

I wanted to snap back, to throw a hundred insults at him, but I didn't. Not when I could see the way his hands flexed at his sides, not when I knew he was ready for whatever we threw at him. He wasn't afraid. He never had been.

"No," I said, stepping forward, my voice steady despite the pounding of my heart. "But we're going to stop you."

The words felt hollow as they left my lips. Because I knew. I knew he was too far gone for words to matter now. This wasn't about saving the city anymore. It was about survival.

The arsonist laughed, a low, sick sound that sent a shiver down my spine. "You think you can stop this?" His laugh died abruptly, replaced by something colder, darker. "You're too late."

Before I could react, he stepped forward, and the world exploded into chaos.

The fire seemed to leap higher, its orange tendrils licking at the beams above us like they were hungry for more. The room was filled with a deafening roar as the flames reached out hungrily, threatening to swallow us whole. I tried to backpedal, but the heat was suffocating. The smoke was everywhere, thick and choking, and my lungs burned with every breath.

Callum was already moving, his hand gripping my wrist with an iron strength that pulled me away from the advancing blaze. "Get out of here!" he shouted, his voice barely audible over the roar of the fire.

I stumbled after him, my legs weak with the weight of the heat pressing down on me, but I couldn't move fast enough. The arsonist was laughing again, his silhouette disappearing into the smoke, blending into the chaos like he was part of it.

"Callum!" I shouted, but the words were lost in the crackle of the flames, the world spinning out of control.

I reached for him, my fingers brushing his sleeve, but there was a movement behind me—too fast, too close.

Then, everything went black.

The darkness closed in around me like a suffocating cloak. I blinked against the smoke, trying to clear my vision, but everything was a haze of red and orange, the air thick with the bitter sting of burning everything. My head was spinning, the world reeling in slow motion. I'd never been good at handling the aftermath of chaos—the way everything felt disjointed, like I was stuck in the middle of a storm that refused to pass.

A voice, low and rumbling, sliced through the haze.

"Hold on."

Callum's voice. He was there, somewhere in the darkness, pulling me from the fire, from the madness that had nearly consumed us. My lungs screamed for air as his hand gripped my arm, his fingers cold, urgent. He was still here. Still with me.

I couldn't help but cough, the smoke forcing its way into my chest, constricting my breath. My knees buckled as I tried to stand, but Callum was there, steady, like a wall that wouldn't let me fall.

"Easy," he murmured, lifting me as if I weighed nothing.

But I wasn't sure I could hold myself together much longer. The fire's roar was still echoing in my ears, and the fear, sharp and biting, gnawed at the edges of my mind. Was this it? Was this how it ended—lost in the flames, with nothing but smoke to remember?

"Callum, we... we can't..." I gasped, my voice hoarse, trailing off as I struggled to catch my breath.

His grip tightened, pulling me into the shelter of a crumbling doorway. The heat was still unbearable, and the world seemed to shake beneath my feet. But he didn't stop. Didn't let me go.

"Stay with me, okay?" he said, his voice hoarse, edged with something I couldn't quite place—worry, maybe. Or guilt. Maybe both.

I nodded, too tired to argue. Too tired to question why I wasn't pushing him away like I should have. The fire, the heat, the smoke—they all seemed to blur into one thing: the knowledge that the arsonist was still out there, waiting. Watching.

The thought made my stomach churn, my heart clench. It was too late to go back, to undo the damage. We were too deep in this, too far gone.

But Callum didn't look scared. Not yet. He just kept moving, kept pulling me through the smoke, his body blocking most of the heat, though I could feel the burn licking at my exposed skin. His eyes—those dark eyes that I'd spent so much time studying—were focused, narrowed with determination. He wasn't giving up. Not yet.

I wanted to say something—something witty, maybe, to break the tension—but my mouth was too dry, and I couldn't get my thoughts straight enough. So I just leaned into him, trusting that he would know what to do. That he would get us out of here.

We reached the edge of the warehouse, the heat becoming more unbearable the closer we got. I could feel my legs shaking, my muscles screaming from the strain, but I couldn't stop. Not now.

"Where is he?" I asked, my voice barely a whisper. The thought of the arsonist, of his twisted grin and his sick games, made my blood run cold.

Callum's jaw tightened. He didn't answer at first, but I saw the grim set of his mouth, the way his shoulders tensed as if preparing for the worst. It didn't take a genius to figure out that the arsonist wasn't done. He was never done.

"I'll find him," Callum said, voice quiet but firm. "You just stay close."

The smoke had thinned out a little as we stepped into the open air, but the smell—the sharp, acrid scent of burnt wood and metal—still clung to my nostrils, making my stomach churn.

I looked up at Callum, my hand still gripping his shirt, and for a second, the world seemed to stop. The fire was distant now, but the danger was still there. The weight of everything—the fire, the man we were chasing, the life I thought I knew—hung heavily between us.

It was strange, really. I'd spent so long hating him, fighting him. And now, in the middle of this mess, I realized how much I still needed him. How much I'd always needed him, in a way I hadn't been able to admit until now. Maybe it was the fire. Maybe it was the fear. Or maybe it was just the simple fact that there was nowhere left to run.

"You don't have to do this alone," I said, my voice coming out shaky but strong.

Callum glanced at me, his eyes hard, unreadable. But something shifted in them, something that almost felt like relief. Or maybe it was just a trick of the light, the flickering of the flames catching in his eyes. Either way, it was enough to make me believe, if only for a second, that we weren't completely lost.

"Good to know," he muttered, before turning his gaze toward the crumbling streets in front of us.

We weren't out of the woods yet, but for the first time in a long while, I didn't feel like I was in this alone.

A sudden movement in the distance made us both freeze. A shadow darted across the street, too quick to catch, but I knew it. Knew him. The arsonist.

"Callum," I whispered urgently, "he's here."

Callum's eyes narrowed, his hand tightening on the gun at his side.

"Stay behind me," he said, voice cold, as he began moving toward the shadow, his steps swift and silent, like a predator stalking its prey.

I followed, my heart pounding in my chest. We were close now—too close—and I could feel the tension building in the air around us. The final confrontation was moments away, but something didn't feel right. My skin prickled, a sense of dread creeping over me.

I opened my mouth to speak, to warn Callum, but before I could say anything, I heard the unmistakable click of a gun.

And then—darkness.

Chapter 33: A Glimpse of Redemption

The smoke had barely settled when I stepped out of the house, the acrid scent still thick in the air. It clung to my skin, made my throat ache. It was a smell I couldn't shake, even when I closed my eyes. Even now, after all the chaos, the relief I'd anticipated felt strangely hollow. The fire had taken so much, but I was still here, and so was Callum, standing a few paces away, his posture tentative. There was a crackling tension between us, an uncertainty that hadn't been there before.

I hadn't expected him to be here. Frankly, I'd almost convinced myself that once the dust settled, he'd slip away like everyone else. But instead, there he was, as if waiting for permission to take a step closer, to step into whatever was left of us. His gaze was soft, vulnerable in a way that felt foreign, almost like I was seeing the person behind the carefully constructed walls he'd built. The man who had always kept his distance, guarded his words like they were precious, now exposed. And it wasn't just the ashes that hung between us—it was everything that had led us here.

"Are you alright?" he asked, his voice low, rough in a way that made it sound like a question he hadn't yet fully asked himself. He rubbed the back of his neck, a nervous habit I hadn't seen him do in years. It made him seem almost... human. The way his blue eyes watched me, the flicker of concern that crossed his face—it was a softening, something I hadn't expected from him, certainly not after everything that had gone wrong.

I wanted to shrug it off, to tell him I was fine. It was the easiest thing to do—wrap myself in the armor of indifference, keep the vulnerability tucked away. But for once, I didn't. Instead, I met his gaze and said, "Not exactly. But I'm still here."

I wasn't sure why I said it like that. Maybe it was the shock of the night, or maybe it was the ache in my chest, the sting of everything we'd lost. But as I said the words, I realized that I wasn't just talking about the fire. I wasn't just talking about the damage that had been done to the house, to the case. I was talking about us, too. About what we'd been to each other, and what we'd become.

The silence stretched, thick with unspoken things. And then, with a tentative step forward, Callum broke it.

"I—" He paused, his voice faltering, something heavy in his expression. "I don't know if I can make up for all the time I've wasted, or for the things I didn't do, but... I'm here. If you'll let me."

The sincerity in his words landed like a heavy stone in my chest. I wasn't sure what to do with it. The old part of me—the part that had spent years building walls against disappointment—wanted to pull away, to shield myself. But the part of me that was tired of pretending, that was weary from keeping it all together, wanted to do something else. Wanted to let myself feel the faintest trace of hope, no matter how foolish.

"I don't know what that looks like," I said, my voice quieter now, the words softer than I intended. "But... maybe we could figure it out."

His expression softened, his mouth twitching in the hint of a smile, something cautious but real. "Maybe," he agreed.

The tension that had been thick between us seemed to ease just a fraction, like a crack in a dam that let the light through. But even as I felt the weight of his gaze lift from me, I could sense something else in the air. Something more dangerous than any fire had been. A reckoning, one I hadn't anticipated, and certainly not with him. Not now.

I glanced at the smoldering ruins of the house, the walls blackened and gutted, the foundation still standing in stubborn defiance. Everything had burned, but somehow, here we were, still standing, like survivors of a war we'd never signed up for. And it hit me then, in a sharp breath that caught in my chest. The fire had taken so much. But it had also given me something, too. A chance for redemption. For both of us.

It wasn't going to be easy. I knew that. Redemption never was. It wasn't just about mending what had been broken; it was about finding a way to live in the aftermath of everything we couldn't undo. But maybe, just maybe, this was the beginning of something that could grow in the charred remains of the life we'd left behind.

I reached up, running a hand through my hair, trying to brush away the soot and ash that still clung to me, as if I could somehow wash off the remnants of everything we'd been through. But I knew that wasn't how it worked. The scars would stay, whether we acknowledged them or not. They were part of the story now.

Callum took a slow step closer, his presence a steadying force I hadn't realized I needed. He didn't say anything more. He didn't have to. His silence was enough. We were both still here, still standing, still breathing, and that—against all odds—was something we could build on. Something that hadn't been completely burned away.

The sun dipped lower in the sky, casting long shadows across the ruins of the house, the remnants of what had once been my safe haven. I stood there for a moment, trying to make sense of the strange feeling gnawing at my chest. The emptiness of the place was overwhelming, the walls hollowed out by flames, the floor charred and warped, the scent of soot clinging to everything. But somewhere in the midst of all that destruction, something else was beginning to take shape. It wasn't clear, not yet, but I felt it—an unspoken shift.

I could feel Callum's presence behind me, steady, grounding, but not intrusive. He didn't crowd me with words or gestures. Instead, he let the quiet stretch between us, the only sound the faint whistle of the wind as it passed through the broken windows. There was a raw honesty in the silence, a tension that didn't feel heavy but... different. It was the kind of silence that made you question everything you thought you knew.

I turned to face him, my eyes meeting his with a sudden intensity that surprised me. "What now?" The words were out before I could stop them, more a thought than a question, but there it was. A question I hadn't even known I needed an answer to.

His lips twisted in a faint smile, but it was a rueful thing, the kind that held more weight than I was used to seeing on him. "Now?" he echoed, glancing toward the horizon, where the sun was making its final descent. "I suppose we start figuring that out, don't we?"

His response, so simple and direct, stung in a way I hadn't anticipated. It felt like the weight of all the unspoken things that had passed between us, the history we had and hadn't shared, all rolled into one small, loaded sentence. It wasn't a promise, exactly, but it wasn't a rejection either. It was a suggestion, an invitation, maybe even a plea. And for a brief moment, I found myself wondering if I was ready to take that first step into whatever that "now" meant.

I glanced down at my hands, still slightly trembling, covered in soot and the remnants of something far more significant than just a fire. "I used to think I had it all figured out, you know?" I said, my voice barely above a whisper. "That I could control everything. Make sure nothing slipped through my fingers." I looked up then, meeting his gaze with a sudden clarity I hadn't felt in weeks. "But I was wrong. Nothing is in my control anymore. Not even you."

The words hung there, a challenge, an invitation, and a confession all wrapped into one. Callum didn't flinch. He didn't try to reassure me with empty promises or smooth over the discomfort that had settled between us. Instead, he stepped forward, closing the distance between us, his gaze unwavering.

"You never had control," he said, his voice low, but somehow softer than I remembered. "Not over me, not over anyone. But you had control over yourself. Over your choices. And you still do. That's the thing about fires," he added, glancing around at the ashes. "They burn everything to the ground, but they can't take that away from you. Not unless you let them."

I swallowed hard, his words sinking into me with an unexpected weight. He was right, of course. I didn't need him to tell me that, didn't need anyone to remind me. But somehow, hearing it from him—hearing it with that quiet conviction in his voice—made me feel like something inside me was finally starting to shift.

"That's a pretty dramatic way to make a point," I said, trying to lighten the mood, to cut through the tension with something that felt more familiar. "Next, you're going to tell me that everything happens for a reason."

He chuckled, the sound a rare gift. "I'd never insult your intelligence with something as clichéd as that," he said, the wry smile playing at the corners of his mouth. "But I will say this—there's something to be learned from every fire. Not just the ones that burn down buildings, but the ones that burn us from the inside out."

I stared at him for a long moment, unsure whether I wanted to laugh or cry. Maybe both. He always had a way of making things seem... possible, even when they were anything but. It was a strange kind of magic, the way he spoke, the way he held himself. As if the world didn't matter so much, as long as he was still standing there, with me.

"You've got a strange way of making me believe in things I never thought I would," I said, my voice quieter now, but still tinged with that sharp edge of defiance I couldn't shake. "You've been gone for so long, Callum. You don't get to just walk back in and expect me to—"

"I know," he interrupted, his gaze firm and understanding. "I don't expect anything. Not anymore. But I'm here, now. And I'm not leaving. Not this time."

The finality in his tone made my chest tighten. I didn't know if I was ready to hear it, ready to accept it. But it was out there now, hanging in the air between us like a promise.

"I don't know if I can believe that," I said, my voice barely a whisper. "I don't know if I can trust that you're really here to stay."

He reached out then, his fingers brushing against mine, a light touch that sent a shock of warmth through me. "You don't have to believe me yet," he said softly. "But I'm here. And I'm not going anywhere."

The simple act of his hand in mine, that tentative gesture, sent something unexpected spiraling through me. Maybe it was the exhaustion, or the fear, or the relief of it all being over. Or maybe, just maybe, it was the start of something new. Something I hadn't known I was ready for. Something we were both hesitant to embrace, but maybe, just maybe, it was exactly what we needed.

The air was thick with the remnants of smoke, the ground beneath my feet uneven and scattered with broken pieces of everything that had once been familiar. My heart wasn't quite in my chest anymore; it had slipped somewhere beneath the rubble, tangled in memories I wasn't sure I could retrieve. Callum's hand, still lightly holding mine, felt as fragile as I did—like it might slip away with a wrong word or a wrong move. I could feel the tension building between us, the pull of something I wasn't sure I was strong enough to confront.

His voice was quiet but steady, like he was waiting for something—waiting for me to give him a reason to stay or a reason to go. I could see it in the way his shoulders were stiff, how he watched me like I was the only thing in the world worth paying attention to. He didn't speak, but his eyes did all the talking, his silence loud enough to fill the space around us with the weight of all that had been said and unsaid.

"You can't keep waiting for a reason to leave, you know." I hadn't meant to say it out loud, but there it was, a truth tumbling out of me like a secret I'd been keeping too long. I pulled my hand from his, feeling the space between us widen with each step backward I took.

He didn't chase after me. That would've been too easy. Instead, his gaze softened, something almost sad flickering across his face, but he didn't retreat either. He stood his ground, meeting me halfway in the unspoken agreement we'd always had—silent, unreadable, yet somehow in sync.

"You're right," he said after a beat, the quiet acceptance in his voice pulling at the knots in my chest. "I'm not waiting for a reason to leave. But I'll wait for as long as it takes for you to figure out if you want me to stay." His words were like a lifeline tossed in the storm, but whether or not I was ready to grab it... well, that was another question entirely.

I opened my mouth to respond, but the words stuck in my throat. What did I want? What could I possibly want from him after everything? It wasn't that I didn't care—God knows I did—but I was so damn tired of the wreckage that followed him. He was like a fire I couldn't put out, a blazing intensity I wasn't sure I could withstand without getting burned.

I turned away, walking a few paces before stopping, my back to him. "You think you can just waltz back into my life after everything that's happened?" My voice cracked as I spoke, and I hated the vulnerability that slipped through. I didn't want him to see me like this—raw, exposed, and at a crossroads I wasn't prepared to navigate.

"You know that's not what I'm doing," Callum replied, his voice harder now, as if the weight of my words had shifted something inside him too. "I never left because I wanted to. I left because I thought that was what you needed."

That hit me harder than I expected, like a slap in the face. The truth of it—he hadn't left because he wanted to. He had left because he thought it was the right thing to do, for me. For my sake. How did I reconcile that with the anger I still felt, with the months of silence, the unanswered questions that had piled up between us like bricks? I felt dizzy just trying to keep up with it all.

I turned back to him, my eyes searching his face for something—anything—that would make this easier. But I didn't find it. Instead, I found him, standing there like he always had, strong, steady, but with that flicker of vulnerability I didn't know how to handle.

"Then why didn't you come back sooner?" The question was out before I could think better of it. My heart thudded in my chest as the words settled in the air between us, and I braced myself for the answer I wasn't sure I wanted to hear.

He hesitated, running a hand through his hair as though he was trying to find the right way to say it. "Because I knew you wouldn't be ready to hear me. I knew I'd mess it up, and I couldn't stand the thought of you pushing me away again." His voice was low, almost a whisper, but it landed with a force that left me breathless.

I swallowed hard, blinking away the sting in my eyes. The admission was raw, unpolished, but it was also... honest. Too honest. And it terrified me because it chipped away at the walls I'd spent so long building. I hadn't expected him to be so damn vulnerable, so... human. And I didn't know what to do with that.

"You always did think too much," I said, trying to joke my way out of it, trying to regain some semblance of control. "Maybe if you'd just come back sooner, we wouldn't be standing in the middle of this mess, trying to figure out if we can make it work."

He stepped closer, just enough to close the distance but not enough to overwhelm me. "Maybe. But maybe it's never about getting it right the first time, or the second time, or the third. Maybe it's about trying anyway, even when you're scared shitless."

I let out a breath I didn't know I was holding, staring at him. His words stirred something deep inside me—something I hadn't allowed myself to feel for so long. A hope, fragile as a spider's web, but there all the same.

"You're right," I said quietly. "I'm scared, Callum. I'm scared that if I let you back in, we'll just burn everything down again."

He nodded slowly, his gaze steady. "We might. But maybe that's the price of trying. Maybe that's the only way to find out if we can make it through the flames together."

I closed my eyes, my pulse quickening. I wanted to believe him, wanted to believe that we could rebuild, that the ashes could somehow be the foundation of something new. But I wasn't sure I had the strength to risk it.

A sound from behind us caught my attention—a car engine, rumbling faintly in the distance, growing louder by the second. My heart skipped a beat. I turned instinctively toward the sound, my body tense.

Callum's expression shifted instantly, a subtle shift in his stance that spoke of danger, of readiness. "Get inside," he said urgently, his voice low but commanding.

Before I could react, the engine roared closer, the headlights cutting through the twilight. Something about the sound felt wrong, unsettling. And as I turned to head toward the house, a figure stepped into the glow of the headlights, and everything inside me froze.

It was him.

The last person I ever expected to see.

Chapter 34: The Quiet Before

The world outside had softened. The edges of the city, once so sharp and unyielding, now blurred in the delicate light of early morning, casting long shadows that stretched lazily across the sidewalks. The hum of life, the buzz of traffic, had mellowed into a kind of gentle, almost reluctant harmony, as if the world itself were testing the waters, unsure whether it was safe to fully exhale. It felt strange, like the air was holding its breath. Maybe we all were.

I sat on the worn leather couch in the apartment, the sunlight creeping through the half-open blinds, tracing patterns on the floor that seemed almost deliberate, as though nature itself had choreographed the scene. There was a fresh mug of coffee on the table in front of me, steam rising in slow spirals, but I hadn't touched it. My fingers hovered over the rim, the porcelain cool beneath my skin. It was the first thing I'd done this morning that wasn't part of the routine. For the past few days, everything had been about routine. A cup of coffee, a quiet breakfast, work—whatever that meant these days. All the small, steady motions that made me feel like I could still find some semblance of control.

But today, that control seemed to slip through my fingers, like sand caught in an impossible wind. I couldn't remember the last time I'd sat still for more than a few minutes without needing to fill the silence with something. Anything. But now, here I was, surrounded by the emptiness of a morning that stretched on too long.

Callum's presence loomed in the background, as it always did these days, but there was something tentative about it, something that had yet to find its way back to the comfort of the familiar. He was in the kitchen, moving with that quiet precision he had, the clink of plates and cups a sharp contrast to the stillness that gripped the rest of the apartment. I could hear the way his feet hit the floor, heavy and hesitant, like he wasn't sure if he should be here at all.

I glanced toward the kitchen, where he stood, shoulders squared, his back turned toward me. The kitchen had always been his space—where he held dominion over the stove and coffee machine as if they were his allies in a silent war against the mess of the world. But today, his movements lacked the easy rhythm that had once come so naturally. There was no music playing, no banter exchanged between us as he flipped pancakes or started the coffee. Just the quiet, stifling kind of silence that makes you question whether you've forgotten how to breathe.

I exhaled, a shaky breath that came too easily, and reached for the mug, finally taking a sip of the coffee. It burned my tongue, but I welcomed the sting, the sharpness that reminded me I was still here. Still trying. It had been two weeks since everything had shifted—since the world we knew fell apart and we were left to pick up the pieces. I should have felt relief. Everyone had been talking about it: the relief that came with knowing the worst was over. But for me, the quiet felt like a weight, a pressure in my chest that made every step feel like I was walking through deep water.

I heard him move then, the soft shuffle of his boots against the floor, and before I could gather myself, Callum was standing in the doorway of the living room, his gaze flicking to the window, the way the light played off the edges of the blinds. He wasn't looking at me directly, but I could feel the tension between us, that strange distance we hadn't known before. The space between us had grown, like we were two puzzle pieces that no longer fit together, and we hadn't yet figured out how to force them back into place.

"Coffee's ready," he said, his voice quiet, almost like he was testing the waters to see if the words would land without causing an echo.

I nodded, not trusting myself to speak. The words I wanted to say tangled in my throat, like I was trying to extract something too complicated for the moment. I could see the effort behind his casual tone, the way his hand gripped the doorframe as if it was the only thing keeping him grounded. And I wanted to reach out, to tell him that it was okay, that we didn't need to be perfect in this moment. But the words wouldn't come. Instead, I just sat there, watching him, waiting for him to make the next move.

He hesitated, his gaze flicking to mine for a brief second before he turned and disappeared into the kitchen again. I exhaled slowly, my fingers tightening around the mug. The tension between us was palpable now, like an invisible force that neither of us knew how to break.

It had been like this for days, these strange, half-conversations where we spoke but never truly heard each other. And I hated it. I hated the way I was pulling away when all I wanted was to close the distance. But the cracks were there, and they weren't going to heal overnight. I just didn't know how to fix them.

Minutes passed, or maybe it was hours, before he returned. This time, he was holding two mugs, his face unreadable. He placed one on the table in front of me, his fingers brushing mine for the briefest of moments. A simple gesture, but it carried weight. He sat across from me, the silence stretching between us again, but now there was something different about it. Something fragile, like a line drawn in the sand, waiting to be erased.

"I don't know how to do this," he said suddenly, his voice rough, like he'd been carrying the words around for longer than he was willing to admit.

I blinked, startled by the honesty. But it was a good kind of honesty, the kind that felt like a bridge had been built between us. Slowly, I set the mug down and leaned forward, meeting his gaze. And for the first time in what felt like ages, I smiled. Not because everything was fixed, but because maybe—just maybe—we could find our way back to something real.

"Me neither," I said, my voice soft but steady. "But we'll figure it out. Somehow."

The days seemed to stretch, as though time itself was refusing to acknowledge the need for anything more than stagnation. We lived in the spaces between movements—silent, waiting for something to break the tension. Every small action felt charged with significance: the clink of dishes, the soft shuffle of feet on the floor, the way the sunlight inched its way across the apartment. Each moment felt weighted, as if it carried the possibility of change, but neither of us had yet dared to tip the balance.

There were mornings when Callum and I would sit together at the small dining table, each of us with a cup of coffee, both of us pretending that this was normal. That the awkwardness between us wasn't an elephant in the room. But the silence would always return. It wasn't a comfortable quiet, the kind that you fall into after years of knowing each other, but the kind that stretches and yawns, uncomfortable and unfamiliar.

I watched him more than I should have, observing the way he pushed the mug around the table as though he were trying to find something that wasn't there. His fingers drummed absentmindedly against the ceramic, his eyes focused on the swirling patterns of steam rising from his drink, as though he could escape inside it. There was a shadow in his expression, something that had never been there before. It was strange—this version of Callum, so distant and elusive, as though he had been carved out of a different mold than the one I had once known so well.

"Are we doing this right?" I asked him, the question escaping before I could swallow it back down.

His gaze lifted from the mug, and for a moment, I thought he might say something reassuring, something to bridge the gap that had formed between us. But he only shrugged, a small gesture that felt more like a barrier than a comfort.

"I don't know," he replied, his voice low, quieter than usual, like he was still trying to find his footing in a world that felt unfamiliar to him, too.

We had always been the kind of couple that didn't need words to fill the space between us—our laughter, the easy glances, the touch of a hand when things got too loud or too bright, those had been enough. But now? Now, the silence was like a constant hum, buzzing louder in the stillness. It wasn't that we were fighting—no, it was something subtler, more insidious. A slow unraveling, like the gentle but persistent pulling at a thread until the fabric begins to tear.

I didn't want to be the first one to acknowledge it. Not because I was afraid of the truth, but because I wasn't sure I knew how to say it aloud. What could I say? That we were both walking around in circles, pretending we knew how to be around each other without everything feeling like a tightrope walk?

The truth was, I missed him. Not the version of him that I had been living with for the past few days, so stiff and distant, but the Callum I had known before all of this. The one who could make me laugh even when my world felt like it was falling apart. The one who would bring me coffee in the morning with a crooked smile, and tell me, without saying a word, that everything would be okay.

But there was nothing in his eyes now that made me feel certain. There was no warmth there, no easy familiarity. Just distance.

"We can't go back to what it was," I said finally, more to myself than to him. "I don't think we can just fix it like that."

The way his jaw tightened told me he didn't disagree.

"No," he said quietly, "but maybe we don't need to."

That stung, more than I cared to admit, but I didn't let it show. Instead, I stared at the dappled sunlight coming through the window, trying to force my mind to settle, to stop running circles around the same few thoughts. But they kept coming back, like a storm cloud gathering on the horizon. What did he mean by that? Was he suggesting that we just let go, that this was the new normal for us? Was that what he was preparing himself for, and if so, was I ready for it?

I shifted in my chair, trying to find something to focus on besides the tightness in my chest. There was a half-finished novel on the coffee table that I had been meaning to pick up again, but I didn't have the energy to pretend I could escape into its pages. Not when my own life felt like it was crumbling just beyond the edge of my peripheral vision.

The air felt thick, and my mind spun in a hundred different directions, none of them going anywhere useful. In the end, I stood up without a word, moving toward the kitchen to give myself some space. I wasn't running away—at least, not exactly. But I needed a moment to breathe, to recalibrate.

Callum didn't follow me, but I could feel the weight of his gaze on my back, like he was trying to read me, to figure out where I was. But I didn't have the answers yet.

I pulled open the fridge and stood there for a long moment, staring at the empty space. The silence felt heavier in here, too, like the walls were closing in, and all I wanted was for everything to feel light again. To feel like I wasn't swimming against an undertow of emotions I didn't know how to navigate.

Then, out of nowhere, I heard him. "I'm sorry," Callum said from the doorway, his voice suddenly clear, like a crack of sunlight after a storm.

I froze, my back still turned to him. The words hung in the air, suspended between us, and for a moment, I wasn't sure how to respond. What was he apologizing for? The distance between us? The silence that had become an impenetrable wall?

I closed my eyes for a second, willing myself to breathe through the moment before I turned around. When I did, I saw the genuine look of regret in his eyes, and for the first time in what felt like forever, I felt something resembling hope stir inside me.

"I didn't know how to fix this," he admitted, his voice rough, as if he were struggling to find the words. "I thought maybe giving you space would make it better. But now I see that was a mistake."

I exhaled slowly, allowing the air to leave my lungs in a long, measured breath. This was it. The moment where we either stayed lost in the quiet or took a chance on something that might still hold a shred of us.

"We'll figure it out," I said, more to myself than to him, but maybe—just maybe—it was something worth believing.

The tension between us hadn't lessened, not really. It was still there, lingering beneath every word, every glance, but it had become quieter, as if we were both trying to ignore the elephant that still sat on the couch between us, pressing its weight into the cushions with every passing second. But, like with all things that are ignored long enough, the discomfort started to wear thin. It was like an itch I couldn't scratch, a flicker of something I couldn't quite place—too subtle to identify but impossible to ignore.

I spent the next few days walking around the apartment, pretending I wasn't hyper-aware of his every movement, trying to convince myself I wasn't searching for any kind of sign that would tell me whether we were drifting or rebuilding. The awkwardness between us was something I could taste—bitter, like a poorly brewed cup of tea, sharp on my tongue and hard to swallow. And yet, every time Callum crossed the room, I felt that warmth, a quiet reminder that, despite everything, he was still here, still trying. I just didn't know if that would be enough.

By the fourth day, I found myself standing in the kitchen at an hour too early for anyone to be functional. I hadn't intended to be there, but my legs had carried me without asking for permission, and the quiet of the morning gave me a moment to think without being bombarded by the noise of the world, the noise of him.

The refrigerator hummed, and the distant sound of traffic outside was a dull echo against the walls. I poured myself a glass of water, the coldness of it a sharp contrast to the heat building in my chest. I hadn't realized how much I missed the simplicity of everything before—before the mess, before the explosion of emotion and words that had fractured us.

"You're up early," came his voice, deep and rough from sleep, pulling me out of my reverie.

I didn't turn to face him. The space between us felt more fragile than usual this morning, like if I moved too quickly, it might shatter. I could feel him there, just behind me, hovering in the doorway with that hesitance that had become his second skin.

"Couldn't sleep," I muttered, trying to keep my voice steady, as if the truth wasn't swimming just below the surface.

Callum didn't say anything for a moment, and I didn't force it. We had long passed the point where silence between us felt natural—it was now something to be carefully navigated, something to be acknowledged but not examined too closely.

"Me neither," he finally said. His words felt like they were laced with something else—guilt, or maybe regret. Maybe both. He stepped into the kitchen then, close enough that I could feel the shift in the air between us, the space he filled with his presence. "Maybe we should talk about it."

Talk about it. The words hung there, an invitation to something I wasn't sure I was ready for. But there was something in his tone, a kind of rawness that I couldn't ignore. It was an opening—an invitation to say what we hadn't been able to put into words before.

I set the glass down and turned to face him, finally letting the weight of the moment settle between us. There was something unsettling about how much I wanted this, how much I needed him to reach out and make the first move. I wanted him to take the lead, to take some of the pressure off me for once.

"You're right," I said, my voice barely above a whisper. "We can't keep doing this, pretending everything's fine when it's not."

Callum's eyes met mine, and I could see the same vulnerability reflected in them that I was desperately trying to conceal in myself. He opened his mouth to say something, then stopped, reconsidering his words before they left him.

"We've never been good at pretending," he said, his lips curving into a faint smile. "But I think we could be better at trying."

His words caught me off guard. There was something about the way he said it—so simple, so matter-of-fact—that made me want to believe him. And for a second, I almost did.

I stepped closer, the space between us shrinking with every breath, but still, I hesitated. There was so much left unsaid, and we both knew it. It wasn't enough to simply acknowledge the distance between us—it was the how, the why, and the what next that haunted every conversation. I wasn't sure if we could just patch things up with a few honest words. It felt like too much, too broken.

But as I stood there, staring into his eyes, I realized something—maybe there wasn't an easy fix. Maybe there wasn't a perfect solution to the mess we were in. But I still wanted to try. I needed to try.

"I don't know if I'm ready," I confessed, my voice trembling, betraying the words I'd hoped would come out steady. "I don't know how to fix it."

Callum's expression softened, and for the first time in days, I saw a flicker of the Callum I used to know—the one who wasn't afraid of the mess, the one who didn't shrink from the hard conversations.

"We'll figure it out," he said again, his voice thick with something I couldn't quite place. "We don't need to have it all figured out right now, but we can't keep pretending it's fine either."

I nodded, swallowing the knot in my throat. It wasn't much, but it was something. A start.

But just as I thought we were about to close the distance, the phone rang. It wasn't a casual ring—no, it was an urgent, insistent sound that cut through the fragile peace we had started to build. I glanced at the screen, and for a moment, I thought I might be imagining it. The name flashing across the display was one I hadn't seen in months—an old contact, someone I'd never expected to hear from again.

Callum noticed the change in my expression instantly, and his own face hardened, the warmth slipping away as if someone had flicked a switch.

"Who is it?" he asked, his tone sharp now, as if this unexpected interruption had taken us both by surprise.

I opened my mouth to answer, but the words froze in my throat. Something inside me recoiled at the thought of answering the call, yet some part of me knew that I had to.

I took a deep breath, my hand trembling as I reached for the phone, but before I could even press 'answer,' the screen flashed once more—and the name disappeared.

But something in the air shifted. The room seemed colder suddenly. And I wasn't sure if it was the call, or something far worse, that had just begun.

Chapter 35: Kindling Trust

I was halfway through re-organizing the café's pantry when the door swung open, the bell chiming like an old friend greeting me. I didn't even look up, too focused on making sure I didn't knock over a bottle of syrup or an entire jar of cinnamon. But then I heard it—the soft click of boots on the hardwood floor, unmistakable and steady. Callum. My heart did that annoying flip-flop thing that it had no business doing, considering the fact that I had sworn, after everything, that I was done being affected by him.

"Need any help?" His voice was quiet but laced with that characteristic warmth, the one that managed to slide under your skin like a soft, reassuring touch. I wasn't sure whether I wanted to punch him or pull him into a hug at that exact moment.

I turned to face him, the air between us as thick as a summer storm. "If you're offering, I could use a hand with sorting through these boxes. They're starting to look like they're breeding in the back corner."

He raised an eyebrow, a smirk tugging at the corner of his lips. "I can't be the only one who notices you're hoarding three types of vanilla extract in here, right? It's getting a little out of hand."

I laughed, feeling the tension in my shoulders loosen just a fraction. "That's a vital ingredient," I explained with a serious tone, though I had no real defense for why there were two types I'd never even opened. "You can never have too many options when it comes to vanilla."

"Right." His voice had a teasing lilt as he reached into a box and pulled out a jar of honey. "This stuff really does look like it's been here since the dawn of time."

"Don't you dare," I said, reaching out to snatch it from his hand. "That honey is a treasure. A friend of mine brought it back from a little market in Greece."

"Ah, Greece. A place I've never been but always thought I should visit one day," he mused, his fingers lingering on the rim of the jar for just a moment too long. He was still a mystery, a bit like that honey—sweet with an edge of something foreign, something I couldn't quite place.

I set the jar back with exaggerated care, my fingers brushing against his for a second longer than necessary. It didn't go unnoticed, but neither of us said anything. Instead, we continued sorting in companionable silence, the hum of the old refrigerator and the soft murmur of the street outside the only sounds between us. I couldn't help but steal a glance at him every now and then. His broad shoulders, the way his dark hair was just long enough to run my fingers through, the way he moved through the small space with that quiet confidence that always managed to make my pulse race.

He was different now. Or maybe I was different. I couldn't tell where one of us ended and the other began anymore.

"I didn't mean to upset you the other night," he said out of nowhere, his voice low. I froze, my hand still gripping a jar of organic peanut butter, the plastic smooth and cool under my palm. "You know, with what I said about my past. I wasn't trying to make you feel uncomfortable."

I could feel the heat of his gaze on me, like he was trying to reach past the layers I'd built, all the walls I'd carefully constructed to keep from feeling too much. But his words, simple and raw, had a way of chipping away at them, piece by piece.

"You didn't," I replied, my voice barely above a whisper. "It was... a lot, but I get it." And I did. In some strange, unexpected way, I did. The way he spoke about the things he regretted, the mistakes that still haunted him—it wasn't just his past that I was starting to understand. It was his present, too. The little things. The way he always had his sleeves rolled up, no matter the temperature, or how his jaw tightened when he was stressed. It all made sense now.

Callum had done things he wasn't proud of. But so had I. We were both swimming in our own regrets, trying to stay afloat despite the currents.

He exhaled, the breath almost like a release, and for the first time in weeks, I saw him soften. The lines around his eyes, the tension in his shoulders—it all seemed to ease.

"I guess," he started again, "I'm just tired of feeling like I'm constantly running from who I used to be." There was a brief pause, the words hanging in the air like smoke. "But I'm not that person anymore. I want to be different. For you, if you'll let me."

I didn't know what to say at first. I couldn't have told him anything profound, not when the truth was so tangled in my chest. But I could give him something else. Something small, yet important. "I'm trying to be different, too," I said. "I don't have all the answers, but I'm willing to figure it out."

A small smile tugged at the corner of his lips, but it didn't quite reach his eyes. Not yet. Maybe it was too soon. Maybe there were still things we weren't ready to say to each other.

But as he turned to pick up another box, I felt it—something shifting between us. Like a door that had been left ajar, just enough for the light to spill through. There was no grand declaration, no over-the-top gestures, just a simple truth. We were both learning how to be present, how to be here—together—without pretending to be anyone else.

It wasn't perfect. It probably never would be. But for the first time in a long time, I wasn't afraid to see where this might go. And maybe, just maybe, that was enough for now.

The morning light filtered through the café windows, soft and golden, casting a halo around the mismatched chairs and chipped mugs that lined the counter. It felt like a new beginning—an illusion, probably, but one I was ready to indulge in. The air smelled of coffee and cinnamon, a perfect combination that always had a way of calming my frayed nerves. As the café slowly came to life, so did the soft, unexpected camaraderie that had begun to grow between Callum and me.

I caught sight of him across the room, standing by the counter, his broad back to me as he carefully arranged the pastries for display. There was something oddly domestic about the way he moved, the way his fingers brushed over the croissants like he was handling something fragile, something precious. It made my heart stumble a little. I couldn't quite tell what it was, but it wasn't the first time I'd felt the pull of something deeper, something that went beyond just passing curiosity.

"Are we planning on selling these today, or do we just want them to look nice?" I called out, not bothering to hide the teasing edge in my voice.

He turned, caught off guard for just a moment before the corners of his mouth quirked upward in that lazy, almost smug smile that I'd come to recognize. "I was just admiring my handiwork. You know, it's important to make sure everything is presented correctly. Art is an essential part of the experience."

I raised an eyebrow. "Art? You're selling pastries, not paintings."

"I know. But you'd be surprised how many people judge the quality of a croissant based on how it's arranged." He raised his arms as though conducting a symphony, then gestured dramatically to the pastries. "It's all about presentation."

I couldn't help but laugh. The sound was light, bright, and maybe a little too free, but I was starting to realize that was the effect he had on me. It wasn't the first time I'd heard him talk like this—like he knew something no one else did, like he had secret knowledge about the world that no one else could understand. But I liked it. It was the same thing that had pulled me in when we'd first met, a mixture of charm and mystery, that unspoken confidence that made him both infuriating and irresistible.

"Well, I suppose you should teach a class then," I said, walking over to adjust one of the pastries that was slightly askew. "I mean, I wouldn't want to disappoint anyone by presenting a crooked éclair."

He stepped a little closer, his gaze still locked on mine, the teasing smirk slipping just slightly. "I think you'd do just fine. You've got a good eye."

The compliment was unexpected, but it didn't land the way I thought it might. Instead of feeling self-conscious, I felt... lighter. Almost as though he'd let me into a private space in his mind, one that wasn't guarded by sarcasm or hesitation. I wasn't sure how I felt about it—this new, unspoken thing between us—but I knew I wasn't ready to turn away from it just yet.

"Don't get carried away," I warned, trying to keep the mood casual, my voice laced with humor. "I don't need anyone thinking I'm the next Martha Stewart or anything."

He raised an eyebrow at me, his lips curling into a smile. "You mean the Martha Stewart who went to prison for insider trading? Yeah, definitely not the vibe I'm getting from you."

I let out a soft laugh, feeling my heart skip a beat at his words. It was strange, how easily we slipped into this rhythm—like we'd done it for years. Like we were two old friends who didn't need to say much to understand each other.

I knew it wasn't that simple. It never was. But I was starting to trust this, whatever it was. I could feel the threads of connection slowly knitting themselves together, one moment at a time.

The bell over the door chimed again, breaking the moment. A few regulars shuffled in, and as I glanced at Callum, I saw the familiar shift in him. The walls, those invisible barriers he kept so carefully in place, seemed to rise again. The easy confidence was gone, replaced by that tight-lipped mask he wore when he didn't want anyone to see too much.

I sighed inwardly. It was a pattern I was beginning to recognize. He let people in, just enough to make them think they understood him, but he never fully opened up. And every time he pulled away, it sent a small pang of disappointment through me, even though I knew better than to expect anything else.

I busied myself with getting the coffee brewing, trying to ignore the knot that had formed in my stomach. But then Callum's voice broke through the hum of the café.

"Hey, could you pass me the sugar?" he asked, his tone quieter than usual. The request was simple, but there was something in his eyes that made me pause before reaching for the jar.

"What's up?" I asked, the words slipping out before I could stop them.

He hesitated for a moment, his gaze flickering to mine, and I swore I saw a flicker of something—something vulnerable—before he masked it again with that signature easy smile. "Nothing. Just—stuff."

"Stuff?" I repeated, raising an eyebrow. "That's all you've got?"

He shrugged, but the smile didn't quite reach his eyes. "Yeah, you know. Stuff."

I didn't buy it. I never had, and I didn't intend to start now. But I wasn't about to push him. Not here, not now. Instead, I set the sugar jar on the counter and gave him a nod, signaling I was ready to move on.

But as I turned back to the espresso machine, I couldn't shake the feeling that we were both standing at a precipice, looking at the same vast, uncertain drop and not knowing if we were brave enough to leap.

And yet, I knew that if we didn't jump, we'd both spend the rest of our lives standing still, frozen in this place where trust wasn't quite earned but wasn't entirely lost either. I wasn't sure if I could take the leap. But I was starting to wonder if I wanted to.

Chapter 36: A New Light

I didn't expect it to happen like this. To wake up one morning and find myself caught in the undercurrent of something I'd spent months swimming against. But here I was, sitting across from Callum, his eyes not just a shade darker than I remembered, but so impossibly warm. The type of warmth that made me think of the rare, lazy afternoons when the sun hung low, and the world felt like it was in no rush. We were in his kitchen, steam curling from the coffee mugs between us, the aroma filling the quiet air.

The silence between us wasn't awkward. Not anymore. It was comfortable. But there was something else there, something unspoken, wrapped around the edges of everything we said. He stirred his coffee slowly, and I did the same, pretending to be absorbed in the pattern the cream made as it swirled into the black. A touch of sweetness. A reminder of why I'd ever let him back in.

"I'm not a man who usually makes promises," Callum said, his voice a smooth baritone, so different from the clipped tones he used when he was all business. "But I'm making one now."

I looked up, not entirely sure I wanted to hear what was coming. "Promises are dangerous," I murmured. "They're easy to break."

"Not this one," he said firmly, locking eyes with me. "Not this one, Lily. I'm promising you honesty. All of it. No more lies, no more half-truths."

It shouldn't have made my heart skip. I shouldn't have leaned forward just slightly, as if the edge of his words could pull me into something deeper. But I did. I did because—against every instinct, every ounce of wariness that had once kept me so tightly wound—I realized I wanted to believe him. I wanted to believe in us.

"What if I can't handle the truth?" I asked, my voice softer than I intended, almost a whisper.

"Then I'll find a way to make you," he said with a faint grin that made the corner of his eyes crinkle. "I've never been good at backing down."

I wanted to argue. I wanted to pull back and tell him not to push so hard, to let me breathe, to keep the walls I'd so carefully built. But somewhere between that promise and the warmth of his gaze, I didn't want to. I didn't want to hide anymore. Not from him. Not from myself.

"So, you're telling me you're here to stay?" I said, trying to sound flippant, but even my own words felt heavy. Too much.

Callum's smile softened, almost as if he could hear the uncertainty beneath the humor I was trying so hard to mask. "That's the plan. What about you?"

I stared at him, the words spinning in my head, but not quite finding their way out. Yes, I could say it. Yes, I could admit that this strange, improbable connection we'd found had turned into something I hadn't expected—something undeniable. But I wasn't sure if I could say it out loud.

Instead, I leaned back in my chair, letting the tension out slowly, and gave him the kind of look that only came when I was trying to be brave but failing spectacularly. "I think... I think you're going to be a lot harder to get rid of than you realize."

He chuckled, that low, rich laugh that made something inside me flutter. "I'm counting on it."

The air between us shifted then, not heavy, but lighter somehow, like a shared breath between two people who had finally exhaled after holding their lungs full for far too long. And I felt it—really felt it—the way the city seemed to quiet, as if it were waiting for something, too. For something new. For something fresh. Maybe even for me. Maybe for us.

There were no grand gestures, no sudden declarations. No, this was something subtler, something that crept up on you like a gentle breeze you didn't notice until you were already bathed in it. But it was there. Something between the mugs of coffee, the soft clink of ceramic, and the lingering look that passed between us. Something real. Maybe that was the difference now—this wasn't just some half-formed connection anymore. This was... us.

"I don't know what happens next," I said quietly, feeling the weight of the truth settle between us like a promise too.

"Me neither," Callum replied, and for the first time, I saw a flicker of uncertainty in him. Just a flicker. "But I think it's going to be worth figuring out."

The words hung there, suspended in the air like the softest thread connecting us to something we hadn't fully explored yet. A future. One that wasn't fraught with secrets, or lies, or questions we were too scared to ask. No. This time, it felt like we could build something solid. It felt like hope.

I took a breath, letting the moment sink in. There would be challenges, I knew that. There would be moments where we stumbled. But I could already feel the shift, the way everything had begun to feel just a little easier, like we were standing in a place where the ground beneath us wasn't so shaky anymore.

And, for the first time in a long time, I felt a sense of quiet optimism. It was the kind of optimism that didn't demand anything from me. It was simple. Peaceful. Maybe even a little reckless, but the good kind. The kind that made me think, for the first time, maybe I could finally start believing in the possibility of something good.

I wasn't ready to call it love, not yet. But I was ready to see where this could go.

And, for the first time in a long while, that felt like enough.

The city hums around me, a familiar rhythm that once felt suffocating but now feels more like a quiet hum in the background of my life, like an old song playing in a room I'd forgotten I was sitting in. I glance out the window, the skyline stretched before me, a mix of glass and steel catching the last light of the evening. It's all so ordinary, and yet, for the first time, I can see it—really see it—like I'm waking up from a long, heavy sleep. Things don't feel as heavy anymore. Not in the way they used to.

The morning after the coffee in Callum's kitchen, I find myself standing in the middle of my apartment, barefoot on the hardwood floors, staring at the painting I've had hanging on the wall for months without really looking at it. The colors are all wrong, clashing in a way that once felt bold but now feels... off. It's the first sign that something inside me is shifting. That maybe I'm ready for something new, too. The walls, once my armor, now seem to be closing in, a little too familiar, a little too stagnant. A sharp knock at the door pulls me from my thoughts.

I know it's him before I even open it. There's a stillness in the air, a way the world seems to hold its breath whenever Callum's near. He's standing on the other side, hands in the pockets of his jacket, the same jacket that always looks a little too worn for the polished version of himself that he tries to project. There's a quiet in him, something that I didn't notice before—the way he doesn't rush to fill silences, doesn't overcompensate with bravado. Just a man standing there, waiting. And for once, it feels like a good kind of waiting.

"You're early," I say, though it's only a few minutes past when we agreed to meet. I'm trying to keep the words light, but there's something that clings to the air between us now. Something that's both fragile and certain.

Callum smirks, that same slow, deliberate curve of his mouth that's become so familiar. "I was hoping you wouldn't mind."

"I think I'm getting used to you showing up early," I reply, stepping aside to let him in. I'm trying to make it sound casual, but it's not. I don't think I'll ever find casual when it comes to him.

He steps inside, the familiar weight of his presence filling the room, and for the first time, I notice the way the light hits him. There's an unspoken change in the air, a subtle difference that's only clear if you're looking for it. I'm looking for it now.

"I brought you something," he says, his hand slipping from his pocket and pulling out a small envelope, worn at the edges. "I thought you might appreciate it."

I raise an eyebrow as I take the envelope. "Is this an 'I'm sorry' gift, or are you trying to bribe me into trusting you?"

Callum's grin widens, but there's a flicker of something behind his eyes, something that tells me he's taking this more seriously than I expected. "Maybe both," he says with a shrug. "I'm not above a little bribery. I'm a man of many tools."

I tear open the envelope, the crisp paper inside almost making me pause for a moment before I pull it out. It's a picture—a black-and-white photograph, old and faded at the corners. It's a shot of the city, but not the one I've come to know. This is an older version—streets I don't recognize, buildings that aren't there anymore, the kind of city that existed before I was even born. I trace the lines of it with my fingers, a strange ache tugging in my chest.

"Where did you get this?" I ask, my voice quieter now.

"I thought you might like it," he says, a little too casually, but the flicker of something in his eyes tells me there's more to it. "It's from a place you're familiar with. Or at least you should be."

I frown, trying to place the image, but it eludes me. There's something about the photograph, something that tugs at the back of my mind, but I can't quite bring it into focus.

He steps closer, leaning against the counter in the way that suggests he's ready to linger, to let the moment stretch. "I thought it might help you remember. Help you see things differently."

I stare at him, a thousand questions dancing in my head, but I don't ask them. Not yet. Something in the way he says it makes me think that maybe this isn't just about the photo. Maybe it's about something else. Something bigger. And for the first time in weeks, the thought doesn't terrify me. It just feels... right.

"Well, it's certainly a new way of looking at things," I say, finally setting the photograph down. "You're full of surprises, Callum. But that's nothing new."

He chuckles softly. "You've barely scratched the surface."

And then, just like that, the moment shifts. The photograph is no longer the focus. I am. He is. The space between us fills with the unspoken truth that we've both been circling around for weeks now—the idea that maybe, just maybe, we've started something that can't be undone. Not this time.

Callum's eyes lock onto mine, steady and unwavering. "So, what do you think?" His voice drops low, almost a challenge. "You ready to see things differently?"

I swallow, feeling the weight of it in my chest. I don't know if I'm ready, but I also know that I don't want to look away anymore. Not from him, not from this.

"I think," I say, a slow smile spreading across my face, "that I'm starting to see things just fine."

And with that, everything shifts. Something in me snaps into place, something I hadn't even realized was out of alignment. I don't know where this will go, or what it all means, but for the first time in a long time, I'm willing to find out.

The days following that promise between Callum and me felt like stepping into a new reality, a world that existed just slightly outside of everything I'd known before. There were no loud declarations, no rushing into the unknown. Instead, it was quiet moments—each one building on the last—that began to change everything. Callum and I were both careful, testing the waters of this new dynamic between us, as if unsure whether we were standing on solid ground or teetering at the edge of something entirely unfamiliar.

It was just past noon when I found myself at the little park near my apartment, the one I used to visit when I needed to think. The city was awake, its usual rush of activity buzzing around me, but it felt muted, softer. I couldn't explain it, but there was a lightness in the air today, as if the promise we'd made was already making things shift. Maybe it was just me, but the place had never felt more alive.

I leaned back against a bench, my eyes closing for a moment as the cool breeze ruffled through the trees. The sharp scent of fresh-cut grass mingled with the faint tang of coffee still lingering on my skin. My mind kept returning to Callum, as it often did these days. The thought of him didn't make me tense anymore. Instead, it made me… smile. I caught myself doing it in the mirror sometimes, a small, unguarded grin that spread across my face before I even realized it. I hadn't smiled like that in a long time. And I wasn't sure if I should blame it on him or thank him for it.

Before I could lose myself too deeply in my thoughts, I heard the soft scrape of footsteps on gravel, a sound I recognized instantly. My pulse picked up, and I opened my eyes, glancing up to see Callum approaching. His shirt sleeves were rolled up to his elbows, and there was that confident, almost lazy smile tugging at his lips, the one that made him look like he knew a secret that no one else did.

I had half a mind to ask him what he was doing here, but instead, I simply patted the seat next to me, not bothering to hide the small thrill I felt at his appearance. I was getting used to him showing up when I least expected it—and maybe, just maybe, I liked it.

"Shouldn't you be working?" I teased, leaning back, my arms stretched out behind me.

"Shouldn't you be, I don't know, doing something more responsible?" he shot back, lowering himself onto the bench beside me with an easy grace that made it look effortless.

"I'm very responsible," I said, raising an eyebrow. "I'm thinking deep thoughts."

"I'm sure you are," Callum said, his voice filled with a sarcastic sweetness. "What deep thoughts? About me?"

I laughed, not because I was trying to be polite, but because there was something so easy about being with him now. It wasn't forced. It wasn't complicated. "Maybe. But mostly about what we're going to do about this whole thing between us." I gestured vaguely between us, not sure how to articulate it. "You know, this unexpected connection that feels like it might actually be worth something."

There was a pause. Callum didn't speak right away, but I could feel him turning the words over in his head, testing them out. When he finally spoke, his voice was softer, more serious. "You're not the only one who's trying to figure that out, you know."

I turned to him then, eyes meeting his for the first time since he'd sat down. There was an honesty there, a vulnerability that wasn't typical of him. It unsettled me in a way that made my heart race. I opened my mouth to say something, anything, but the words didn't come. Instead, I just nodded, absorbing the weight of what he'd said.

"I guess that's the thing," he continued, running a hand through his hair. "We've been so busy keeping our walls up, trying to make sense of things that we didn't even stop to ask if we're actually ready for whatever happens next."

I didn't have an answer to that. It felt like a question we were both afraid to face. And yet, there was something in the air that made me think we might be closer to an answer than I'd been willing to admit. The tension between us was thick, but it wasn't uncomfortable—it was alive. And as much as I wanted to run from it, I also couldn't ignore it anymore.

"I'm not afraid of what might happen next," I said, finding the words at last. "I'm afraid of missing the chance to find out."

Callum's lips quirked up at the corners, his gaze softening as he looked at me. "I thought you might say that."

We sat there in silence for a while, neither of us rushing to fill the space between us with words. There was something comfortable in that. Something reassuring. And for the first time, I felt a deep, undeniable sense of peace settle in my chest. Maybe we didn't need to figure everything out right away. Maybe the journey was just about showing up and seeing what came next.

But as I looked at him, that certainty I had started to feel wavered just for a second. Because behind his smile, I saw something else. A flicker of doubt. Not in me, but in himself. And it unsettled me more than I cared to admit.

"Callum," I started, but he cut me off before I could say anything more.

"I need to tell you something," he said, his voice suddenly serious, the warmth fading from his eyes. "Something I should have told you before."

My heart skipped. The casual air between us disappeared in an instant, replaced by the sharp edge of something unspoken. I sat up straighter, suddenly aware of how quiet the world had become around us, how heavy the silence had turned.

"Tell me what?" I asked, my voice barely above a whisper.

He was staring at me now, eyes narrowing, the weight of the moment pressing down between us.

"I'm not who you think I am, Lily," he said, and I felt the air shift, like a storm was rolling in on the horizon.

Chapter 37: Embers of Love

The kitchen was still warm, the lingering scent of freshly brewed coffee clinging to the air like a promise. I leaned against the counter, watching him as he flipped through a stack of papers, his brow furrowed in concentration. The morning light filtered in through the half-drawn blinds, casting a soft glow over the room, and for a moment, I felt like I was caught in a still frame, the world outside moving at a pace far too quick to match the steady rhythm of my heartbeat.

His shirt sleeves were rolled up, the cuffs just barely brushing the underside of his forearms as he adjusted the papers, and I couldn't help but trace the outline of his muscles in my mind. It was ridiculous, the way he still made me feel like a teenager with a crush, the way my thoughts sometimes veered into places I wasn't sure I was ready to go.

He glanced up, catching me watching him. His lips curled into a smile, a lazy thing, one that made my stomach tighten in all the best ways. "What?" he asked, his voice low, that familiar warmth threading through the words.

I smiled back, tilting my head as I crossed my arms, an instinctive shield even though I knew I didn't need one. "You're handsome," I said, the words slipping out before I had a chance to second-guess myself.

He chuckled, setting the papers aside, clearly not fooled by my casual tone. "You've said that before."

I shrugged, a small laugh escaping me. "Well, it's still true. Just thought you might need a reminder."

I walked toward him then, the cool tiles beneath my bare feet grounding me, steadying me in a way that nothing else ever had. His gaze followed me, soft and searching, and when I stood in front of him, I let my fingers trail down his chest, a familiar but still thrilling gesture.

"I don't know how you do it," I said, the words tumbling out before I could stop them. "How you make it look so easy, like everything in my life just... fits with yours. Like I don't have to force it."

He placed his hands on my waist, drawing me closer as his thumb gently traced the curve of my hip. The heat of his touch made me close my eyes for a moment, my breath catching. "You think it's easy?" His voice was quiet now, sincere in a way that sent a shiver through me.

I opened my eyes, meeting his gaze, and saw something there, something that mirrored my own feelings. "I do," I said, my voice softer this time. "I do think it's easy. But maybe it's because we make it easy. I never thought I'd find something this... steady. Something this good."

His lips pressed gently against my forehead, and I closed my eyes again, savoring the feeling. The world outside, the endless to-do lists, the looming responsibilities of the future, all seemed to disappear when I was with him. When I was in his arms, nothing else mattered.

"You're my home," he murmured, the words so simple yet heavy with meaning. And in that moment, I knew it was true, more than any words could express. I had found something rare in him, something I hadn't even realized I was searching for.

The sound of a car engine outside broke the quiet, and I pulled away reluctantly, glancing toward the window. It was early, still too early for anyone to be visiting. I furrowed my brow, a sense of unease creeping over me. "I'll be right back," I said, reaching for the door, but he caught my arm just before I could turn the knob.

"Wait," he said, his grip firm but gentle. "What's going on?"

I hesitated for a moment, the unease still clawing at me. There was something in his voice, something that made me stop and turn back to face him. "I don't know," I said slowly, trying to push the feeling of dread aside. "It's probably nothing, but I'll just check. You stay here."

His gaze hardened for a brief second, the protective instinct flickering in his eyes. "I'm coming with you."

I opened my mouth to protest, but the look on his face stopped me. He wasn't asking, not really. And in that moment, I realized it didn't matter whether I wanted him to come or not. He was already a part of this, part of me, and nothing was going to change that.

We stepped outside together, the cool air a stark contrast to the warmth inside. The car was parked across the street, an unfamiliar one, sleek and dark, its engine still running. My pulse quickened as we approached it, the feeling of unease not letting up.

Before I could ask him what he thought, the door to the car swung open, and a man stepped out. Tall, with dark hair and an air of confidence that immediately set me on edge. He smiled, but it didn't reach his eyes.

"Can I help you?" I asked, my voice steady even though my insides were twisting.

The man's eyes flicked over me, and then to him. A recognition flickered in his gaze, though it was gone almost as quickly as it appeared. "I hope I'm not disturbing anything," he said, his voice smooth, too smooth. "But I need to speak with you." He directed the words toward me, but his focus was on him.

I could feel the tension between us like a taut wire, ready to snap at any moment.

And then the man spoke again, this time his voice colder, sharper. "It's about your past."

The man's words hung in the air, thick with an unspoken warning, and I felt a strange chill crawl over my skin, despite the sun still rising high, casting everything in a false warmth. He wasn't just here to chat, that much was clear. His eyes—sharp, calculating—drilled into me, as if he could peel away the layers of my life and expose everything underneath, whether I was ready or not.

"You don't know me," I said, my voice coming out steadier than I felt. But my heart pounded, faster now. "And I have no interest in whatever you think you know."

He smiled, though it was more a baring of teeth than a gesture of friendliness. "I'm sure. But you might want to listen. This is more important than you think."

I glanced at him quickly, but only enough to gauge his intentions—was he sizing me up, or had he done his homework, tracing my steps back through the life I thought I'd left behind? It was unsettling, to say the least. My mind went to places it hadn't dared visit in months. My past wasn't something I spoke about often. I had built this life, this fragile bubble around us, and I wasn't about to let someone from the shadows ruin it.

He gestured to the car behind him. "I'm not the one you need to worry about. But there are people... people who've been asking questions. And they don't take kindly to anyone who hides things." His eyes lingered on me with an unsettling intensity, like he was daring me to ask who "they" were. I wasn't going to bite, though. Not now, not when it felt like the walls around me were closing in.

I could feel him standing just a little too close now, his breath warm against the back of my neck. A part of me wanted to step away, but another part—the one that refused to show weakness—stayed rooted in place. "What are you offering?" I asked, already knowing the answer.

A grin spread across his face, but it didn't quite reach his eyes. "I'm not offering you anything. You've got nothing to give me that I want. But if you want to keep things simple, if you want to keep him safe..." He paused for effect, letting the weight of his words settle. "You'll come with me."

I couldn't tell if the air had suddenly grown heavy with tension, or if it was just the sudden sharpness of the situation pressing against me, trying to push me into submission. I looked back at him, searching for something that didn't feel like a threat, but found none.

A hand brushed against my arm, and I didn't need to turn around to know who it was. His presence was always a comforting thing, steady and unwavering. But now, as he stepped forward, I felt the sharp divide between us—between the life I had with him and the one I had left behind, one I hadn't even realized still lingered in the corners of my mind.

"You're not taking her anywhere," he said, his voice like gravel, low and controlled.

I turned then, my gaze locking with his. There was a question in his eyes, an unspoken plea for an explanation I wasn't sure I had the answers to.

The man didn't flinch, his eyes narrowing as he took in the sight of him. "Doesn't matter to me, really. She's just a piece in a larger game."

"Don't talk about her like that." His voice cracked with something dangerous.

"Fine," the man said, shrugging off the exchange like it didn't matter. "But you'll want to know who's playing this game before you get too far into it." He glanced back toward the car, where the darkened windows seemed to reflect the tension in the air. "I'm just a messenger. I'm not the one you need to worry about."

The words rang in my ears, echoing like a warning bell, each one bouncing off the walls of my mind, threatening to overwhelm me. I wanted to ask what he meant, to demand answers, but something stopped me. I glanced at him—at my rock, my steady hand—and saw the storm brewing behind his eyes, the flicker of doubt that hadn't been there before.

He took a step closer to me, wrapping his hand around my wrist, pulling me gently but firmly toward him. "We're going inside," he said, his tone brooking no argument. "Now."

For a moment, the man didn't move, but his eyes flicked toward the car again, the implication clear. He wasn't about to let us go so easily.

"Not today," I said, surprising myself with the clarity in my voice. The man's expression hardened, but he didn't push further.

Instead, he simply nodded. "You'll regret this," he warned, his voice quiet but no less menacing. "People like me... we don't forget."

With that, he turned and walked back toward the car, the door slamming shut with a finality that made the hairs on the back of my neck stand up. The engine roared to life, and he pulled away, his car disappearing into the horizon like some shadow chasing after us, relentless and unyielding.

We stood there, in the wake of his departure, the silence between us thick and heavy.

He turned to me then, his grip loosening around my wrist, but his concern still evident in the furrow of his brow. "Who was that?" His voice was strained, as though even he didn't know how to process what had just happened.

I swallowed hard, the truth lodged in my throat like a bitter pill. "I don't know," I said quietly. "But I have a feeling we're going to find out soon enough."

The words felt hollow, like I was only half speaking them, the rest of me still stuck in the space between the past and the present.

But when he took my hand in his, when he pulled me close, the knot of fear in my chest loosened, just a little. Whatever came next, we'd face it together.

I never expected things to spiral the way they did, but there was no mistaking the shift in the air. Even as I stood beside him, feeling his warmth seep into me, the heavy sense of impending change lingered, dark and undeniable. The man in the car hadn't left us with much—just a cryptic warning and an unsettling sense that I was somehow trapped in a game I didn't want to play. But there it was, hanging between us, an invisible thread pulling me back into a past I thought I'd escaped.

I wanted to push it away, to shut the door and pretend it had never happened, but something in the back of my mind told me it wouldn't be that easy. As much as I longed for peace, for that quiet rhythm we'd found together, life had a way of kicking down doors when you least expected it.

We stood on the porch, the sound of his retreating car still ringing in my ears, the hum of the engine fading as the world seemed to hold its breath. I tried to focus on him—on the solid presence of the man beside me—but I felt something shift between us, a subtle but undeniable tension.

"I'm sorry," he said, his voice so quiet I almost didn't hear it. But the apology in his tone, unspoken but clear, made my heart ache. "I should've known. I should've protected you from all of this."

I shook my head, turning to face him, willing him to see the truth in my eyes. "You didn't know. And you can't protect me from everything. This is my mess."

His hands dropped to his sides, fingers flexing as if he didn't know what to do with them. He studied me carefully, the concern in his eyes deepening. "But it's not just yours anymore. I'm in this with you. You know that, right?"

I nodded, a lump forming in my throat. His words should've been comforting, but instead, they felt like the weight of a promise neither of us could keep. The world outside had shifted, and nothing would ever be as simple as it had been just an hour ago.

He stepped closer, his presence a silent shield, and I allowed myself to lean into him for a moment. The warmth of his body, the solid assurance of his embrace, was the only thing keeping me grounded. But even then, the gnawing uncertainty didn't let up. There was a danger now—something lurking just beyond our reach.

"What happens now?" I asked, my voice small against the overwhelming silence.

He hesitated, and for a fleeting second, I saw the conflict in his eyes. He didn't have the answers. Neither of us did. "I think we need to find out who that guy really is," he said finally, his words firm, but laced with a tension that didn't escape me.

I pulled back slightly, a frown tugging at my brow. "You don't think he was just some random person, do you?"

"No," he said with a shake of his head, "I don't think he was. I've seen that look before. Those kinds of people don't show up without a reason." His jaw tightened as he spoke, and I knew—without a doubt—that whatever this was, it wasn't just a misunderstanding. There was a real threat behind it, something we couldn't ignore.

I closed my eyes for a moment, trying to steady my breath. "So, what do we do now? Do we go digging into my past?" The thought of unraveling everything, of opening doors I'd buried for so long, made my stomach twist. But the more I thought about it, the more I realized we didn't have a choice. We were already knee-deep in something we couldn't walk away from.

His gaze softened as he reached out, brushing a lock of hair behind my ear. "We don't have to do anything you're not ready for. But I'm not going to let you face this alone."

I wanted to believe him. I really did. But even as the words settled between us, the truth was clearer than ever: we were already in this together, whether we liked it or not.

The sound of my phone ringing broke the fragile stillness, and I pulled it from my pocket, expecting to see a random number flashing on the screen. But it wasn't a stranger's call.

I glanced at the name, my heart skipping a beat. It was from my old hometown.

My finger hovered over the screen for a moment, the weight of everything pressing down on me. Finally, I answered.

"Hello?" My voice was steady, but there was a tremor in the back of it that I couldn't shake.

"I don't have much time," the voice on the other end said, low and urgent. "You need to listen carefully. They're closer than you think. You've been compromised."

My breath caught in my throat. "What do you mean? Who is this?"

"I can't explain everything right now," the voice continued, "but they're already looking for you. They know where you are."

My pulse began to race, the room closing in around me. "Who?" I demanded. "Who's looking for me?"

There was a long pause, and then, the voice came again, this time sharper, more desperate. "It's not over. Don't trust anyone. Not even him."

The line went dead, leaving me standing there, phone in hand, my thoughts spinning out of control.

I turned slowly to face him, my breath shallow, my heart pounding in my chest. The look on his face was a mixture of confusion and concern, and I felt the weight of his stare like a heavy burden.

"What is it?" he asked quietly.

I swallowed hard, my throat dry, and I opened my mouth to speak, but the words refused to come. The warning, the phone call, the stranger with the dark eyes—it was all too much, and I didn't know how to make sense of it.

He took a step toward me, but before he could reach me, the sound of a car engine roaring to life echoed in the distance.

I didn't need to look to know it was them. They were here.

And we were running out of time.

Chapter 38: Forged in Fire

The air was thick with the scent of smoke and charred earth, the kind of smell that clings to the back of your throat long after the fire has died. I stood at the edge of the clearing, hands pressed against my knees, trying to catch my breath. It wasn't supposed to feel like this—not after all the planning, not after all the rehearsing in my head. But there it was, the heat of the moment searing through me, pushing me to confront everything I had buried deep inside.

The forest around us was still and silent now, as though it had been holding its breath, waiting for the storm to pass. The fire—raging in my chest since I'd seen the look on his face just hours before—hadn't quite burned itself out yet. We had come so far, faced so many battles together, but the ghosts of our pasts had a way of creeping back in when you least expected them.

And yet, here we were again, on the precipice of something that might either shatter us or strengthen us. I wasn't sure which, but it didn't matter. What mattered now was that he was here, his presence a steady warmth behind me. And I needed him in a way I had never needed anyone before.

"Hey," his voice was low, a rumble of comfort against the tension in my shoulders. "You alright?"

I didn't answer at first, because no, I wasn't. But I wasn't sure how to tell him that without unraveling everything we'd fought for so far. How do you admit that you've been holding on by a thread, terrified that any wrong move will tear it all apart? I took a slow breath, steadying myself. "Just... thinking."

"You always do that," he said, moving a little closer, his boots crunching on the dirt. I could feel the heat of his body next to mine, a reminder that I wasn't alone, even though the past had a way of making me feel like I was drowning in it. "And when you do, you get that look. Like you're trying to solve a puzzle that doesn't have a solution."

I turned to him, meeting his eyes for the first time since the tension had started to build, since the words had been left unsaid between us. I could see it in his face—he didn't know what I was thinking, but he could feel the storm inside me, the way it was threatening to break everything wide open.

"Maybe I am trying to solve a puzzle," I said, my voice quieter than I intended. "Maybe that's the problem. I thought we were done with all this. But it feels like every time we take a step forward, something else drags us back."

His expression softened, and I could see the shift in his eyes, a flash of understanding. "I know it feels like that. But we can't control everything, love. We can only deal with it as it comes."

He was right, I knew that. But sometimes, the weight of the past—of everything we hadn't said, everything we hadn't dealt with—had a way of pressing down on me until I could barely breathe. And I had no idea how to make it stop.

"Do you ever wonder if we're just... repeating history?" I asked, almost afraid of my own words. I hadn't meant to say them, but once they were out, I couldn't take them back. "Like we're destined to keep making the same mistakes over and over?"

He was quiet for a long moment, his eyes searching mine, trying to find the piece of me that had gone missing. "I don't believe that. Not for a second."

His voice was steady, sure, but I could see the shadow of doubt creeping into his gaze. We both knew too well how easily the past could unravel everything we thought we understood about the present.

"I'm scared," I admitted, the words slipping out before I could stop them. "Scared that we'll get it wrong. That we'll hurt each other in the end."

He reached out, taking my hand, his grip firm and steady, a reassurance that I didn't know I needed until that moment. "You won't hurt me," he said, his voice soft but unwavering. "I trust you. And I believe in us. Whatever happens, we'll figure it out. Together."

There it was, the thing I'd been waiting for. The promise of something more than just the firestorm of our fears. The quiet strength that only he could offer, the one thing I had never truly let myself rely on before.

"I'm not perfect," I whispered, my voice barely above a breath. "I don't always know what to do. But I'm trying. I swear I am."

"I know," he said, squeezing my hand once more before letting it fall back to his side. "I'm not perfect either. But I'm right here. And that's not changing."

I wanted to believe him. I did. But my heart, battered and bruised from years of trying to protect itself, struggled to let go. To let him in. To trust that maybe, just maybe, this time was different. That the fire we'd walked through together wasn't something to fear, but something that had forged us into something stronger.

He took a step closer, his presence consuming the space between us, and for a moment, everything else faded into the background. It was just the two of us—no past, no future—only the here and now.

And then, with the smallest of smiles, he whispered, "We're going to be fine. I'm not going anywhere."

The warmth of his words wrapped around me like a blanket, and for the first time in what felt like forever, I allowed myself to believe it. To believe in us. The fire we'd faced had burned us, yes, but it had also forged something in its wake. And whatever came next, I knew we would face it together.

I should have known that when the phone buzzed on the table, it was never going to be good news. Call it intuition or just the fact that life had a way of throwing curveballs when you were least prepared for them. We hadn't even had breakfast yet, the sunlight barely streaming through the kitchen window, and there it was: a call I should have ignored.

But I didn't.

"Hello?" My voice was a bit too sharp, a touch too defensive, as if I could ward off whatever trouble lurked behind the unknown number.

The voice on the other end was familiar but not in the comforting way I wanted. "We need to talk. Now."

I clenched my jaw. I knew this voice. It was a ghost from my past, the kind that had no business still hanging around. It wasn't the first time it had found its way back into my life, and I had always managed to push it away before, but this time... this time, there was no escape.

"I don't think there's anything to discuss," I said, trying to keep the tremor from my voice. But of course, it was there, lurking under the surface, and whoever was on the other end had a way of sensing that kind of weakness.

"You'll want to hear this. Trust me," the voice said, its casual tone making my blood run cold.

I glanced over at him, still asleep on the couch, tangled in a blanket that had somehow ended up draped across him despite the heat of the room. He looked peaceful—like nothing could touch him. And for a split second, I let myself believe that nothing would. But then the phone call dragged me back to the here and now, and I knew. I knew that peace was a fragile thing.

"I'll be there in an hour," the voice continued, hanging up before I could protest.

I stood there for a long moment, the phone still clutched in my hand, the weight of the conversation pressing down on me. This wasn't just some stray phone call. This was a reminder—of who I used to be, of things I hadn't finished, of consequences I couldn't outrun.

I knew what I had to do. But I hated the thought of it.

"Hey," I said, my voice quieter than I'd meant it to be, as I shook him awake. The last thing I wanted was for him to see the fear in my eyes. He deserved better than that. "We need to talk."

His eyes flickered open, the hazy remnants of sleep still clouding his gaze. "Mornin'?" His voice was thick, a lazy drawl that made me want to smile. But I couldn't. Not right now.

"I'm sorry," I said, pushing a hand through my hair, suddenly feeling the weight of the world. "Something's come up. Something from before." I bit my lip, the words suddenly seeming too much to say. How could I explain it all to him when I wasn't even sure how it all fit together myself?

He sat up, his expression shifting from confusion to concern, but he didn't push me for answers. He just waited, that steady gaze of his never leaving mine, as if he knew there was more I wasn't saying. And I knew I couldn't keep it from him forever.

"What happened?" he asked, his voice no longer groggy but sharp with intent.

"I—" I paused, taking a breath. "I need to go. I'll explain later, I promise. But this... this is something I can't handle alone."

He stood up, running a hand through his hair, and for the first time, I saw a flicker of the same unease that had been growing inside me. "What's going on?"

I shook my head, fighting the panic that was rising in my chest. "I don't know. I just know that if I don't deal with this now, it'll catch up with us. All of us." I moved toward the door, my heart hammering, my mind racing.

He caught my arm, gently but firmly, and for a second, I thought he might stop me. "I'm coming with you."

I met his eyes, and for all the times I had pushed him away, I realized that this was one of the few moments where I couldn't afford to hide the truth from him. Not anymore. "No. This is something I have to do on my own."

His jaw tightened, but he didn't argue. He understood me more than anyone ever had, but he also knew when to give me the space to handle my own mess.

"Alright," he said, letting go of my arm. "But you're not doing this alone in my head. If you need anything, you call me. Immediately."

I nodded, swallowing hard. His words were like a balm to the wound I hadn't let him see. I wasn't alone. Not in the ways that mattered. But this—whatever this was—was something I had to confront in the quiet of my own mind first.

The drive was long, the streets unfamiliar in the way they always seemed to be when you were running away from your past, but somehow they became more claustrophobic when it was coming for you. The car hummed along, its engine a steady drone beneath the increasing thunderstorm in my chest. I could feel the weight of everything that had happened before. It was impossible to outrun the past, no matter how far you tried to go.

The place wasn't far from here—too close, really. It was just another reminder that no matter how many miles you put between yourself and the ghosts, they never stay buried for long. They always find their way back. Always.

As I pulled up, I could see him standing outside, arms crossed, waiting. My heart sank. I knew what was coming. The very thing I'd hoped to avoid. But there was no turning back now. It was time to face it. Face him.

The moment I stepped out of the car, I felt it—like stepping into a different world altogether. The air was thick, sticky, the kind that pressed against your skin like a warning. The silence was oppressive, broken only by the soft rustling of leaves as the wind tried to find a path through the overgrown yard. He was standing there, arms folded across his chest, like he'd been waiting for an eternity. And in some ways, he had.

"Did you think you could just walk away?" The words hit me before I could even find my footing on the gravel driveway. His voice was low, controlled, but there was a bite to it—like a man holding back a storm. "Did you really think I'd let you disappear again?"

I swallowed hard, every instinct in me telling me to run, to pretend I didn't hear him. But I couldn't. Not this time. Not when I knew what was at stake.

"No," I said, my voice steadier than I felt. "I never thought I could get away from you. From this." My hand waved vaguely in the direction of the house behind him. The one that had haunted my memories, the one that felt as much a prison as it did a home. "I just thought maybe if I didn't come back, maybe it would all fade. Maybe I could forget. You could forget."

He took a slow step forward, his eyes narrowing in that way I knew so well. He wasn't one to rush in, but when he moved, it was always with purpose. "You think I forgot? You think I didn't see everything you left behind? You think this"—he gestured to the house again, his tone thick with contempt—"was something I could just let go?"

I didn't know what to say to that. The truth was, I didn't want to face him again. Not like this. Not with all the mess still between us.

"I didn't want to come back," I said finally, my throat tight. "But I had to. I don't know what you expect from me, but I'm not that person anymore."

His lips twisted into a half-smile, one that didn't quite reach his eyes. "You never were. Not really. But you never stopped pretending. That's the problem."

I took a deep breath, trying to steady myself against the rush of emotion that threatened to swallow me whole. "I didn't know what else to do. I didn't know how to fix things."

He scoffed, the sound bitter, cutting through the tension like a knife. "You didn't fix anything by running, you know. You just gave up. You think that's how it works? You think you can just walk away from all of it?"

"I didn't walk away." I was almost shouting now, the words spilling out faster than I could control. "I was trying to protect you. Don't you get that? I wasn't trying to be selfish. I wasn't trying to run—I was trying to keep you safe."

He took a step back, his hands raising slightly as though he was trying to hold up a barrier between us, a gesture that didn't make me feel any better. "You think you were protecting me?" His laugh was cold, full of sharp edges. "You think you're the only one who needed protection? You think I don't have scars, too? That I didn't see everything, just like you did? Just like everyone did?"

The air crackled with the weight of his words, and I could feel the edges of my resolve starting to slip away. How had we ended up here, in this place where everything seemed so impossible? I didn't know how to fix what we'd broken. And worse, I wasn't sure I even could anymore.

"I'm sorry," I whispered, the words heavy in my chest. "But you need to understand—there are things I can't undo. Things I can't take back."

He looked at me for a long moment, his expression unreadable, his jaw clenched. I knew that look. I'd seen it too many times in the past. The way he tried to hold back everything he was feeling, trying to keep control. But I knew, as I looked at him now, that he wasn't sure what came next either.

"You think I don't understand what you're saying?" he asked, his voice barely a whisper. "I understand. But I also know you're still running. You're still hiding from the truth."

I took a step forward, the distance between us closing faster than I would have liked. "I'm not hiding anymore. I'm here. I'm facing it, okay?"

He shook his head slowly, his eyes dark with something unreadable. "Are you? Are you really?"

Before I could answer, a loud crash broke through the stillness, a noise that sent a jolt of panic through my chest. Something in the house. The door—slamming open? No, it was worse than that. I couldn't place it, but the sound was unmistakable. Something was happening.

We both froze, listening, the tension thick enough to cut. My heart was racing, thudding in my chest, every instinct screaming at me to run, to get out. But I didn't.

He turned sharply, looking toward the house. "What was that?" he muttered, his voice low, dangerous.

"I don't know," I said, my throat tight. "But I don't think it's over yet."

He turned back to me then, his eyes searching mine, his jaw set with a sudden, grim determination. "Stay here," he ordered, turning to move toward the door.

"No." My voice was stronger now, more urgent. "I'm coming with you."

He glanced at me, his eyes filled with the kind of warning I knew all too well. "You don't know what you're walking into."

"And you don't either," I shot back, stepping forward, my heart pounding in my chest. "But I'm not standing here while something happens inside that house. We go in together, or not at all."

He hesitated, his gaze flicking between me and the door. Finally, with a grunt, he nodded. "Together. But don't get in the way."

We reached the door just as another crash sounded from inside, louder this time, followed by the unmistakable sound of someone—or something—moving through the house.

I didn't think. I didn't have time to think. With a shared glance, we pushed the door open.

And then we both froze.

Chapter 39: Healing the Heart

I used to think peace was something elusive, like trying to catch a sunset in your hands. But now, as I sit by the window, the morning sun pouring in and warm on my skin, I realize it's not fleeting. It's right here, in the steady rhythm of my breath, in the quiet of the room, and in the weight of Callum's arm across my shoulders. The world outside is bustling—people rushing to work, cars honking, the usual noise of city life—but none of it touches me. Not anymore.

I've started to recognize the difference between contentment and happiness. For the longest time, I thought they were the same thing, but they're not. Contentment is the calm you find in the aftermath of a storm, when the winds have settled, and the rain is nothing more than a memory. It's the sigh of relief you release when you realize you've survived. Happiness, though—it's the warmth of a hug when you least expect it, the laughter that bursts from your chest like a well-kept secret finally spilling out. It's the touch of Callum's hand on my lower back as we walk to the market, a simple thing, but it means everything. That's happiness. The moments I thought I might never have, but now, I'm savoring each one.

I glance over at him now, lounging on the couch, a book in his hands, his dark hair falling into his eyes. He looks up at me and smiles, a crooked thing that lights up his entire face. It's a smile that used to be a rarity, an afterthought almost, as though he was never quite sure it was allowed. But now, it comes more easily. I'd like to think it's because of me, because of us, but I know it's also the kind of smile you get when you start believing in second chances.

"Can I help you with anything?" His voice is quiet, but there's an edge to it that makes my heart flutter. He's always so aware of me now, as though he can sense the slightest shift in my mood. I never asked for that kind of attention, never expected it, but

I've come to crave it. I guess that's love, in a nutshell—recognizing the smallest details, the unspoken things, and understanding them without explanation.

I laugh lightly and shake my head, walking over to the kitchen counter. "Nope. Just thought I'd stand here and be in awe of your ability to make my heart beat faster with a single look. No big deal."

He chuckles, setting the book aside and stretching, his muscles rippling beneath his T-shirt. "You're not fooling anyone, you know. You like the way I look at you, just as much as I like looking at you."

There's that charm again, the one I used to resent, the one that made me think he didn't take anything seriously. But now, it's different. There's depth to it, a tenderness I hadn't realized was there, hidden beneath the surface all along. The teasing, the flirting, they're not just games anymore. It's a way for him to reach out, to show me that, despite everything, we're still here. We're still fighting for this.

I grab the half-empty jar of honey from the counter and pour it over my tea, watching the amber liquid swirl. It's a small, simple thing—pouring honey—but it feels significant. Every action, every word between us feels like we're weaving a tapestry, one stitch at a time. And maybe that's what healing is: finding meaning in the smallest things and realizing they're not so small after all.

"You still think about the past?" Callum's voice cuts through my thoughts, gentle but insistent. He knows me too well. Knows that my silences speak volumes.

I pause, my fingers stilling on the jar, before turning to face him. "I think about it," I admit, my voice barely above a whisper. "But it doesn't hurt anymore." I take a slow sip of my tea, the warmth of it spreading down my throat. "I think I've learned to carry it, rather than let it carry me."

He nods, his expression softening. "I get that. I think I'm getting there, too."

For a moment, we're silent, just two people who understand each other in ways no one else can. It's a quiet understanding, a bond forged in the fires of our separate storms. It's not perfect, but it's real. And that's enough.

The doorbell rings, a sharp interruption to the calm we've found. I set my cup down and glance at Callum, who looks as surprised as I feel. "You expecting anyone?" I ask.

He shakes his head, already standing and moving toward the door. "No idea."

I follow him, the air in the room suddenly shifting, thick with anticipation. When Callum opens the door, I'm not sure what I expect, but it definitely isn't her.

A woman stands there, a little out of place, her blonde hair caught in the wind, her eyes wide as though she's unsure if she's made a mistake. But the recognition hits me first. I know her. I know her from the past, from before everything came crashing down. She's the one who was there when Callum's life spiraled, the one who helped pick up the pieces when I couldn't.

And as her gaze locks with mine, I can see the storm rising again, like it never really left.

I don't know how long we stood there, staring at her. The woman on the doorstep. Her name slips my mind for a moment, but then I remember—Lydia. Of course, it's Lydia. The woman who knew Callum in ways I never did, the one who occupied the spaces in his life I had once thought were mine to claim. The sight of her, standing there with that hesitant half-smile, makes the air in the room thicken. I can feel the unease settle over my skin, a tingle I can't shake.

Callum seems frozen too, his hand still on the doorknob, like he's unsure whether to pull her inside or shut the door in her face. He glances at me, a brief flicker of something in his eyes—guilt, maybe, or uncertainty. It doesn't matter. She's here now, and we have to deal with it.

"Can I help you?" I ask, my voice a little more brittle than I want it to be. I've never been great at hiding how I feel, and I'm sure my irritation is written all over my face.

Lydia looks at me, her expression unreadable for a second before she opens her mouth to speak. She's older now, more put-together than I remember, but there's a wariness in her gaze that betrays her calm exterior. "I'm not sure if you're going to like this, but I need to talk to Callum."

Her words hit me like a slap, but I force a smile, even though I'm anything but amused. "I'm sure Callum can speak for himself." I try to sound casual, but the words come out tighter than I expected. It's as though I've forgotten how to hide the rawness of everything that's been happening, how I feel like the edges of my heart are still bruised from the past.

Lydia's eyes flick over to Callum, and I watch his shoulders tense. "I think you should let her in," he says softly, his voice an odd mix of caution and something else. Regret? Maybe. Or guilt, again. I can't quite tell, but I can see the flicker in his gaze that tells me there's more to this than he's letting on.

I don't want to let her in. I don't want her here. But I can see the way his jaw tightens, the way his fingers tap against the doorframe, and I know I've lost this one. Callum hasn't said it outright, but it's clear he owes her something. And for reasons I don't fully understand, he's not ready to burn that bridge.

I step aside reluctantly, and Lydia enters, her perfume filling the space between us like an unwelcome memory. It's not a bad scent—floral, warm, with an undercurrent of something deeper, muskier—but it's enough to make me feel like I'm stepping into someone else's life. I don't know what to make of this woman, but I'm pretty sure I don't want to.

She looks around the apartment, as if she's measuring something, then turns to Callum. "I didn't know where else to go," she says, her voice quieter now. There's a vulnerability there, a crack I can see if I look closely enough. I'm not sure I believe it, but I'm also not sure I care. The woman's been a part of Callum's life when I was just a blip, a shadow, and I hate how easily she falls into the space between us, like she owns it.

"You've got nothing to apologize for," Callum says, his words low and steady. He walks into the kitchen without waiting for her response, clearly not wanting to deal with the confrontation in the doorway. "I just didn't think it was necessary to—"

"No, you're right," Lydia interrupts, her eyes snapping to mine. "I should've just kept my distance." There's something about the way she says it that feels rehearsed, as if she's trying too hard to sound casual about something that's clearly eating at her. I don't care. Let her feel guilty. I have every right to feel the way I do.

I cross my arms and lean against the wall, my gaze fixed on her. "So, what exactly do you want?" My tone is sharper than I intend, but I'm done with games. Whatever this is, I'm not playing along. I've worked too hard to get to where I am, to let some ghost from Callum's past come in and disrupt everything.

Lydia looks at me for a long beat, her eyes flicking from me to Callum. She's measuring me, trying to figure out what I want to hear. I'm not sure I care about her intentions anymore, but I'm curious what she has to say. The silence drags on, heavy, before she speaks again.

"I never meant for things to get as messy as they did," she says, and for the first time, there's a crack in her armor. Her voice falters, just for a second, and I catch it. "I just... I wasn't prepared for how quickly everything fell apart." Her gaze turns to Callum, and there's a sadness there, an old wound she hasn't learned to heal. "I thought we'd have more time, you know? To fix things."

There's a long moment of tension, a beat where Callum doesn't say anything. I can see the conflict in his eyes, the pull between his past and the life he's built with me. It's not easy, trying to balance the two. I know that now. I don't envy him. But I can't ignore the feeling of being caught in the middle, like a pawn on a chessboard. And I'm not the type to let that slide.

"You don't get to just come back in and say things like that," I snap, my voice cutting through the air like a blade. "You don't get to apologize for a past you left behind, then act like it's okay to pick up where you left off."

Lydia flinches at my words, but I can't stop now. The truth needs to be said. "You're not a part of his life anymore. You don't get to waltz in here and make him question what we've worked for."

There's a quiet intensity in Callum's eyes now, his expression unreadable. For a second, I wonder if I've gone too far, but then I remember why I'm doing this. I'm protecting us. I'm protecting him.

"I'm not asking you to," Lydia says, her voice softer, almost pleading. "I'm asking for one thing. One chance to fix it."

One thing I've learned about love is that it has a funny way of turning everything upside down when you least expect it. Here I am, thinking I'm finally getting the hang of this relationship, that we've put the past behind us, only for Lydia to waltz in and remind me how fragile everything can be. I feel the air grow dense around us, a subtle shift in the room that weighs heavy on my chest. She stands there, looking like she's come to make things right, but I'm not sure how much of this I'm willing to entertain.

"One chance," I repeat, my words dripping with disbelief. I cross my arms tighter, almost as though I'm trying to hold myself together. "Do you really think that's enough to fix everything? Do you honestly believe one conversation can undo all the damage?"

Lydia looks at me, her face softening, as if my bitterness has caught her off guard. There's a flicker of vulnerability in her eyes that almost makes me second-guess myself, but I can't afford to. Not now. I won't let this woman disrupt everything I've worked for, everything Callum and I have fought to rebuild.

"I don't know," Lydia says, her voice quieter now. She seems to shrink into herself, her shoulders hunching just slightly. "But I know I can't move forward until I've tried."

The sincerity in her voice hits me harder than I expect. I can see it—she's not just apologizing for the sake of it. She's struggling with something, and I think it's more than just trying to make amends with Callum. It's a little like watching someone try to navigate a labyrinth of their own regrets, but at the same time, I'm not sure how much I want to let her in.

I glance at Callum, whose face has gone unreadable again. He's standing by the kitchen counter, fingers brushing against the edge of it, almost like he's lost in thought. His silence is maddening—he's caught between the woman who used to matter to him and the life he's slowly building with me. He doesn't know what to do either.

"You can't expect to waltz back in here like nothing happened," I say, my tone firmer now, a little sharper. "You don't get to just apologize and walk away with a clean slate."

Callum shifts slightly, and I catch the glance he gives her, the way his jaw tightens. It's enough to set me on edge. Maybe it's the way he looks at her, like there's something unfinished, unresolved. And as much as I want to brush it off, it feels like the weight of the past has shifted back onto my shoulders.

"I'm not asking for a clean slate," Lydia says quickly, almost too quickly. "But I can't just leave things hanging like this. Not with him. Not with... with you." She directs her gaze at me then, a flicker of something unspoken passing between us, a moment where everything feels too raw. "I owe him, I owe you, an explanation."

I laugh, though it's more a sound of disbelief than anything else. "An explanation? You owe us both the truth, Lydia, not some half-baked apology about things you can't change."

She takes a slow breath, her hands twisting in front of her, like she's afraid to speak too loudly, afraid to say the wrong thing. There's a hesitation there, but I can't decide if it's genuine or just another ploy to make herself feel better. I've seen people use words like shields before, deflecting the sharp edges of the past until they don't have to face them.

But then her voice drops, quieter, almost breaking. "I didn't mean to hurt either of you," she says, and for a brief moment, I believe her. "I thought I was doing the right thing at the time."

I shake my head, biting back the urge to interrupt. The truth is, I can't trust her, not yet. I've come too far to let the past creep in like this, to let someone waltz in and shake up the delicate balance Callum and I have built. "I don't know what you're trying to do here," I say, my voice trembling slightly. "But I'm not going to sit here and let you tear us apart again."

I want to make it sound firm, but I can feel my resolve slipping. I don't want her to win, don't want to let her back in, but I can't shake the doubt that's creeping in. There's too much tension in the room, too many unspoken things, and all I want is for this to be over.

Callum clears his throat, his gaze shifting between Lydia and me. His lips are pressed together in that familiar tight line, the one that makes me wonder what he's really thinking. "We can't just ignore the past," he says quietly, almost as though he's trying to reason with both of us. "It's not about whether we forgive or forget. It's about understanding why it happened."

I feel my heart clench at his words, a tightening that makes everything seem sharper, clearer. Because he's right. As much as I want to run from this, to shove Lydia out and shut the door, the truth is, the past can't be ignored. Not for me. Not for Callum. It lingers, in the spaces between us, in the things we haven't said aloud.

"Fine," I snap, the words coming faster now, before I can stop them. "You want to explain? Fine. But make it quick. Because I'm done letting your ghosts haunt us."

Lydia seems to brace herself, her eyes closing for a moment as if gathering her courage. When she opens them again, there's a heaviness to them, a weight that makes my stomach twist. "I wasn't the only one responsible for the way things went wrong," she says, her voice steady now, but there's a crack in it that catches me off guard. "Callum... he didn't want you to know everything."

I freeze, my breath catching in my throat. "What?"

And before she can answer, before any of us can process what's just been said, the door slams open behind us, and a voice I don't recognize calls out, sharp and urgent. "Callum, we need to talk. Now."

Chapter 40: The Promise of Forever

The evening air hung with the weight of promise, thick and fragrant with the scent of jasmine blooming in the garden just beyond the terrace. I could almost taste the sweetness of it on my tongue as I stepped out into the fading warmth of the sun, the last golden rays dappling the stone steps beneath my bare feet. Callum was there, leaning against the railing, looking out at the horizon with his hands tucked into the pockets of his well-worn jeans. He was always a bit too casual for his own good, but somehow it suited him, the perfect mix of comfort and mystery.

"You really should wear shoes," I teased, crossing the space between us, my voice soft in the quiet. "It's not proper to go barefoot in public."

Callum grinned, that lazy, confident smile that always made my heart flutter, as if I was the only one in the world that mattered when he looked at me that way. "Says the girl who's been barefoot for hours," he shot back, lifting an eyebrow. "Besides, no one else is around to care."

That was true enough. We'd had the place to ourselves for the better part of the day, a rare and precious thing in our chaotic lives. There was a peace in the silence that stretched between us, but it was the kind of peace that was comfortable, not unsettling. As if the world had stopped just for a moment, allowing us to be the only two souls that existed.

I slid my hand into his, feeling the warmth of his skin, the calluses on his fingers from years of hard work. There was something grounding about him, something steady and sure. And in this moment, as the soft breeze whispered around us, I felt it—the promise. It had been building, slowly, over days, weeks, months, a quiet understanding that neither of us had dared to name until now. But now, it was impossible to ignore.

"I don't think I've ever been more certain of anything in my life," I said softly, my gaze fixed on the sea stretching before us. The sky above had turned a brilliant shade of pink, the last blush of the sun as it sank lower, teasing the edges of the water with its dying light.

Callum's fingers tightened around mine, and he shifted slightly to face me, his expression open, but with an intensity that I couldn't quite place. "Are you sure?" His voice was low, almost hesitant, as if the weight of his words could shatter everything if he wasn't careful.

"Of course, I'm sure." I turned to look at him, catching the flicker of doubt in his eyes, and my heart gave a little twist. There had been so much uncertainty between us over the last few months—misunderstandings, old wounds reopening, fears that threatened to pull us apart at the seams. But now, standing here with him, I could feel the threads of something stronger weaving between us. "I've never been more sure."

His lips quirked, a half-smile that didn't quite reach his eyes. "Then let's make sure we're both on the same page," he said, taking a step closer. The air around us shifted, charged with the weight of his words.

I could feel my pulse quicken, a flutter of nerves in my stomach that I hadn't expected. He had a way of making everything seem like a turning point, as though whatever came next would change the course of everything that had come before it. And maybe it would. Maybe this moment would be one we'd look back on, the beginning of something we both hadn't dared to imagine until now.

"Tell me," Callum said, his voice soft but steady. "What do you want from this... from us?"

I hesitated. What did I want? My mind raced through all the possibilities, all the roads that could lead from this moment. But the answer felt so simple, so clear. "I want this. I want us. I want to know that no matter what happens, we'll face it together."

Callum's eyes softened, his hand lifting to cup my face, his thumb brushing gently over my cheek. The touch was tender, almost reverent, as if he was committing the feel of me to memory. "I'll always be here," he said, his voice barely above a whisper. "Always."

A shiver ran through me at the weight of his words, a warmth spreading through my chest that had nothing to do with the late afternoon sun. The promise was in his eyes, in the steady way he looked at me, and I felt something inside me shift, settle into place.

"I don't know if I deserve that," I murmured, the words slipping out before I could stop them. The truth of it was, I didn't. I had a history, one filled with missteps and mistakes, things I couldn't erase, no matter how much I wished I could. And yet, here he was, offering me something I hadn't dared to hope for—a future.

"You do," he said firmly, almost fiercely, as if the very idea that I might think otherwise was absurd. "You deserve all of it."

I looked up at him, my heart swelling with something I couldn't quite name. There was a tenderness in the way he held me, a certainty that made my insides feel warm and soft. For the first time in my life, I didn't feel like I was standing at the edge of something that could fall apart. With Callum, I felt like I was finally home.

And in that quiet moment, with the world fading away around us, I made him a promise of my own. Not in words, but in the way I held his gaze, in the way my heart beat steady with his, knowing without a doubt that no matter what the future held, we would face it together. Forever.

The evening stretched on, quiet and expectant, as if the world itself was holding its breath. We didn't speak for a while, just stood there, letting the soft hum of the night settle around us. Somewhere in the distance, a bird called out, its voice echoing in the hollow spaces between us and the horizon. The stars were beginning to flicker into existence, tiny pinpricks of light scattered across the inky canvas above, each one a reminder of something vast and unknowable. But here, in this moment, with Callum's hand still wrapped around mine, nothing seemed more certain.

"I think," I began, breaking the silence, my voice almost a whisper, "I think I've forgotten what it feels like to be truly happy."

Callum turned slightly toward me, his brow furrowing, just enough to show he was listening closely. "Is that so?" he asked, his tone soft, measured. His eyes searched mine, looking for the truth behind the words.

I nodded, a small, rueful smile tugging at the corners of my lips. "I've had... moments, I guess. Bits and pieces. But this—this feels different. Like it's more than just fleeting. More than just a good day."

He didn't answer immediately, his gaze thoughtful. There was a flicker of something in his eyes, something I couldn't quite place, before he leaned in, brushing a lock of hair away from my face. The touch was so tender, so deliberate, that it took me by surprise, like he was trying to memorize the way I looked at this very moment.

"Maybe that's because you're not running from it anymore," he said, his voice quiet but steady.

I froze, the words sinking into me with an uncomfortable weight. He was right. For so long, I had been running—running from myself, from things I didn't understand, from the future I couldn't quite grasp. Fear had always been my constant companion, shadowing my every step, whispering in my ear that nothing good could last, that nothing was safe. Even now, I could feel it lurking, just beneath the surface, waiting for the right moment to remind me of the rules I'd lived by for so long.

But in this moment, with Callum so close, his presence steady and warm, it felt like maybe, just maybe, I could stop running. That I could finally trust what was right in front of me.

The thought scared me more than I was willing to admit. I opened my mouth to speak, but the words wouldn't come. Instead, I just stood there, staring at him, feeling the pull between us, a magnetism that seemed impossible to ignore.

He smiled then, a slow, knowing smile, as if he could sense my hesitation, could feel the battle waging inside me. "I'm not going anywhere," he said, and it was a promise, simple and unequivocal, like the rhythm of a heartbeat.

His words hung in the air, settling around us like a shield, as if he could somehow ward off the doubts and fears that I knew were still gnawing at me. But in his eyes, there was nothing but certainty. There was nothing but us. And for the first time, I believed it, or at least, I wanted to.

I exhaled slowly, allowing the tension to drain from my body, my shoulders sagging slightly as I finally allowed myself to relax. I let go of the fear, just for a moment, and let myself be swallowed by the warmth of his presence. I was here, with him, and that was enough. For now, it had to be enough.

"Tell me something," I said after a beat, my voice teasing now, lighter, as I leaned in a fraction closer. "What's the worst thing you've ever done?"

His eyebrow arched, a flicker of amusement passing over his face. "That's an oddly specific question," he remarked, though there was no judgment in his tone, just the kind of playful curiosity that always made my heart skip.

I shrugged, a wry grin on my face. "Everyone has skeletons in their closet. I'm just curious what yours look like."

Callum laughed softly, the sound rich and warm, like a note struck on a well-tuned piano. "Well," he said, drawing out the word,

"I may have once convinced my best friend to skip a wedding, claiming we had an emergency that required us to 'rescue' a cat from a tree. Turned out the cat was perfectly fine, but the wedding wasn't, and well... let's just say I wasn't very popular after that."

I couldn't help but laugh, the sound light and genuine, bubbling up from somewhere deep inside me. "You're a terrible person," I said, half-amused, half-mocking, though I couldn't have been more charmed.

He shrugged, his grin widening. "It was for a good cause. But no one ever appreciated my good intentions."

"Of course not," I said, shaking my head. "People don't appreciate being lied to about cats in trees."

We both stood there for a moment, laughing softly, the kind of easy, unburdened laughter that came when two people were finally comfortable enough to share the smallest, most ridiculous parts of themselves. It was a connection, deep and effortless, and in that moment, I realized that it wasn't just the promise we'd made earlier that was holding us together—it was these moments, these tiny revelations, these moments of vulnerability and shared humor, that were weaving the fabric of something much stronger.

I glanced up at him, catching the quiet tenderness in his gaze. "What about you?" I asked. "What's the worst thing you've done?"

He looked at me, his eyes flicking between my own, and then, with a tilt of his head, he said, "I once let someone go when I should have fought for them."

The words hung there, heavy and unexpected. The easy banter faded, replaced by something deeper, something raw. The weight of his confession settled in the space between us, and I realized that there was more to him than I'd ever imagined. More than the man who made me laugh, more than the man who held me when I needed him most. He had his own wounds, his own regrets, and they were as real as mine.

But somehow, that didn't scare me. It made him more real, more human. And I wasn't sure where this was going, or how it would turn out, but for the first time in a long time, I wasn't afraid of the future.

The night unfolded around us like a slow-burning fire, each flicker of flame illuminating the spaces between us, those quiet, intimate moments that felt suspended in time. I couldn't help but notice how the air seemed to hum with something unspoken, something that swelled just beneath the surface, threatening to overflow. We were no longer just two people standing together. We were something more, something forged by the shared promises and the weight of everything we had yet to say.

Callum turned slightly, a thoughtful expression clouding his face for just a second. It was the kind of look that made my stomach knot with a strange mixture of anxiety and excitement, like the first drop of a rollercoaster, and I couldn't help but wonder if he was feeling the same thing I was. The weight of this, of everything we were standing on, seemed to press against us, as if the world was holding its breath, waiting for the next step.

"I've been thinking," he said, his voice lower than usual, like he was testing the words on his tongue before letting them loose. "About what comes next."

I tilted my head, curious. "What do you mean?"

He paused, searching for the right way to phrase it, his eyes flicking to the stars above, as if they could give him the answers he was looking for. "I know we've made promises. And I'm not saying I'm having doubts, but..." He trailed off, exhaling slowly, like he was trying to let go of something that had been gnawing at him for a while. "But we both know life has a way of throwing curveballs."

A knot formed in my stomach. This wasn't what I expected him to say, and my first instinct was to pull away, to distance myself from the possibility of whatever that meant. "Are you saying you're not sure?"

He shook his head quickly, as though to erase the words before they could settle between us. "No, that's not what I mean. I'm sure of you. I'm sure of us." He looked at me then, his gaze steady, unwavering. "But I don't want you to think that I have some perfect plan for us, or that everything will be easy. Because it won't be. I've seen how things can fall apart. I've been there."

A chill ran through me at his words. I had, too. The world we lived in was rarely kind, and even when it seemed to give you something beautiful, it had a way of pulling it back before you could savor it. And still, I couldn't help but believe—this was worth fighting for. It had to be.

"Callum," I whispered, stepping a little closer, feeling the cool night air brush against my skin. "We don't need a perfect plan. We just need to know we're in it together."

His eyes softened at the sincerity in my voice, but there was still a tension there, a layer of something he wasn't saying. And that something—the unsaid things—began to gnaw at me, just like the fear I couldn't quite shake. We were standing on the edge of something beautiful, but I could sense the precipice, that sharp drop just below us. The question was, would we leap together?

"I know that," he said, his voice quiet now, almost reverent, as if the weight of my words was grounding him in a way nothing else had. "But I need you to understand one thing, more than anything else."

I raised an eyebrow, my heart skipping as I waited for him to continue. "What's that?"

He took a slow, deliberate breath, as though gathering his thoughts. "If you're with me—if we're doing this together—then you have to understand that I won't let anything come between us. Not again. No matter what."

My chest tightened at the intensity in his voice, the heat of his words curling around me like a protective cloak. The sincerity in his eyes made my heart flutter, and for a moment, I almost believed it. But then the weight of his statement hit me, and something flickered—something that made me question whether we were truly ready for the kind of commitment that came with such a promise. Could I handle that kind of intensity? Could we survive the weight of those words?

Before I could form a response, the sound of footsteps in the distance caught my attention, sharp and sudden, pulling me out of the bubble that had formed around us. I turned quickly, my gaze snapping to the figure emerging from the shadows at the edge of the terrace.

The world seemed to pause. Everything slowed, even the air, which felt suddenly thick and heavy. My stomach flipped, and I didn't even realize I was holding my breath until Callum's hand tightened around mine.

The figure was familiar, though I couldn't quite place it at first. But then the realization hit me like a slap across the face, and I felt the blood drain from my cheeks. Standing in the doorway, looking every bit as imposing as the first time I had seen him, was Daniel—Callum's brother.

"Hello, little brother," Daniel said with a wry smile, his voice smooth and calculated, as though nothing was amiss. But the tension in his posture was unmistakable. "I hope I'm not interrupting."

The words hung in the air, thick with unspoken challenges, the weight of past grudges pressing down on the air between us. Callum stiffened beside me, and I could feel his body go rigid, the subtle shift in the atmosphere unmistakable. There was no mistaking it now. This wasn't just a visit. Daniel was here for something, and whatever it was, it had nothing to do with catching up or making amends.

"Daniel," Callum's voice was tight, controlled, though I could see the muscle in his jaw twitching. "What the hell are you doing here?"

Daniel's smile widened, a knowing glint in his eyes. "Oh, I think you know exactly why I'm here."

Chapter 41: A Love Rekindled

The coffee cup clinked against the saucer with a soft, almost apologetic sound. I should've taken that as a warning. After all, nothing good ever started with coffee at 9:15 a.m. on a Tuesday. The steam curling up from the mug, a little too thick for this time of day, was the only thing comforting about it. That and the faint scent of vanilla that lingered in the air.

I couldn't quite put my finger on what was different about today, but there it was—a strange weight, like something was about to shift, and I wasn't sure if I was ready for it. Or if I wanted it to happen.

Outside the café window, the rain was coming down in sheets, blurring the world into soft watercolor smudges. It was one of those rare days when the world felt still, like everything was caught in a collective exhale, as if the universe were holding its breath for something that hadn't yet arrived.

"Don't you think this rain's a bit much?" he said, his voice cutting through the quiet like the perfect line of a melody. I'd know that voice anywhere. The one that always seemed to get to me, no matter how many times it should've lost its power.

I looked up from my coffee to find him standing there, his coat a little damp from the downpour, but his eyes as clear and confident as ever. He had a way of looking at me like I was the only thing worth seeing, even in a crowd.

"Did you just ask me about the weather?" I grinned, the corners of my lips lifting before I could stop myself. I couldn't help it. His charm was an old, familiar friend I wasn't ready to say goodbye to.

He leaned in, pulling out the chair across from me and dropping his coat on the back. "I know it's not the most riveting conversation starter, but I'm trying to ease into this." He smiled, a grin that had the power to knock the breath out of me every time.

I knew I should be angry. I should be anything but amused. After all, the last time I'd seen him, we hadn't exactly parted on the best terms. Words had been exchanged, accusations thrown, and in the heat of the moment, things had been said that I could never take back.

But here he was, as if time had simply decided to erase the distance we'd created between us.

"So, is this your idea of easing into a conversation?" I teased, swirling my coffee.

He chuckled, leaning back in his chair. "You know it's a little more complicated than that, don't you?"

I raised an eyebrow, the playful smile still lingering on my lips, though it was harder to maintain than I liked to admit. "Is it? Because from where I'm sitting, you just waltzed back into my life, acting like nothing ever happened."

The smile faltered just a fraction, a shadow of something deeper flickering in his eyes. It was gone before I could name it, but it made me pause. The sudden stillness between us was thicker than the rain outside. "I wasn't acting like nothing happened," he said quietly. "I've been thinking about it every single day."

I glanced at him, unsure of how to respond to that. His honesty was disarming. It made me want to believe him, even when I knew better. Even when I'd spent months convincing myself that what we had was a thing of the past. But here he was, looking at me like he hadn't given up on us. Like he hadn't given up on me.

"You've been thinking about it?" I asked, my voice softer than I intended. "For how long?"

"Too long," he admitted, pushing the mug of coffee away, though it remained untouched. "I messed up. More than once, and I'm not proud of it."

His words landed in the space between us like stones in water, the ripples spreading wider and wider with every second.

"I didn't ask for that," I said, my voice trembling despite my best efforts. "I didn't ask for you to mess up. Or for you to come back now."

I could see the apology in his eyes before it even left his lips. "I know. I know. But I'm here now. And I'm not leaving without fixing this. Fixing us."

The quiet tension felt heavier than the storm outside. The air between us was charged, thick with all the words we hadn't said yet. But it was more than that, too. It was the unspoken weight of the love we'd shared, the kind that burns just as hot in the absence of touch, as it does when you can't get close enough.

I looked down at my coffee, taking a slow sip, needing something—anything—to distract me from the thudding of my heart. It was foolish, I knew. Foolish to think I could simply ignore the way he'd affected me, how effortlessly he'd slithered back into my life with a smile and an apology.

"I never stopped thinking about you either," I finally said, my voice low. The words slipped out before I could hold them back. They felt like a confession, something I'd buried deep, only to unearth it now, in the strangest moment.

His gaze softened, but I could see the edges of his usual cocky grin creeping back. "Well, that makes two of us."

"Does it?" I raised an eyebrow. "I thought you were too busy 'messing up' to think about me."

He winced, but it was brief. "Touche," he murmured. "But I'm here now. And I'm not running away from this, from you, again."

His words should have scared me. They should have made me want to get up and walk away before this whole thing became another mess. But instead, something inside me softened, like I'd forgotten how to build walls where he was concerned. The truth was, I was tired of the games. Tired of pretending I didn't feel the pull every time he was near.

"You really think you can fix this?" I asked, my voice almost daring him to say it again.

"I don't think," he said with quiet certainty. "I know."

I didn't know what I expected when I agreed to sit down with him, but it certainly wasn't this. His presence was like a familiar scent—a blend of citrus and leather that somehow made me feel both grounded and unsteady, as if the earth beneath me was shifting, but I wasn't sure where it was taking me.

The rain outside had finally let up, though the clouds still clung to the sky like an unspoken promise of more to come. We were still sitting there in that tiny café, the minutes ticking by like they were trying to tell us something we hadn't figured out yet.

"So," I began, not knowing how to navigate this fragile truce between us. "What exactly do you think you can fix? I mean, it's been months. And honestly, I didn't spend all this time working on myself just to let you waltz back in and make everything magically better."

He looked at me, his fingers tracing the rim of his coffee cup as if he was carefully choosing his words. "I never wanted you to have to work on yourself. I never wanted you to have to do anything alone."

It should've been easy to dismiss him. I could've laughed at the sentiment, could've stood up and left—gone back to my life without him, the life I had built after he shattered everything. But there was something about the way he said it, like he truly believed it. Like I mattered to him in a way that transcended the mess of us.

I didn't answer right away. Instead, I leaned back in my chair, studying him the way one might study an old map, full of familiar places and forgotten landmarks. His jaw was a little more squared now, his hair a little shorter. But it was the eyes that had changed.

They no longer held that easy arrogance, that cocky defiance I had once wanted to shake from him. Now they were guarded, like he'd seen too much to be naive, yet still hopeful enough to want to try again.

"I'm not asking for you to fix anything," I said, my voice quiet, almost to myself. "I'm just trying to figure out what happens next."

His lips parted as if he was going to speak, then closed again. "I don't want to rush you," he said, his voice surprisingly steady. "But I think we owe it to ourselves to be real with each other now. No more games. No more pretending we don't still want this."

The words felt like a dare, and I hated that I wasn't sure how to respond. I wanted to argue, wanted to say something that would make him second-guess this entire conversation. But I didn't. Instead, I found myself nodding. Not because I was ready to forgive him. Not even because I was certain I wanted him back. But because, deep down, I realized that part of me always had.

"I think," I began, tapping my fingers against the side of my cup, "we need to address the elephant in the room."

His brow furrowed. "What elephant?"

"The one where you vanished off the face of the earth without a word. The one where you broke everything, and then I had to pick up the pieces while pretending like I didn't care." My heart was pounding now, but I couldn't stop myself. The words came rushing out, carried by an anger I thought I'd buried long ago. "I was fine without you, you know. I built a life. I moved on. And then you just waltz back in here like—"

"Like I'm the one who walked away?" he interrupted, his voice sharp, but not unkind. "Because believe me, if I could've stayed, I would've. I wasn't doing any of this because I wanted to hurt you, okay?"

I blinked, the heat in my chest suddenly turning cold. "I'm not asking for your excuses," I said, my voice more bitter than I intended. "I'm just trying to figure out why you think you can come in here and act like nothing happened. Like we're just supposed to pick up where we left off."

He shifted forward in his seat, eyes intense. "Because nothing's changed. Not really. You and me—we've always had this connection. The kind that doesn't just go away, no matter how many mistakes I've made. I'm here now. And I'm not asking you to forgive me right away. But I want to try."

There it was again. That pull. That quiet certainty in his voice that made me feel like maybe he wasn't lying. Maybe there was something in him, something real, that was willing to put in the work this time.

"Try?" I echoed, almost laughing at the absurdity of it. "I'm not some project for you to fix, you know."

His lips twisted into a rueful smile. "I'm not fixing you. You're already whole." His gaze softened. "But maybe I can help you remember that."

I couldn't help it. A laugh bubbled up, light and bitter at the same time. "You have a way with words, don't you?"

"I've had time to practice," he said, a grin creeping back onto his face. "But seriously, I know I've screwed up, and I know you're probably expecting me to grovel or something. But I'm not going to do that."

"You think I want you to grovel?" My eyebrow lifted, the faintest trace of challenge creeping into my voice.

"No," he said, leaning in just a bit, his eyes glinting with that familiar spark. "But I do think you're waiting for me to do something I haven't done before. Something that makes you believe I'm serious. That makes you trust me again."

And just like that, the air shifted again. My breath caught, but I didn't back away. I wasn't sure if I wanted to run, or if I was tired of running at all. He'd always known how to make me question everything I thought I knew. And, for the first time in a long time, I wasn't so sure I wanted to fight it anymore.

I should have known better than to think that anything between us could be simple. But I was here, leaning across the table, barely an inch from the man who had broken me—who had left without a word, like I was some forgotten chapter in his life. And now, just like that, he was back. He was here, with the same steady, determined gaze, the same soft curve of his mouth that made me feel both terrified and utterly undone.

"I'm not asking you to make it easy," he said, his voice low, deliberate. "I'm asking you to give me the chance to make it right. That's all I want. A chance."

It should have been easier to turn him down, to tell him that there was no room left for him in my life. It should have been simple to stand up, gather my things, and walk away—leave the man who had left me drowning in a sea of unanswered questions.

But I wasn't that person anymore.

The woman sitting here wasn't the one who used to wait for him to show up, to ask for forgiveness, to beg for the life we'd planned together. No, this woman had learned how to stand on her own, how to pick up the pieces of her life and glue them back together, even when everything had shattered. She didn't need him to fix her anymore.

Yet there was that pull. That stupid, magnetic pull that made it almost impossible to breathe without considering what would happen if I gave in.

"I've spent so much time convincing myself that I was better off without you," I said, trying to keep the tremble out of my voice, but failing miserably. "That I could move on, and everything would be fine."

He didn't speak, just watched me, his dark eyes full of something I didn't know how to read. Maybe it was regret. Maybe it was guilt. Or maybe it was something else—something I wasn't ready to confront.

"But the truth is," I continued, my voice thickening, "I haven't been fine. Not really." I let out a sharp breath, looking away from him as if I could somehow escape the weight of those words. "I've missed you. More than I want to admit."

His expression softened, and for a moment, the distance between us seemed to vanish. But that was the problem, wasn't it? The distance never truly disappeared. It was there, hovering between every word, every touch. There was so much unsaid, so many things left to untangle.

"Do you know how many times I've wished I could take back the things I said to you?" he asked quietly, the hurt in his voice unmistakable. "How many nights I lay awake, thinking about what I could've done differently?"

I swallowed hard, trying to ignore the flare of hope that sparked in my chest. "You can't just erase the past, you know," I said, trying to sound resolute, trying to push away the part of me that still cared, that still wanted this to work. "We can't pretend like everything's fine."

"I'm not pretending," he said, his voice barely above a whisper. "And I'm not asking you to forget. I'm asking you to trust me again. Slowly, if that's what it takes."

I looked at him, really looked at him, and something inside me shifted. I wasn't ready to let go of my anger, not entirely. But what I was ready for, I realized, was the truth. The whole truth. No more lies, no more half-hearted apologies. Just the raw, unfiltered reality of what had happened—and what still might be.

"You've had your time to think," I said, surprising myself with how calm I sounded. "But I need to think, too. I need to figure out what I want."

He nodded, his lips pressing together in a thin line. "I can give you that. But don't take too long. I'm not going anywhere this time."

The tension between us tightened, and I felt the weight of his words settle into the pit of my stomach. It was impossible not to feel the pull, not to wonder if this was the moment I'd been waiting for all along. Maybe I wasn't ready to give up on him, on us. But I wasn't ready to dive back in, either.

"I don't even know where to begin," I murmured, more to myself than to him. "What do we even do now? How do we go from where we are—where we were—to something new?"

His gaze softened, and he reached for my hand. I flinched instinctively, but he didn't pull back. He just waited, his fingers gently brushing mine. I could feel the warmth of his touch, the electricity that had always existed between us, surging to life again.

"We start with honesty," he said quietly. "We start by saying the things we've been too afraid to say. No more hiding. No more pretending."

I could feel my pulse quicken, my breath catching in my chest. His words were an invitation, a challenge, and I wasn't sure if I was ready to accept it. Not yet. Not when the wounds were still so fresh.

But then he leaned closer, his voice dropping to a whisper. "Tell me you don't still feel it. Tell me that when I touch you, when I look at you, you don't feel the same thing I do."

My heart pounded, and I tried to swallow the lump in my throat. I wanted to be strong. I wanted to say no. But all I could do was shake my head.

"You're right," I whispered. "I do feel it."

His breath hitched, and for a moment, everything seemed to stand still—like time itself was holding its breath, waiting for us to make a decision. To choose.

And then, as if the universe itself had decided for us, the door to the café opened with a loud crash, and a voice, cold and unfamiliar, cut through the air.

"Well, well," the voice said, dripping with sarcasm, "this is interesting."

I turned, my stomach plummeting, and found myself staring into the face of someone I hadn't expected to see. Not here. Not now.

"Seems like you've got some explaining to do."

Chapter 42: Rising from the Ashes

The sun dipped behind the jagged skyline, casting long shadows that stretched across the city below, its fading light a bittersweet reminder of the day's end. I stood at the window, my fingers pressed lightly against the cool glass, watching the world shift into a softer version of itself. The clamor of the street below, once a constant hum in my ears, now felt distant—like it belonged to someone else's life, not mine. Not anymore.

I glanced over at him, the man who had somehow become more than just a part of my life. He had become my life. He leaned against the doorframe, arms crossed, eyes narrowed in that thoughtful way of his, the one that made me feel like he was always a step ahead of me. A quiet observer, always watching, always thinking. But then his gaze softened, just for a moment, as he caught my eye. It was like he was seeing me for the first time all over again.

"Lost in thought?" he asked, his voice low and rich, like honey poured over a forgotten secret. I liked that about him, the way he could make the simplest words feel like a melody.

I turned to him, smiling. "Just... thinking."

"About what?"

"About how far we've come. From where we were, I mean."

He pushed himself off the doorframe and walked toward me, his steps sure, the weight of his presence filling the room. His hand slid over mine, warm and grounding. I let out a soft breath, a sound I hadn't realized I'd been holding in.

"It feels like a lifetime ago, doesn't it?" he said, his voice tinged with something unspoken, something I couldn't quite place but knew was there, hiding in the spaces between his words.

I nodded, the memory of everything that had led us here suddenly sharp and vivid—fights we thought we'd never win, days spent in silence, in anger, in regret. The weight of it all had once been unbearable, but it was in that weight that we had found each other, learned each other's truths, and built something we never expected. Something real.

"More than a lifetime," I murmured, reaching up to brush a strand of hair from my face. "And yet, here we are. Standing on the edge of it all."

He caught my hand before it could drop, pulling me closer, his thumb tracing lazy circles against my skin. "We didn't just survive, you know. We rebuilt."

I smiled at him, that wry smile of mine that had become as much a part of me as the pulse of my own heartbeat. "Rebuilding isn't always as pretty as it sounds."

"True," he agreed, his lips twitching into a grin. "But I think we've managed it better than most."

He kissed my forehead then, soft and lingering, as though he needed the reassurance as much as I did. And I let him, leaning into him, allowing the familiar scent of his cologne to wash over me like a balm. The scent of home, of safety, of things I hadn't known I was capable of feeling.

"Do you ever wonder," I began, my voice barely a whisper, "if we would have found each other if things had been different? If everything hadn't fallen apart?"

His hand tightened around mine, his voice steady. "I don't know. But what I do know is that we're here now, and nothing else matters."

A silence settled between us then, a silence heavy with the weight of years spent apart and together, the space we'd both inhabited alone before we'd found one another. And in that silence, something shifted—a kind of knowing that we had moved beyond the past, beyond the pain that had once held us in its grip. We had evolved, transformed into something stronger, something unbreakable.

I let my head rest against his chest, feeling the steady rhythm of his heartbeat, a steady drumbeat that matched my own. His arms wrapped around me then, pulling me closer, as though afraid I might slip away. And I understood that fear—it was a fear I shared. The fear that, despite everything we had built, the world could still come crashing down.

But as I stood there, wrapped in his warmth, I realized something. I wasn't afraid anymore. Not in the way I used to be. The fear of losing him, the fear of not being enough—it had all dissolved into something else, something purer. We had learned to stand side by side, not as two broken halves, but as two whole people who had found their place in each other's lives. And that, I thought, was enough.

"I used to think," I said, breaking the silence with a quiet laugh, "that love was supposed to be easy. That it was just supposed to… happen. But now I know better."

He chuckled softly, his lips brushing against my hair. "And what do you know now?"

"That love is a lot like this city," I said, looking out at the lights below, flickering like stars. "It's not perfect. It's messy and complicated. But somehow, it works. And when it does, it's beautiful."

His hand found mine again, and I felt him squeeze it, grounding me. "You're right," he said, his voice thoughtful. "But just like this city, we'll keep building. We'll keep rising, no matter what happens."

I looked up at him then, really looked at him, seeing the promise in his eyes. And for the first time in a long while, I let myself believe it. Believe in us. Believe in everything we had been through and everything we had yet to face.

"I like the sound of that," I whispered, pressing my cheek against his chest once more.

And for the first time, I wasn't afraid of the future. Because I knew we would face it together.

It was a strange thing, this peace we had found—like the calm after a storm, when the air still hummed with the electricity of what had been, but there was a quiet now. A quiet that felt like the world had paused just for us, holding its breath, waiting to see what we'd do next.

I stood there, leaning against him, feeling the warmth of his body against my back. It was the kind of warmth that made me forget the chill of every storm we'd weathered, the kind that made me believe, just for a moment, that we might actually have it all figured out.

But the truth was, there were still pieces of us that weren't quite healed. Not completely. And I knew that no amount of hope could erase what had happened, what we had lost along the way. That kind of grief didn't fade easily. It lingered, like smoke in the corners of a room you couldn't quite clear.

He seemed to sense the shift in the air, the sudden tension in my shoulders, and his hand came to rest gently on mine. I hadn't realized I'd been gripping the edge of the windowsill until his fingers touched mine, sending a calm through me that I hadn't expected.

"Hey," he said, his voice quiet, but with an edge of concern. "What's going on in that head of yours?"

I let out a breath I hadn't realized I was holding, staring out at the skyline again. "Just... wondering," I murmured, my voice barely a whisper. "What happens when the ashes start to settle? What happens when the fire's burned out, and all that's left are the embers?"

He was quiet for a moment, and I knew he was trying to find the right words. The thing about him was, he always thought before he spoke. It was one of the reasons I had come to love him more than I ever thought possible. He wasn't like everyone else. He didn't rush in with a quick fix or an answer that didn't make sense. He thought about me, about us, about everything.

"We keep going," he finally said, his voice steady, like he knew exactly what I needed to hear. "We keep going because there's nothing left but forward. And you're not doing this alone anymore."

I shook my head, even as warmth spread through my chest. "But what if forward is harder than we think?"

He laughed then, a low sound that tickled the back of my neck. "If I've learned anything from you, it's that we don't just think about things. We do them."

I smiled, despite myself. It was true. I'd spent most of my life second-guessing, worrying about what could go wrong, about what I might lose. But he—he had taught me that sometimes, you just had to take the leap.

"I don't know if I'm ready for another leap," I admitted, turning to face him, my hands finding his. "What if I fall again? What if I mess everything up?"

"Then we fall together," he said, his grin playful now, but his eyes sincere. "And we get back up. Together."

It was impossible not to believe him in that moment. I wanted to, more than anything. The thought of falling, of losing him, still weighed on me. But the idea of rising again with him at my side felt like something I could grasp, something solid and real.

"You make it sound so simple," I said, rolling my eyes but unable to hide the smile tugging at my lips.

"It's not simple," he said, his expression turning serious again. "It's messy and complicated and all sorts of hard. But it's ours. All of it."

I studied him then, really looked at him—the slight crinkle around his eyes when he smiled, the way his shoulders relaxed when he let go of the tension, the warmth in his voice when he spoke of the future. He had been through so much, just like me, and yet he still believed in the possibility of us, of everything we could be.

"I think I'm still learning how to believe," I confessed, my voice barely above a whisper, as though saying it out loud made it somehow more real. "How to believe that we've really made it through. That this is it."

He reached up then, cupping my face in his hands, his thumb brushing over my cheek. "You don't have to believe it all at once. You just have to believe it now. Believe that right now, this is where we're supposed to be."

I closed my eyes, letting the sensation of his touch fill the gaps in my heart, the gaps I hadn't known existed until I'd met him. The spaces where doubt once lived were slowly being replaced by something else—something softer, something better.

"I'm trying," I murmured. "I really am."

"I know you are," he said softly. "And that's enough for me."

I looked up then, meeting his gaze, and for the first time in a long time, I wasn't afraid. Not of him, not of the future, not of the fire that had burned us so badly. I wasn't afraid of the ashes, either. They were just part of the process. What mattered now was what we did with them. What we could build from the remnants of everything we'd survived.

He smiled, and I smiled back, a true smile this time, one that reached my eyes.

"Together," he said again, as though reminding us both.

"Yeah," I replied, feeling the weight of his promise settle in my chest like a warm blanket. "Together."

There was something about the evening air that made everything feel different—like it was holding its breath, waiting for a moment to settle. The streets below buzzed with their usual frenzy, but here, on the rooftop, the world felt quieter, as though time itself was taking a break, letting us catch up. The city stretched out before us, a patchwork of glowing windows and darkened alleys, a city I had once feared and now couldn't imagine living without.

It was strange how something could be both a sanctuary and a battlefield. But that was the thing about the places we loved, wasn't it? They had their sharp edges, their tangled histories. They weren't always easy. And yet, somehow, they became home.

I could feel the weight of his gaze on me, and when I turned to him, his eyes were softer now, more sure than they had been before. The playful spark was still there, but something deeper, something that spoke to the long days and longer nights we'd spent building this life, was there too.

"Okay," he said, breaking the silence with a smile that reached his eyes, "enough of the serious stuff."

I raised an eyebrow. "Serious stuff? I thought that was your favorite thing."

He snorted. "Only when I'm pretending to be a brooding philosopher." He paused, eyes flicking toward the edge of the building, then back to me. "But right now? I'm more in the mood for something a little more... lighthearted."

I couldn't help but smile. "Lighthearted? Are you suggesting we play charades or something equally ridiculous?"

His grin widened, a full-on cheeky smile that made me roll my eyes. "Well, charades might be fun, but how about something a little more... unconventional?"

I stared at him, trying to read his face, but it was impossible. He always had that slightly mischievous look, like he was on the edge of revealing something important or just about to pull a prank. "Unconventional how?"

"Come with me," he said, nodding toward the stairwell, his tone playful, but there was an underlying urgency, like he was trying to push me into something I hadn't seen coming.

My heart skipped, but I followed him without question. It was always like this with him—one moment, I was bracing for a conversation about the future, and the next, I was swept up into whatever wild idea he had conjured.

We moved quickly through the narrow hallways, the familiar clatter of his boots on the floor echoing in the silence. His hand brushed mine again, just for a second, and I felt it—this tiny spark, a whisper of what had once been and what was still here, simmering beneath everything we'd been through.

We emerged into the alley behind the building, where a few distant lights flickered in the windows above, but the street itself was quiet, almost forgotten. It was here, in this quiet, unremarkable space, that he stopped, turning to face me.

"Okay, now close your eyes," he said, his voice low and filled with mischief.

My pulse quickened. "What are you doing?"

"Trust me," he replied, that same smile curling on his lips.

I hesitated for only a moment, and then, as I had so many times before, I trusted him. I shut my eyes, feeling the cool breeze tug at my hair, the soft brush of his fingers against my wrist as he guided me forward.

"Ready?" he asked after a beat.

"Ready for what?" I said, my voice tinged with humor, though I couldn't mask the thrill of the unknown that was starting to bubble up inside me.

Without warning, I felt his lips brush against mine, quick and soft, just a whisper of a kiss, and then he pulled away, his breath warm against my cheek.

"Now open them."

I did, and for a moment, I could hardly process what I was seeing.

There, in the middle of the alley, was a makeshift stage—a small, weathered podium with a couple of old chairs and a beat-up guitar resting against it. String lights were draped haphazardly across the walls, casting a soft, golden glow. It was like something out of a forgotten memory, an idea he'd pulled out of thin air and decided to make real.

And standing at the edge of the stage, guitar in hand, was none other than Alex.

I blinked. "Is that... is that Alex?"

He laughed. "The very same. I told you I had a surprise."

I was still trying to process what was happening when Alex looked up, his familiar grin spreading across his face. "You two coming up or what?"

I shot a confused glance at him. "You... you're playing?"

He shrugged, the playful twinkle in his eye never fading. "Turns out, I'm more than just a pretty face with an impressive guitar collection."

I crossed my arms, trying to stifle the laugh that was bubbling up inside me. "This is... this is really happening, isn't it?"

"Oh, it's happening," he confirmed, strumming a chord on the guitar that sent a ripple of sound through the quiet air. "Your man thought you could use a little impromptu concert. So, what do you say?"

I glanced at him—at the man who had a way of making everything feel spontaneous and exciting, even when it was completely unexpected—and I felt a rush of affection that nearly knocked me off my feet. "You know," I said, a smile tugging at the corners of my mouth, "I think I'm in."

"Good," he said, pulling me toward the stage, his fingers interlacing with mine. "Because this song is for you."

I stopped dead in my tracks. "What?"

He just winked at me, and before I could process what was happening, he gave Alex a subtle nod. The guitar started up again, and the first chord hit me like a wave.

The song was slow, intimate—too personal. It wasn't just for me, it felt like it was about me. My breath caught in my throat as the words flowed from Alex's lips, and I realized something in that moment, something I hadn't expected: I wasn't ready for this.

The way the words swirled around me, the intensity behind the music—this wasn't just a surprise. This was a confession, and it was happening right here, in front of me. My heart raced as the realization hit.

I opened my mouth to say something—anything—but before I could speak, a shadow moved across the alley, drawing my attention.

The figure was tall, dark, and completely unfamiliar. And they were staring directly at us.

I froze, every instinct telling me to turn away, to escape, but the figure wasn't moving.

And then, in the stillness of that moment, everything changed.

Milton Keynes UK
Ingram Content Group UK Ltd.
UKHW031153251124
451529UK00001B/101